Praise for
Ivy Cole and the Moon
by Gina Farago

"Werewolf Ivy Cole rocks! Cool, collected, yet caring, and blessed with a deadly focus, she is the new heroine of horror fiction. Gina Farago's gripping novel is sure to please genre fans and mainstream readers alike."
—Elizabeth Massie, Bram Stoker Award-winning author

"An intriguing morality play, featuring sharply drawn, engaging characters and loaded with rural southern atmosphere. With her stark descriptions, authentic, colloquial dialogue, and characters possessed of deadly secrets, Gina Farago gives us a tale with both dark, subtle undertones and wild, graphic action—kind of like Flannery O'Connor meets *The Howling*."
—Stephen Mark Rainey, author of *The Lebo Coven*

"Fast-moving…Fiction has a new, thoroughly engaging leading lady…Farago's novel immediately captures the imagination with its setting in the deep dark North Carolina mountains and its action spanning those mysterious nights when the full moon shines and wild creatures go wilder. We're looking for a sequel and looking hopefully out the window for the next full moon."
—*Greensboro News & Record*

"It is rare when an author has the ability to let the reader see, hear, feel, and smell so vividly what they are reading. Farago lets the mind's eye travel beyond the printed page so one may experience this well-written story. At last, an unusual and entertaining book for werewolf enthusiasts!"
—Robert Harris, actor, *Cabin Fever*

"What's not to like about a sweet thirties-something southern belle who feeds on the entrails of her enemies under a full moon? This is the kind of book that can make you cry, giggle, throw up, and stroke your chin page to page."
—*Insidious Reflections*

LUNA

LUNA

Gina Farago

NEDEO PRESS

The characters and events depicted in this novel are fictitious, as is the town of Salty Duck, North Carolina (although loosely based on Beaufort and Morehead City, North Carolina). Any resemblance to actual people, events, or places is entirely coincidental.

Published by
NeDeo Press
116 South Main Street
Randleman, NC 27317
www.NeDeoPress.com

Bible scriptures quoted from The Scofield Study Bible,
Authorized King James Version,
printed by Oxford University Press, Inc., New York, copyright © 1945

Library of Congress Control Number 2007939418

ISBN 978-0-9763874-6-6

Cover Design and Illustrations by T. Glenn Bane
Author Photograph (with gray wolf Deneb, Wolf Park, Battle Ground, IN)
by Karl Farago

Printed in the United States of America

1 3 5 7 9 10 8 6 4 2

In loving memory of
Lesten "Dan" and Lois Sutphin

Acknowledgments

Special thanks are in order for those who have assisted me during the writing of this book:

To my husband Karl, a former Marine and expert marksman, for his guidance on weapons and boats in general. Thanks, honey.

To my editors, Barbara and Theresa Bane, for their candid and insightful notes. Your comments (and criticisms) are, as always, invaluable. And to Karen Grossman for her impeccable copyedits on the Ivy Cole series.

To T. Glenn Bane, my award-winning cover artist, who captures the mood of my writing so eloquently within his dark landscapes.

To Jennifer K. Johnson, a second-grade teacher at Gladesboro Elementary School in Hillsville, Virginia, for her educational expertise in guiding my passages involving the school system.

To the Farago family—Charles, Mary, Rick, and Donna—for their continued support and European influence on my writing, and to Ted and Becky Bennett, for their many years of support as well.

To the cities of Beaufort and Morehead, North Carolina, for being the foundational blueprints on which the fictional town of Salty Duck was laid, and to the beautiful wild sanctuaries of the Outer Banks, just because.

And to the red wolves of the Alligator River National Wildlife Refuge—may you find peace at last and thrive.

Prologue

*F*LASH OF *moonlight. Flash of teeth. Splash of blood.*

Blood.

Everywhere. On her coat, filling up her jowls. Engorging her stomach. Her muzzle buries in it, breathing it as it bubbles with fading life.

More, she demands through the rage. More!

Claws and teeth slash in a fury, and blood-rain pours down around the female wolf. Black fur and chunks of flesh fly to litter the ground. With head thrown back, she releases a howl that shatters the night and reverberates to the heavens. Then she plunges her mighty wolfen head into the black werewolf's chest and tears the cavity wide....

"Miss, are you all right?"

Ivy Cole abruptly sat up. A hand was on her shoulder, shaking it gently.

"Yes, I'm fine." She wiped the long blond hair out of her eyes. They sparkled a fathomless emerald green, and the train conductor seemed momentarily dazzled. He smiled underneath the brim of his navy cap, but there was uncertainty there.

"You were dreaming," he said. "I hope it wasn't so bad?"

Oh good Lord. Was I talking in my sleep? Ivy blanched at the horrifying notion. There was no telling what she'd said. "It wasn't, and I'm okay now," she replied simply. "Thank you."

"Good. Beautiful young ladies like yourself shouldn't have bad dreams." Lines across his brow crinkled, pulling the cap even closer over his generous nose. Was it flirtatious amusement or concern in his expression? Ivy didn't know.

"You might want to ready yourself for deboarding," he continued. "We're stopping in Chicago, if you'd like to get off and stretch your legs. We've still got a ways to go before the final stop in Winnipeg."

She nodded and he walked away, only to rouse another passenger somewhere down the aisle behind her. The train clacked and shuddered, punctuating the conductor's muted comments.

Ivy looked out the window, expecting the blushing autumn countryside to have dissolved into pavement and gleaming towers. But it was not the station nor the rise of city skyscrapers that she saw. Instead, remnants of her dream floated past the window, images like silent film rolling at the speed of the slowing train. The misted swells of Appalachia's Blue Ridge lay within her inner vision, and the characters who played out the last scenes of her life there were tragic at best. She'd fled them all—a relentless lady sheriff bent on exacting what *she* thought was justice, a man turned beast who met his ill-fated end at Ivy's own judicious hand, and a deputy who had stolen Ivy's heart and permanently scarred his own by doing so. The future without him, Melvin Sanders, would be a lonely future indeed. But she'd left him with a special gift to remember her by.

And one of them—the deputy or the black werewolf she destroyed—had left her with a special gift as well.

The train clattered on, toward the unknown, for this town was merely a layover in a greater journey she had yet to venture. Ivy looked down at an indiscernible curve pressing against her waistband, still no more significant than a raised welt beneath her skin.

She laid a cool hand across it. There was a stirring there, she instinctively knew. A small life gathering, a part of herself. But would the child be born with the kind heart of her deputy or the unconscionable soul of the black werewolf, she did not know.

But Ivy did know this: The child would be born a girl. And she would call her Luna.

PART 1

"There shall be weeping and gnashing of teeth."

—*St. Matthew 25:30*

1

Sandpiper Bridge rattled loudly as the Jeep Wrangler made its way over the iron causeway leading across the bay into Salty Duck, North Carolina. Wind tore at the already mussed hair of the vehicle's occupants: a blond lady in a white T-shirt and cutoff denim shorts; a strapped-in little girl, her ponytail flying in a messy tangle around her face; and one big black dog *(wolf)*, his tongue hanging out and the sea air rushing over the roll bar making him squint.

The child, Luna, threw her hands in the air like on a thrill ride and her high-pitched giggles competed with the rat-tap, rat-tap of the Wrangler's wide tires traversing the bridge's grated metal. Ivy slowed the vehicle to twenty-five to better take in the view. Gliding to the left and right across water painted golden by the noontime sun were sailboats, cruisers, and speedboats souped up like race cars. The drawbridge had just been let down in front of them, having allowed passage of a shrimp trawler on its way to the open sea. A flock of gulls rode its frothy gilded wake like a swarm of downy bees.

The Jeep bumped hard at the bottom of the bridge, eliciting another delighted squeal from Luna, and Ivy accelerated past the gray weathered sign that read "Salty Duck, circa 1709." Fish shacks on either side of the potholed road welcomed them to town, their wares listed on rustic hand-painted planks that advertised fresh clams, oysters, and fish with exotic names like croaker and sheepshead.

Live oaks dripping moss and a smattering of loblolly pines shielded their advance down Sandpiper Lane, and Ivy slowed again looking for one street in particular.

"There it is, Mommy! There it is!" Luna screamed in her ear, and Ivy laughed. She herself had been such a quiet, reserved child, but this one was Mach 2 all the time, and everything was an event. But Ivy did not stifle it. Her child could read letters before she could tie her shoes.

"And so it is, Boo. Good eye."

Ivy put on her right blinker and whipped the Jeep down Battery, a street even narrower than the small main drag they'd left. Historic two- and three-story houses with hip roofs and double-decked porches lined both sides of it, tucked amid more twisted oaks. White picket fences and black wrought iron protected lush, almost jungle-like gardens in front of each 18th- and 19th-century home. Old wood painted in cream, yellow, light blue, and weathered colonial white fronted facades that predated the Civil War. Pirates had once roamed local waters, Ivy had learned upon researching her new home—waters that were broken by a hopscotch patch of marsh and islands just one short block away.

Ivy fell in love with Salty Duck the minute she read about it in, of all places, a Canadian library book about vintage sea ports of the Atlantic. She spent six months making phone calls to real-ty companies, anxious for a rental to become available long term. The agent's return call couldn't have come at a better time. Life on the chilly outskirts of Winnipeg had played out, and Ivy was restless to move on again. Although she knew better, she could-n't help herself—she could no longer deny the yearning in her heart to come back home. Ivy wanted her baby to grow up knowing from where her deepest roots came, the roots of her mother, in North Carolina. The warm Southern sea air welcomed Ivy and her daughter, and she knew she'd not made a mistake.

"Sixty-one-o-three Battery Street. Do you see it, Boo? The house should be coming up on the left." Ivy drove slowly, and even Aufhocker, her four-legged guardian and best friend since childhood, seemed to strain alongside Luna to search out their destination.

"Six thousand. Sixty-one-o-one…Sixty-one-oh there it is!" Luna started grabbing at the seatbelt before the Jeep had pulled to a complete stop. She was on the street and running off behind the house in question before Ivy could stop her. Auf hopped onto the hot sidewalk and trotted around the house after the child.

Ivy leaned on the steering wheel and surveyed her new home. Buttercream paint flecked and chipped from nearly three-hundred-year-old wood stacked beneath a bluish-gray tin roof. The front of the house was flat, two-story, cut by a sturdy front porch that rose above a narrow yard. Cranesbills bloomed alongside sea oxeye daisies, their purple- and yellow-blossomed faces crowding the sliver of yard between porch and walk. A knobby circle of whelk shells imprisoned the flowers at the foot of the porch steps. The front door of the house was freshly painted bright red, in striking contrast to the subtle tones of the rest of the home, and beside it hung a plaque and testament to the significance of the place: Captain and Lord Manfred Woodside of Parish Keep Court, 1755.

So this was once the home of a nobleman and captain. Yet it was one of the most modest residences in the entire historical district, its status now reduced to tourist vacation rental. Only Ivy had managed to commandeer it indefinitely with a handsome deposit that for most people would have amounted to a mortgage down payment. But she was not anxious to go down that road again. Renting was more freeing, especially when one had to flee in the wee hours of the morning like the last time she left North Carolina. There was another cottage once, not so unlike this one, that had stolen her heart. She dreamed of her little house often and wondered what finally became of it after being abandoned. The sheriff of Doe Springs in the Blue Ridge Mountains surely knew Ivy was never coming back. She pictured it, rumpled in vine-cover, her gardens overgrown, the white picket fence collapsing under neglect.

No matter. Here were other gardens, other white picket fences. Doe Springs was a state length away, and Salty Duck was her home now. And Luna's and Auf's.

"Mommy, get back here!" a voice called from somewhere behind the house.

"Not so bossy, Luna. Remember your manners!" she hollered to the sun sprite that had taken over her life.

"Mommy, get back here, *please!*"

Ivy shook her head and rolled out of the Jeep. She stretched one good time, feeling the road leaving her legs and the wadded-up bundle of vertebrae that was her spine. Her flip-flops clapped across a threadbare yard of sparse grass and sand as she circled the side of their new home.

"Look!" Luna pointed triumphantly at the cause of all the excitement. It was a simple rope swing dangling from a giant live oak with limbs as tortured as arthritic hands. Ten feet up the coastal tree, the branches arced downward and crested upward into bark-laden swells that invited an introspective spirit to come drift quietly among them. It was a Thinking Tree, and Ivy pictured herself there with her new journal, whiling away hours while Luna swung below and Auf slept in the grass.

"I'm going to like this place, Mommy."

Swing forgotten, Luna sprinted off to explore the rest of her new world, all one-quarter acre of it. Ivy walked around to the front of the house after her child and stood on the sidewalk. Tight on both sides and across the street were the rest of the neighbors: the Salty Duck historic district, still named Parish Keep. Captain Woodside would have been pleased, not just by the name but by what Ivy saw. Her neighbors' houses were as meticulously kept up as her own, particularly the handsome Victorian facing Battery.

"You got the wrong house, Woodside. After your time, I reckon."

New screams and squeals grabbed Ivy's attention. Another momentous discovery had been made apparently. Ivy saw the heavy drapes in the Victorian pull back and then abruptly fall into place again as her eyes landed upon them.

"Boo, keep it down over there, okay?" Ivy might as well be speaking to the pelicans passing overhead. As much control as she wielded over her canine companion—indeed, Ivy was an amazing dog trainer by trade—she seemed to lack all authoritative alpha traits when it came to her own daughter, who was now captivated by another swing, this one on the front porch.

A familiar warmth nuzzled Ivy's leg and her hand fell absently to stroke it. Aufhocker's black fur sifted through her fingertips as she contemplated unpacking her few possessions from the mini tag-along trailer she'd rented, or hoofing it a block and a half down to the waterfront for some lunch.

No. She was here and stalling wouldn't change things. Unpacking (once again) was inevitable, and she'd better get to it. There wasn't much—just some clothes, the mantel clock from her mother, her ancient tome *Lykanthrop,* dog food, and a few children's books for Luna. Ivy's idea of home and a safe place was really wrapped up in those items anyway—the house was just the structure that guarded them.

Ivy went to the side of the house where her Jeep was parked and stepped onto the wide patio deck, skirting a usable charcoal grill and a picnic table that didn't look half bad despite its apparent age. Keys jangled in her pocket as she opened the side door into a cheery yellow kitchen. Even though the appliances were old, the room smelled of fresh lemon.

A miniature rocket hurled into Ivy's back and clasped its tiny fingers around her waist. "Gotcha, Mommy!"

Luna matched her mother step-for-step as they wandered room to small room, making the space theirs with every footfall. The furnishings swam in ocean blues and sailor whites and accents of yellow and red. Pickled cabinetry and whitewashed walls of old, splintered wood brought the ocean tide inside. Ivy could *feel* the coast and the marshes and the sway of sea oats in the confines of Captain Woodside's former home. It was not just good, it was better than good, and Ivy let a smile of hope get past her. Maybe here, maybe this place, maybe this time it could be home.

Salty Duck on a Saturday afternoon was not a crowded place, even here on this late August crossroads between summer and fall. Tourists tended to flock farther south to the larger beaches, where amusement park rides and live theaters and mega movie complexes competed with the quiet of the shore.

Ivy liked that just fine. Salty Duck was truly quaint in its solitude, and more than a little uppity about it. The Realtor had warned her before she arrived: "The neighbors are quite about newcomers who look like they're sticking around longer than a week. Nothing personal, so don't hold it against them. They're just clinging to the last sandbar they've got before the developers sniff them out and take over." Ivy couldn't blame a place for that. If folks here liked to keep to themselves, that suited her just fine too.

"What'll it be, ma'am?" A burly man in jeans and an "Eat at The Bluewater Lady" T-shirt stood beside her, pen and notepad ready. He'd sneaked up as she peered across the inlet, lost in thought and relief that unpacking had not taken too long. Luna too was startled, her own attention riveted to three wild ponies that grazed beyond the silver streak of water dividing mainland from islands. Breeze from Marshy Bottom Sound stirred the napkins on the restaurant's outdoor deck, and Auf dozed a few feet from their table on the cobblestone sidewalk. Big fishing charters and smaller single-engine boats were moored right alongside yachts just on the other side of it.

Ma'am. It used to make Ivy feel old, until a particular young deputy with mountain-sky blue eyes changed her perspective on it. She had learned to quit thinking of him on a daily basis, then something would come at her from an unexpected angle, like a waiter on an evening in Salty Duck, and he'd be there with her all over again. *Stop it, Ivy. Let him go....*

"Ma'am, your order?"

"Yes, I'm ready. Oysters with plenty of tartar sauce, please, and the squirt here will have the shrimp basket."

"Fitting." The man grinned, hiking his trimmed goatee upward a notch.

Ivy glanced at her daughter. *Yes,* she thought, *Luna was a little on the tadpole size, even for a five-year-old, but if the stranger only knew—*

"I am not a shrimp, you know," Luna said, her head thrown straight back to glare up at the waiter. "A shrimp is a crustacean. But maybe a waiter wouldn't know that."

The man's eyes rolled over to Ivy, who just shrugged. He snatched the menus and left.

"I hope he only spits in your food for that," Ivy said.

"Ooooh, Mommy, that's gross." And then she was a child again, lost in the ponies across the water.

Ivy strolled down Front Street, flanked by Luna and her large black "shepherd." After a delicious calabash dinner, they'd wandered north, away from town, and farther into the marshes. The inlet paralleled them on the right, but Spartina grasses and a quagmire of crab-encrusted black mud thickened to push the waterway farther from the street. A boardwalk jutted out into the wetlands on their right, a pier into a heat-sultry wonderland.

Luna's and Aufhocker's feet drummed in hollow cadences across the wood planking as they ran together through the marsh, Ivy still strolling casually behind them. The boardwalk bent to the right around an impenetrable thicket of yaupon holly, but Ivy could still hear Luna's laughter as she and ever-faithful Aufhocker headed for the walk's end.

Ivy stopped and leaned against the railing, careful to avoid the white splatters courtesy of the gulls and plovers that flew overhead. From below, reaching up to her, were thick stands of saw grass, their sharp blades softened by the spiraled pyramids of periwinkle snails. Along the grasses' stalky bottoms marched armored armies of fiddler crabs, creeping things with spiny skeletons and oversized click-ing claws. On closer inspection, their sapphired shells looked like bits of gem glass moving across the rich black mud of the marsh. Pluff and brine stirred together in Ivy's sensitive nose, new smells that were so different from the lovely Blue Ridge she pined for. There would be much to explore and discover here—for Luna especially, who had only known urban life in Manitoba's capital. The ocean horizon could become her daughter's very own cherished blue ridge.

Ivy closed her eyes and let the clitter of restless fiddler crabs lull her, when a low growl from the hidden end of the boardwalk snapped her aware. It was Aufhocker, warning.

Ivy jerked away from the railing and her stride lengthened as she strode down the boardwalk. "Luna! Auf!" Her steps quickened until the thump of her footfalls pounded into a jog.

She rounded the bend to a broad, covered area at the end of the pier. A man crouched among picnic tables, his hand outstretched toward the wolf. Aufhocker stood his ground between the stranger and Ivy's little girl.

Luna pulled on Auf's tail. "Stop it, Auf. Bad dog. Bad dog!" Aufhocker ignored the assault on his longest extremity, his lips still rumbling over inch-and-a-half canines.

"Luna, let him go." Ivy stood with her wolf and child.

The man stood as well. "I didn't mean to scare everybody, but seems I'm trapped back here, unless I start climbing over picnic tables or leap over the rail. But I kind of like these shoes." He offered a friendly, albeit uneasy, smile.

Ivy saw it was true, Auf had him penned in, the pup in his charge safe and secure. Aufhocker was the gentlest animal Ivy had ever known—with the ones he loved. Outside the familial limits of the pack, however, his instinctual protective nature could turn from lov-ing to lethal. Ivy should have known better than let the two ramble off together out of her sight. But the man didn't seem too terribly upset. Maybe he wouldn't go running to report her "dog" to some-body who cared more about leash laws than liberty. Her first day in Salty Duck and already she'd screwed up.

"Aufhocker, out!" Ivy said. To the man: "I am so very, very sorry.

Auf is all talk and no bite, believe me." *Oh, please believe me. Please, please believe me.* "It's just he gets very defensive when anyone comes near Luna."

"No problem. I admire a good dog like that. Big fella. What is he?"

"He's a wo—ouch, Mommy!" Luna looked at her mother, irritation scrunching up her young face. The sudden hand on the girl's shoulder was uncomfortably firm, but then the look in Ivy's eyes reminded her: *Dog. Always call Auf a dog. It's a habit we must keep, Boo. Wolves get into trouble in these parts.*

Ivy relaxed her hand on Luna's shoulder when she saw the little girl understood. "He'a shepherd mix," Ivy said casually. "Just a big ole goofy mutt who gets too protective and shows off. Aufhocker, heel!"

Auf immediately relaxed and sat by his mistress's side at her command, but his eyes never left the stranger's, whose own were the light aquamarine of a Caribbean cove. Ivy looked up into those eyes, and for a moment she was lost in another time, in blue eyes of a deeper hue, mountain misted and kind. Her guard wavered at feigned familiarity. She shook it off. There was nothing familiar about this man, nor would there ever be with any man again if she had anything to do with it.

He was still smiling at her through a rugged beach-tanned face, but the wear in the slight lines about his eyes and forehead were too gentle to be caused by the sea. The fishermen here wore mugs carved by thirty-knot winds and month upon month of baking under shadeless skies. So, not a fisherman, nor a seasoned lifeguard either. A newcomer like herself, perhaps? Or a tourist? Why did she even care? She didn't.

"No harm done then. Good. Let's go, gang," Ivy said. Auf moved to the side, making room for the man to pass ahead of them. The man extended his hand instead.

"I'm Caleb." His white shirt was rolled up to the elbows, accentuating the bronze of muscular forearms, which matched the copper-tinted brown of his hair.

"Well, that's nice. Luna, Auf, I said let's go." Since the man apparently wasn't leaving first, Ivy took Luna's hand and spun her around.

"I think we're neighbors," Caleb called after them. "At least for the summer, anyway. I thought I saw you pull in earlier. Army green Wrangler, right?"

Ivy turned, pivoting Luna with her. Auf, too, faced Caleb again, his expression blank.

"You don't live across the street, do you? In the Victorian?" Ivy said.

Caleb chuckled, a deep but lighthearted sound in his throat. "Tried to. Mrs. Pitchkettle owns that house and I couldn't get her out for love nor money. Mr. Pitchkettle had it open to boarders briefly, but his wife closed shop on the whole operation. Right after she met me, in fact."

Ivy didn't reply, her expression as void as the wolf's.

Caleb tried again. "I'm actually several houses down from you, across St. Mary's. Hey, what I said before was a joke. A bad one. Trust me, my personal resume usually impresses most people. I don't want you to think you've got a bad neighbor."

"I won't think anything of it at all. Excuse us." Ivy was walking away again, but the child attached to her right hand was becoming increasingly heavy. Luna peered over her shoulder at the nice man. He waved good-bye to her and leaned against the rail to continue enjoying the view. Luna dug her heels into the boardwalk, and her mother finally stopped.

"What is it, Luna? I feel like I'm dragging a sack of potatoes here."

"Mommy, you're acting mean." Luna's lips pooched out and her free hand was on her hip.

My oh my, Ivy thought. But maybe Luna was right. Rudeness was not in her mother's nature and certainly not what she wanted to teach her child. They'd both been raised better than that. It was the South, for heaven's sake, and some neighborly hospitality was in order. And he was a neighbor, after all. If this was to be home, it was time to act like it. Let the walls fall. They'd been in place since leaving Doe Springs. Long enough. Too long.

Ivy sighed and looked back at Caleb, who appeared captured by the last light of the evening. Somewhere in the Pacific, the water readied to swallow the sun, but even here, on the East Coast, the sunset could be quite dazzling.

"Caleb," Ivy called to him.

He looked up. "Yes?"

"Have a nice evening," Ivy said.

It was the best she could do.

2

THE COVERS tucked up to Ivy's chin were choking her, and the random creaking of the settling house against a late-night roaming wind had become the chatter of a ghost in the walls, urging her to rise. (*And flee,* she thought ruefully.) She fought against the goading notion just as she fought the sheets to the other side of the bed to free herself. The ceiling she stared at above was a bare white expanse, a boring nothingness that should lend relief to an overstimulated mind, but it didn't help. It was as it always seemed to be in a new place: first-night jitters, an unwillingness to unwind taut senses that seemed always to be on the defensive, especially since becoming a mother. Ivy just couldn't sleep.

Irritated but resigned, she sat up. She clicked on the hurricane lamp on the nightstand and groaned. The clock read twelve forty-three a.m. After midnight, and a new day already. Who needed sleep anyway? Thankfully, the other two-thirds of her family had not shared her problem. Luna went straight to bed after getting home from their dinner and walk in the marsh, her energy finally winding down into the feathers of her comforter in the bedroom upstairs. Ivy put Aufhocker to bed beside the child, a canine pillow that would endure endless nightly kicks and wallowings by the five-year-old without a whimper.

Then Ivy had made her own bed downstairs with a comforter that matched her daughter's. She ran her hand over the plain quilted squares, remembering a rose-colored coverlet made by the loving hands of her mother. It was gone now, last wrapped around the gray fur of an injured terrier. Ivy smiled at the thoughts of Simple Rex, the scrappy little warrior who had fought for Ivy's life in the mountains under the full moon. She missed him, missed all of her other dogs, especially at nighttime when their choral snorts and dream barks and paddling feet had lulled her to sleep. Perhaps that was what she'd been missing all these years to keep insomnia at bay.

Now her family was quite small, and yet, with the addition of Luna, it was larger than life. She'd never planned on children, had preferred the life of the disperser wolf—alone, free, and lonely. But fate had other plans, just like for tonight apparently, for sleep was not in the cards.

Two feet hit the hardwood floor, and Ivy abandoned the bedroom for the kitchen. Ten minutes later she was on the front porch swing with warm cocoa in hand, a homemade treat made a childhood habit by her Aunt Ava Pritchard. Perhaps the soothing milk and chocolate could accomplish what good old-fashioned exhaustion could not.

Ivy let the wind take her as it fluttered through the cotton of her nightshirt and pushed the wooden swing gently. Only a block from Front Street and the marsh, the salty breeze found her easily. The whisper of air on her bare legs was soothing, but atop Captain Woodside's roof was a widow's walk, and Ivy debated going topside instead of staring at the street, where the Pitchkettles' imposing Victorian filled her view. Standing on the railed platform above, she could see Marshy Bottom Sound, the Banks with their wild ponies, the skippers coming in and going out to sea, the lighthouse down by Pious Cape, and beyond it all, to the vast map of the ocean itself, as wild and untamed as any forest or mountain she'd traversed in her lifetime. At least, that's how it looked when she'd ventured there briefly this afternoon after unpacking Luna's things.

"Here's to wide-open spaces, whatever form they may take or however they may find us," Ivy said to the briny air. She saluted with the cocoa, completely inappropriate on such a warm late-summer's night, and sipped.

A movement across the street interrupted the toast. Ivy stopped the swing and peered hard into the darkness. Someone was afoot in the Pitchkettles' garden. She could see a vague, shadowy silhouette moving in and out between the fortress of forsythia and crepe myrtles the neighbors used as a balustrade to shield their already formidable home. He crept along with the lurching, low-to-the-ground stealth of someone wanting to move unseen.

Ivy lowered her feet to the plank floor and quietly stood to get a better look. The figure stopped abruptly, bent over, and then Ivy watched as something rose and fell rhythmically into the soil of the side yard, near the corner where house and street met. The person beat the ground again and again, and Ivy saw clods of earth flying into the air with each determined swing. He—or she?—stood upright, tossed the spade, and reached for something else. A shovel now, Ivy could just make out over the scant view afforded through the wrought iron fence and thick shield of brush cover. The stranger grunted with each thrust into the ground. More dirt flew. A mound grew.

Peculiar, these neighbors, the Pitchkettles. What could they possibly be up to in the garden at this hour? And not a light on anywhere to guide their work.

Images from old movies rolled through Ivy's mind like grainy black-and-white film. Here, in this quaint seaside town, the seemingly placid and unassuming neighbors harbored secrets in their charming *(spooky)* old house. Under the veil of forbidding darkness and the scant light of the Pious Cape beacon, corpses piled in the couple's basement were tendered as garden fertilizer for summer roses and corn.

Don't be silly, Ivy! She shook off the creeping misgivings. Perhaps the neighbors weren't mass murderers, but their late-night visitor was sure no gardener either and curiosity was getting the better of her. Ivy set her cocoa on the porch rail and slipped down the steps to the sidewalk. Without the shelter of the porch, the ocean breeze turned teasingly aggressive and snatched up the ends of her nightshirt. It flew straight into her face, and the wind rushed over her bare belly with a balmy kiss.

"Oh!" Ivy batted the gown back down to her knees.

The digger in the garden looked up suddenly. Ivy froze. Upstairs in the old house, a light snapped to life and the heavy drapes drew back. A woman's face appeared at the window. The sash flew open and she leaned out, her long black hair falling over her shoulder and through the window like a Rapunzel braid.

"You down there! What are you doing?" a terse voice called. Ivy assumed the woman referred to the trespasser in the garden, then realized the unfriendly inquiry had been directed at herself instead.

Ivy opened her mouth to explain when a man, Mr. Pitchkettle, Ivy gathered, appeared beside the woman in the window. Mrs. Pitchkettle said loudly to him, with every intention for Ivy to hear, "It's the newcomer, Leland, the one who just moved across the street. I told you she was a tart. It's been only a day and already she's flashing the neighbors."

The sash slammed closed and the curtains yanked back into place behind it.

Ivy stood in the street, holding her gown to her knees and speechless. Should she bang on their door to alert them to the trespasser in their garden? Holler at them from the road? Throw a rock at (through) their window? That might be more satisfying.

Ivy looked back across Battery. The digger was gone. It appeared they'd scared the yard-working night crawler away. Whatever had been going on over there, Ivy should do the neighborly thing and tell the Pitchkettles about it on the morrow, whether they deserved her neighborliness or not. But getting involved with anybody in town, particularly over something that could involve talking to the police, was the last thing Ivy wanted—or needed—to do.

She thought about it. The digger was gone. Really, what harm was there in walking around in someone's garden with a shovel any-way? He didn't appear interested in breaking in. Probably just a teenager doing a silly prank of some sort. Considering the friendliness of the folks in their antiquated Victorian stronghold, that scenario seemed highly likely.

"No harm, no foul, you cranky old thing," Ivy muttered to herself.

Shortly thereafter, she climbed back into bed, the cocoa working magic on her high-strung nerves. She slept very soundly, dreaming of big earthy holes, and her hateful new neighbors falling into them.

3

IVY COLE'S former house looked lonely. He didn't believe that a house, a structure, an inanimate *thing* could possess a soul or a spirit, but this cottage surely did, for the very essence of its hollow core seemed pained. Mournful. Pining, perhaps, with no hope of solace. No hope at all for the mistress's return. A corpse.

The house was not the only one who longed. Deputy Melvin Sanders sat in his black Dodge pickup looking at the dark, empty sockets of the vacant soul in front of him. Just as he did every Saturday night around this time, with midnight closing in and specks of stars shimmering over his head like chips of distant ice. Uncaring. Silent and uncaring. Like *her,* maybe. By now. After so long. He was a memory in her wolfen brain, if even that. Less, like a speck. An ice-chip star in the firmament above, no more important surely. Did she gaze at the same sky as he and ever think of him, too? No. He did not believe she did.

Melvin opened the truck door and got out. He stretched his six-foot five-inch frame, as muscular as it ever was, heavenward. That had taken time. Lots of it, even to stretch like this. Broken ribs, excessive blood loss, and his right side, decimated, harrowed to the bone—both the right bicep and the right calf. But all fully mended, miraculously. Impossible, the doctors exclaimed. A miracle. It had been in all the papers: the Devil of Doe Springs's final assault, on the sheriff department's only two deputies, no less. One died, horrendously. The other lived, recovered fully, hallelujah. Yes, a miracle.

If they only knew what hell a miracle was.

Melvin walked to the old picket fence fronting Ivy's cottage on the outskirts of Doe Springs, North Carolina. A slight limp drug at his right leg. *Stop that,* he thought. It was habit. The locals hounded him so much about overcoming his injuries that he had learned to feign a gimp leg. The act was second nature in public, where children and curious adults alike thought nothing of stopping him on the street and asking to admire his scars. He was a hero to Doe Springs, but to himself? A farce. There would be no need to pretend after tonight.

Melvin pushed through the gate, through a wild garden turned to weed, up the steps, and through the front door. Jack Lutsky saw no call to keep the place locked up. No one did because no one owned it but Ivy Cole, and she was gone. Lutsky had waited for word from her for years (and graciously paid her property taxes in the meantime). But then he'd finally given up and rented the house—unrightfully, as Ivy had bought it kit and caboodle from Lutsky a year before she disappeared—for a while to his cousin. She stayed three months, swore the place was haunted, and moved to her sister's basement in neighboring Pine Knot.

A house like this should be haunted. It was tortured and at a loss. Love ripped away. Ivy had treasured her own private corner of the mountain, marked it as her own in a thousand ways, with gardens and flower boxes and the sweat of female handiwork about the house that he still saw evidence of: the pots of long-dead plants hanging from the porch eaves, a wind chime, more terra cotta planters falling down the steps, now broken and busted like the rest of the place.

The living room was exactly as she'd left it, with several added layers of dust. Lutsky's cousin did little to change things or clean up, and any disturbed dirt had resettled quickly. The yellow sofa was still there, where Melvin sat with Sheriff Hubbard the first time they came out to question Ivy about Clifford Hughes, whose mangled remains lay within a mile of her house. How naïve he and the sheriff must have looked to Ivy then, with their rooting questions and warnings to be careful at night for the creature could still be lurking about. And there the creature was all along, sitting right with them, offering lemonade and an innocent ten-million-dollar smile.

Melvin moved on through the house to the kitchen, which opened onto a backyard of nothing. Ivy's dog fence was down; it started crumbling at the spot Aufhocker had gnawed his way through, determined to get to the startled deputy in front of him. Melvin remembered scuttling away from the black wolf, only to run into Deputy Meeks with his gun drawn, ready to save his partner.

Melvin almost laughed at that. Almost.

Lutsky's cousin was right: There were ghosts here, floating in shrouds of brume above the weed-browned carcasses of lawn and cottage and memory.

Melvin turned his back on it. All of it. He strode through the house, out the front gate, and into his truck. The engine started and Melvin stared ahead, his eyes mirroring the emotionless ice of the night sky. He had come to the cottage for the last time. He had made up his mind. It'd taken a long time coming, like the healing. But once arrived, it was permanent.

He would do it at last. He would find Ivy Cole. God help her when he did.

4

"Mommy, I want a pony."

"Of course you do. Finish your cereal." Ivy flipped to the middle of the newspaper, looking for something interesting. She was searching. The full moon was only a week away and here she was, brand-new in town, knowing nobody, which meant she knew of not one single person who—

"Really, Mommy. A pony, like the ones we see across the pond."

—not one single person who might need fixing on a full-mooned night. News here was ridiculously upbeat. The Salty Duck Historic Society, rampant in charity work. The Salty Duck Women's League, holding a bake sale for the church every other Sunday until winter. The Salty Duck Sailors Corp., hosting a fishing tournament for the homeless. And Salty Duck didn't even have any homeless, as far as Ivy could tell. The town was full of do-gooders. Ivy flipped to the obituaries just for the fun of it and tasted the names like appetizers, until...

"Mommy you're not listening I want a pony!"

Ivy put the paper down. "First of all, Luna, Marshy Bottom is a tidal creek, not a pond. Secondly, those ponies are wild so no, you cannot have one. And third, lower your voice. I don't appreciate yelling in my ear, and you're spraying Cheerios everywhere."

"Sorry." Luna meant it. She did not pout; indeed, she was not wired like other children in a lot of ways. She could turn from storm clouds to rainbows in a single breath, the happy side of her nature always outweighing the dark. But that was another consideration, too, for Luna's ideas of light and dark could be oddly skewed, a perception of right and wrong that worried Ivy sometimes.

"But," Luna closed her eyes and whispered loudly, "I wish, I wish, I wish I had a pony, even if it's not just like the ones across the pond. Just so you know." She finished the last Cheerio in her bowl and tipped it up to drink. Milk dribbled from the corners of her mouth and she wiped them with a slender arm. Today she wore a blue denim halter and matching shorts that turned up at the cuffs. Her blond ponytail sat high on her head—genie-style, she called it— and her eyes were her mother's all over: wide emerald cuts under impossibly long, dark lashes.

Ivy's heart turned over just looking at the child. It was like peering into a mirror of the past and seeing her own reflection from thirty years ago. If only Ivy could have been as happy as this one. She worked hard to make sure every day was a good one for Luna Cole, despite having no male role model, no strong father figure in her life to help guide her. Ivy felt cheated of that in her own childhood as well, but she reckoned she turned out all right anyway.

"Are you hunting, Mommy?" Luna's elbows were propped on the table, her feet in her chair, ponies temporarily forgotten.

"No, Boo, I'm reading the newspaper." A day of play awaited them both, but the fun would be all Luna's. Ivy would be looking for a job as they trekked about town and perhaps a future meal as well. But Luna didn't need to know that last part, and Ivy was suddenly reminded of lessons learned concerning stalking in her own backyard anyway. Past mistakes quelled her local interest, and broadening her territory seemed like a good idea. She'd scout some surrounding towns later in the week. Perhaps they would have grimmer news.

"'Cause if you're hunting, I know who you should eat."

"Oh, you do."

"Yep." Luna smiled brightly. "That waiter. He said I looked like a shrimp."

"He said no such thing." Ivy was buried in the paper again, the Lifestyles section. A craft festival was in town, just down the street in the Parish Keep Courtyard, to be exact. Local artisans of paint, pottery, driftwood carvings, basket weaving, quilts...

"I'd gobble him up, Mommy, every last bite." Luna made a slurping sound as she rubbed her tummy.

"Luna! For heaven's sake, go outside and play till I've cleared breakfast. And no more talk of who's eating who, got it, young lady?"

Luna hopped down from the table and wrapped her little arms around her mother's neck. She planted a kiss on Ivy's cheek. "Got it. I love you, Mommy." And she was out the door before her mother could reply.

"Gladys, look at this. Will you just look at this?"

Ebby Brown, wife of July and house servant to Leland and Missouri Pitchkettle, stood in the couple's side yard with a hoe in one hand and pruning shears in the other. "Missy's done lost her mind. I knew it was bound to happen sooner or later. I was hoping for later, least till I could get July to his retirement."

"Holy criminy. The old gal's lost it for sure. As if we'd had any doubts, though, eh?" Gladys, assistant to Ebby and the Pitchkettles' personal gardener, leaned on her own hoe and stared. "Where you think they all came from?"

"Danged if I know. Look out, here comes Leland. I wish he didn't have to see this latest bit of work. You know how he feels about his wife."

"Well, he has to know about it. I don't want to go changing things up with no witnesses. Sure's I put that woman's garden back together, she'll be all over me for disturbing her latest *sign*."

"What's going on, ladies? We paying you to work or sit on your green thumbs?" Leland was bearing down fast, sure he'd caught his two housekeepers up to lazy no-good.

Ebby's solicitous thoughts toward the elder Pitchkettle evaporated with every step he drew closer. The merchant's face was a map of angry lines and unrightful suspicion. If Leland was going to be cranky at them this early in the morning, let him get a healthy dose of Missy's craziness. Who was she, the lowly servant, to protect him?

"You'll be wanting to see the latest, Mr. Pitchkettle." Ebby motioned to Leland, who reached them at last and stopped dead.

"What the hell is all that?"

"Hoping you might could tell us."

Leland, Gladys, and Ebby looked across a new yard. A yard, which once grew fragrant clusters of oleander and trellis-crawling bunches of moon vine. Now it sprouted a wasteland of human arms and legs. Toes stretched skyward out of the buried thighs, and red-tipped nails clawed their way from holes previously occupied by azaleas. Twenty separate limbs jutted from the over-fertilized sod, imported from inland to make the native sandy landscape more agreeable to Missouri's varied taste in flora.

A screech erupted from behind the trio, jolting Leland out of his shock. Missouri Pitchkettle stood there in her long-sleeved lace blouse and old-fashioned ankle-length skirt, clutching a rosary.

"For God's sake, Missy, they ain't real." Leland rubbed his chest. *But the heart attack you about give me might be.*

"They're just mannequin parts, see there?" Leland kicked the nearest plastic protrusion and a foot flew off into an uprooted bush.

"It's the devil again." Missouri's heavily jeweled hand fluttered to her throat, the rosary dangling. "He left this for us. I keep dreaming about him. See, Leland, I told you. It's a sign!" She waved the rosary toward the plastic limbs, which annoyed Leland on another level—the Pitchkettles were Protestant.

Gladys and Ebby exchanged glances. Ebby said, as gently as she could, "You sure you didn't do this, Mrs. Pitchkettle? Maybe you forgot, like the other times?"

Missouri wrenched her head around, her customary braid lash-ing like a bullwhip. "Are you an idiot by nature, Ebby Brown, or has too much fertilizer soaked into that empty cornhusk on top of your shoulders? Of course I didn't do this. When would I have done this?" She stared the woman down until even Gladys looked away. Her gaze softened to imploring when it landed on her husband. "Leland?"

"'S all right, Peaches. Somebody's playing mean tricks. We'll get it cleaned up for you. Plants are still here strewed about. We'll get them back in the ground, won't we, ladies?"

"Yes, sir," Ebby said through a sigh. The "we" of it meant her and Gladys. But Ebby was tired of cleaning up Missy Pitchkettle's messes. First it was all her clothes, laid out in the front yard in complete outfits like someone would come along and step right into them. Then it had been her jewelry, strung from bush to limb about the property like an exploded treasure trove that had been hurricane-blown into the trees. Gladys and Ebby, women on the backside of middle-aged themselves and used to having all feet firmly planted, scaled oak trees and retrieved every last bauble under Leland Pitchkettle's watchful eye.

And now this. Dismembered mannequins planted in the garden. July's retirement better come quickly.

"You did it!" The rosary pointed at Gladys and Ebby now. "Confess, you scheming harpies."

"That's it." Gladys threw the hoe down and started to stomp off. Leland caught her arm. "Wait, Gladys." To Missouri: "Missy, won't you go round front for a spell till I set these ladies straight on a few things?"

Missouri's lips pursed and buckled under the strain of holding back, but hold they did. She nodded at her husband and, picking up her layered skirts, disappeared to the front of the house.

"Set us straight! I'll set you straight with my bare knuckles right now, Leland Pitchkettle. We've taken a lot of guff from you and the missus, but I've had it. Look at this yard. And she accuses us!" Gladys's matronly fists were balled at her sides. She had a good twenty pounds on the master of the house, and Ebby would have paid money to see what she was about to witness for free. The housekeeper stood back to give her stout friend room. If Leland was going to take a licking, she didn't want to get caught in the collateral damage.

"Now, now, Gladys, Ebby—y'all just calm down, will you? Can't you see she's not...she's not thinking right?" Leland's voice strained and faltered over the words. "She must have got these from the store warehouse somehow. She was up all last night. I lost track of her when I drifted off. Maybe she sneaked out. I don't know. I just don't know." He stared across the violated yard, his words drifting away with grim thoughts left unsaid.

Ebby looked at her employer of fifteen years, really looked at him, for the first time in a long time. His black hair, graying ever quicker. The haggard dip of the sallow bags under his eyes. The clothes showing stains he didn't bother to hide, when once his countenance had been so meticulous. Ebby listened, heard the truth in the tone of that voice, a truth that pained her a little. Despite what a hateful old coot Leland pretended to be, he loved his "Peaches" more than life, and he was worried. *This is more than worried,* Ebby thought. *Leland is scared.*

"I know she's been a pill here lately," he continued. "But please don't desert us now. Missouri needs you." Leland's voice cracked and he quickly turned his back. "I need you." He wiped his eyes with the back of his hand and found a stern voice again. "There'll be a little something extra in the paychecks from now on. Now put this yard back in order." Leland walked to the house and went inside.

Missouri Pitchkettle couldn't be fooled. There was foulness afoot, she'd sensed it coming early. Summer was nigh over, and the visions in her dreams said the evil was moving in with the fall. The fall—of Salty Duck, it would be. Autumn leaves would turn blood-red this year, and death would follow. That's what her dreams told her, and these attacks to her person were proof. Evil sought her out because she *knew.* Knew...something. She wasn't sure what, but no matter; it sorted itself in the dreamscape, revealing pieces of the puzzle at its own ready.

"Ahhh!" Missouri screamed again. A hobbit was bouncing along her fence on the sidewalk. It stopped and peered through the wrought iron bars.

"Hello," the hobbit said.

Missouri clutched the rosary and ventured closer. "You there, little girl. What are you doing?"

Luna jumped up and down trying to get a better view of the strange lady talking to her. She gave up and scaled the fence instead, landing squarely in front of the older woman, who leaped back when Luna's feet hit the ground.

"I'm Luna Cole," she announced brightly.

Missouri looked around, seeing no other neighbors in sight. "Where did you come from? Who sent you?"

Luna knew her address and phone number by heart; should she recite them? And nobody sent her, certainly not her mother. She would be furious Luna left the yard and even more furious she was talking to strangers.

"*He* sent you, didn't he?" Missouri leaned to peer at the child eye level. Colorful beaded necklaces clicked and tinkled as they swayed together by gravity's pull.

Luna could smell the woman's face powder. It tickled her nose like old dust beat from a carpet. The red lipstick she wore bled into the fine cracks around the perimeter of her lips. A long braid of salt-and-pepper dark hair fell over her shoulder and for one instant Luna debated snagging the lock and giving it a sharp yank.

"You look like a gypsy," Luna said instead.

"And you look like trouble." Missouri Pitchkettle frowned, if it was possible to frown any more than she already was. She grasped Luna's chin with sapphired and rubied fingers. Her eyes widened and she abruptly let Luna go. She staggered back a step, the rosary she still held now trembling. "You…"

Luna stood quietly, looking up at the gypsy lady backing away from her. She smiled uncertainly and reached out a tiny hand. "It's okay."

Missouri shrank farther back. "He sent you, didn't he? Didn't he?" She abruptly jumped forward and grabbed Luna by the shoulders. "I saw it! In your eyes...Your father is the devil, child."

"Mrs. Pitchkettle!"

Caleb stood on the street, leaning casually over the fence. "Got a visitor, I see. Hello, Luna, how are you this morning?"

Luna ran to Caleb and away from the woman with her scary words and witchy appearance. Caleb lifted her over the fence, and she grasped him around the neck, reluctant to be set down.

"Missy, who are you talking to?" Leland called from the porch. He came down the steps and put a light hand on Missouri's arm. "Caleb. What are you doing here?"

"Not a thing, Leland. Just being neighborly and saying good morning is all."

"Be neighborly somewheres else. You know you get Missouri all stirred up. Is that your young'un?"

"No, sir. Escapee from her mother's house across the street, I believe."

"Fine, then. Keep your kids in your yard where they belong. Come along now, Peaches."

Missouri half-heartedly tried to jerk her arm away, but she let Leland lead her toward the house. At the bottom of the steps, she turned to face Caleb and Luna, who watched from the street.

"There is a pox upon this place," she hissed before allowing her husband to take her inside.

5

T EE HUBBARD, former officer and professional tracker for the State Bureau of Investigation, was dead. His ex-wife, Sheriff Gloria Hubbard, knew it all along; he'd been dead to her even before a bullet tore through his chest, nicking his left ventricle, and the dirt had piled so heavily across his body and face he could barely breathe. No, he had been dead to her the day he left North Carolina for Montana and never looked back.

But he did come back, ran back, the second she called. Eager to assist her with the mutilation cases in Doe Springs, eager to see her, just eager to be near her again, whatever the gory reason.

And that's what killed him.

The black night, a clear full moon, him and his beloved bloodhound Zeke parked in a borrowed pickup in the brush, surveying a scene, spying on the woman's house—Ivy Cole—who'd come under suspicion for the murders in Doe Springs.

And then a light shining into the truck, blinding him. A familiar voice, a friendly voice, putting his guard down, but still he could not see the face. And then a gun shot, point-blank, into the cab and the bright glare of the flashlight growing dimmer, dimmer, to dark.

Dirt. Dirt in his eyes, his nose, pressing down. Crushing weight, suffocating weight. Pain in his chest. Unbearable.

Help me, can anyone hear me? Zeke!

But these are only unspoken appeals, for his mouth is full of dirt. His fingers turn into claws, but they cannot reach up to clear the dirt away for it is all around him, embracing. Entombing. He lies still, breathes evenly, thinks. But the thoughts are not about the dirt at all, nor the pain. It is Gloria he sees, his sweet Glory, and she is with him, holding him, smiling on him again like after they first got married. This was a good place, and Tee did not want to leave....

Tee!

Sheriff Gloria Hubbard sat straight up in bed, sweat plastering her chestnut hair to her forehead and cheeks, the old gray Army T-shirt she slept in a wet sheath on her skin.

"Tee." She whispered his name into the dark room, and the words were answered by a tongue on her cheek. Chester, chocolate Labrador and loving roommate, kissed the tears away like he did most nights when this dream awoke her. It was not the same dream every time. There were different scenarios, more gruesome details, or less, when Fate was feeling merciful. But the premise of her sleeping mind's story never varied: an ambush, and his last thoughts—of her.

Fact was crueler than five years of nightmares, however, because the truth was this: She did not know what became of her ex-husband and could only live on assumptions alone. The man who supposedly killed him was now dead himself, dead before revealing his grim secrets—the hows, the wheres. Those were the two missing pieces Gloria cared about most. At least if she could find Tee, she could give him an honorable burial. She had a plot here in the Blue Ridge. She would lay him to rest overlooking the mountains he once loved, to be joined someday by a woman she was sure he had always loved. Even when she denied it. Even when she had pushed him away because of their one failed case together. Annie. The little girl killed by the same outlaw that ironically admitted to killing Tee. Little Annie of Gloria's past, a young girl devoured by a wolf in the woods with no thoughts to her innocence at all. Even though not her and Tee's own and merely a case number, to be cold about it, they had grown closer to Annie as time tortured with remembrances of failure, their failure, at saving the daughter of strangers. Or at least finding her body and giving the remains peace, if there were any remains. Werewolves did not tend to waste much, Gloria had learned. Not the efficient ones, anyway, although the rogue male that took Annie's (and presumably Tee's) life could be described as nothing complimentary, even in his killing, whether it be as the wolf or in his human guise.

But just like Annie, Tee's body had never been discovered, nor Zeke's either, for that matter. The faithful tracking hound must have met the same fate as Tee that night, and Gloria could only pray that it was a quicker end than the ones she witnessed again and again in her dreams. The ambush, however, she felt was not a vision delivered from divine sources, but rather, an instinctual notion based on police training and the intimate way she knew her ex-husband. There was no one alive who could have taken Tee and Zeke had they seen it coming.

Gloria wiped the moist hair away from her face. She gave Chester a hug before pushing his seventy pounds out of the way so she could start her day. Since the summer of the Devil, she had not needed an alarm clock. Tortured sleep was something she sought to escape every night; arguing with the sunrise over getting out of bed was never an issue. The moon greeted her most mornings. Today was a welcome exception. Dawn peeped over her windowsill, and she was grateful to see that despite the horrific nightmare, she had managed to make it through the entire night in slumber.

Chester dropped two raggedy corduroy night slippers by the side of the bed, and Gloria slid her feet into them. She went straight to her top dresser drawer, the image of Tee still hauntingly real. Times like this she could almost smell him, almost feel the stubble of his face next to hers instead of Chester's velvety muzzle trying to draw her back from the land of the dead. And when Tee was so ethereally present, she would go to her dresser and pull out the crisp legal document tucked in a drawer all its own. It was a deed to a spread in Montana, Tee's five-hundred-acre ranch just south of Glacier National Park. The executor of his estate, a lawyer named Bradshaw, had sent her the papers shortly after Tee disappeared. Gloria had not been aware, until the day the manila envelope arrived, that Tee had also listed her name on the deed.

The sheriff held the ranch papers like she held onto hope. She had never gone out to see the place. Had never even seen a picture. She didn't want to. Tee may have made her the co-owner of his property, but it was not hers. It would never be hers. It was Tee's, and he would come back for it one day. She would hold it for him until then.

"Sheriff Hubbard? Are you there? Sheriff, please pick up. This is Delores."

Gloria's answering machine talked to the old house in the voice of her administrative assistant. She picked up the bedside telephone.

"Hubbard here. What is it, Delores?"

"It's Melvin, Sheriff. I came in this morning and his desk is cleaned out. There's a letter for you, too. Do you want me to open it?"

Gloria sighed. "No. I'll be there in a few minutes."

"Oh, okay, then." Delores sounded disappointed.

Gloria hung up the phone and briefly clutched the ranch deed to her chest. Then she safely tucked the papers back into the dresser and got ready to face her day.

Deputy Melvin Sanders was gone. Gloria had tried his house first—the jangling phone went unanswered, the knock on his door the same. His truck wasn't there anyway, not that she expected it to be. There was only one other place to look, and she was there now, sitting in her cream-colored Cherokee, an old faithful vehicle that was becoming more sentimental companion than useful. Before her, crouching amid a garden gone to seed, was Ivy Cole's old house, falling down without her. Gloria came here often, but not as often as her former deputy.

That didn't sit right. Former deputy. Yet, she knew that's what he was, because this morning Gloria stopped by the office, and the letter lying on her desk was exactly what she knew it would be: resignation on crisp white paper, professional to a point, just like the man himself. Resignation, or giving up. Sanders was not one to ever give up, so she knew he was leaving for a personal cause. The sheriff wasn't too surprised, really. She had expected him to take off much sooner than now, but that was all right. Time called folks to arms at different junctures. Gloria had read between the lines of Sanders's brief note, words that dripped of five-year-old guilt. He blamed himself for what happened on that cool Blue Ridge night, when they each had almost lost their lives to two fantastical beasts pulled straight from a Grimm's tale. Melvin had what-if'd himself into despair unnecessarily, for the sheriff never blamed him. She ran her tongue over her repaired front tooth, chipped while fleeing a were—

No. Even after all she'd seen and lived through that night, even after all that horror, she still couldn't own up to it. To say the word meant to admit the impossible, and Gloria's mind still worked in universes where one plus one always equaled two and humans did not run on all fours through the forest.

Gloria looked at the rundown house. She came here knowing Sanders would never leave Doe Springs without telling it good-bye. She'd hoped to catch the man early, persuade him to come back, tell him they would muddle through the demons he must still be wrestling—they were all toting their own private crosses these days, she could certainly relate. If he needed a support group, she'd do the best she could, or find him somebody better at consoling than she.

But he wasn't here after all, and the sheriff saw no need to go inside. She knew every line on the walls, every skidmark in the hardwoods, every sound that resonated in the echoes of silent memory: Ivy's dogs greeting them with barks and howls, Ivy's pleasant Southern drawl quieting them, the wind pulling the strings of the porch chimes when anyone passed.

Gloria started the engine and glanced at the cottage one last time.

I hope you find whatever you're looking for, Melvin. I hope you find peace.

Someone rapped on the Jeep's window, and Gloria jerked around, hoping to see a big black Dodge pulled up beside her. It was not Sanders after all. She rolled the window down.

"Hello, Sheriff," Police Chief Wilkerson said. "I found her."

6

"LUNA COLE! What did I tell you? Just what did I tell you?"

Ivy crossed Battery Street in her bare feet, heading strong for the neighbor's house and the stranger holding her child. When she looked out the kitchen window onto an empty backyard, her heart had double-flipped into her stomach and now they both thumped and ached together in a jangled mishmash of nerves. Ivy was not very familiar with this particular feeling, but Luna had had the ability to elicit it in her mother on more than one occasion. It was fear.

"She's fine," the stranger who dared to still hold her child said.

"Mommy, it's Caleb," Luna said, her arms tight around the man's neck. "He saved me from the gypsy woman. She's gone now."

"Gypsy? What?"

Caleb laughed and set Luna on her flip-flops. "Mrs. Pitchkettle gave her a fright. Heck, the woman even scares me. They're an odd flock of birds over here."

Ivy knew that was true. To the side of the monstrous Victorian structure and toward the back she could see two ladies hard at work setting plants. A pile of flesh-colored plastic was stacked against the fence. Yep, she'd been right. It was just a silly prank after all, involving a little cleanup and nothing more. Should she wander over and tell the women about what she'd witnessed anyway? No, she'd let it be. Right now there was other pressing business to tend to.

"I told you to play in the yard, Luna, not run amok up and down the Keep. I'm getting worn out with your not listening to me. Do I need to ground you? Keep you in your room and not let you play outside at all? Do you remember what happened in Winnipeg?"

Luna looked up at Ivy through glistening gems. The floodwaters were perilously close to spilling over, and Aufhocker appeared at Luna's side. He nuzzled up under her arm, and Luna buried her face in his broad black neck, hiding from her mother's wrath. Ivy hated when the wolf coddled her—she felt undermined—but being stern on the child was hard for both of them. It was for her own good, though. That's what mothers did, even when it killed them inside.

Caleb studied cracks in the sidewalk, embarrassed to be a part of the fracas, yet not willing to give up ground till he'd tried an introduction one more time. When it looked like the nor'easter was merely going to be a mild blow of wind, he stuck out his hand. "Let's start over. I'm Caleb, slayer of evil gypsy women everywhere, at your service."

Ivy's attention lifted from the depressed duo to the hand offered her. She paused, then took it.

"I'm Ivy, mother of the properly chastened. At least, I hope so."

"That's quite a grip you've got there, Ivy. Arm wrestle for a living, do you?"

"Only part-time. Thanks for, well, whatever happened here. Luna has a knack for getting into sticky wickets. Keeps me a nervous wreck."

It did indeed. Winnipeg apartment living had been a challenge. Luna had learned to walk by the time she was eight months old, and opening doors was her specialty. The uppity neighbors in the old brownstone did not appreciate finding the toddler standing in their living rooms or bedrooms at odd hours while her anxious mother ran up and down the halls calling her name. But what was a young mother wolf to do when the pup was of wandering age and wouldn't stay put? Locks. That had been the answer. And plenty of them.

Ivy was not anxious to imprison her daughter like that again. She wanted her to have freedom here, to run with her hair loose in the wind and sand between her toes, to feel safe without the necessity of deadbolts.

"I'm glad I could help," Caleb said. "Hey, even your dog seems to have warmed up."

"Don't press your luck with him. He's not warmed up, he's just occupied."

"Trust me, after our first meeting, I don't intend to test him."

Aufhocker listened but paid the adults little mind. He felt Ivy's tension leave the minute Luna was out of the man's arms and by her side again. Things were all right, and sensing this, the wolf was all about the girl in his ruff, her sniffles giving way to giggles as he tried to reach around and lick whatever he could reach. Her knees, at the moment.

Ivy saw the change. Luna was turning all smiles again, her reprimand forgotten.

"Well, then, I guess that's that," she said to Caleb. "We'll be on our way. Thanks again."

Caleb bent down to Luna. "I'm sure I'll be seeing you around, little miss Luna. Maybe one of these days you would like to take a ride up the sound, maybe tool around the island and pony watch? I've got a fishing boat collecting barnacles down at the dock. So you cheer up, okay?" Caleb tugged her ponytail and stood up. "Oh, and you're invited, too, of course," he said to Ivy. "Have a good day." Caleb strode up the street, whistling.

Ivy smelled the festival halfway down Battery Street. A nose not even as fine-tuned as hers could detect the sugary sweetness of funnel cake or the salted steam of boiling shellfish on the air. After the to-do this morning, Ivy'd decided to forget job hunting altogether and visit the craft festival instead. She could find a job anytime, but steamed oysters and chowder cooked in an outdoor tent on the sound—how often could she get that? Besides, Luna needed a taste of local culture. It would be good for the whole family. All three of them.

"Mommy, do you smell it? Do you smell it?" Luna clapped her hands and jumped up and down. Auf sidestepped to avoid the child's trampling feet. "I'm going to eat crab cakes till I pop." She skipped ahead, past rows of turn-of-the-nineteenth-century homes, which only got older as they approached Parish Keep Courtyard, the Salty Duck Historic District's grassy communal area overlorded by live oaks and magnolias that rivaled each other in size if not age.

Ivy and her small pack turned left off Battery, through a trellis dripping vines of wisteria, and into the crowded square. The visitors center, itself a restored 1800s apothecary, was wide open and flooded by folks in island wear, brimmed hats, suntan oil, and shades. But it was the colorful ice-cream-colored tents that had drawn the crowd, for therein were the artisans: the potters, quilters, sculptors, photographers, basket weavers, shellers, jewelers. Laughter and the low hum of excited babbling wafted with the smells of the food, and Luna could hold back no longer. She was off for a booth touting homemade apple dumplings, Aufhocker trotting alongside to keep up. Satisfied Luna was not leaving yelling distance, Ivy lingered by the nearest vendor, a painter's tent, his oil work laid out on heavy canvasses and gray wooden frames that resembled honed driftwood.

"'Tis beautiful, aye, love?"

Ivy looked up. A man sat on a stool at the back of the tent dressed in pirate garb complete with eye patch and peg leg. A large plume wavered above his black buccaneer hat.

"You're the artist?" Ivy asked.

"Aye, that I am. Painted it with me very hook." The man held up his left hand, covered by a gray plastic crescent from the dime store. Ivy tried not to laugh. As silly as his tourist-friendly approach might be, the artist had talent. The rendering of a milky moon hovering over Marshy Bottom and the ghostly spire of the Pious Cape Lighthouse rising from it was the most beautiful she'd ever seen. She was captivated by the opal light and felt her eyes involuntarily start to shimmer orange. She quickly looked away from the painting and its unearthly pull like the true moon itself. A wolfscape it was, dark like the hiding woods, only these shadows of moonlight bore ripples from black water.

"How much?"

"For you, me pretty lady, a mere three hundred shillings will cover it."

"Oh, I didn't bring enough for that." Ivy looked longingly at the oil.

"'Tis but a pittance of the regular cost, me lady. Five hundred after today. Three is a discount for the lovely wenches of the Duck." The pirate wiggled his eyebrows, dislodging the black patch. He quickly reseated it and stared at Ivy expectantly through one uncovered brown eye.

"Bruce, you're a thief," a new voice said from Ivy's side. Startled, she turned to see who had joined her.

"Caleb! Man, I didn't think you were ever coming back. My butt's numb from sitting on this stool, and I've got a boot-scootin' boogie night planned," the pirate said, his swashbuckler accent suddenly morphing to Low-Country cowboy. "How am I s'posed to dazzle the gals on the dance floor with my cheeks all squeezed up in a knot like this? Next time get the balloon lady to watch your stuff when you need to high-tail it out for something." Bruce looked at Ivy. "As for you, good looking, you could've bartered this painting down to nothing. I'm a pushover for the women. If you want to come cut a jig at the Boondocker, me and this peg can do some real fancy footwork. Be there at eight. See you then." He tipped his hat and hobbled off with a loud "Aargh, ahoy mateys" to a group of children who had wandered his way.

"He's not serious, is he?" Ivy said.

"Hopeful is more like it. What do you think?"

"Cut a jig at the Boondocker with Bruce and his fake peg leg? I don't think I could keep up."

Caleb laughed. "The painting. I meant the painting."

Ivy smiled. "Oh, that. Well, Blackbeard would have been proud of Bruce. Three hundred, he said. Sounds like piracy at high seas. But, I have to admit, it's worth it. So you're an artist as well as friendly neighbor and rescuer of small children everywhere. Where do you find the time?"

"You'd be surprised how much downtime superheroes really have. Now seriously, you like this?" Caleb raised a brow looking at his work. "I couldn't decide if it looked like a moon coming up over the Outer Banks, or a big searchlight stuck in the middle of a bad hotel portrait."

"Motel art has its own niche, you know. Your market's covered, either way." *I'm flirting,* Ivy thought with sudden horror. One pretty picture with the moon and suddenly she was moony herself. "Well, good luck with all that. I appear to have lost my child again. Excuse me."

"Wait, don't run off. Luna's fine. Look—the pirate's found her."

It looked to be the other way around. Luna and Auf had Bruce the Buccaneer backed against a tree. She was firing a chain of questions at the man concerning Captain Hook, buried treasure, Peter Pan, and improbable death by tick-tocking crocodiles at sea.

"Here, take this." Caleb picked up the painting and handed it to Ivy.

"As beautiful as this is, I don't have three hundred dollars. I don't even have ten dollars left, by the looks of all the stuff I've seen Luna eating since we got here. I hope the vendors have been more honest with my money than your helper. Otherwise, I'm broke."

"Bruce is not my helper, but I have to admit, I'm a lot like him when it comes to the ladies. I want you to have it. Think of it as a housewarming present."

I would so love to have it, Ivy thought, while looking longingly at the picture. But it was too much, in more ways than perhaps Caleb was intending, and she couldn't take chances. If it was in every way Caleb intended, the friendship should stop here. *What friendship?* her inner voice chided. It had never even started. She was making sure of it.

"Thank you, but I can't let you do that. It's too valuable."

"Okay, let's try something different. It just so happens I'm looking for some help. You can work off the cost of the painting."

"You don't even know me."

"I don't know anybody in Salty Duck except for the Pitchkettles, so you're as good as the next guy, I'd say."

"What about Bruce over there?"

"Too many handicaps, and I'm not talking about the Wal-Mart prostheses." Caleb tapped his temple. "What do you say?"

"I say what's the job?"

"Hi, Mommy. Look what I got." Luna held a drippy strawberry cone up to her mother. It was half-melted and lopsided. "It's for you."

"Oh, great. Thank you, Boo. How much have you had to eat, by the way?"

"I'm almost full, Mommy. Hi, Caleb. Here's mine, if you want it." Luna held out her own strawberry blob barely hanging on to the edge of the sugar cone. "Or you can have this." She fished a deviled crab out of her pocket, the moist breading leaving a stain on her denim shorts.

"That's just about the nicest thing anybody's ever given me, Luna, but I'd rather you keep it." Caleb said. To Ivy: "My boat is a wreck. When I said it's down at the marina collecting barnacles, I wasn't kidding. If you've got some time to spare, you could help wipe the deck down, get the mildew cleaned off, stuff like that." Caleb shook the painting like fish bait. "Interested?"

Ivy eyed the jiggling moon, but it was tethered to a hook of obligation. And yet, wouldn't the artwork look amazing over the white brick fireplace in her bedroom, just above the precious mantel clock that had belonged to her mother?

"I'll consider it."

"Well, then," Caleb said, setting the painting behind the table, "I'll just hold on to this until you decide."

Marcus Daywright was an opportunist when it came to picking women, and opportunity was across the courtyard in hip-hugger jeans, sandals, and a cute little cut-off T-shirt that showed her trim waist. Long blond hair was bound up in a messy ponytail on top of her head; how he'd love to set that hair free and run his big hands through every strand of it. Like sugar sand, the locals might call it. That's what it would feel like.

But gals like that never went for his kind. Oh, below the neck got plenty enough attention. Years on his daddy's farm had grown his corn-fed son into a powerful man. Then working docks up and down the coast had kept middle-aged spread at bay. But the knob on his shoulders was average at best, and slinging fish for a living was a smelly occupation that proved to be female repellent guaranteed. Some women he'd known in the past, bar maids and strippers mostly, said he was "nice looking, in a way that grew on you." He reckoned it was true, but he never could trust a woman who was taking his singles in her teeth. He'd moved on to better work, upped his stock value, so to speak. Gotten on the right path at last.

This one, Goldilocks, was unmarried. Marcus could tell by the way she flirted with the man at the painter's tent. By her age—thirties, he guessed, a little younger than him—and the fact she had a kid tagging along, she must be divorced. The available looks of her announced it to every red-blooded male in the place. The pirate had given it a shot. And got shot down, too. Marcus got a chuckle out of it. He'd seen the whole thing. The other man seemed to have more to offer, but in the end she had wandered away from him as well. Now Marcus just took stock of the woman as she sauntered his way. Slutty clothes. Broken marriage. One child the spitting image of the woman even down to the ponytail, a bastard most likely, hanging on to Mama's apron strings while she threw herself at whatever man fell across her path. Just to pass 'em on by anyway. A tease. The worst kind of woman, the kind of woman who had made Marcus's life hell. The kind of woman who laughed when you asked her out because your daddy weren't rich and your clothes weren't made in town and your face didn't look like it belonged on a damn magazine cover.

Marcus was done analyzing. Sinful. That was his bona fide assessment. Pure-T sinful. Women like that deserved what they got. Or what they lost.

Marcus took another bite of his hotdog and watched the woman, child, and shepherd browsing from one tent to the next on their winding course around the courtyard. The dog would be an issue. Big. What? Near two hundred pounds maybe. Stupidly big. Who the hell kept a dog like that? "I'll tell you," Marcus said around his hotdog, "scared women, that's who. Women with no man in the house to protect them. *Divorced* women."

He wiped his mouth with a paper napkin, then threw it in the wastebasket beside his bench. Slowly, Goldilocks and her entourage were making their way in his direction. She paused over handmade beaded jewelry. Sweet grass baskets up from Georgia caught her eye. She moved on to wind chimes constructed from shell. These she purchased. Marcus watched patiently as the crone at the booth gingerly wrapped the chimes in newspaper and the two engaged in pleasantries.

Here she comes. Marcus pretended to watch the crowd in front of him as the woman edged into his peripheral vision. She glided right by without a look. Not even a glance.

Marcus was not surprised. He could have thrown himself off the bench in front of her and she probably would not have even bothered to step over. His back had plenty of footprints on it. Well, that had all come to a stop, hadn't it?

Go to church and find a nice girl there, Marcus, he could hear his dear ole mama saying. *You won't never find nothing but white trash at those places you hang out in. Are you listening to me, boy?* Whap. There came the broom. Even in his twenties, his mother still smacked him with it when she thought he wasn't listening. His daddy thought it was funny. That all ended, too, when he was twenty-six. And nobody had been laughing then.

But he had to hand it to the old witch: She was right. Nothing but white trash if it weren't hanging out in church, and even there Satan masqueraded in the guise of beautiful women. A God-fearing man had to be careful. Evil was all around, and it was, decidedly, effeminate.

"Marcus, you still with us?" Ellory Roak poked him with a wooden spoon, and Marcus's head snapped around. The look on his face must have been similar to the one his mother saw before he ripped the broom from her hands and beat her with it until she lay in a heap, unconscious.

"Whoa, Marcus, it's just me. Your crab pots are starting to boil over, and we're out of coleslaw," Ellory said, the spoon held high in surrender.

Marcus's face softened into a genial smile. "I'll get right on it, Ellory. Be there in a second."

Ellory did a mock salute and Marcus put his attention back on Goldilocks. She was laughing at something the kid must have said. They clasped hands and left the courtyard, heading west up Battery. Marcus's gaze bore into her back, imagining...

On the woman's other side, the black shepherd paused. His head swiveled around and eyes the color of char locked on the man on the bench.

Marcus sat up straighter. The hairs on his arms did the same.

"Reverend, I hate to keep bothering you, but we're lined up ten deep, and there's no slaw."

Marcus turned to Ellory. "Coming, son. You're doing a fine job over there. The church will raise a fortune this weekend thanks to young deacons like you." Ellory beamed at the praise and walked back to the Parish Keep Ministry tent.

Reverend Marcus Daywright looked back up Battery Street, but the woman and strange dog were gone.

7

FORMER DEPUTY Melvin Sanders checked the address on the mail-box again, but it was pointless: He couldn't read it. Kudzu swaddled the stone and mortar structure till it was barely visible, save for the hole for the mailman, and even that looked to be a battle soon lost. Behind the vine-claimed box, a once-elegant wrought iron gate hung halfway open between two more supporting stone columns that were crumbling around rusted hinges. A crest graced the middle of the gate; it was a rose encircled by a tangle of thorns, but "choked" came to Melvin's mind, much like the state of the mailbox and the creep-ers climbing over the wall that separated the estate from the rest of the world. This was once known as Briar Rose Plantation, but today, according to the farmer who had given Melvin directions from his John Deere ten miles back, it was now simply called Cole's Old Place.

Melvin hopped out of the Dodge and swung the eight-foot-high gate the rest of the way open. Ahead of him lay a cracked paved drive now sprinkled by some early leaf fall. Autumn was nearing the Blue Ridge—indeed, he was only an hour away from Doe Springs—and by the looks of all the old-growth poplars and maples lining the driveway, this path would soon be aflame in the vibrant shades of the season.

As he rolled toward the plantation mansion looming ahead, Melvin pictured horse-drawn carriages and the stately gentlemen who may have driven them. It was all Southern Goth, with soaring columns and a sweeping front porch that perhaps once entertained society's finest. *Impressive,* he'd thought, until the truck pulled closer and he saw how the grand dame's once elegant façade had cracked. Like a fading starlet attempting to hide her age with powder and face paint, so too had this once graceful home lost its battle with time. When Melvin climbed the steps to the porch, he was careful to side-step rotting boards in the floor.

Melvin raised his hand to knock on one of the heavy double doors and was startled when the door jerked open ahead of him.

"I've done been ordered to tell any of you meddlesome squirrels to scurry on out of here. Mabry ain't well, so git." A woman in her early twenties stood before him, fists on the hips of her white nurse's uniform and her brown hair wound up in a bun too matronly for her age. She backed up a step and slammed the door before Melvin had a chance to say hello.

He knocked again, harder, and when her face appeared through the door's window this time, it was eye to eye with his badge, which, for reasons sentimental, he had neglected to leave in Doe Springs with his resignation.

"Hello, ma'am. I'm Deputy Melvin Sanders, and I need to speak with Mr. Cole, please."

The door whipped open again. Thin lips pursed with displeasure and Melvin noticed on close-up that three hairs poked from a mole on her chin.

"What's all this about? You come to arrest a poor old sick man on his deathbed? Is that how y'all are running it down at city hall these days?"

"Ma'am, I'm not from city hall and this is concerning personal business. I didn't realize Mr. Cole was so ill, but it will only take a minute, I promise you." Melvin made sure she got another good look at the badge before tucking it away.

"Well, reckon I can't keep you out, you being the law and all. I better announce you before you go running up there, though, and if

Mabry won't receive you, I'm calling the city and making a complaint. Now you wait right here," she pointed to a spot of chipped parquet just inside the foyer, "and I'll come get you when he's ready."

The nurse stepped aside, letting the big deputy into the entrance hall. High above Melvin gleamed a chandelier. Or, at least at one time it had gleamed. The sparkle was now dimmed by dust, and a long, tenuous thread of cobweb connected its base to the top of the stairwell. A staircase wound toward it, and the nurse climbed it now, leaving her intruder alone in the large, echoing room.

Melvin ran a hand through his closely cropped dark hair. Ivy had told him a long time ago that the relatives on her daddy's side were all crazy, and he wondered if this girl might be one of them. Maybe a cousin. She certainly was not going to be any help, and the thoughts of going to battle for answers just made Melvin tired. Truly, he could let this go right now. Get back in his truck and drive home. Not Doe Springs or even Asheville where he'd been raised, but all the way to West Virginia, where his roots were strongest and his dead daddy's sweat had splattered the coal he shoveled.

But he'd tried to let this go for five years now, and it wasn't a matter of *him* letting *it* go. It had grabbed hold of him with a vengeance too terrible to utter, and the only way to stop it— maybe—was to find the source. And the first key to finding that source lay inside this house. With Ivy's crazy cousin and sick uncle.

"He'll see you, but you better make it quick." The girl stared down at Melvin from the top of the stairs.

"Thank you," he said. "I won't be long."

Melvin stood at the foot of a massive four-poster mahogany bed, its duvet and velvet pillows the color of spilled blood. Woodland animals chased one another from one end of the kingly headboard to the other, and the posts were just as intricately carved. Huddled in the center of it all was a small, dwindling man the color of grave ash. Tufts of white hair sprouted over his ears, and the lines in his face were as deeply etched as the ornamental bed he lay within. *Inquisitor* ran through Melvin's head, a first-impression response he immediately shamed himself for. The man was old, sick, dying apparently, and Melvin felt only compassion.

Mr. Cole drew in a raspy breath and released it like a death rattle. Then he spoke.

"I been meaning to come down to city hall and give you a rank piece of my mind, you dung-wallowing, pig-filth loving, scum-sucking puddle of dog vomit. Let me show my gratitude for saving me the trip." Mabry Cole, in a surprisingly agile move for one so frail, snatched the telephone off the end table and flung it at Melvin's head.

"Mabry, stop it!" The young nurse stood in the doorway and had barely ducked the flying phone. "He ain't from city hall. I done told you that two seconds ago, don't you remember?"

"He's not? You're not?" Mabry squinted at Melvin, raking his eyes up and down the man as if hoping they'd snag on something identifiable. "This isn't about the taxes or the auction?"

"No, sir," Melvin said, standing upright from his ducked position. "I'm from Doe Springs and I'm not on duty. This is personal, a Cole family matter."

Mabry Cole sat up straighter, and suddenly he didn't look so very sick at all. "Well, then, let's start again. Pull up a chair. Nurse Ratched, go get us some tea with plenty of lemon. Make mine hot."

The girl frowned and left the room.

"That's not really her name, Nurse Ratched. Gets all over her when I call her that, though. Now what's all this about? The only visitors I get anymore are ones with their hands out. For some reason, you don't strike me any different. What do you want?"

"Sir, like I said, it's regarding the Cole family."

"Are we kin? You're not some nephew I don't know about, are you? Because I've had nephews and nieces popping out of the woodwork since word got out I'm only fifty percent on this side of the dirt. Put a foot in the grave and you'd be mighty surprised how many concerned family members you'll suddenly get, like Nurse Ratched in there, but she's earning her keep, I'm making sure of that.

So if you're sniffing for a piece of the estate, she'll get whatever bone's left. There's nothing much but scraps here anyway after those vultures at the tax office went after us. And that was just before the hyenas at the bank ran their teeth over us. So if'n it's money you're looking for, forget it."

"No, sir, it's nothing like that. But it is about one of your nieces—Ivy."

"My brother William's girl? Ah yes, weird little withdrawn Ivy. I remember her well. All grown up now with five kids and fifty extra pounds, I'll wager. She sent you?"

"Actually, no. I'm looking for her, and I was thinking maybe she'd been in contact with you at some point. I understand she doesn't have a lot of family left, but you're nearby to where she used to live. Doe Springs."

Mabry settled deeper into his pillows, sighing, and the lines on his face slacked. A couple of minutes passed with him staring at some unknown location on the ceiling, and Melvin feared the old gent had fallen asleep right there in front of him. Or died. His eyes were wide open after all.

"Mr. Cole?"

"Been a long time," Mabry finally said, his eyes dropping from the ceiling to refocus on his company. "I was just studying on it all. Sure do miss my brother, even if he did betray the lot of us and run off to New York instead of taking over the family textiles like he was supposed to. Probably wouldn't be in this hellhole if he were still around to run things. But no, Will had bigger fish to fry than sticking around in Podunk. Married that German woman, Catherine. What a looker. Sweet, too. Daddy couldn't stand her, the sour old bigot, but a shame what happened just the same. Whole family was destined for tragedy. Ivy couldn't have done much better if the police are looking for her, am I right?"

"She's not in trouble. I..." What? What could he possibly say? Melvin didn't know how to end the thought, how to explain to this bitter old man that he was more bitter still, not for losing what he thought was owed him, like Mabry seemed to be, but for gaining a Cole "gift" he knew he never deserved.

Mabry's watery green eyes slitted like a python's at Melvin's stumble. He leaned forward and jabbed a nicotine-stained finger the deputy's direction. "You her husband? She run off and leave you? Is that what this is about?"

"Something like that." It was close to the truth, and Mabry saved him from lying. Melvin went with it.

Mabry nodded like he knew it all along. "Coles are cursed, that's what it is. You might've married her, but she'll always be a Cole."

Cursed? An odd word choice. Significant, or mere coincidence?

"My advice is cut your losses and let her go," Mabry continued. "I couldn't help you even if I wanted to. Haven't seen that girl since she lived up North and weren't more than a freckle-faced teenager."

"That's too bad," Melvin said. It surely was. He was hoping Cole could give him the easy answer and save the trouble of doing heavier footwork. But Melvin was prepared to play gumshoe for as long as it took to track the quarry down.

"What about on her stepmama's side? Have you tried any of them?" Mabry said. "That trollop Will married after Catherine passed, Una—she had a passel of brothers and sisters. Come to think of it, doesn't one of them, Ava, still live in Doe Springs? She'd be right long in the tooth these days if she's even still alive, but Ivy might still be in touch with her. She's got another uncle too. Stefan, I think's his name. Kraut, lives in Germany. Try one of them."

Melvin had. They were the obvious choices, but Ava denied knowing anything about her niece's whereabouts, and Stefan seemed to have disappeared. If Ivy were still in the States, it would be easier tracking her here than trying to hunt down Stefan Heinrich across the ocean. As for Ava—the Widow Pritchard, as she was called about town—Melvin knew she was a liar, but what could he do? Throttle an old woman until the truth came out? *Shame on you, Melvin Sanders. There was a time when even the speculation of that would not have entered your mind.*

" 'Course, I wish she had've called, Deputy, or we might not be in the fix we're in right now." Mabry interrupted Melvin's musings and kicked at his covers in disgust. "William's trust could have pulled this pile of rubble back together, made it look like an estate again.

But I doubt Ivy would give the Coles a dime of it, after the way we shunned Catherine all those years and took up with Una so quickly after her death. Ah well, nothing to be done about it now except look back and regret."

"Mr. Cole, about the trust—was it in Ivy's name?"

"She inherited it, but it was in Will and Una's name originally. Since they were killed at the same time—murdered, God rest their souls—it all passed to Ivy then."

"But still in the parents' names?"

"Ivy's now, of course. But if she's running, a smart girl would be using an alias for legal matters and accounts. It's a substantial amount of money, Deputy Sanders. You find that money, you'll find Ivy. But a husband would know all about that. You ain't her husband, are you?"

"No, sir. I'm sorry to have misled you before, but I have to find your niece, and it is personal. That part was true. Can I ask you something else?"

Mabry shrugged. His gaze began to drift upward, and Melvin jumped in before losing the old man to the ceiling once more.

"You said before that the Coles are cursed. Do you—how do I put this? Do you know anything about Ivy's special abilities?"

"Special abilities?" Mabry snorted. "Only thing special about that girl was the way her two mamas and Daddy felt about her. After losing them, she didn't have nothing else, save all that money she was too young to manage and a god-awful black dog she toted every-where. Ivy left home and lost touch with all of us. I heard she was a fine dog trainer, if that's what you mean, but I'd hardly call that spe-cial."

"Yes, someone like yourself would certainly be in a position to judge."

Mabry's liver-speckled lips drew up into a spiteful grin. "You got it bad, don't you, boy? I feel sorry for you. Love and hate when they're twined in a heart can pull a man apart, can't they? Good luck with your hunt, Deputy Sanders."

"Thank you, Mr. Cole, you've been very helpful. I appreciate your time."

"Time's all I got, and it gets away from me a little more every day." Mabry watched Melvin walk to the bedroom door. "Deputy?"

Melvin turned.

"You be careful out there now, you hear? When the wolves are knocking at your door, don't let them in, son. Don't ever let them in." Mabry winked, and then his eyes rolled up toward heaven again and he began to snore.

8

THE RED light blinked. On. Off. Continuously. Reverend Marcus Daywright, his face bathed in its scarlet glow, had come to see it as a beacon of sorts. A warning light, of hellfire surely. Red as sinner's blood, red as the flame of Satan. This was a place of Sodom he dwelled in, under the deceptively peaceful name The Sea Mist Motor Lodge.

Tonight the reverend knelt by his bed, both knees on the cold floor, hands clasped together under his chin, elbows propped on the mattress, the red blinking light his reminder of eternal damnation and the promise of God's love. In front of him, open to the First Book of Samuel, lay the Old Testament, and he recited it now. He did not need to look at the Good Book to say the words for he'd heard them plenty growing up, right before the broom bashing would begin.

"'The Lord killeth, and maketh alive: he bringeth down to the grave, and bringeth up. The Lord maketh poor, and maketh rich: he bringeth low, and lifteth up.'"

Someone walked by the window, their silhouette bulky behind the red-lit blinds. The figure paused, and then ambled on. Marcus paid the passerby no attention. He canted—loudly—every night, and the regulars of the rundown inn were used to him by now, accustomed to the random shouts and citations coming from behind the closed doors of Room 37.

Marcus's lids began to droop as the sweet verses poured from his mouth like the Last Supper's wine. He ran his tongue over his lips, tasting the words, tasting the law of the Book. Smoky gray irises disappeared behind vein-strung runny whites as the Word gripped him, and on he prayed.

"'He raiseth up the poor out of the dust, and lifteth up the beggar from the dunghill to set them among princes, and to make them inherit the throne of glory: for the pillars of the earth are the Lord's, and he hath set the world upon them.'"

Marcus's hands trembled in their mighty clasped grip. Spittle dripped down the reverend's chin. "'He will keep the feet of his saints.'" A hand slid from the grasp of the other and moved lower, lower, unzipping the pants, the hand sliding inside. "'And the wicked shall be silent in darkness.'" Marcus's voice rose, the deep tones breaking adolescently over long vowels and stiff consonants.

"And the wicked shall be silent in darkness." The words flowed faster. "The wicked shall be silent in darkness." Faster. "Wicked shall be silent in darkness." Faster! *"Andthewickedshallbesilentindarkness."*

Frantically, the hand. Frantically, the words. Flinging the verses heavenward in a crescendoed flurry of slurred speech. His body shook, his eyes rolled farther back, the red light warned, he was bathed in the blood of the light...

And with...a...final...gasp: *"THE WICKED WILL BURN IN HELL YOU SORRY MOTHERFUCKING COCKSUCKERS!"*

Marcus slumped over the mattress, sweat matting his hair and dripping onto the pages of his Bible. He grasped the edge of the dingy white bedspread and wiped his face with it. It smelled faintly of urine, and he thrust it away in disgust. Outside his window, another figure had paused.

"Get out of here!" Marcus screamed at the backlit shadow. The person moved away, a drunken sway to their lilt.

Marcus rose to his feet, mindful of the creaking in his knees. He should be praying on floors of pure gold, not floors of harvest gold carpet pockmarked by Marlboro Lights. This room was too drafty, too, what with fall coming on; he'd most likely need to find a better place before winter or his whole body would be nothing but aches and pains come ice weather. He couldn't help the church in a condition like that, but what would Parish Keep Presbyterian think of him if they saw him living like this anyway? Some folks just wouldn't understand what he was about, and that's why he stayed here, fifteen miles outside Salty Duck and out from under watchful eyes and curious noses.

The reverend zipped his pants and grabbed his Bible. Not the one on the bed, but this one from underneath it. A larger version, which he found much more useful in moments like these. And the moment was, indeed, at hand. Prayers said, it was time to go to work.

Marcus got into his pickup—an obscure, disappear-into-the-background brown—and drove to the end of the parking lot. He turned toward the coast, the flashing red motel sign disappearing in the rearview behind a swinging cross pendant, a gift from his late, sainted mother.

"Boo! Where are you? It's bedtime." Ivy stood at the intersection between dining and living rooms, at the foot of the stairs. It was House Central, and yelling at the top of her lungs could usually reach her rambunctious child whatever her coordinates.

No matter this night—Ivy heard them both, Aufhocker and Luna. They were on the roof, in the widow's walk.

Ivy mounted the stairs, through the second floor loft past the door to Luna's bedroom, and up another narrow flight of stairs onto the roof. Two butts faced the door, one child, one lifelong companion who had appointed himself guardian of the house. They enjoyed the moonlit view, over other rooftops, beyond Salty Duck's Front Street, past the Intracoastal Waterway, or the "Ditch," as mariners called it, and all the way to the Mother Sea herself. A damaged circle of moon balanced on the tightrope of a black horizon. Nearly round and perfect, it was. But just nearly. *Soon,* Ivy thought.

She joined her family and scratched Aufhocker's head, the love of her life since a young teen herself. He leaned against her leg slightly.

"Isn't it beautiful, Boo? See that constellation? It's Orion the Hunter. And there," Ivy shifted her pointing finger a fraction, "is his eternal companion, Canis Major."

"A major dog?"

"Sort of. It means 'the Big Dog.'"

"Like Auf!"

Ivy laughed. "Yes, just like Auf. That white dot in Canis Major is called Sirius, the Dog Star. It's the brightest in the sky, even brighter than the sun, if it were closer to Earth. Appropriate, don't you think?"

"It's not the brightest," Luna said, unimpressed. "Look over there. See it, Mommy?"

"That's not a star. That's the Pious Cape Lighthouse." *In Caleb's painting,* Ivy thought. It was the same breathtaking night sky with a wisp of haze wrapped around the lighthouse and a corona of gold soft about the moon. It had been two days since the craft festival, and still Ivy had not answered Caleb's offer. But seeing his canvas brought to life here from the top of her cottage made her answer a little easier. She would call on him. In time. Yes, she would. Maybe.

Auf's head jerked under Ivy's massaging hand. He craned his head around to stare at the rooftop door behind them, ears perked.

Ivy heard it, too, her own senses more well-tuned than even her wolf's. A latch in the house had opened and closed. The wind had picked up; surely she had not forgotten to close the front door.

"Luna, honey, stay here for a minute, okay?"

Luna didn't answer. She was still mesmerized by the phantom light radiating from Pious Cape.

"Stay with her, Auf. I'll be right back."

Ivy descended through the cottage, her senses suddenly on keen alert. There was an interesting odor coming from the living room, a new smell that did not belong here. Something wrong was in the house.

"Hello? Anybody home?" a voice called from that direction.

A man stood just inside the front door, a wide-brimmed hat in one hand and an oversized Bible tucked in his arm. "There you are. I'm sorry to barge on in like this, but I knocked and the door was open." He waved the hat toward the door as if to assign it the blame.

Ivy stared at him from across the room.

The man smiled and tried again. "I swore I heard someone say come in." He shifted the Bible and the letters of the gilded title poked above his forearm more prominently. "Anyway, I'm Reverend Marcus Daywright. I'm with the Parish Keep Presbyterian Chapel down here on the corner of Mission and Cemetery Cross." He held out his free hand.

Ivy noted the calluses on the large palm from across the room. "They work you that hard at the ministry, Reverend?"

Marcus's brows knitted, puzzled. He looked at his hand—the hand she did not rush over to accept—and redeposited it by his side.

Ivy breathed in deeply, inhaling the sweet and sour of her uninvited guest. He did not smell of a chapel. She searched her inner database and came up with the unsanctified scents of moldering wood paneling, musty carpet, and a wafting of...urine?

"The pastor's name is Reverend Holliday. I've passed the church many times," Ivy finally said, the coldness in her voice a nearly tangible barrier between them.

"True, and how good of you to notice. We don't get much recognition, sure enough, so we mighty do appreciate when somebody does take the time to pay attention. I'm a visiting pastor, from a fellowship in South Carolina. Reverend Holliday is my spiritual brother, and I'll be up for as long as he'll have me."

Ivy nodded and peered hard into his face. "Wait. I do recognize you. From the craft festival. You were sitting on a park bench eating a hot dog."

Reverend Daywright's eyes widened slightly. "Why, yes, young lady. I was helping the church raise some money with a fish fry."

Ivy remembered the tent behind him, the steaming kettles of crab, the large canisters of homemade coleslaw, the savory ears of roasted corn. He was with the church after all. She tentatively extended her hand at last and he gripped it firmly.

"I'm sorry, Reverend. I'm Ivy Cole. I'm new in town and finding strangers inside my door can be unnerving to say the least." Her strong grip belied the lukewarm way in which the handshake was delivered, and her tone barely warmed past frigid. "Is there something I can help you with? I'd be glad to give a donation, but isn't it late to be calling on folks for such a thing?"

"It's never too late to do the Lord's work." Reverend Daywright still held Ivy's hand. He looked down at her, but the smile that he offered was by no means fatherly. "They call me the Preacher Man back home. Tell me, child, have you found the Lord?"

The man's eyes bore into Ivy's harder through the soft resonance of his words. Ivy looked from his face, across the width of his oak-crossbow shoulders, back to the hand that still gripped hers. It trembled slightly. The hat slid from his other hand to rest on the floor beside dirty tennis shoes.

It was wrong, those shoes, the placating tone, the hour. The man made no move to retrieve the hat. It lay there, prone beside his ankle, an anchor holding time still now, for neither man nor woman moved.

Marcus's grin deepened despite himself, a sideways sneer that slid up one corner of his mouth into his cheek like a scythe pulling up the skin. Did she know? Did the lamb suddenly realize there was a culling a-coming? That the blade of the Lord was about to smite the unholy from the flock? A chuckle followed the grin, Marcus couldn't contain it. His hands tremored worse as desire to do God's work coursed through his veins with liquid fire and brimstone. The woman didn't move, which surprised him a little and pleased him a lot. She was paralyzed with fear, it seemed, his shaking and sneering and chuckling behavior rooting her like a spotlighted deer.

Reverend Daywright gathered his composure. "It's all right, child. Don't be afraid." He spoke to her gently, the shepherd calming his wayward sheep. He could not have her sprinting off, out of control, no sirree bob. That's when things could get messy. Her fingers were small sticks in his palm. He could begin there. Could. But he'd wait.

Ivy jerked her hand away, and he let her have it. She did not move otherwise, but the reverend saw her eyes narrow to slits. An orange glimmer seemed to emanate from beneath her heavy lashes, a trick of the light, surely, or a trick of the whore to distract him. She spoke, her voice low and even. "It's late, and I think you should go, Reverend Daywright. I'll bring a donation by the church next Sunday. You can count on it. Good night now."

Marcus continued to stand in front of the door, blocking it. He shook his head sadly, but the grin was still in place and his eyes danced in the half-light of moon and evening lamp. There was no real sadness about him, only joyful anticipation, and Ivy read it easily. The man was mad.

"Listen to me very carefully, sir. You don't know what you are about to bring upon yourself. I am going to give you an opportunity to *think*. And then I am going to give you the opportunity to leave. You have fifteen seconds to accomplish both."

Her words were bold, sure enough. Marcus respected that. But there was an uneasiness there he detected, a waffle in her bravado that was most likely concern. Marcus suspected her thoughts had drifted to the child's safety now, an instinctual reaction that even the lowest of animals possessed. *Where was the little snippet, anyway,* Marcus wondered, *and the dog, too?* He'd been prepared to deal with the four-legged menace right off, but so far he'd seen neither hide nor hair of either one. Didn't matter. The real business of the evening was standing in front of him with her arms crossed and a hip cocked like her shit stank of perfume and he was dirt.

Marcus gently laid the Bible on the floor beside his fallen hat and then reached into his pocket. He pulled out a thin white rope, cotton, nonabrasive, not that that mattered much. He wound the ends around his palms and pulled the cord taut between them.

"Think, you say," he said as he took a step toward her. "Get out, you say." Marcus took another step. "How impolite that all sounds. Reminds me of my ex-wife a bit, but I won't tell you how she ended up." He snapped the rope taut again.

"Yeah, you saw me at the festival a few days back," he continued. "I saw you too. Watched you sashaying around the park with your

belly showing and your tight jeans outlining every curve. You wanted me to see you, didn't you?" Marcus continued to advance and now
he saw what he was aiming for: apprehension was creeping into the
woman's confident face, the face of an angel, damn her. How Satan
loved to tempt him and mock him with all he could never have. A
scourge on the earth, these jezebels, these Babylonian harlots. "Tell
me, child, have you read the story of Abraham and Isaac?"

Ivy looked uncertain. "Yes. I know of it." She took a step backward, away from him.

"And what would you know of it?"

"Abraham offered the life of his only son, Isaac, to the Lord."

"Good. Very good. It's a tale of willing sacrifice. Sacrifice, my
child, is the only way to truly free a soul. We all have to learn about
sacrifice." Marcus edged closer as Ivy took another step back.

"What are you talking about? Luna? Are you talking about Luna?
You stay away from my daughter."

Arms uncrossed now, defiant at her sides, her little hands curled
into fists. It was almost cute, Marcus thought, when anger competed
with their most basic instincts to flee.

"The sins of the parents are visited on the children, Ivy Cole. I
can't spare you. Either of you."

Marcus lunged, and Ivy fled for the stairwell. Marcus caught her
easily, wrenching a fist through the hair he had so sinfully lusted after
at the festival. He slammed the light switch off and then shoved Ivy
to the floor. "I'm setting your soul free, girl. Think of me when you
get to hell."

Marcus grabbed Ivy's wrists and began binding them. She kicked
upward, her foot missing the soft of his groin but connecting
painfully with his inner thigh instead. He grunted, releasing the binding, and Ivy's palm shot straight up to flatten Marcus's nose against
his cheek.

The man bellowed and cupped his face as blood poured through
his fingers. The woman on the floor, incredulously, smiled up at him,
mocking him. Rage dampened the pain and Marcus lunged for her
again.

Ivy rolled away, still trying to make it to the stairway. "Aufhocker!

Stellen!" she screamed before the rope choked her words to a cough. She clawed as the noose tightened and her breathing wheezed to a halt.

A growl from the shadows. Something at the foot of the stairs. The room was illuminated only by streetlamps and the dim pale of moonlight. But the shaggy outlines of something coming at Marcus fast were easy to make out. Then another figure moved from behind it, another huge form in the dark as if the shadows themselves had massed into something tangible. Something…terrible.

Marcus fell back, releasing his hold on the woman.

"Aufhocker, *stellen! Angreifen!* Kill him!"

Ivy scrambled to her feet just as Marcus found his. She kicked him again, this time connecting with a kneecap that went spongy under her shoe. He stumbled backward, flailing, his pinwheeling arms hitting the light switch again and flooding the room brightly.

Two wolves braced before the man, the black one he'd seen before and mistaken for a dog, a grave error, he saw now. The other animal he did not know. It was polar white and as large as the first wolf, but strange yellowish-orange eyes blazed above a muzzle too long, too keen, to be mere wolf. Marcus nearly slumped unconscious, looking into those eyes. It was hellfire in an ivory demon's face.

The world slowed on its axis and the two advanced toward Marcus as if through a wall of shimmering water. Orange Eyes seemed to smile at him, the black rimmed lips opening over razor fangs nearly the length of his finger.

Marcus blinked, trying to stay focused. The situation had reversed itself unexpectedly, and the reverend needed help. His Bible. He dragged himself toward it, his ruined nose and displaced kneecap unmindful annoyances compared to what he faced now.

The wolves' heads lowered. They stalked him slowly as if in a game, for the prey was too injured to run any longer.

Marcus dug his fingers into the old plank floor, pulling himself along and pushing with his one good leg. The Bible was within his grasp. He clutched it and opened to the middle, the Book of Jeremiah. But salvation in scripture was irrelevant at this moment. Marcus pulled a gleaming object from the hollowed-out center of the Good Book. It was a hunting knife, eight-and-a-half inches of stainless steel with a curve at the end that doubled an inch and a half back. The blade was called, fittingly, before tables had turned, a guthook.

Marcus held the knife in front of him, his confidence renewed. "Come on, you sonsabitches. Come on!"

The wolves needed no encouragement. The black wolf's hindquarters bunched, but it was the quicker white wolf that sprang for him first.

Marcus readied the blade and sank it to the hilt in the animal's throat as its crushing weight leveled him to the floor. But the force of the wolf's attack drove the beast into him regardless of the knife, and fangs found the meat where neck and shoulder met. Tendons snapped as the massive head drew back, pulling Marcus's flesh with it, but only then did it seem to realize it was injured. The white wolf swayed, then staggered off its feet. The black wolf was ready to take its place. One hundred fifty pounds leaped onto Marcus's chest as the room went feral with the stench of blood.

Screaming, screaming…first the woman, now Marcus: "Oh God, save me, I'm dying." Blood gushing from his body as the black wolf worried him…Hot on his shoulders, an inferno on his chest, pieces falling into his hands, an ear chunked onto the floor. He could no longer speak, no longer see, no longer feel as the pain ebbed into the dark of the wolf's fur on top of him, all over him, *inside* of him, gnawing at bones and pulling organs from secret places.

And then, only the dark…

"Luna! Luna!"

Ivy scrambled to the white wolf now cradled by a puddle of crimson, more Marcus's blood than the wolf's own. Aufhocker, his chest slick wet and his muzzle dripping red foam, joined Ivy by the other wolf's side. Ivy slid against the wall, pulling the white wolf's head into her lap. She gripped the knife's handle and withdrew it from the animal's thick neck.

"Luna, my Luna, why did you come? I told you to stay on the roof." Ivy stroked the large head as tears coursed down her cheeks to mingle with the wolf's blood. "Don't change back, Boo. It's going to be okay. Stay this way a little longer, and it will all be okay." Aufhocker lay beside the wolf and licked her wound.

Three a.m. or there'bouts. It was hard to say, but the sun was not yet up, and Ivy's back, still iron board straight against the living room wall, ached her awake. Aufhocker looked up, ever alert, and Ivy scratched his head gently. "It's okay now, boy, you can relax."

The little girl in Ivy's arms was leaden with slumber. Her breathing was even, past dreaming, and Ivy knew she was lost in that wonderful dark abyss of deep sleep. Ivy buried her face in her daughter's blond locks, taking in the scents of baby shampoo and powder. There was another scent too, one that only those such as Ivy could detect, a musky underlayer of the other embedded deep within the skin. Skin that was again porcelain perfect, unscathed.

"Thank you, thank you, thank you," Ivy whispered. She kissed Luna's cheek, and for a moment, the serene look upon her daughter's face and the painfully innocent youth of it took Ivy to another place, another moment when she'd first cradled her sleeping love. The child had been born an anomaly in the Canadian hospital.

Ivy remembered the nurse bringing the baby in shortly after the trouble-free birth. The other nurses were clustered around the door, peeking in, whispering. The nurse had lowered the infant quickly, nearly dropping her in Ivy's arms, before backing to the door and the comforting circle of her colleagues.

Ivy pulled back the blanket to nearly translucent skin and a full head of shockingly white fine hair. She glowed, like a seraphim, like a celestial body, like the full moon.

And then the baby opened her eyes to the mother. Orange irises as melon-bright as a jack-o'-lantern's stared out of the cherubic face and a smile split the pink cheeks. Already Ivy could see the saw-tooth nubs of emerging teeth.

The nurses did not speak, only quietly closed the door. Ivy and the child were gone when the doctor returned to her bedside. A reporter had come too, but they never found her again. The bill was paid in cash.

Luna was different from the very beginning, but Ivy had no idea exactly what that meant. Until the first feeding was late and a tantrum morphed into more than Ivy had bargained for. There could never be such a thing as babysitters or preschool, and the thoughts of enrolling the girl in kindergarten soon stressed the mother greatly.

But tonight Luna's gift—what made the child so special and different from other lycanthropes indeed—had saved her mother's life.

Ivy cradled her again like a babe, scooping her up in both arms. She carried the precious bundle to her own room and laid her under the covers. Aufhocker was by her side before she'd even called for him.

"Stay with her, Auf. I've things to tend to."

The former Reverend Marcus Daywright lay about the living room. Most of him was near the front door where he'd crawled, as good a place to start as any. Had it been the night of the full moon, tidying up would have been much simpler. Unfortunately, Aufhocker's appetite, although substantial at twenty percent his own body weight, could not rival her own. There would have been little to none of the Preacher Man left to clean up had Ivy made a meal of him. But the full moon was still days away, and Marcus could not hang out in the house that long. Mess aside, the smell would be unbearable. And noticeable to nosy neighbors who apparently didn't like Ivy much anyway.

Ivy gathered a garbage bag, a cinder block, and an old tarp from the garden shed in the backyard. She rolled Marcus's torso onto the tarp, then collected the rest of him in the bag: a shinbone from under the coffee table, a glob of—what? who could tell?—from the bottom bookcase shelf. At least in this dismembered, half-devoured state, she could carry him. She threw his knife and desecrated Bible in last, and tossed his hat atop it all.

Collection finished, Ivy leaned against the wall again, exhausted. She wiped a strand of hair from her eyes, leaving a bloody swipe across her forehead. Then she pushed off the wall. Only one more thing left to do.

Marshy Bottom's pier creaked lonely at this hour. The boardwalk, despite the clear sky and lighthouse beacon in the distance, was surprisingly dark once entering the fortresslike tangle of yaupon. Ivy dragged the tarp down the weathered walkway, the garbage bag and cinder block perched on top of it. The marsh could be sultry at night, but the late season and a cool ocean breeze blowing in over the islands kept mosquitoes at bay and Ivy's eyes clear of sweat. Crabs skittered through cracks in the planking as she progressed toward the picnic shelter, a place where she'd come with Luna not so long ago. Never could she have imagined that only a short time later she would be dragging a half-eaten reverend's body to the very same spot in the middle of the night. And what a truly sad development it was, after all her painstaking concerns about not hunting in her own town again and lying low to keep out of the spotlight. So much for that.

"Here we are, Preacher Man."

Ivy pulled the tarp to the edge of the pier and the flaps fell open. The man's head lolled off the spinal string holding it to his torso, but the damaged cord snapped and the head splashed overboard before Ivy could catch it.

"Dang it!" She grabbed the flashlight from her jacket pocket and shined it into the water. The head bobbed and turned, minute jerks in the water from multiple tiny attacks. Already the small fish—and whatever else—that lived under the boardwalk had found it. They plucked at the cheeks, the eyes, the forehead, while Ivy bound up the rest of her cargo with the cinder block and pushed it over the side as well.

She shined the light in the mud-puddle-colored water once more to see only a few final bubbles burp along the murky surface. The head and the body were gone.

Ivy clicked the flashlight off and let the threads of moonlight that found her through the thicket and shelter illuminate the scene. It was not within the Parish Keep Cemetery and its distinguished roster of seafaring captains and community founders with whom Marcus would be buried. It was here, in the black brackish water of the sound and in the company of carnivorous fishes with whom Marcus would finally rest. Some final words seemed in order. Ivy bowed her head.

"'And cast ye the unprofitable servant into outer darkness,'" she whispered. "'There shall be weeping and gnashing of teeth.' St. Matthew, chapter twenty-five, verse thirty.

"Rest in peace, Preacher Man."

9

ADELAIDE PROCTOR was right on schedule. The twins were already at band practice, and she had thirty-five minutes to tidy this kitchen before carting Billy off to his soccer game. The days just flew by; thank goodness she kept a tight itinerary or her whole family would be lost.

Addy stood in front of her kitchen sink, rinsing this evening's dinner dishes and placing them into the dishwasher. The wide double windows over the kitchen counter focused on an even wider backyard, which linked up to a narrow strip of beach on Marshy Bottom Sound. Bixby, the Proctors' two-year-old Irish setter, was out there now, roughhousing it with one of Billy's old soccer balls.

Addy's to-do list ticked off in her head as she rinsed and placed, rinsed and placed. "Feed the dog" was the only thing left before taking Billy to Salty Duck High at six-thirty for pregame warm-up.

"Billy!"

"Geez, Mom, I'm right behind you."

Addy jumped and turned to her fifteen-year-old son. He was only half-dressed for the game. His knee pads weren't even on yet.

Time wasters. Addy's family was full of them. Running off schedule was a real risk now—they'd have to hurry.

"Go rustle up Bixby. I have to feed him and then we have to go."

Billy just stared at his mother, slack-jawed, and reached for a
cookie from a plate by the sink.

"No!" Addy swatted his hand. "Bixby. Now. Scoot."

Billy frowned and shuffled out the French doors. His mother
was always in such a hurry. One cookie. Just one lousy cookie. It
wouldn't have killed her to give him at least that.

Bixby darted around the yard, back and forth, to a ball on the
ground. He barked at it, then leaped in to bite, then leaped away to
bark again. His red shaggy tail wagged with each jump and turn.

"Come on, Bixby. Let's go!" Billy called from the top of the yard.
The dog ignored him, rapt in his new game.

"Bixby, come!" Billy clapped his hands and whistled, but the setter continued his rough-and-tumble with the ball. Billy glanced back
at the kitchen. His mother's face scowled from the windows. She
held up an arm and tapped her watch impatiently.

"Good grief." Billy trudged toward the bottom of the yard
where grass met beach and marsh. He'd have to drag Bixby up by the
scruff of the neck, looked like.

The boy drew closer, then started to slow. And slow.

Bixby the Irish setter looked at his young master happily. He
snatched up his prize and pranced toward Billy. The dog dropped it
at the boy's feet.

"Mom!"

"No. No, no, no. No."

Ebby and Gladys traded glances in the parlor as Missouri Pitchkettle
read the newspaper and mumbled to herself. Ebby had seated Missy in
the sunniest corner of the house, overlooking her lovely restored garden, for a dainty breakfast of homemade crepes and mimosas.

But it didn't make any difference. The woman's heavily painted face drooped with despair despite the cheery surroundings and Ebby's best efforts to please her.

"No, no, no, no," Missouri mumbled again, but louder.

"Missy, is there something the matter?" Ebby asked as Gladys hovered nearby. The latter had come in for a quick breakfast herself before getting down to the business of rose snipping. As for the mannequin parts, Leland had disposed of them in a burn pile at the dump, guaranteeing they would never make an eerie resurrection. That would seem unlikely, except the unlikeliest of things had been happening lately and Leland didn't want to take any chances.

"Ma'am?" Ebby tried again.

Missouri slammed the paper down on the etched glass table. "I *knew* it! Leland! Leland!"

"He's down on the Front already this morning, ma'am. Said he had to open the store. Mr. Praig called in sick."

"Sorriness follows us whomever we hire, doesn't it? Leland could have at least told me he was leaving."

"You were still sleeping, ma'am. He knows you don't do that much anymore, and he didn't want to disturb you."

Missouri pursed her lips like she might keep the big news all to herself, but no such luck.

"Don't you want to know what's going on in this town, Ebby?" she blurted. "Or are you content to run around with your nose buried in your skirt and yours stuck in the root cellar, Gladys?"

Gladys nearly choked on her orange juice. She was hoping to eat her toast in peace and escape to the yard without much notice.

"Tell us, ma'am, just what is happening in Salty Duck these days?"

Missouri jabbed a long-tipped nail at the headline on the newspaper. "Murder!"

And it was true. Gladys and Ebby moved closer to gaze at the front page. A grainy picture showed police deputies milling around the Marshy Bottom Pier alongside an indiscernible covered mound on a stretcher.

Ebby scanned the article, her brows knitting in concern. "Oh my God! She's right, Gladys. Adelaide Proctor's boy found a man's head—a head!—in their backyard. The family dog was playing with it." She read silently to herself, then sucked in her breath. "Oh my God! It was Marcus Daywright! He was pulled from the marsh yesterday—in pieces! They found his abandoned pickup nearby."

"Marcus Daywright?" Gladys said. "The Reverend Marcus Daywright? Our visiting pastor?"

"Yes. And no. You won't believe it—"

"He was a liar!" Missouri spouted. "Had us all fooled, and now he's the fool."

"Let me see that." Gladys grabbed the paper and read for herself. "A former con? Released from prison two years ago after serving time for assault and battery?"

"Of his ex-wife. They have a statement from her. Says when she asked him for a divorce, he tried to kill her. That sounds a little worse than assault and battery to me." Ebby tsked and shook her head. "And listen to this. He was not even an ordained minister. He made it all up. This is scandalous. Poor Reverend Holliday will not know how to handle this."

"I knew there was something wrong about that man the minute I saw him passing around the collection plate," Missouri said smugly. "Something about the way he looked at me. Crazy, burning eyes. I felt the evil sloughing off him like fish scales."

"Well, there you go, Missy. The evil you predicted has come and now, apparently, gone. You can rest easier at night," Ebby said quietly. But she would never rest easy again. Salty Duck had not known anything as gruesome as this in her lifetime. And if Reverend Day— if Marcus Daywright were an evil man, what greater evil put him in the marsh in multiple pieces?

Missouri seemed to study on the article a moment longer, her own eyes burning with an intensity that could be alarming in its own right. Gladys nudged up closer to Ebby. "Looks like a spell might be coming on. Want me to get her medication? I'm thinking I could use a little of it."

"No, let her be. I think she'll be all right."

Missouri's head pivoted in the women's direction, her eyes wide, pupils slightly dilated. "I hear your whispering," she hissed, a bit of spittle running down her chin. "But it won't be all right. I see it, something else. The washerwoman came to me in my dream last night. The omen of death—she showed me. Blood. Blood in the water, blood in the sand, blood washing up on the shores in a tidal wave over this town.

"This man, this Marcus Daywright...he was not the end, ladies. He was only the beginning." Missouri went to the window overlooking her garden, Battery Street, the house just across the way. A shrewd leer passed over her face and a shiver shook her thin shoulders as she gazed down upon Captain Woodside's rented cottage. "Only the beginning."

10

IVY FELT terrible. It was Doe Springs all over again, when her best friend's husband, Clifford Hughes, had been discovered so quickly after a full moon attack, eventually leading the police (and the ill-fated love of her life) right to her doorstep. At least the tussle with Clifford, before he met the wolf, had taught her a useful lesson. Those self-defense classes at the college in Winnipeg had bought her the time she needed with Daywright. She'd held her own before the cavalry arrived, and a smidgen of pride started to turn the awful feelings around.

She put the newspaper down on the shell-colored comforter, leaving the speculation of Marcus Daywright's death—and town deception—to lean back on her plush feather pillows. She stared at the empty space above the mantel in her bedroom (and her late mother Catherine's beautiful but broken clock) and immediately felt the weight of her daughter in her lap.

"What are you doing, Mommy?"

"Nothing, Boo. Just thinking is all."

"About the bad man?" Luna glanced at the newspaper, but her real thoughts were on getting out of her Eeyore pajamas and getting on with the day. The morning sun was streaming through the lace curtains, beckoning her.

"No, I was thinking about that painting at the craft fair again. It would look good up there over your grandma's clock, yes?"

Luna swiveled her head to look above the fireplace, but then the picture of the policemen and the black body bag suddenly riveted her attention.

"He was a bad man, right, Mommy?"

"Oh yes, Boo, definitely. A very bad man. I have to say, though, I've never had a meal choose me before. Too bad it was before the full moon."

"That was fun, Mommy. Can I pick next time?"

"No, you may not." Ivy tweaked her nose. "Not until you're older and know what choosing is all about."

"I already know. I choose that waiter."

"Boo, let it go. I don't want to hear any more about the waiter. He didn't do anything to you, okay?"

Luna looked sulky for all of two seconds, then nuzzled up underneath her mother's chin. Ivy stroked her hair. It worried her, this flippant attitude toward death. While it was true Luna had been through a tragic ordeal and Ivy was grateful for her safety, the magnitude of what actually transpired seemed to have eluded the child. Was that immaturity due to youth, or an indication of her father's genes coursing through her? If that one *was* the father.

Ivy shuddered to think it. Her hopes had always been that Luna's father was the other man from her past. She searched for him in the child daily, little clues to indicate Deputy Melvin Sanders's blood coursed through her daughter's veins and not that of the cold-blooded werewolf she'd run with so briefly in the Blue Ridge. But oh what a magnificent-looking creature he had been. If only Ivy could have turned his nature, taught him to be the true wolf such as herself and less the beast dominated by his wicked human side. Ivy studied her daughter again. Luna did have a sweet temperament most the time. At least there was that.

Never mind all that now, though. The past was far, far behind them, and the future was all that mattered. Hopefully, that was not suddenly jeopardized by the discovery of Daywright in the marsh. Ivy continued scanning the newspaper article. A quote of remorse from the good pastor, Holliday, tugged at her heart: "We wish we had known that Marcus was in trouble of some kind. As upset as we, the church, are that he deceived us, we are more upset thinking perhaps we failed him somehow. That was no way for a brother and a friend to die."

Ivy put the paper down again. *Good people, conned and betrayed,* Ivy thought. Good people who had no idea whatsoever what kind of monster they had let into their house. To them, Daywright was a reformed criminal trying to find salvation in their ministry. They would never know the truth, and she could certainly never tell them.

"Can we go to that place, Mommy?" Luna poked a tiny pinkie at the grainy photo of Parish Keep Presbyterian.

"What—church? You want to go to church?"

Luna nodded. "It's pretty."

Ivy smiled. "Yes, Boo, it is a very beautiful building. We'll walk by there today, if you like, and you can take a picture of it."

But on second thought, why not go to church for real? Should I really be so quick to dismiss it? Isn't that what good, wholesome families did together, to give their children guidance? To teach them the importance of life and death? To give them…gravity?

"You know what, Boo? Forget what I said. Instead of just going by there, how about we actually attend church on Sunday? Would you like that?"

"Yeah! Can I wear a new dress?"

"Yes, and I'll buy one too. New dresses for a new mother-daughter tradition."

"Thank you, Mommy. I can't wait!" Luna straddled her mother's lap and covered her face with kisses.

PART II

"Hound of God..."

11

THE TALL, thin man, cloaked in a black wool overcoat against the gray mist of the rain, meandered through the paths of the Ohlsdorf in Hamburg, Germany. It was the second largest cemetery in the world and the first place of his greatest comfort, even in the cold blanket of a German drizzle. This was an elephant graveyard of sorts—for him, a place to seek solace with family long dead. He communed with them here because so little of his kin remained on this earth.

None were buried in this cemetery park among the nearly three hundred thousand other graves, ironically. His long-deceased parents, his uncles and aunts, his beloved sister Catherine, all rested in their homeplace outside Cologne. But he had left Cologne after Catherine Cole's brutal murder nearly three decades ago and not gone back. Dead was dead and ghosts followed him wherever he fled to, so he assumed one cemetery was as good as another for speaking with them.

And surely none was as elegant as the Ohlsdorf, an open-air museum of sorts with its nineteenth- and twentieth-century sculptures eerily white and wraithlike among the memorials for the dead.

But heaven was all around him, not spectral deities of harm. Angels graced curving lawns and whimsical gardens now preparing for fall. Indeed, there were more than two hundred angels in the cemetery park, their placement on high socles allowing mourners to look up into their beatific faces for consolation. But there was one sculpture in particular that called to Stefan Heinrich, and he walked steadily to find her, rising gracefully in perfect alabaster outside the ornate bridge leading into the *Rosengarten*.

She was there, as always, welcoming him from her eight-foot stature. Her carved wings were demurely folded, her eyes cast lovingly down at her hand. It rested on the head of a regal dog that stared up at her with as much devotion.

Stefan settled on a marble bench beside the sculpture, not minding the chill of the stone nor the rain soaking into the tails of his coat. He needed comfort today, comfort only coming here could provide. And privacy.

His cell phone rang promptly at one p.m., as he expected. It was an international number.

"I'm here."

"You were right," the voice from another continent told him.

Stefan shut his eyes. Rain collected in droplets in his gray beard. He sighed and opened his eyes again. "Tell me."

"They found a body in the sound. A former convict, posing as a preacher."

"And the signs were all there?"

"More details are coming out, but my contact at the morgue told me everything. Ripped to pieces. Beheaded. Parts missing. He wasn't in the water long enough for that kind of damage, although the police don't seem to be making that conclusion. The fish and crabs did do their part, but I'd say yes, the signs are all there."

"Before the full moon." Stefan put a wavering hand atop the angel's, just as his heart reminded him that he was old. It kicked him rapidly, snaring his breath, and he coughed to catch it again. He had been waiting for news such as this for a time, but even knowing it would one day come, he still did not feel prepared.

Dread spiked with excitement could be a deadly combination to an aging anatomy such as his own.

"Hello," the voice an ocean away said, his deep tenor heavy with the American accent.

"I'm still here," Stefan said.

"Now that we're sure, do we carry on with the plan?"

He nodded, then realized his friend could not hear him. "We carry on with the plan," he said, his reply strong, resolute. "I will send the Benandanti in the meantime, for protection."

"Protection for her—or me?"

"Both. He is well-trained. When the time is at hand, he will not harm you. Only others who may try to get in the way."

"I understand."

Silence on the line. A click of static.

The American spoke. "Stefan?"

"Yes?"

"I'm sorry."

"You can come out now, Simon. You have learned all you need-ed to know."

A dark figure moved hesitantly from behind the bushes, his own overcoat jeweled in water droplets and damp leaves. He, too, was tall but heavier than Stefan, with a square jaw and piggish black eyes that were both hypnotic and penetrating. *A mobster's eyes,* Stefan thought, looking at someone he used to call friend.

"You knew I was here the whole time?"

No, Stefan thought angrily. *How much did you hear?* "Of course. Come, sit." He slid over to give the other man room.

Simon sat on the cement bench and stared at the gardens through the light drizzle.

"You look good, my old friend. A little too thin, but...good," Simon said.

"And you as well."

The rain lightened but held. Droplets pattered off foliage, the only sound in the nearly deserted cemetery. Stefan pulled his coat closer about him, but it was not the weather that suddenly chilled him.

"We have found one at last, have we not?" Simon said.

Stefan did not answer.

"The Order of the Lykanthrop has waited centuries for this impossible thing, Stefan. Did you ever think we would see it in our lifetime? A child that can change without the aid of our moon? It is a miracle for us."

Stefan knew it all too well. He wished Simon did not know it at all, but it was not a surprise. Stefan suspected for years that the Order had been following Ivy too, keeping up with her despite her unpredictable moves, her flighty behavior. It pained Stefan that she fled about North America without any thoughts of her uncle at all, however. Were it not for Stefan's close relationship with the Widow Pritchard, his niece may have been lost to him forever. Perhaps that would have been just as well. Stefan could not be certain that it was not through him that the Order had been able to find Ivy time and again. Most unfortunate, especially now.

"Your niece, Ivy," Simon said, seeming to read his thoughts, "does she still possess the Lykanthrop bible? We will be needing that as well."

"As well?" Stefan said.

"Yes. The child and the book."

Stefan's jaw ground at the presumptuous "as well," at calling him "old friend," at assuming the Order had any rights to his lupine family line.

"They are not a part of the Order, Simon, and I have been out for a long time—"

Simon cut him off. "We are ready to induct you back in. Your breeding program with the special wolves has been well noted; their intelligence and longevity are beyond exemplary. But it was the mixing of Ivy's blood with that of your pack's—Fenris was the alpha, I believe—that has earned you legendary status with the Lykanthrop. You bred her, Stefan. Ivy was born from Fenris's line."

"Ivy was born from William and Catherine."

Simon laughed. "You were always too humble. Or too stubborn. Ivy became unique by what you did, with her ability to choose her victims, to spare life if she so chooses it. To walk like the true wolf with control and rationality, a thinking being. Ironic, isn't it, that the animal should be more evolved than the creature the Lykanthrop becomes, eh?"

"I only did what I had to, to save her life."

"You did that and more. Your efforts with Ivy, my old friend, have led to Luna." Simon's narrow marble eyes danced under hooded brows. His teeth shone too white against the pallor of his skin and the gray of the whitewashed day around them. "We watched for five years, Stefan, waiting to see if there would be evidence of anything exceptional about Ivy's child. I did not need to eavesdrop on your conversation to know what I know. I followed you to inform you."

"Inform me?"

"We want the girl, Stefan, and we want you back in the Order to raise her. And to repeat the process."

Stefan nodded. All was as he expected. His American friend would be amused that he had been right in his predictions about the Lykanthrop.

"You nod. I am pleased. I will tell the others you have agreed to rejoin us. You will be promoted immediately, of course."

"The child, Luna. I will bring her to you."

"No need, dear, considerate Stefan. We have a man in the States already. He will be taking possession of the girl shortly."

Stefan's heartbeat quickened, followed by another jab in his chest. He fought back the cough. "No. Absolutely not."

"It is too late. Steps are in motion. Your niece, Ivy, will not be harmed if at all avoidable." He patted Stefan's hand. "We will send for you when Luna has arrived. Until then," his hand, resting so gently on Stefan's, clutched with viselike intensity, grinding Stefan's bones like twigs to kindle flame, "until then, you are to tell your friend in Carolina to back off. The Benandanti cannot save him, and I know you would hate to lose even more of your fine *Canis lupus* companions. Such sentimentality." Simon shook his head and released the elder's hand. Stefan grasped his injured fingers, rubbing them to restart circulation.

Simon straightened his overcoat, shaking water from the lapels. "You will hear from me," he said, then he walked across the *Rosengarten* bridge and faded into the tangled garden of vines and roses and mist.

"The American," as his friend and mentor Stefan Heinrich liked to call him, clicked his cell phone shut and leaned into the railing overlooking Marshy Bottom Sound. The pier from where a body was dragged recently lay to his left, farther down Front Street leaving town, and he had no desire to go that direction again. It was cordoned off with police tape anyway, and gawkers hanging out of their car windows kept that end of the street's traffic in a snarl.

Behind him, the main section of Front Street was just beginning to stir. Delivery trucks brought shipments of fresh fish to merchant doors. Engines sputtered to life on daysailers and catamarans lining the docks off the cobblestone walk. Restaurants threw open windows and coffee pots rattled against cups for early patrons who enjoyed breakfast on patio decks. Birds called and dove into the water for their own morning meal, and, if one listened closely, a wild pony's whinny could be heard, carried across the breeze from the islands.

He loved these sounds, the awakening of a day in Salty Duck. He admired the rugged men who manned the big fishing vessels that went out beyond the Gulf Stream for weeks at a time, and equally the grizzled local sailors who trolled the shores on smaller crafts, looking for enough catch to feed their families for another month. And it all depended on the kindness of the sea, what she would yield for the day, whom she would allow to dock and drop anchor.

It was a good, honest life in a yin-yang, love-hate relationship with Mother Nature. She could give abundantly and take with vicious, unexpected abandon.

Perhaps that was what had drawn him to Stefan Heinrich. The yin and yang, the balance of nature, the give and take required to maintain that balance. There was no such thing as good and evil in Stefan's world. Only an equilibrium of forces, to keep the earth upright and spinning on its axis.

The American appreciated that philosophy, but he appreciated what Stefan offered as a reward even more. It made all the risks worth it, and thus he would help Stefan "restore the natural order," so to speak. But he felt true sadness for his friend just the same. Stefan loved his niece, Ivy Cole, and her child, although the latter Stefan had never met. To hurt Ivy was unforgivable, but, just like Mother Nature, Stefan, too, could take with unexpected and vicious abandon.

The man watched a tourist ferry glide by, its gaily dressed passengers huddled together on the boat's deck. One of the women raised her hand and waved to shore. He smiled and lifted his own hand. Then he turned and walked down Front Street, the order of the upcoming events heavy on his mind.

12

"How do I look, Mommy?"

Ivy had finished the clasp on Luna's pearl necklace, and now the girl twirled round and round for inspection.

"Like a doll, Boo, an absolute little lady."

With Luna's upswept curls in ribbons, pink taffeta dress, and white Mary Janes, she looked like a collector's porcelain come to life. The delicate string of pearls completed the exquisite picture—they were purchased, along with the dress, at one of the trendy beach shops on the waterfront just the day before. The pearls were real, an extravagant gift for a five-year-old, but Ivy couldn't help herself. Auf was not the only one guilty of spoiling, particularly after the near tragic course of events with Daywright.

"What about me, Boo? Will I do?"

Luna squinted and examined her mother from head to toe. "You're too pretty for church, Mommy."

"I don't know what that means, but I'll take it as a compliment."

But Ivy checked the mirror again just the same. She hadn't been to church in a long time (since when she was barely older than Luna, in fact) and the rules were rusty. But the high, round neckline and mid-calf hem seemed conservative enough. Ivy was not a flashy dresser by any means—comfort ruled her wardrobe in denim, sandals, and tees—but since drawing the Preacher Man's eye, she had started second-guessing her selections.

"Let's go, Mommy, let's *goooo!*" Luna was on the porch already and running down the steps.

"All right, all right, I'm coming."

The Parish Keep Presbyterian Chapel, on the corner of Mission Street and Cemetery Cross, was gearing up for one of the largest congregation attendances in twenty years. Normally holding a crowd of one hundred fifty on a good Sunday, the masses swarming through the arched entranceway today looked to be nearing three hundred. Among the regular faces and curious newcomers were a smattering of reporters, eager to get quotes from church members concerning their take on Parish Keep Presbyterian's very own Marcus Daywright.

Ivy almost turned around upon seeing the throng of people. She had a good relationship with God, felt like they were on the same side on most issues, felt like He looked after her and forgave her when she made bad "choices" on a rare occasion ("once in a blue moon," one might say). So was she sure, absolutely sure, she wanted to start a new routine now?

Yes you do! the little voice called her matronly conscience snapped. *Luna needs some good old-fashioned Southern church raising and moral spiritual guidance, remember?* Yeah, she remembered. Being a single mother was hard. Luna needed…balance.

Ivy squared her shoulders and gripped her daughter's hand. They waded forward and let the congregational current carry them in.

• • •

Reverend Matheson Holliday, flanked by deacons and backed by a fifteen-member choir, straightened his suit jacket at the pulpit. Salty Duck's other churches must have been empty this Sunday for it appeared all of the town filled the pews before him. There was standing room only at the back, and Holliday could see a line of black suits and feathery ladies' hats filing out the open doors, their wearers straining to see in from the street.

The pastor took a deep breath. He was never nervous spreading the Lord's word, but today was a different day indeed. Reporters did not show up because they were interested in his awe-inspiring message. In fact, Holliday had been accused of being rather bland in the pulpit, although his sincerity had kept parishioners loyal for years.

No, the multitude and media were here because today, Reverend Matheson Holliday would be addressing a murder in the church, a murder of a man he'd invited into the fold with open arms, good intentions, and too much trust. He never checked Marcus Daywright's credentials. He never made follow-up calls to the church in South Carolina from which he claimed to hail, a church Holliday had since discovered was burned to the ground twenty-five years ago and Daywright had spent three years in prison for it. Holliday, in his blind trust, had potentially endangered his entire congregation by bringing not only the unsavory Daywright in, but also whatever animals had followed him to Salty Duck seeking some kind of payback.

"Drug affiliates, Reverend," Sheriff Buckley informed him. "Daywright had connections with runners all the way down to Miami, and their bosses are not good people, I can promise you. They're the kind of folks who'd hack a man up and toss him in the drink."

It had not been reassuring news, and it was only a fraction of Daywright's transgressions. Holliday had read the sheriff's full report on Daywright and his crime sheet going back to his teens. The reverend was ashamed of himself for letting a character such as this slip by undetected, and standing here before all these expectant (accusing?) faces, he wasn't even sure where to begin. Rehearsing an appropriate presentation had been a waste of time. The reverend had wrestled with the right words all night long, coming up short. He decided this morning over coffee and a pack of Rolaids that he would put the sermon in God's hands and hope he said the right thing to reassure everyone.

And let them know just how truly sorry he was for letting them down.

A prayer seemed like the best answer. It usually was.

Reverend Holliday finally spoke. "Let us pray."

Three hundred people obediently bowed their heads in silence, while dozens of camera flashes sparked about the church like a cascade of clicking fireworks.

"Dear Father in Heaven, we call on you today to ask for," Holliday paused, searching, and then the next word and the whole theme of the sermon lay before him clear as if written on parchment, "*forgiveness,* dear Lord. Forgiveness. Not just for Marcus Daywright, but for those of us here who feel ill will toward the deceased for his deceptions. He fooled us, Lord, yes he did. He fooled me, too. But help us to pray for understanding of a troubled child who grew up in an abusive home. A troubled youth who turned to a life of violence against others instead of to God. A troubled man who maybe, upon coming to our town and this church, was searching for a way to find Jesus after all, and acceptance. We gave him that—a home in our parish, a new light to follow. We gave him a choice and a chance to change. And he was doing it!

"So help us forgive him for lying and for his unstable past, I beg of you. And as for those who hurt Brother Marcus...," Holliday stumbled. It was hard to say, being merely a man himself, but right was right and he knew what God expected, so the words scraped through his teeth anyway, "we pray for them too, no matter how heinous, how foul, how utterly void of good these men must have been to have killed in such a way. As it is said in the second Book of Samuel, chapter three, verse thirty-nine: 'The Lord shall reward the doer of evil according to his wickedness.' It is not for us to judge. Amen."

Three hundred people raised their heads and stared at their pastor. Miniature tape recorders strained forward from the reporters in the front row.

"Forgiveness," Holliday repeated, looking over the crowd before him, "will be the subject today. There was a wolf among the flock, and your humble shepherd, your reverend, failed to detect him. So just as I pray that we ask for the Lord to forgive Marcus Daywright and consider his soul in the afterlife, I pray that you will forgive me too.

"Let us turn to Corinthians...."

Ivy, who had managed a decent seat near the middle back of the church, stole a glance at her child while Reverend Holliday preached. Luna listened intently to the pastor, her head cocked to the side, her eyes slightly narrowed like when she was seriously taking something in and concentrating hard to process it. Ivy guessed that was good, although a few of the references in the sermon had rankled her greatly, and explaining them to Luna later might be difficult indeed. *Heinous? Foul? Void of good?* Really, now. Daywright was going out with a parade of angels and here she was, marked the bad guy again. Her whole life she'd only chosen the weak, the undesirable, the miscreant to cull from the human herd. There was not a righteous soul alive who had a thing to fear from the white wolf, and sometimes Ivy just wanted to scream it from the rooftops. She felt so misjudged, as the wolf had always been. Heinous? Please.

Ivy shook it off and took a moment to glance around at the rest of the congregation. A few faces she recognized from the craft festival. The pirate was here, four pews up on the left and all of his limbs miraculously intact. Not far from him was Luna's waiter *(oh Lord, hear my prayer—please don't let Luna see that waiter)*. In front of him, turned completely around in her seat and staring her dead in the eyes, was Ivy's neighbor, Missouri Pitchkettle. The woman's frown drug her ruby lips so low they looked like they could almost touch in an inverted point to form a circle around her chin.

Missouri's gaze did not waver when Ivy's green eyes locked on the woman's own, but then they dropped to Luna and Ivy swore the woman's frown, impossibly, furrowed deeper. Leland Pitchkettle, sitting ramrod straight beside his wife, nudged her in the arm and her head whipped around to face front again.

Sixty-five minutes later and Ivy and Luna were caught in the human current again, this time in a backwash that flowed out the door and past Reverend Holliday and his wife, Prill. They grasped Ivy's hands, Prill the left and Holliday the right, and she was trapped.

"It's nice to see another new face," Prill said. "We've had so many newcomers today. I hope that it's not a one-time event and that you'll join us again."

"Yes, please come back next Sunday," Holliday said. "I promise you the sermons are usually more uplifting and not so grim."

The reverend and his wife smiled, and Ivy could feel the warmth from them like sun on her skin.

"I enjoyed it, and I will," she answered.

Holliday and Prill squeezed her hands before letting her go and moving on to the next in line.

Ivy was out the door at last and considering a stroll through the adjacent cemetery, then a lunch at The Bluewater Lady, when she heard her name calling from somewhere in the thinning crowd. Caleb emerged past a well-groomed family of six making their way to a minivan parked on the street.

"Hey! I thought that was you." He was by her side, a tanned man in a handsome navy suit and smelling of the ocean on a summer's day.

"So you go here too?" Ivy gestured toward the medieval arched doorway of the chapel that finally appeared to be empty.

"Just like everybody else today it seems. But if you're looking for some variety with no shady connections thus far, I hear there's a pretty good Baptist revival going on, on the north side of Salty Duck. The Catholics and the Lutherans are squared off over the west end, and the Methodists keep a quiet corner on the southern edge of town. But me? I prefer whatever's within walking distance."

Ivy blinked. He really did try so hard. "Thank you for the rundown on your nondenominational loyalties. If you'll excuse us, we're thinking of taking a walk in the cemetery."

"Good idea. It's just the day for it." Caleb fell in step right beside Ivy, and Luna's smile made it clear that at least one of them was delighted he'd joined them.

"You've been thinking about the painting again," Caleb said as they entered through the cemetery's old iron gates to amble beneath oaks dripping resurrection moss.

"What makes you say that? It wasn't *that* good."

Caleb laughed. "Well, you're right about that, but I saw how you looked at it. Have you thought any more about my offer? My boat is a wreck and I sure would like to get her prettied up again."

Ivy knelt by a scroll-topped tablet carved from brownstone. The words were barely legible, the centuries of coastal erosion taking their toll on the historical record. A lamb was carved into the marker and beneath it, just a single name and date: Our Precious Liza, August 28, 1864-September 16, 1865.

"So young," Ivy said.

Caleb knelt beside her. "Probably yellow fever. This area was plagued with it during that time. But you're not answering my question."

Ivy stood up and wandered on, past graves of blockade runners, privateers, militiamen, victims of Tuscarora Indian massacres when the town was first settled. The cemetery was a time capsule to be relished, and she wished her meddlesome company would go away, leaving her to enjoy the burial ground in peace.

"I'm not going to go away, if that's what you're thinking," Caleb said, as if reading her mind. "I'm in sales by trade and perseverance is how I get my way. At least, until I get an answer or a boot in the butt. Which will it be? And if it's the latter, tell me now so I can get a running start out of the way."

Ivy tried not to laugh, but she couldn't help it. "Are you very good at what you do, Mr. Salesman?"

"Top of my field. Are you buying or not?"

Ivy mulled it again. Just recently she had made up her mind to call him and accept his offer, yet by the next day she'd forgotten all about it. But what were her excuses, really, other than excuses? She didn't have a job yet so her days were free. She'd debated starting up her dog-training business again, but to be honest, the vacation atmosphere of Salty Duck had sapped her motivation and made her lazy. She was perhaps one step away from whiling whole days away in her Thinking Tree, watching Auf and Luna play while she doodled in her journal and fought sleep.

What's wrong with that? she thought.

Plenty, her conscience squawked again. *You don't want to be a no-account and set that example for your child, do you?*

Ivy frowned. Her conscience had become a real pest since she became a mother.

"Time's a-wastin'." Caleb crossed his arms and feigned impatience.

He was persistent, she'd give him that. She'd done nothing to encourage his friendship, yet here he was, hanging around anyway. Yes, terribly, aggravatingly persistent. And Ivy was wearing down.

She smiled at Caleb, a real smile at last, and the man's face flushed under her sudden affability. He looked away to hide how pleased her attention made him feel.

"You know what? Why not? Luna, come over here!"

Luna left the inspection of a cannon-topped crypt to run to her mother's side.

"Would you like to help me and Caleb clean up his old rickety boat? He promised us a ride, you know."

"He promised *me* a ride, Mommy. Yes, yes, yes!"

"Well, there you go, Caleb. You've got yourself a couple of deck-hands."

That night Ivy sat in Luna's bed, a place she'd hesitantly moved her child back to after Daywright's attack. Mother and daughter were propped on pillows and reading *Where the Wild Things Are* together. Luna could identify most of the words already, and Ivy felt so proud at how advanced the little girl was before even starting kindergarten.

Luna abruptly closed the book and set it on her lap. "Mommy?"

"Yes, Boo—are you sleepy now?"

"No."

That was usually the answer.

"Then what is it? We didn't even finish the story tonight."

Luna fidgeted with the edges of the book pages, something heavy obviously on her young mind. Even Aufhocker looked up from the foot of the bed, sensing a shift in the atmosphere.

"What is it, Boo? You can tell me anything."

"I have to ask you something."

"Okay, shoot."

Luna rolled the book over in her hands. And back again. The pages fluttered. Finally, "Mommy, are we bad?"

Ivy's eyebrows jumped a notch.

"Why do you ask such a thing?"

"Today Mr. Holliday said that killing is bad and that the people who did that to Mr. Daywright were bad. He said there was a wolf in the flock that was bad. How did he know, Mommy?"

Oh, wow. You knew this was coming. Okay, think, think, think.

"Luna, Reverend Holliday was not talking about us."

"But he said—"

"Just listen. Yes, Reverend Holliday was right when he said killing is bad. People should not kill other people; that is absolutely true. But we are not like other people. You and I are very—special."

Luna paused on that, as if to mull it. Ivy let her take her time. Finally: "I don't feel any different from other people, Mommy. I don't feel special."

"Of course you're special! You're my little Boo. But let me put it another way: Is it wrong for the lion to kill the gazelle to eat? Is it wrong for the wolf to hunt the elk who also shares his forest? They have to have food too, right?"

Luna blinked and Ivy tried again.

"These wolves, Luna, the good ones, cull the weak and the sick from the herd so the rest of the *flock,* to use the reverend's word, can thrive. Just like when we hunt, right? We may be the wolves among the flock, sweetheart, but we'll never be like Marcus Daywright."

"Mr. Daywright was sick?"

"He was very sick, honey. We helped Mr. Daywright. Do you understand?"

Luna nodded, but her hands still bent and unbent the edges of her book and her gaze still lay across the bedspread in a thoughtful "I'm not sure" way.

"Tell you what, Luna, you liked Reverend and Mrs. Holliday, didn't you? And all the folks at church today?"

"Yeah."

"Why don't we make them our adoptive pack? We will be the guardian wolves of the Parish Keep Presbyterian Chapel—how about that?"

Luna still stared at the squares of her white comforter, but she nodded again, slowly, imperceptibly.

"I would like that very much. And, Mommy?" she said without looking up, "I'm glad of what you said. Because I didn't feel bad about what I did to that man, Mommy. I didn't feel bad at all."

13

*T*HE MOON, *the moon, damn the goddess moon and her power over lore and darkness....*

It was a chant that wrapped through Melvin Sanders's mind often, looping like an endless tape with no variation, only singsong, repetitive clarity. He did not even know where it came from. Maybe he made it up, or maybe it was from one of the many ancient books he'd explored, trying to find some insight into his...disease.

Melvin was home again, and it was dusk. He'd sneaked back in this early Monday morning, rolling into the garage with his lights off at three-thirty a.m. Then he'd immediately gone to the seclusion of his bedroom, where he'd been all day, waiting for nightfall. It would not do, chancing a neighbor seeing movement in the house, seeing a light on, seeing a shadow pass by a window. The town, and especially Gloria, needed to know he was gone. He did not want to have to *explain,* or be forced to defend his decision to leave the department, or talk with anyone from Doe Springs period. So today, when he should be starting a brand-new work week, the cream-colored walls of this simply furnished room were his refuge, and his prison.

For the Melvin of five years ago, before Ivy Cole, dusk in his two-story gingerbread cottage had a different meaning altogether. Dusk would have meant a nice dinner after a fruitful shift with the sheriff's department. A relaxing jog down to Watershed Mill. Maybe a baseball game on the tube or a movie with a friend. Before Ivy Cole, dusk could have meant a lot of pleasant things.

Now, it meant dread. And then the terror would follow.

Melvin stared dully at nothing at all as the details of his sparse, immaculate bedroom became fuzzy with retreating light. The grandfather clock chimed from elsewhere in the house, and Melvin's stomach roiled. He'd lived on Tums the whole summer he spent with that woman—that beautiful, wretched, deadly woman—and now, out of habit or some queer nostalgia perhaps, he found himself reaching for one in the nightstand. An emergency bottle was there, nearly untouched since the day she left.

Melvin closed the drawer, leaving the bottle where it lay. Tums couldn't help what he was about to face. Again.

Melvin pushed off the bed and straightened the heavy impression he left in the white spread. His hands shook as they grasped the edges of the material, and he knew he'd better get on with it. He was running out of time.

The basement was unfinished, a gray block of cement with a hollowed-out center, depressing as an isolation chamber in every nondescript feature.

Renovating the room was a chore he'd meant to tackle whenever he found the spouse and family of his dreams. Melvin pictured them, his wife and kids, finishing this space together—whatever they wanted. A playroom? A craft and hobby room? An entertainment center for themselves and company to enjoy? It would have been painted in happy colors and decorated in children's joy.

Melvin almost laughed, thinking of it now. Never in his wildest nightmares could he have perceived of the room being used like this.

There was a routine. First, barring the door. It was made of twelve-gauge steel construction, two inches thick, five hundred pounds, and painted white from the outside so it wouldn't look conspicuous. Four heavy-duty metal hinges welded into a triple-reinforced frame held the door to the left, and, symmetrically, four custom-made industrial-strength combination locks ran down the right side. Melvin had found that, after dark, although his senses were heightened and images and details were enhanced in his instinct-driven brain, he could not remember numbers nor manipulate the dials on a combination lock for the life of him.

Second, there was the pole. The twelve-by-sixteen wooden post, hewn special for him at the very mill where he enjoyed his runs, was alone in the center of the empty room. It ran from concrete floor, where it was buried four feet, straight up to the low ceiling. A Clydesdale could not move it, and, yet, he still had doubts every time.

Next step, the clothes. Melvin had gotten tired of replacing outfits, even the ones he bought at Goodwill for just this occasion. He stripped bare and tossed the sweats in the corner. He was in better shape than ever from weights and jogging thanks to his motivation to stay fit for the police force, yet sitting down here naked in the cold basement still made him uncomfortable. Uncomfortably…embarrassed. He'd tried at least giving himself an old couch to sit on and a blanket, but the shredded mess to clean up afterward hadn't been worth it.

Finally, the shackles. Tractor chains rattled against the pole as Melvin fitted specially-made metal cuffs around both wrists and then his ankles. He tossed the keys in the corner with his sweats. It would take him half the night or better to break free of the chains wrapped around the post, then the rest would be spent clawing at the steel door and worrying with locks that refused to give to long, clawed fingers.

Melvin sat on the floor, ignoring the bite of the cold cement on his skin. Already he could feel a pulling in his gut, out his limbs, like the moon were a magnet shifting not merely tides, but blood and bone and sinew with as much ease.

Was it like this for her? No, he knew not. Ivy did not hide her "talents" in a dank, underground room. She would be out tonight, relishing the blue moonlight on her ivory coat, her nose to the soil, sniffing out a trail of prey she'd long chosen before that night. She would revel in the transformation, the hunt, the release of anxious anticipation as wolfen fangs sank into yielding flesh.

There was no shame in this act for Ivy Cole.

Melvin leaned against the post of his confinement, not caring if the support offered him comfort. He was increasingly uncomfortable regardless, with his limbs beginning their tell-tale ache and the prickling, itchy, crawling skin that felt like it'd come alive and was shifting itself around his body, a loose blanket suddenly pulled askew.

And still he thought *of her, of her, of her.* She was forever in his mind, every waking hour of normalcy and every primal, dark moment such as this. He hated her, he still loved her, he loathed what she'd done to him, he longed to forgive. The emotions wrestled in his mind as forcefully as the physical anatomy of his body fought the full moon. But the violence of his fantasies, whether as man or while morphing into wolfish beast, was more troubling still. Torn, his reveries were—between grabbing her thankfully in his arms, a complete man with his love again, or grabbing her throat in one iron fist and crushing it until her head bobbed as lifelessly as a doll's.

It would all be addressed soon enough. Melvin had found her, had jumped on an old money trail that had long since petered out. And just when he thought he would never pick up the scent again, there it was in the most unusual of places: the *Doe Springs Gazette* right in front of him at morning breakfast, page 4B. A killer had come to North Carolina's coast, it seemed, and there in a photograph accompanying the article stood Ivy Cole amidst a church crowd, her face in profile as she looked far away at something he couldn't see. The journalist had snapped away, unnoticed.

After this full moon, Melvin could leave the safety of his basement prison to go confront her once and for all. He would have twenty-nine days to take care of the Ivy Cole situation and make it back to Doe Springs before the moon cycled full again. Hopefully, he would come home with a remedy, a vaccine—a freakin' magic potion, if that's what it took—and life could be normal again.

Melvin winced and grabbed his leg. A cramp lingered in his calf and then crept upward for his thigh. It sledge-hammered across his knee, and his face broke out into a sweat. The pain was coming. Did she feel pain right now, just as he? Or was it pleasure as the lunar fingers gripped her bones and pulled them apart to reshape anew? And worst of all, who would die tonight at the maw of the ivory hunter?

"The moon, the moon, damn the goddess moon and her power over lore and darkness."

Former Deputy Melvin Sanders chanted in rhythm to his laboring heart and waited for the wolf to come.

14

THEY SLIPPED out together, a ghostly pair wrapped in a gray-white mist, one large, the other, horrifyingly huge. They moved with spectral precision, silent footfalls landing one in the pad of the other, yet leaving not a single print upon the sand as if erased by an eldritch enchantment.

The beach was deserted at this hour, as was expected. Only the beacon from the distant lighthouse shed any intermittent illumination into the black of a coastal horizon. The full moon herself was in hiding behind clouds carried up the Gulf Stream like on the ocean current.

But they did not need light, preferred to move without it. Their brilliant yellow-orange eyes saw the nightscape as if brightened by full sun instead of the moon. There was no crevice nor shadow their vision could not penetrate at any hour.

The larger wolf—the Silver—led the way, her companion trotting obediently at her flank. Every now and then, the young White stopped to nip at a washed-up jelly fish or stringy piece of kelp. A large broken clam shell snagged the youngster's attention. She clamped it in her jowls and carried it a ways down the shore before losing interest to drop it, only to replace it with another shell, which she tossed high in the air. It landed behind the pup, startling her, and she skittered forward into her mother's side. The Silver turned and with only a look sobered the pup's play for at least a moment.

The ocean rolled in on a low tide beside them, and when the waves roared back out, they left in their wake pillowy mounds of sea foam, thick and white like clotted cream. The youngster could stand it no longer. She broke from the Silver's side again and dashed amid the airy knolls, snapping and leaping from one to the other, as the sea continued to replenish her with playthings.

The mother wolf sat on her haunches and watched the antics of the pup. She cocked her head to the side as the white wolf left the defenseless foam to begin attacking the waves themselves. She ran after them in their retreat, then fled herself when they turned and chased her to shore, their pearly crested tops growing ever larger until they plunged over the big pup, tumbling her off her feet in a comic roly-poly somersault with the tide.

The Silver's black-rimmed lips drew back over her four-inch canines, a look to those who knew canids that could only be interpreted as a smile. A silly dog's grin, at utter joy of being alive and the sight of her sputtering pup staggering out of the water, no match for the ocean and defeated. The young one shook herself mightily. Diamond sea drops sprayed the mother wolf, and she turned her head away from the watery onslaught to look down the beach.

Down the beach. A figure moved, a form was taking shape out of the darkness. It was distant still but headed this way.

The pup was beside her now, ears perked in the same direction. Down the beach. A faint sound carried up to them over the boom of the surf.

"Little Miss Caroline, ain't you a-lookin' fine, wish oh wish I had the time, to makin' you my la-a-dy."

A song. A man's voice. And a scent. The Silver knew it, but it was strange to the youngster. Liquor. The pup's nose wrinkled as the odd smell wafted toward them.

"Little Miss Caroline, wouldn't you like some wine? Sit with me and we shall dine, while makin' you my la-a-dy...."

• • •

Hobo Joe was feeling just fine himself. There was three hundred dollars in his pocket—cash—and he'd just dropped a twenty on this pert-near-perfect bottle of Jim Beam he was chuggin'. He was off work for six days straight (as for a hobo, Joe only aspired to the nickname; in truth he kept an on-again, off-again job gassing up boats at the marina). Six days to go through three hundred bucks in booze and women, a fine way to spend a week indeed.

"*Little Miss Car*—what the hell?" Hobo Joe's crooning and chugging came to a halt. "Who's up there?"

It was hard to tell, what with the black of the sea-oat-covered dunes molding uneven, hackled silhouettes to his left and the unforgiving wash of salty ink to his right drowning all sound. Farther down the beach, well beyond the little points of light that had caught Joe's attention, development in the way of condos and hotel highrises offered a shimmering oasis of Vegas-lit beauty spooning with the shoreline.

But not up here. Up here there was nothing but sand, dadblamed sand always blowing in your shoes or up your shorts and itching out your privates. Sand, and those four little pinpricks of orange light.

"Who's up there? I see the fire from your smokes. Hey, is that you, Raeford?"

Hobo Joe took a swig of Beam, then staggered on toward the glowing fireflies that bobbed at first and then had grown completely still at the sound of his voice.

"Got any smokes you can spare?" he yelled over the wind. "Anybody? I got a bottle of bourbon I'd be willing to share for a Pall Mall, if you got it."

The four lights that had drawn the man up the beach were closer now, unwavering and welcoming. Hobo Joe could use some company. He could use a smoke too, maybe get his hands on Raeford's Johnny Walker Red. Whoever else was with him tonight might have some jerky or a candy bar on 'em. He hadn't eaten all day. "I'm singing you a song, good buddy. You best be a-joining me. *Little Miss Caroline…*"

The song sputtered to a halt. The orange lights had split up. Two went to the left of Hobo Joe and two circled to the right and disappeared. Joe rubbed his weepy eyes with his weather-raw hands. He looked about, a little lost at the moment. This was not his area of the beach, come to think of it, nor Raef's either.

"Where the hell have I wandered off to? Who's there?" he yelled at the ocean, which had seemed to swallow up the lights to his right. When he looked back, the other pair were gone as well.

Night was back, the lights were gone, but the man felt anything but alone. He had heard Salty Duck was full of haints, but all the years he'd lived here, he'd thought that to be just a bunch of jerkwater hooey to draw the tourists. But the prickles crawling up the back of his neck and the hair standing up on his arms was not from the steady breeze blowing in from the gulf.

"*Little Miss Caroline…*" the man's voice tried to pick up the song with the bluster and gusto he'd felt before. But the words now only squeaked out in tinny, stilted syllables before dying completely on the name of his long-lost beloved.

"Caroline? Are you here? Are you haunting me, woman?" he whispered. "It's the will-o'-the-wisp. Dad-blamed will-o'-the-wisp floating along the beach. Caroline! Get on back to your grave, woman!" Hobo Joe wasn't whispering now. He shouted at the top of his lungs. Grandaddy had told him about the beach lights that flickered eerily up and down the coast sometimes. Smarty-pants out-of-towners called it the *ignis fatuus*—combustible gases produced from decomposing critters and plants in the marsh. But there was no marsh righ'chere, only the ocean and the sea grass and the dad-blamed irritatin' sand.

Hobo Joe squinted up the shoreline. Ignis whateverus or haint from the other side—the glowing orange sparks had vanished and the only lights left now were those distant lanterns of civilization a half-mile away and the beam of the candescent full moon, peeping now from behind a rampart of hovering storm clouds.

He rubbed his head like greasing up a basketball. "It's the booze, the no-good booze." Hobo Joe pulled a second bottle from his pocket, a half-pint of Cutty Sark, and made like he was going to throw it. Common sense got the better of him, though; what was the point in wasting good whiskey? He turned up the Scotch and downed the last quarter cup, then dropped both empty bottles in the sand.

And then he felt it. A presence, something with him, near him.

"Caroline?" Joe's back muscles tensed as the air around him seemed to compress.

Whatever lurked on the beach this night was directly behind him.

A breeze, softer and warmer than what wailed in from the sea, caressed the back of his neck like a lover's breath. He heard another blow, barely audible, and then felt the warmth again.

Hobo Joe slowly turned around, and the lights were back, steadfast-still a good foot over his head. He looked up at them, into them, the disembodied embers of his dead wife's ghost come to torment him.

And he saw.

Pointed ears, tufted triangles close to the head. An ebony-tipped muzzle, breathing hot only inches from his forehead. Jowls with fangs dripping saliva onto his upturned face. A thick, powerful neck ringed in bone-colored fur...

Hobo Joe looked into that furious, beautiful, horrific face, captivated, and could not look down to see the rest of what held him. But he would not have wanted to, for out of the darkness rushed another animal toward the shock-bound man.

His body shuddered as the force struck him midwaist from the side. Hobo Joe buckled forward. He grabbed the fur of the thing standing in front of him, his eyes still cast upward into those of the monster's, pleading with it, it seemed, or praying.

Then Hobo Joe's intestines slid out in long ropy loops next to his liquor bottles, and he released the fur to topple onto his ruined lower half. The devastation of his torso was immediately windswept with sand, and Hobo Joe's last thoughts were of the mess of the sand in his gaping wound and how he would never be able to clean it....

15

"IT'S STARTED," Sheriff Gloria Hubbard announced to no one in particular. She was seated on the top step of her back deck watching Chester chase a leaf skipping across the grass. He was slower now, a little age catching up to her only child, but the puppy was still in him enough to pursue anything that moved erratically: rabbits, squirrels, or even quick-scooting leaves attempting to escape the yard on a late-night breeze.

It was eleven forty-seven p.m., the moon was full, and Gloria was angry. Her fingers drummed their familiar cadence on the edge of an empty coffee mug. Da-da-da-*da*. Da-da-da-*da*. She should be on her way to mission completion right now, hunkered down low somewhere within the village limits of Salty Duck, North Carolina, and observing her target. But complications had arisen. Her one remaining deputy since Melvin walked off the job, Officer McKaye, suddenly developed chicken pox, of all things, and she couldn't leave the department unmanned save for Shirley, the detention officer/dispatcher, and Delores, the administrative assistant. Only a handful of applications for the open deputy position had trickled in, which would have been surprising except since the massacre that occurred five years prior in Doe Springs, nobody wanted any part of sheriff-ing and deputying in this tiny backwoods town.

Even me, Gloria thought. She thought it often. She never meant it. Maybe.

Gloria looked up at the sky, at the big gray boulder called the moon. She used to love the full moon, the way it lit up the Blue Ridge Mountains at night, casting them in gossamer beams of pur-ple-black light.

Used to.

"It's started, I can feel it. I know it," she said to the moon again.

It answered her with indifferent, deadly silence. And what she knew was a wolf hunted and someone tonight would die. Yet she had no proof. She could not call Salty Duck—the place where Police Chief Wilkerson of Pine Knot had tracked Ivy to once she appeared back on the radar screen, apparently from some other country—she could not call Salty Duck authorities and say, "By the way, you have yourselves a werewolf running amok down there. I suggest you lock her up before the mysterious disappearances begin."

And that's all there would be. No bodies, no traces, nothing to connect the sweet, attractive, law-abiding Ivy Cole to anything. Gloria would look like a fool.

The sheriff stood up and whistled. Chester bounced to her and then up the steps inside.

The kitchen they entered together was an armory. Gloria sur-veyed her arsenal, spread across the kitchen table, propped against cabinet doors, lying across the stove, even, for cooking had become a thing of the past. Food was no longer about pleasure but subsis-tence only, and the microwave handled all that just fine.

For a normal villain, this was definitely overkill. For Ivy Cole, Gloria hoped it would be enough. All the guns wouldn't be going with her, of course. She had carried the some twenty-plus weapons here to debate over and choose. When it all came down to it and her plan was in place, the sheriff had settled on three: the Remington 7615P pump-action patrol rifle with .223 hollow-point rounds that go in pretty but scatter large on the exit; the ever-rugged and ever-faithful police officer and military favorite Remington 870

Wingmaster shotgun with an improved cylinder choke capable of firing tear gas, if need be; and for close encounters, the gun she wore
on her hip every day and felt as comfortable with as a third hand, her
Glock .45. It was large for a woman's grip, but Gloria had always handled the firearm well. Gloria could handle anything, she'd always
thought of herself. This task, she prayed, would be no exception.

The phone rang. That would be unusual, except it had rung at
this hour on a full moon night for a few years now. She picked it up.

"Hello, James."

"Hi, Gloria. You getting ready to settle in?" Police Chief
Wilkerson said.

"In a little while. Maybe after another cup of coffee."

"Hope it's decaf, or it's going to be another long night."

"I don't sleep, you know better than that."

He laughed, deep, resonant. "Want some company?"

It was her turn to smile. The question—and the answer—were
always the same. "No. I'm doing okay tonight. Maybe next time."

"Just thought I'd ask."

"Never hurts."

"Only me, but maybe someday...?"

She didn't answer him. She didn't know how.

"Well, if you need anything, Gloria, I'm right here."

"Thank you, James. Thanks for...being there for me. You're a
good friend."

Quiet on the other end. Summing it up. Friend. "You went
through a lot back then. Losing your deputy that night the way you
did, almost losing Sanders..."

"I'm okay, I promise. All these years checking up on me, aren't
you exhausted?"

"Public service is my duty."

"I'll put in a good word with your boss."

He laughed again. "Good night, Gloria."

"Good night, James."

Gloria set the phone gently back in its cradle. She leaned against
the sink, feeling the poke of a semi-automatic in her lower back, a
reminder to get the guns back to the station, now that she had made

her selections. *You're a good man, James Wilkerson,* she thought, as the kitchen clock ticked over to a minute past midnight. It was the chief who had stepped in to aid her after the plague of the Devil of Doe Springs lifted from their town and Ivy Cole alighted with it. He had been a godsend, him and his department, who had assisted her for months after the last wolf attack that left her own department crippled. Three of Wilkerson's best officers were assigned to her until Sanders was back on his feet and Alan McKaye hired.

Wilkerson didn't know about Ivy's connection to the Doe Springs murders. Had he known, Gloria would not be able to carry out her plan alone, the way it had to be done. Wilkerson was an exceptional lawman, bent on following procedure to the letter, a characteristic they at one time had in common. Secondly, he was sweet on her with that typical, overly testosteroned policeman confidence he made no attempt to disguise, and that had kicked his protective instincts into high gear. He was reminiscent of Tee in so many ways, yet she had not been able to reciprocate.

Gloria was a sheriff—she didn't need a mate, protection, or a chaperone least of all. Her plan did not involve textbook procedure or the messy worry of a love interest. How could it, with the kind of thing she was up against? There was no procedure taught for this at the academy.

Gloria glanced at the calendar hanging on the wall by the telephone. Whatever happened tonight—or on all the full-mooned nights in the past five years—she could not help. But there was a twenty-nine-day window of opportunity opening, starting tomorrow, in which she could save the next life. And this time, Gloria was not concerned about the law or proof or the courts because, just like Wilkerson, they would not understand what this was all about.

Sheriff Gloria Hubbard reached for her rifle and cradled it in her shoulder. She hefted the barrel and in one smooth motion aimed it at the full moon outside the window.

Gloria was not going to Salty Duck to arrest Ivy Cole. This time, she was going to kill her.

16

"GOOD MORNING, Mr. Haskell!" Caleb waved to a man on the marina pier. He was much older, with a grizzled beard offset by skin baked the color of chewing tobacco. The man glanced up from his task over a deep sink, which was being fed water by the cut end of a green rubber hose.

"Hullohhh to you, Caleb. See you got yourself some shipmates today. Hitting the water finally, are ye?" Haskell's heavy Down East brogue (from his papa's side) combined with some kind of southern mountain twang (all from his mama) was nearly impossible to decipher, but Caleb's ear had tuned to it.

"Hitting the scrub buckets is more like it," Caleb answered as the trio drew up beside a mess of magnificent blue-striped wahoo by the fisherman's feet. A thirty-pounder was laid out on the beaten white counter, its belly slit and guts spilling into the sink.

"Aye, finally going to take that rust bucket to task. Don't believe you could have rounded up a prettier pair of first mates anywhere." Haskell pretended to tip a hat on his bare, sunburned head and then offered them a gap-filled grin. Something gray and gelatinous clung to his forehead where he touched it, but he didn't seem to notice—or perhaps care.

"Mommy, his teeth are—"

"Thank you, sir," Ivy said, understanding Haskell perfectly and cutting off her daughter's observation on dental hygiene, or lack thereof.

"Don't say 'tif I don't mean it." He scooped up the stringy fish guts and slung them into the water. "Wishin' I had some help today myself."

"Hobo Joe leave you hanging again, Mr. Haskell?" Caleb asked.

"Sorry lot he was cast from, I'm telling ye. Drunkard's about as dependable as using a colander for a lifeboat. Can't say as I miss the singing, though. Heard about enough out of him and his sweet Caroline 'round here."

Luna's eyes suddenly brightened as she snagged on one of Mr. Haskell's words with unerring clarity. She opened her pink lips wide. *"Little Miss Caroline, wouldn't you like some wine? Sit with me and we shall dine, while makin' you my la-a-a-a-a-dy!"*

The song belted out of the tiny child, surprising both men and a pelican perched on a piling above Haskell's head. It fluttered off to a different perch three boats down. Luna beamed at the adults. Her mother's mouth fell open, speechless.

"Well now," Haskell said, dropping his knife in the splattermuck in the sink. He squinted at the girl. "Sounds to me like somebody else is a-knowing ole Hobo Joe."

"No, not at all." Ivy laughed as casually as she could fake it. "Luna listens to everything on the radio and parrots it to show off. Goodness knows she's quite the little entertainer." Ivy's teeth gritted through a forced smile.

"Naw, now, that song is particular to Joe. She couldn't have got it off no TV or radio show neither. He made it up and has tormented me with it for nigh eight years. I'm only shed of the whole two repeating verses when he's out on a binge somewhere."

"We must have passed him on the street then. It was nice meeting you." Ivy, with Luna in tow, abruptly walked off, past dozens of occupied boat slips.

The fisherman turned to Caleb. "Not much of a talker. But then, looking like that, it's not what she says that counts, eh?" Another gappy grin, and he was back to the wahoo. A second fish flopped into the sink, and the knife went to work.

Caleb stepped away from the thorny old salt and his penchant for slinging whatever he cleaned. He watched mother and daughter saunter away, but the set in Ivy's neck and the rigid bend of her arm around Luna, hurrying her along, was anything but relaxed. Caleb's eyes narrowed just a bit as he studied them.

Ivy and Luna stood in front of a beaten-up fishing vessel, glad to be away from the curious Mr. Haskell but terribly dismayed at what they'd located in his stead. It was the worst boat on the row, and Ivy knew it must be Caleb's, even though it was in even worse shape than she'd imagined. There were no other fishing boats in such disrepair tethered to any of the pilings that Ivy could see, so this had to be it. Browbeaten by the sea, barnacled mercilessly by the harbor's watery inhabitants, and cared for seemingly not one iota by its neglectful owner, the poor boat looked like it could barely float here, let alone handle a cruise around the Banks. Ivy was seriously beginning to doubt Caleb's judgment—in both their ability to help save his sinking ship and in Ivy's willingness as a mother to let her daughter board it.

Caleb caught up to them and stood looking at the sad little craft.

"It's a mess. Just a complete mess," Ivy said.

Caleb nodded in agreement. "A regular horror show, I'd say."

Ivy sighed. "I guess it is what it is. We had an agreement. Where do you want us to start?"

Caleb pursed his lips. "Hmmm. How about over there?" He pointed farther down the wharf, toward another connecting pier that jutted right. "As much as I'd like to help this fella out, whoever he is, I doubt he'd appreciate us climbing around on his boat. Come on."

Luna skipped after Caleb, leaving her mother behind. Ivy

watched the blond waif curl her fingers around one of Caleb's and they both strode on, ignoring Ivy's aggravated sighs. As Caleb and Luna disappeared around a moored sailboat, she threw up her hands in exasperated defeat. "Hey, wait for me!"

17

"You, sir, are a liar of the worst sort. I feel bad for calling Bruce a pirate when I had no idea whom I was really dealing with." Ivy flipped her hand at him, feigning disgust.

"Fibber. I prefer 'fibber' over 'liar,' thank you," Caleb countered, grinning.

"But you made it sound like your boat was falling apart!" Ivy leaned back and let the ocean breeze brush her hair as her retort carried away over the water. She was seated on comfy cushioned benches lining the bow, and Luna was across from her, up on her knees and her face smiling into the wind. Caleb was at the helm of the thirty-two-foot center-console Regulator, bright yellow and aptly named the *Yellowfin*. It was an angler's dream and a far cry from the modest fixer-upper he'd described when negotiating the painting.

"Okay, maybe I exaggerated when I called it a wreck," Caleb said. "But admit it—aren't you glad, just a little bit? I mean, I can turn this bad boy around and take you back to the lobster boat, if you like. You seem to have a soft spot for it."

"I like riding above the water, if you don't mind." Not that she'd really minded any of it, exasperated as she pretended to be. After

Caleb had helped the girls climb aboard, the "cleaning" Ivy was hired to do consisted of wiping condensation off the seats along with a few misguided missiles from overhead gulls. Then Caleb had tossed the towels into the head and came back out carrying a cooler filled with soft drinks. It had been an unexpected and surprisingly pleasant way to start their day together.

Ivy enjoyed a cola now as the twin outboard engines powered effortlessly through the water. Sipping her drink, she watched Caleb, who did look rather captainly behind the wheel. A baseball cap shielded his alert eyes and the breeze billowed his sky-blue shirt like a pirate's blouse. This was joy for him, Ivy thought, his commanding a boat toward the solace of open water the same way she found peace trekking gravel back roads and grassy meadows in bare feet. The way he had guided them so smoothly away from the dock; the way he manipulated the obstacle course of other boaters coming into the marina, waving to them as they headed out; the way he revved the engines outside the wake zone, carefully so as not to rock his passengers in their seats—all of these things were with expertise and concern, and Ivy felt like she really could just sit back for the first time in a long time and enjoy the view.

They rode the slight chop through Marshy Bottom Sound, passing the charming waterfront of Salty Duck on their left and a thin ribbon of island on their right, which was part of Shackleford Banks. A few wild ponies grazed along the island's shoreline, their feet buried in what appeared to be liquid gold as the sun glinted off the waterway. An osprey soared low overhead, heading for a nearby nest with a fish gripped in its talons. Beside the boat, a gray dorsal fin broke the water briefly, followed by another. The blunted head of a dolphin emerged to chase their wake. Luna was mesmerized by all she saw, and, for once, completely speechless.

"You know why it's called 'Salty Duck'?" Caleb hollered above the breeze and the engines. Ivy squinted toward shore, where the historic buildings that once housed cargo shipments and fisheries now catered to waterfront restaurants and eclectic boutiques. They began dwindling to a speck as the boat picked up speed and roared farther away.

"No." Ivy shook her head.

"Editing. Altered the whole town."

"Oh, come on."

"No, really. Bad proofreading and one deaf old man robbed the town founder of notoriety."

"Okay, tell me. How did an editing mistake alter history?"

"All right, disbeliever. I'll tell you. The town was founded in the early 1700s by a member of the British navy. His name was Theodore Salter. He used the sound as a trade-route shortcut through the Banks and into the many inlets out here. Where the town now lies was one of his favorite layovers because of its accessibility. He named the community and its waterway after himself: 'Salter's Aqueduct.' Residents began shortening the name. They called it 'Salter's Duct.'

"Well, seven years went by between Theodore's founding and his next visit with goods bound for America. When he inspected the town's management records, he saw the ratification documents had been redrawn, the originals, he learned, lost to a fire at the first town hall. The transcriptionist at the time, as it sadly turned out, was a man who was half-deaf and turning blind in a hurry. To his ear, 'Salter's Duct' had always been 'Salty Duck,' and no one caught the error behind him. After the American Revolution, patriots took up with officially calling the seaport Salty Duck as a snub to the British.

"The man who started all the hubbub, the transcriptionist, was Smitty Pete, and that, if you'll look ahead of us, ladies, is his island."

Caleb pointed straight ahead. Salty Duck and the islets of Shackleford Banks were mostly behind them now. This lone stretch of land was far removed from the rest—isolated and populated by a maritime forest of scrubby trees that appeared to be clawing their way away from the wind-torn beach.

"Why is that Smitty Pete's island?" Luna asked.

"Because, Luna, that's where Captain Salter sent Smitty to live out the rest of his days. He was punished for his error."

"See where bad spelling and not paying attention can get you, Luna?" Ivy said.

"Exiled," Caleb nodded gravely and winked. "There are a lot of ghost stories surrounding that bar of sand. Folks coming into the Banks at night claim to still see Smitty, wandering up and down his lonely stretch of beach carrying a lantern."

"Will we see him? Will we?" Luna asked, straining over the bow toward Smitty Pete's Island.

"Dunno. Reckon it's possible. But I'll tell you something else even more amazing: This spot," Caleb cut the engines about fifty feet from shore, "is the best place in the whole Outer Banks for catching flounder. Grab some poles, girls, we're going fishing."

It was nighttime, and the fire crackled and wavered on the shore. A log shifted, sending sparks floating upward in a whirling mass like lit confetti. Around the fire's edges, Ivy lounged on her side in the sand, her head propped on one hand and a paper plate containing nothing but flounder tails in front of her.

Caleb sat across the fire, occasionally poking it with a stick to stir up the rocket sparks and make Luna giggle. That worked for all of ten minutes, then she was up and off, racing down the beach to find Smitty Pete.

"That was the best fish dinner I have ever eaten, Caleb. Thank you."

Caleb grinned and poked the fire again. "Wish I could take credit for the catch. Good thing I brought backup."

The amateur anglers hadn't caught a thing, not even a nibble, despite Caleb's expensive rods and patient efforts at teaching his crew how to bait and cast. But he had come prepared for the hungry worst: His cooler revealed stacks of flounder filets, peeled shrimp, and potatoes wrapped in tinfoil to throw into the embers. The storage compartment under the captain's seat had held a picnic basket, which Caleb waded to shore once they'd anchored close enough.

Ivy tried not to think of another picnic she'd shared with a man she had close feelings for. No, her deputy was long gone, and this person—this sweet, considerate, competent stranger—was here now.

And admit it or not, Ivy found his company and attention welcome. He certainly seemed to care about Luna, and Luna had taken to him immediately. It was an encouraging sign, and Ivy found herself giving over to it.

"Look, Caleb, look!" Luna rushed back into the firelight and pushed something inches from Caleb's nose. "I found it for you." The sand crab was drawn up tight in its egg-shaped shell. She dropped it in his palm.

"Well, I sure do appreciate that, Luna."

"And look at this!" She thrust a small black object at him as well. It was three inches long, rectangular, and with a dried-up curly horn at each of its four leathery corners.

Caleb took it and held it to the light. "Hmmm. A mermaid's purse. Very good, Luna. These are rare."

"A mermaid's purse! A mermaid's purse! Did you hear that, Mommy! I'll go find lots more!" She turned on her bare heel and sprayed the adults with sand as she fled back down the beach in pursuit of another discovery.

"And what, pray tell, is a mermaid's purse?" Ivy asked lazily.

"It's what some folks call a skate egg case. I thought mermaid's purse sounded much more intriguing to a five-year-old."

"It's all I'll hear about for weeks. Don't be surprised if she comes back here dragging a real mermaid, or even, heaven forbid, Smitty Pete."

Caleb laughed and then remembered his present. He set the crab in the sand, outside the circle of light. Soon it would be brave enough to make its way back to the ocean.

"I've never seen her take to someone the way she has you, Caleb."

"It's my natural charm. Women of all ages find me irresistible." He wiggled his eyebrows and poked the fire again. Another shower of sparks flamed up to block out the stars.

"And that's why you're still single?" Ivy arched a brow of her own.

"Touché. Maybe I'm not *that* irresistible. I mean, I did have to lie and kidnap my dinner dates, didn't I?"

"If we've been kidnapped, then this is the most enjoyable abduction I think I could have ever experienced. But you could have just asked me."

"And risk brutal, humiliating rejection? Nah, somehow I thought if you were treating our date as a job, I'd have a better shot. Oh, wait—I don't think that came out right."

"There's some more of that 'natural charm' you were bragging about. Well, just for the record, I hate it when people trick me, Caleb. But under the circumstances..." Ivy looked around her. The *Yellowfin* bobbed just offshore in the moonlight; Luna's laughter floated in with the waves; the fire cast a halo of warmth that kept the cool evening zephyr comfortable.

"The food was worth it?" Caleb finished her thought.

Ivy laughed. "Yes. Under the circumstances, the food was worth it."

"What about you, Ivy? Any husbands in your past?"

"Oh, okay, that was sudden. I see we're back to the serious stuff."

"Pardon my lack of segue; I'm trying to be interesting. You know—dazzle you with varied and clever conversation. You're supposed to find me funny, smart, and devilishly unpredictable. Isn't that how these things work?"

"I haven't been on a...date?...in so long, I don't remember. But to answer your question, no, I've never married."

"Being a single mom must be tough. Staying in all the time, hanging around with a much younger and demanding crowd."

Ivy laughed again. "It's not so hard. Actually it's nice having a little person to talk to. Prior to that, I only had four-legged companions. I'm a dog trainer on hiatus, if you want to know. My shepherd, Aufhocker, is my other child."

"Sounds like a fun job, the dog training. Why don't you do that here, now that your employment with me has run out?"

Ivy was long on answering and Caleb took the quiet moment to watch her through the flickering fire. He caught another glimpse of that shy, reluctant smile and bright eyes that reflected the firelight so well they looked nearly orange themselves.

"You know, maybe I will," Ivy said finally.

"What's that?" He'd been lost in shimmering eyes and waves of shiny gold-spun hair pouring across the sand.

"Restart my business. My hiatus is starting to turn into early retirement, if you want the truth. I haven't trained dogs in several years. I lost my pack, you see."

"Your pack?"

"Yes. I had lots of dogs once, eight total, back when I lived in the mountains. One in particular I miss most of all. His name was Rex—Simple Rex, my vet used to call him." Ivy smiled, remembering the compact and tenacious little terrier, a mere pittance of a dog when she'd first found him who later became the biggest of heroes. Rex had been anything but simple. Extraordinary, he was, and even beyond that. Leaving all her dogs, but especially leaving Rex, had been one of the hardest decisions of her life. And one of her greatest regrets.

Ivy sighed and came back to the fire, leaving sweet canine memories to wilt away in the draft of the flames. "I had to move and I couldn't take everyone with me, only Aufhocker. I've been so sad since then, I quit training."

"You feel guilty."

"Yes."

Caleb squinted at her. "I know you, Ivy, better than you think. I'm a good judge of character, and I can tell you wouldn't be the sort of person to just abandon something you love. I'm guessing those dogs went to a wonderful home."

"The best, actually. And thanks for thinking so. But enough about me. What about you, Caleb? What do you do?"

"Oh, I'm part of the exciting world of—are you ready for this?—yacht sales. Or I was, until recently. I quit everything in Chicago and came here. You could say I'm on a hiatus too. I cut my teeth on boats in Lake Michigan when I was just a kid, but it felt confining, despite its vast size. Nothing compares to the boundless ocean."

"We have that in common."

"The ocean?"

"The appreciation for no boundaries."

Caleb wished there was more behind the statement—a hint, a suggestion, an innuendo. But it was not a flirtation of any kind, merely a fact stated simply in that honest way she had. If only the fire did not separate them, if only there truly were no boundaries. But since the first day meeting this enigmatic lady, he knew there were boundaries aplenty where men were concerned.

Ivy abruptly sat up and brushed sand from her clothes. It was a sign of finality, the evening was ending. As if sensing her mother's mood, Luna appeared in their intimate camp again. Her cheeks were flushed from running up and down the beach, searching for treasures.

"Look, Mommy, I made some new friends."

"New friends, Boo?" Ivy wrapped her arms around the child's waist and pulled her close. "Don't tell me you rustled up Smitty Pete after all."

"No, I couldn't find him," she said, a comically adult look of consternation wrinkling her tiny brow for a moment.

"Then where are these new friends? You don't have a starfish hiding in your pocket, do you?"

"Ivy, listen. Something is out there." Caleb stood up. He had heard a noise, rustling, cautious but definite. He hefted the stick he'd been stirring the campfire with, testing its sturdiness.

Ivy stood beside him and stared into the darkness.

"Don't worry, Caleb. I told you—they're my new friends. You can come out now!" Luna called toward the thick line of trees that had been shielding their backs and dividing shore from maritime forest. "Don't be afraid!"

Twigs cracked, first from one spot, then another, and another. Something—some *things*—were moving through the trees toward them.

"Luna, what did you do?" Ivy looked down at her daughter, whose eyes sparkled up at her mother in the color of a harvest moon lit by pumpkin light.

"Stop it," Ivy hissed and turned her daughter away so Caleb could not see the emerging bright glow that even lit up the girl's cheeks.

And then…other eyes, bright, cast in deep burning amber. Six pairs of them at the tree line, hovering, watching. Forms began to take shape as they melted out of the forest and onto the sand.

"This is incredible," Caleb whispered, gripping the stick even firmer. He was ready to wield it like a baseball bat in the hands of a maniac to protect them all, if necessary. But for now, he watched. "Incredible…" he whispered again. "What are they, Ivy?"

"*Wa'ya,*" she breathed, transfixed by this glorious gift. It had been so long to see a brother in the wild….

"What is *Wa'ya?* Coyotes?" Caleb asked quietly. He was torn between herding the girls toward the safety of his boat and standing here all night, in awe of the magnificent animals just yards away.

Ivy shook her head. "*Wa'ya* is what the Cherokee Indians called them. They're wolves, Caleb. *Canis rufus,* to be exact. Red wolves."

The canids crept closer, just outside the safety of tree cover. There were, indeed, six of them. Seventy pounds of lean muscle, long slender legs tipped by large white feet, feet that padded over pocosin habitats and dune ridges with fluid ease…They were smaller than their cousin, the gray wolf, but the intelligent, feral eyes bore the same ancient wisdom.

The alpha male stood slightly ahead of the rest, his head lowered with pointed ears airplaned to the side, a stalking posture crossed with caution. A cinnamon swathe of fur ran up his muzzle and across his head, merging with a ribbon of sparse black along his buff and brown back, camouflage shades that painted him a phantom in this beige coastal landscape. He and his pack watched the humans impassively. It was not their nature to approach man at all, and Ivy looked down at her child. Luna had drawn them. Luna…had called them.

And they came. Despite every survival instinct bred into them for centuries, despite at one time being hunted to extinction in the wild, here they stood, facing their most dreaded predator, and, unbeknownst to Caleb, their greatest allies.

"Wolves, Ivy? On the island? I've only heard of them running free in the Alligator River area of North Carolina. How did they get way out here?"

"I'm not sure. This could be one of those experimental reintroduction sites, like Bulls Island in South Carolina. It's a mystery. But here they are, just the same."

The wolves shuffled nervously at their voices, all but the alpha, who had not moved.

"Okay, it doesn't matter. Start backing up. Move real easy toward the water. I don't think they'll follow us into the ocean," Caleb said. The big wolf in front was starting to alarm him. It looked at them too keenly, particularly at the small girl. Caleb put his arm in front of Ivy and started ushering her backward.

"Mommy, Caleb is silly. Tell him there is nothing to be afraid of. We're here and—"

"And Caleb is absolutely right, Luna. They won't hurt us if we leave them alone." Ivy glared at Luna, daring her to say one more word.

Luna's visage clouded like the moon in a thunderstorm. "I don't want to go. I want to stay with my friends. You'd let me play with them if *he* wasn't here."

She was right. They would both sprint off into the woods with the pack, Ivy on two legs and Luna on four. What a wondrous, magical night it would be, to run and howl with a pack of real wolves under a crescent moon borne across the sky by an ocean wind. Ivy had not had such an opportunity since she left the West and its meager population of grays that eluded man like spirits....

Nevertheless, Caleb *was* here, and there was nothing Ivy could do about that.

"That is enough." Ivy scooped Luna up and propped her on her hip. "Caleb knows what he's doing and we need to listen to him." She let Caleb continue to back them into the ocean. He stood between them and the pack, who had not stepped any closer. Their heads bobbed down slightly, then back up, as they tasted smells on air currents and noted the change in the little she-wolf's mood. Her anger made them wary of coming closer, although Ivy, quietly amused, was sure Caleb thought his gallant stick was holding them at bay. The braveness of the gesture, albeit one she and Luna would giggle over later, warmed her heart further. She said a wistful good-bye to the pack under her breath as the cool Atlantic water closed over her knees and thighs.

Back on the boat, Caleb turned a spotlight to shore. The wolves were gone.

18

IVY FELT happy, genuinely happy. It had been awhile. But moving to Salty Duck had been the best thing she could have done for herself and her child. They had a sweet cottage, nice keep-to-themselves neighbors (except for grumpy old Mrs. Pitchkettle), a membership at Parish Keep Presbyterian, and Luna was completely smitten with one particular handsome boatman who seemed to delight in the girl's company as much as Ivy's own.

And he had inspired her, it was true, for right this minute she and Luna were walking down Front Street placing flyers on cars and in store windows that would allow it: *Professional Dog Training in Your Home! Over a decade of experience. First session free. Call Ivy for an appointment.*

Luna gleefully thrust the flyers into people's hands as they passed on the cobblestone walk. She paused at a lamppost. Affixed to its side was another flyer: *Have you seen this man? "Hobo" Joe Rouger, last seen at Sea Ray's Tavern...*

"Mommy, that's—"

"Come on, Luna, let's go." Ivy snatched the little girl's hand, sending flyers fluttering to the ground. She didn't want to be reminded of Hobo Joe yet again. It was not a good kill—good kills were planned, victims stalked and studied, her motivation based on a person's deserving her predatory release. There had been none of that with Joe. He was a random soul staggering drunkenly across the wrong patch of beach at the wrong time.

But worst of all, and what had kept Ivy lying awake for many nights: There was no chance given to the victim to repent. Before transforming, Ivy always liked to grant her victims a choice, just like she had choice in choosing them. It was easy. If they were sorry for the miserable state of their lives, sorry for the abuses they inflicted on others, sorry for the bad they brought into the world, Ivy would let them go.

So far, it had never happened. Folks looking at a petite, righteous blond woman telling them how to live tended to get belligerent, not remorseful. Until, of course, the silver wolf arrived. They were full of penitence then, but then it was too late. The wolf did not bring out the best in people, only the worst of the worst. Liars lied more in their pleas for mercy, cowards fought the least and ran harder than ever, and the violent became more violent to no avail.

Hobo Joe was given none of these choices. No contrition. No time to reflect. No moment to evaluate his erring ways, if there were any, and say a simple "I'm sorry." Ivy didn't like drunks, could have smelled Hobo Joe even against the direction of the ocean breeze, but that's all she had known. Was it enough to lay his guts open on the sand and devour every piece of his flesh, even the bones?

Maybe. Maybe not. But still, the kill was not intended to be a kill at all. A frolic on the moonlit beach was to become a game of cat and mouse when the singing man had headed their way. It was to be a teacher's moment, mother to pup, in stalking only. Even if seen by the man, there would have been little cause for concern. After drunks passed out, they usually forgot the night before and even if remembered, they themselves usually blamed the bottle for bad hallucinations. Ivy credited herself on two occasions for scaring drunken men sober, and one even went into the monastery. It was some of her finest work and not an ounce of blood had been shed.

But the pup had struck before the mother wolf could stop her.

The suddenness and ferocity of the attack surprised even Ivy. And once the blood flowed, there was no turning back. Mercy then was a quick release, and the silver wolf had delivered it. The jugular tore between her teeth as easily as warm bread as soon as the man's body had hit the ground.

The silver wolf disciplined the pup soundly after it was over, sending the youngster whimpering onto her back with tail tucked tight to her belly and her sweet tongue licking submissively at her mother's muzzle. The bigger wolf could taste the coppery taint of the man's blood in the pup's kisses as she begged for forgiveness. But the deed was done and there was no bringing Hobo Joe from Sea Ray's Tavern back after that.

Ivy shook it off, and the present moment rushed back to her. She was in Salty Duck on a beautiful day and her daughter Luna was staring up at her.

"Mommy, that hurts!" Luna's little hand was clasped in Ivy's and turning red.

"Oh, Boo, I'm sorry. I got distracted," Ivy said, redirecting her attention to the task at hand. There would be time later for talks on morality and choices with her child. Today was for happy thoughts and new beginnings, and Ivy was determined to let nothing spoil it. "Let's move on to the next store. Tear me off some tape, honey."

Luna stuck two pieces on the corners of another flyer and pressed the paper against the glass door of The Scotch Bonnet, prettily named after North Carolina's state seashell. They had been to this place before—it was the same waterfront boutique where Ivy had purchased their clothes for church. Merry hats and flowery sundresses adorned sewers' dummies in the window. Oversized faux shells leaking strings of fabulous pearls entwined around the dummies' feet. Ivy was just about to comment on a lovely pair of earrings that would match Luna's necklace when…

"Hey, you can't put that there." A short fussy man wearing a tan corduroy sport jacket (*in this heat—he must be mad*) and askew toupee emerged through the doorway, pushing Luna back.

"Oh!" Ivy jumped at his sudden appearance. "I'm sorry. There were other local flyers stuck here—I thought it would be all right."

"You thought wrong." His nose twitched rapidly to the right, then the left, and his toupee seemed to shift slightly with it. He reminded Ivy of a mole that had just surfaced from the dark earth and was adjusting to bright lights.

"Caswell, what's the ruckus?"

An older man with a slight paunch and a full head of real hair, black peppered gray, came out into the bright coastal light and squinted at them. It was Leland Pitchkettle and Ivy felt an inward groan. She'd had no idea when she shopped here before that this was his store.

"More flyers to litter our storefront," the mole now known as Caswell said. He snatched Ivy's eggshell stationery from the heavy glass door and shook it accusingly.

"Let me have a look at it." Leland fished out a pair of wire-rimmed glasses and untwisted them onto his face.

"A dog trainer. That be you?" he asked.

"Yes, I'm Ivy Cole."

"We're neighbors and attending church together—I'd think I'd know who you are. You're giving my wife fits, in case you haven't figured it out."

Ivy had no response for that. She just looked at him blankly and wished she were anywhere else on the planet.

"You're Mr. Pitchkettle," she said finally, for lack of anything else.

Leland glanced up at the store sign. "Would make sense, now wouldn't it?"

Ivy followed his gaze to the decorative "Scotch Bonnet" plaque hanging above them. For the first time she noticed the small print burned into the wood underneath the swirly letters of the store name: "est. 1977, Pitchkettle."

"Right. We're sorry to bother you. We'll be on our way." Ivy reached for the flyer Leland still held.

"Now just hold on a minute. I'm all for supporting free enterprise and working mothers. Don't see no harm in putting a piece of paper on the wall for a time, long as it's over there with all the others and not smack-dab in the middle of my door. Here, Caswell, stick it." He thrust the flyer back at his twitchy counterpart, then winked at Luna. "Ladies," he said, and left.

Caswell slapped the piece of paper alongside an ad for a bake sale and huffed back inside after Leland.

Luna tugged at Ivy's shirttail. "Is he a good man or a bad man, Mommy?"

"Who? Mr. Pitchkettle?"

Luna nodded.

It was an important question, one that should never be answered lightly in this company. "I think," Ivy said slowly, "that Mr. Pitchkettle is a good man disguised as a bad man. Do you understand?"

"It means he acts all mean and hateful but deep down he's nice?"

"Yep. That's right."

"What about Mrs. Pitchkettle? Is she wearing a disguise too?"

"You got me on that one, Boo. But good, bad, or otherwise, you stay away from over there, got it? Now, let's forget about the Pitchkettles. We've passed out enough flyers. I think it's time for some ice cream at The Bluewater Lady!"

"Well, look who's back. If it isn't the mighty crustacean."

It was Luna's waiter, standing tall over them at their outdoor table. Dark eyes the opaque color of obsidian bore down on them above the amused grin parting his goatee. In his hand were two menus.

Luna stared straight ahead as if he weren't there. She didn't even smile.

Ivy did it for her. "Hello again. I think we're just having ice cream today. Two banana splits, please."

The waiter put the outstretched menus back under his arm. Ivy noticed the bottom of a tattoo peeking beneath the shirtsleeve of his usual "Eat at The Bluewater Lady" T-shirt. It looked like a Celtic symbol wrapping around his large bicep.

"For such attractive ladies, I'll make sure you get double whipped cream. Here, I'll even leave you with some extra napkins." He carefully placed them in front of Ivy and Luna. His hand brushed Ivy's and her eyes darted up to meet his. She saw her reflection and nothing else in the dark pupils. He looked at her a little too long before straightening up.

"Back in a jiffy," he said and walked away. There was a swagger to his stride, right down to his scuffed-up cowboy boots, that reminded Ivy of the old Westerns she loved as a kid. Bruce the Pirate-Cowboy flitted through her mind; he could learn a thing or two from this guy.

"He likes you, Mommy, but I don't like him," Luna said.

The latter was obvious, but maybe Luna was right about the first part too. The man seemed to make it a point to wait on them every time they came in, despite Luna's obnoxious attitude. Ivy was used to fending off—or outright ignoring—casual male attention, but her outspoken and overly observant daughter made the ignoring part tricky. Avoidance was usually the best answer.

"You don't like him too, do you?" Luna said. It was half accusation, half plea, and Ivy tried not to laugh. She knew her daughter well, and what she knew was the child had already set her sights on the man she thought should be in their life.

"I don't know, Luna. He's very handsome, in a roughneck kind of way. Rugged and strong, don't you think so?"

"I think he's stupid."

Ivy sighed and set to studying on finding a new favorite place to eat while waiting for the ice cream to arrive.

The waiter stood half in and half out of the kitchen, waiting on two large banana splits. He knew they wouldn't eat a third of them, but he'd upsized their order anyway. It would take about five minutes or better for the food to be ready—good a time as any to make the call. He pressed a small cell phone to one ear while holding the other closed against the clatter of the kitchen.

"Yeah, Gage here. I can barely hear you. Hold on," he said into the phone. The lunch rush noise in the restored dockside tavern-turned-restaurant proved to be too much, and he moved out the side door just beyond the patio seating on Front Street.

"That's better. Listen, I'm calling because they're here again....Yes, that's right. I'm looking at them right now." Ivy's and Luna's profiles were to him as they faced one another over their table.

The garbled voice on the other end of the line spoke and his face scrunched in frustration.

"Well, how much longer do you want me to wait?"

More static, cleared by a firm answer.

"Oh. It was delivered today? That was quick. Should it make any difference at this point? I could just follow them down the street a ways before they even get home...."

A raised voice, commanding in strong German.

"Okay, relax. I won't do anything yet," the waiter said. "You're the boss."

He dropped the phone in his pants pocket. It was nearly unbearable, watching the clock ticking by and being held to inaction. Granted, the next full moon was weeks away—there was plenty of time. But why take chances? As for the delivery—what was even the point in that? It seemed so ridiculous. But Stefan Heinrich believed it to be so, despite the fact the Order was completely undeterred.

Gage Rowland, The Bluewater Lady's most recent hire, watched Ivy laugh and tweak the little girl's nose. Luna swatted at the hand, then reached up to tweak her mother's nose in return. Observing such a sweet moment, it was hard to believe that lycanthrope blood ran through her veins. Hard to believe—if he had not seen the lupine forces at work for himself. Not Ivy, to be sure—he had never encountered the likes of her. Her disciplined judgment wrought from the true *Canis lupus*—the ability to kill or not kill, choose or not choose—was unmatched in the werewolf's world. For that, she was one of a kind.

One of a kind—until now. Until Luna.

"Order up!" called from the kitchen.

The waiter hurried in to get the desserts. He didn't want the ice cream to melt and stir up the rebellious little she-pup further. She didn't like him right now, no, she surely did not. But that would change.

Very soon, a lot of things would change.

19

Ivy and Luna moseyed home, sticky from jumbo banana splits and tired from a day on their feet. How surprised the waiter had appeared when retrieving their empty dishes, every last banana, cherry, and gooey walnut devoured. And how sweet of him not to charge for the obviously upsized desserts, even more of an affirmation in Ivy's mind to change eating establishments. She'd left him a huge tip and vowed to Luna they would never dine there again.

Luna seemed very pleased by her mother's decision, and Ivy was pleased with another decision, that of moving forward with her life. The anticipation of immersing herself in dog training again—a job she felt so passionately about—had buoyed Ivy's spirits like the tide. If she could get just one or two good clients, word of mouth would fill her date book. It always had. No, she and Luna did not need the money—her inheritance set them for life and would take care of Luna long after Ivy was gone. But that was never why she worked with dogs in the first place. They were her love, those four-legged guardian souls. And if the house was lonely with just her small pack right now, she could fill it up again by enjoying other people's pets and seeing the relationship between canines and humans blossom.

Ivy was tingly with the prospects, despite the aching feet that told her with a brand-new whining blister how glad they were to be turning up Battery Street for the homestretch. The lane was blissfully quiet and peaceful, until Luna started yelling and tugging at her tired legs. "Mommy—on the porch! On the porch! Look!"

Ivy was so accustomed to the outbursts, she didn't even startle. But they were home, and, indeed, something large and brown hunkered on the front of Captain Woodside's cottage. It was a large animal crate adorned with airline stickers. From inside the house, Ivy heard the unmistakable low-toned deadly warning of Aufhocker. His gaze alone could turn even big men away; when he became vocal, it was the fool indeed who would stick around to learn what lay behind that menacing growl. The bearer of this package had been no fool.

"Mommy, what is it?"

"I don't know, Boo. I'm not expecting anything, other than the painting from Caleb." Which this certainly was not.

The crate rocked slightly and was still again.

Ivy and Luna halted at the foot of the steps, frozen. They looked at one another, then back at the mysterious carrier. Aufhocker's head popped into view through the front door's glass window, then he dropped out of sight again. Ivy heard his feet working at the door casing, trying to get out.

"Luna, stay back. Let me get Aufhocker before—"

But it was too late. Luna bounded up the steps and pulled the crate open before Ivy could stop her. A monstrous black head lunged out of the container, straight for Luna's face. Ivy screamed and was up the steps after her daughter, but not before a pink tongue had covered Luna's cheeks in wet, sloppy kisses.

"A puppy, Mommy! Somebody sent me a puppy!" Luna grabbed the animal around the neck and hugged it tight. It wiggled in her grasp, nearly taking her off her feet.

"A puppy? He's nearly grown." The chiseled head, broad between the eyes but honed at the muzzle, was nearly as large as Luna's own noggin. The young dog was about nine months old, Ivy guessed, and by the looks of it, on its way to overtaking Auf in stature. She knew those fathomless intelligent eyes, the low elegant ears, the huge feet that would pad in a near straight line, unlike any "ordinary" shepherd, as this might appear to some unfamiliar with the line.

Ivy knew the bloodline all too well, would know it even if the crate weren't marked as freight from Germany to the United States.

Ivy opened the door and marched inside. "Auf, you've got a cousin on the porch. Watch him. Watch!" she pointed to the door and Auf skirted out, his tail up in the dominant stance of a wolf about to put a newcomer in his place.

Ivy picked up the phone and dialed. It rang three times, six. On the seventh ring, a honey-dipped, deep-Southern, genteel voice worthy of Scarlett O'Hara answered. *"Hel-lo?"*

"Miss Ava, it's—"

"Ivy! I have been waiting and waiting to hear from you, sugar. I'm pleased you've finally decided to give a lonely old lady some of your time." The words pealed soft as wind chimes wrapped in velvet, velvet masking thorns that pricked Ivy in places only her aunt knew they would. Miss Ava, known as the Widow Pritchard to most in Doe Springs, could curdle even the heartiest with her subtleties.

"Hello, Ava. I'm sorry I haven't called sooner. I wanted to get settled in first before boring you with all the trivialities of beach life."

"Trivialities at my age can be scandalously exciting, dear, and you've had weeks and weeks to settle. How's my little towheaded beauty, by the way? When will you bring her to see me?"

"You know we can't come back there." Ivy had called in a riled-up state of supreme aggravation, but now, hearing her beloved aunt's voice, she felt only shame for not calling more, writing more, being more. It was a tiring dance of guilt with her aunt, but a familiar one Ivy couldn't change. She really *was* sorry, because Ava loved Ivy like the daughter she herself had never had.

"I know that, but I can wish, can't I? Now, let me settle back with this cup of tea, and I want to hear all about Salty Duck, the new house, how Luna's adjusting—everything!"

"Miss Ava, we'll get to all that, but something happened today and you're the only one who can clear it up."

"I'll help any way I can, sugar. Pray tell, what's happened?" A teacup clinked in a saucer a few hundred miles away.

"A surprise arrived today. It's wearing a pink ribbon with a card that says 'For Luna' and nothing else."

"Don't be so cryptic, sugar. Guessing games wear me out. What's got a ribbon?"

"A dog. A big black *special* dog. Ring any bells?"

"Oh my."

Ivy could picture a fluttering hand adjusting diamond-rimmed glasses, then patting the silvery upswept bun of hair for security. But the voice that replied was steady as a battalion ship on glass-smooth water. "I didn't know he would actually *send* something."

"Oh, Miss Ava," Ivy half snapped, half sighed. Her suspicions were correct. "Why did you tell Uncle Stefan where we are? It's enough of a risk letting even you know."

"I hope that's not an implication you can't trust me?" Firm now, a trace of arsenic in the honeycomb.

"Of course not. But I know how persuasive—and sneaky—the Doe Springs police can be. The more people that know where I am, the more dangerous it is."

"If you're talking about your handsome young deputy, you can think again."

"What does that mean?"

"He quit, dear." Ava paused. "And not only that, he left town."

"Melvin is...gone?" Ivy's tidy little world suddenly spun off its axis and bounced away through the stratosphere. How could this be? Even though she and Melvin hadn't spoken since their last night together in the Appalachian woods, Ivy felt she had not lost him completely, via updates on his well-being through her aunt. She knew about his recovery in the hospital. Had seen newspaper clippings of him receiving a medal of honor for his heroics against the Devil of Doe Springs. Knew he still lived alone, unmarried, not even dating, according to the waitress at Etta's Diner who meted out the latest gossip to Ava over her brunch there every Sunday. And now he was—

"Gone, sugar. There's an ad in the *Doe Springs Gazette* for his replacement."

"I can't believe it. Where did he go?"

"Well, according to Viola at the diner, folks are speculating he went home to West Virginia. He still has people up there."

"Did he see you before he left? To try to…"

"Find you again? No, he didn't."

It was the right answer, but one that broke Ivy's heart. As a deputy, sworn to uphold the law, his finding Ivy was the last thing that needed to happen. Melvin knew what she was; he had discovered the people she had…eliminated.

But Ivy hoped it wasn't as a deputy that he came around the Widow Pritchard, inquiring of her whereabouts, skimming for any telltale information. Ivy hoped the real reason he frequented Ava's parlor was driven not by the fact he was a lawman—but just a man. One whose heart had once been owned by her.

"Don't fret about it, Ivy. He's moved on with his life apparently, and so have you. Let it go, sugar. Let *him* go. It's time, don't you think?"

Ava was right. She would miss Melvin only in the lonely wee hours, when her daughter could not hear her cry. But she wouldn't let him steal her daytime happiness too. There had to be a point when she saw the future and quit looking to the past. Salty Duck and Luna were that future. Not Melvin. Not anymore.

"Stefan's gift to Luna, Ava. Let's talk about that."

"Enjoy it! Auf could use a break. He's been your sole guardian for too long, and you know the quality of what Stefan breeds." Then, before Ivy could protest: "Stefan loves you, honey. I wish you'd quit blaming him for what happened to your mother. It wasn't his fault he came too late to save her."

Ivy didn't like to be reminded of it—the Christmas Eve in Cologne, Germany; the smashed mantel clock that died chiming midnight; the werewolf that tore through the house, tore apart Catherine Cole in front of her, and then tore into her own tender body, only to be saved by Stefan's timely arrival and survive the guilt that came later, knowing she lived and her mother had not.

But Ava never minded playing the prickly pear, even when it came to poking barbed sticks at age-old self-flagellating guilt. She let truths and opinions fly and land wherever they may. And if that hit somebody square in the gut, she expected them to shore up like a true Southerner and take it like a man. Or a lady werewolf who'd wallowed in her own self-pity for too long.

"Ivy, are you there?"

Ivy shook her head, and the reverie from Cologne blew softly away like the pattering snowflakes from that blood-brightened night when she was only ten.

"When you talk to Uncle Stefan again, thank him for us. Tell him Luna loved the puppy."

"You should tell him yourself. I've been the go-between for too many years now."

Silence. Then: "I have to go, Ava. I'll call again soon, promise. I miss you."

"I love you too, sugar. Good-bye."

20

THE WIDOW Pritchard seated the phone in its cradle and carried her tea to the sunroom in the rear wing of the antique Victorian. The delicate Wedgwood rattled as she set it on the patio table and peered out the soaring glass walls at her meticulous yard. Every shrub, every tree, every vine and flower and ground creeper had been seeded by her own loving hands over a lifetime. But the plants that pleased her senses did nothing to alleviate her loneliness. And there had been plenty of that since Ivy left town. Ava had barely gotten used to the idea her beautiful niece was home before she was gone again—this time for good.

But it was necessary, her leaving the country, going into hiding to protect herself and the baby. Coming back to the States—back to North Carolina, for Lord's sake—was another example of how fool-hardy her confidence could make her. Did she truly believe five years was enough time to make folks forget what happened, to back off on their search for more fading clues? The lip service she gave to the concern about the police…how worried could she truly be to come back to the East Coast?

No, Ivy wasn't worried about getting caught—she was inching

back closer to somebody she was having trouble leaving behind. But Deputy Melvin Sanders was as good for Ivy as a wooden stake for a vampire. A werewolf involved with a police officer? It had almost been Ivy's undoing. And no matter what Ava just told Ivy on the phone about the deputy going home to West Virginia, Ava didn't believe it for a minute. What she did believe, she certainly wasn't about to tell her niece: that she suspected Sanders had found his lost love/nemesis at last and was hot on his way to confront her, with sparking as the last thing on his mind and justice quite likely on the forefront. Telling Ivy he might be coming would only make her naively glad; surprise, however, could provoke her instincts of survival. Could, but it was a crapshoot, depending on how slick Sanders played it. He was not a deceitful, manipulative man by nature, but time had hardened him. Ava was not sure what Sanders might be capable of in his efforts to bring Ivy in.

Ava patted herself on the back for saving Ivy from Deputy Sanders once before. Looks like she'd have to step in and do it again.

A bell sat by the saucer and teacup. It was hand-cut Polish lead crystal, a gift from her late sister Una in her travels about Europe. Ava rang it twice.

"Did you call me, Widow Pritchard?" A young woman in her fifties—young by Ava's standards, anyway—peeked around the corner, a frizzy swatch of permed red hair covering one eye. She tucked it back under her prim navy-colored hat. Ava rolled her eyes. She did not know why her housekeeper wanted to wear the silly maid's uniform; a sturdy pair of gardening overalls had always suited Ava just fine. But the woman seemed bent on formality. "Is too grand a house to go slopping about in my sweatpants, Widow Pritchard," she'd told Ava her first day of work.

"Gert, I need you to pack me a bag. Make that two bags, plenty for an extended stay, if need be."

"Taking a vacation, ma'am?" Gert sounded hopeful. The Widow Pritchard stayed cooped up here day in and day out, when she wasn't piddling with her landscape. It wasn't healthy. Elderly or not, a little adventure was good for any soul, and Gert had been on the widow for months to get away.

21

"I SUPPOSE he needs a name," was the first thing Ivy had said to her daughter after hanging up the phone with Ava. But on closer inspection, that had been an erroneous statement, for the new arrival had not been male at all. Clever Uncle Stefan had known better than to send a challenge to Aufhocker's position in their hierarchy, and the wolf was already grudgingly falling prey to the female's puppyish charms.

They were all in the backyard by the Thinking Tree now, the youngster dancing around the older wolf and licking at his muzzle. He took one massive paw and mashed her to the ground, then cleaned her ears before letting her go. Ivy placed a bowl of chow at the base of the tree, and the puppy wolfed it down while Aufhocker sat atop the back steps of the deck watching, a not-too-completely perturbed expression on his insouciant face.

"It has to be a good name, Luna. Anything in particular grab you?" Ivy asked, as she leaned against her tree and watched the female eat. Ivy had wished to extend her pack, and now, magically, that wish had been granted all the way from across the ocean. She would take Ava's advice and embrace it.

"I think her name is Ben-and-Anti," Luna said. "Is it a first and last name, Mommy, like Luna-and-Cole?"

"How do you know that's her name?"

"On the back of the card. There was more writing, see?" Luna handed it to her mother.

Benandanti, 1694.

It was the wolf's lineage name and its first recorded date. Aufhocker's line ran through Fenris, a mighty sire of coal black wolves, all who were now deceased, save Auf himself. Apparently Stefan was back in business with a new mated pair through, Ivy suspected, Auf's maternal side.

"Benandanti, Boo—one word. It means 'hound of God,'" Ivy said. "The Benandanti were werewolves who fought witches to protect crops, keep livestock healthy and fishing grounds flourishing, and the people of their area safe. Your great-uncle Stefan has sent you a guardian angel, just like he sent me when I was a girl."

"I love her, Mommy. She's so cuddly and beautiful, like a twin Auf, just not as big yet and no old gray hair around her neck and nose."

Auf sniffed loudly from the deck, as if he understood every word and found the reference to his age insulting.

"Can we call Uncle Stefan to thank him?"

Ivy thought about it. It would so please him, and the gift really did warrant some kind of reply. But it had been a long time—since she was a child herself. How do you start a conversation after that many years have passed? The telephone would be awkward in her hand, the long silent pauses punctuating their discourse even worse. There was so much to say, and nothing.

"Let's start with a letter, how about that? I'll help you write it."

Luna smiled and ran to her new charge. The bowl was empty and brown gravy rimmed the young wolf's jowls. She met Luna with more kisses, and soon the girl's face was covered in gravy too.

"Help me decide what to call her, Mommy."

"Okay. It needs to be a special name, unique like Aufhocker's. And powerful, too—she's got a very important job ahead of her, looking after you. How about..." Ivy tapped her fingertip to her chin and let the Thinking Tree inspire her. "I've got it. How about Calopus, after the great mythical wolf? It was a ferocious predator, black as a bog on a moonless night with horns on its head and spines covering its body."

Ivy and Luna looked at the young female, who had suddenly left Luna to flop over on her back. All four paws waggled in the air as she twisted to the left and right, frantic in her efforts to rub out some unreachable itch. She paused to look at her new family from her upside down view, and her tongue lolled out in a silly pink flag by her head.

Luna looked at her mother doubtfully. "I don't think that fits, Mommy."

"She'll grow in to it. Just try the name on for size."

"Calopus. Cali." Luna said the words slowly, tasting the letters, weighing the syllables on her tongue. The name rolled agreeably off her palate. "All right. I like it. Here, Cali!"

The wolf flipped over and jumped to Luna's side. Luna beamed, her arms wrapping tightly about the animal's thick neck once more. Aufhocker stood from his watchful perch on the deck, then hopped off to join them.

22

DEAR JOURNAL,

A new home, a new start, a new life. Salty Duck is proving to be all I hoped for and more. We started off a little rocky with some nutcase con man posing as a preacher and a run-in or two with a peculiar neighbor Luna now calls the Gypsy Woman. But things have settled, and just today we received a marvelous—albeit unsolicited—surprise from Germany. I had been thinking of extending my family via my dog-training business, and as if reading my mind—there she was, another black wolf on my doorstep per Uncle Stefan. Luna is smitten, and Aufhocker, despite his usually suspicious I-hate-all-who-enter-here protective ways, seems a bit taken with the new gal as well. Uncle Stefan insists on watching over us it seems, and Ava is applying the guilt trip. I think it might be working.

Oh, and if a particular man ever asks, I might, just might, go on a date again. His name is

"Whoa! What is that?"

A deep voice called from below, halting the pen's progress. It was late evening, and they were still in the backyard. Ivy found herself snuggled up in the palm of her Thinking Tree with her journal, while Luna and Cali rested below her, spooned in the grass in a nap. Aufhocker was curled amid the roots of the oak, waiting for his lofty mistress to alight from the branches he could not reach.

"Hello, Caleb. I'm up here—in the tree." Ivy waved to him. Luna sat up at her mother's voice, rubbing grass and sand from her cheek. Calopus and Aufhocker were immediately alert by her side.

"I didn't mean to disturb everybody." Caleb returned Ivy's wave with his free hand. The other held a large, flat item wrapped in postal paper and tied with twine.

Ah, finally. Ivy closed the journal—a new one, since her original was lost sometime ago when she left Doe Springs—and made her way down the gnarly stair step limbs to the ground.

"Looks like somebody new has joined your family," Caleb said. He squatted and clapped to the unfamiliar dog, but the big black "shepherd" stayed by Luna's side. Aufhocker's chest rumbled and a lip curled. Calopus took his cue and a surprisingly deep growl forced through the whites of her impressive teeth as well.

"The puppy is a gift from a relative. Her name is Cali."

"Puppy? You could have fooled me."

"They grow 'em big overseas." Ivy put her hand atop Auf's head and the thunder calmed. Cali settled as well but remained at attention, eyes and ears trained on the man in their yard.

"With a new pup in place I guess you won't be needing this now. But I'll give it to you anyway." Caleb propped the painting by his leg and produced another small package he'd been holding behind it. "It's for you, Luna, for helping me with the boat."

"We didn't do anything," Ivy said. "I feel guilty for accepting even the painting from you, let alone something else."

Caleb glanced at Ivy. "What? This old thing?" He nodded toward the wrapped package that was obviously a frame of some kind. "This is just a replacement window for my rental house. But now this, little Luna, is for you."

Luna toddled over to Caleb, sleep quickly receding at the

prospect of another present. Caleb handed her a small square box.

"Careful with it. Don't shake it or turn it upside down. It's very delicate."

Luna took the package as if receiving an egg. Cali stretched her nose out to sniff the box, and Aufhocker advanced a couple steps closer. Ivy, too, now stood over her daughter. Luna looked up at her.

"Go ahead, open it," Caleb said.

Luna gingerly tore the paper from around her fragile gift. It was a terrarium with a green top. Inside was a turtle no bigger than Ivy's palm, his tiny nose pressed against the plastic wall. When he noticed his cover was blown and the faces peering in, his head quickly retreated into his army-helmet shell.

"A turtle! A cute itty-bitty turtle! Look at it!" Luna thrust the terrarium at Ivy.

She smiled tightly. "Great. A new dog and a new turtle, all in the same day. Wow."

"And don't forget about this," Caleb said.

"The replacement window? No thanks, we're full up here, on pets *and* windows."

"Okay, maybe I lied and it's a particular painting that you once couldn't stop raving about. Can I carry it in for you?"

Ivy tucked the journal under her arm and slid back into the flip-flops at the base of her tree. Dusk was folding and it was time to go in anyway. "I don't recall *raving* about the picture, but sure, come on in."

Ivy led her two- and four-legged entourage through the kitchen to the living room. Her bedroom lay to the left and the fireplace was visible through the open door.

"There, above the mantel," Ivy said, pointing. "I've even got a hook up already for it."

"You must have trusted my word to have prepared in advance."

"I know where you live. Besides, I collect debts in convincing, horrible ways." Ivy smiled crookedly and one eyebrow arched high.

Caleb looked at her sideways. "Glad I make good on my promises then." He ripped open the twine and brown paper. The moon shone through the first revealing tear like a miniature beacon of grace. Ivy noticed Luna's eyes shined a little too brightly looking at the oils. An emergent yellow-orange hue as luminous as the moon on the canvas began to break through her daughter's green irises.

"Luna, honey, why don't you get your turtle all settled in your room?" Ivy quickly spun the child around and patted her bottom.

"Yes, Mommy," she said dreamily and wandered off, the terrarium clutched in her hands and Cali on her heels.

Caleb hoisted the heavy frame on the hook above the mantel and a charming, wood-carved clock.

"There. You're all set," he said. For one horrifying instant he almost sat down on her bed to admire the painting, then caught himself.

"Oh, Caleb, it's perfect," Ivy breathed. The room was dim, but suddenly she felt like the golden faux moonlight bounced off the rippling painted water of Marshy Bottom and filled every corner of her room. The limpid beam of the lighthouse, gently scintillating in saffron light, was hardly visible beneath the overshadowing moon. Ivy could be lost in his painting for hours, mesmerized by her controlling goddess and succumbing to meditations of adventures past and hunts yet to come. Her own eyes sparkled with emerald happiness— and control. They blazed orange only when she allowed it, a skill her daughter had yet to master.

"Caleb, you are truly talented."

Caleb's cheeks pinked slightly, a boyish reaction that apparently he could not control either. "I'm glad you like it. Really, if I didn't sell it at the craft festival, it would have ended up in a closet somewhere or on a motel wall—I don't know which would be worse."

Ivy didn't seem to hear. She was still staring at the moon over the waters of Salty Duck.

"Ivy?" He gathered his courage. It was now or never.

"Yes, Caleb, that would be nice," Ivy said absently. She traced her fingertips over the gray weathered wood of the frame.

"I didn't—"

"Seven o'clock tomorrow would be good. Perhaps I can get a sitter."

"Oh, uh, great. I'll pick you up at seven."

She turned to him then. "Don't be silly. I'll meet you on the side-walk and we can walk down to Front Street together."

"I'll wear comfortable shoes."

"Tomorrow then. Good night, Caleb."

He was dismissed. Caleb left her with the artwork and let him-self out. As he ambled down Battery toward his house, he couldn't deny the extra spring in his step. Tomorrow he was going on a sec-ond date with the aloof Ms. Cole, and this time it looked like she trusted him—or liked him—enough to be alone. Caleb suddenly felt an incessant urge to whistle. He went with it and let the tune carry over the evening air.

Had the marina keeper Mr. Haskell been there, a chill may have carried up his spine as the familiar tune wafted eerily across Parish Keep all the way to the sound. Perhaps he would have sung the words to accompany the vocals.

"Little Miss Caroline, ain't you a-lookin' fine, wish oh wish I had the time, to makin' you my la-a-dy...."

23

M<small>ISSOURI</small> (OR "Mis'er'y," as her husband sometimes teased) was having that dream again. It tore at her maddeningly—something did—but she could never see it in the black void of abysmal nothingness around her. It struck from one side, then the other, and while her body whipped and writhed with each searing attack, she could not run to escape it, nor could she even turn in time to catch a glimpse of the demon whose teeth and claws were shredding her skin from her bones in thick, flayed strips. And just before she woke with blood coursing down her raw, laid-bare arms, torso, and legs, two orange dancing lights appeared right in front of her face, filling the blackness around her till there was nothing but blood and pain and ember light.

"Leland!" Missouri screamed.

Leland Pitchkettle bolted straight up in bed, knocking the telephone, alarm clock, and their King James Bible to the Persian rug in his panicked fumble for the lamp. "Jesus Christ, woman, what is it? Are we under attack?" He struggled out of the bedcovers and squinted into the darkness which, surprisingly, wasn't very dark at all. Dawn seeped through the heavy velvet drapes obscuring the windows.

"No! *I'm* under attack. Something's after me, Leland, and I don't know *why.*" The last word screeched across the stable blackboard of Leland's mind. His patience geared up to give out, but in the end, it held. He came around to his wife's side of the bed and sat beside her.

"Was it that dream again, Peaches?"

"It was a vision. You know it's not a dream!"

Missouri's head bobbed like it would shake loose from her frail neck, and the braid lying coiled on the pillow beside her shook like a rattlesnake readying to strike. A streambed of tears flowed through the crevices of crow's feet around her darting eyes and leaked onto the down beneath her head.

She was the most pitiful thing Leland had ever seen, and his heart broke with the realization he could hide from this no longer. He'd acquired prescription pills to calm her, hired two servants to take all the workload off at home when they could barely afford one anymore, put his own watchful eye on her every minute, which was hurting their business downtown—Caswell was no kind of store manager to speak of. But despite Leland's best efforts, none of it seemed to be making a difference. Maybe he should have sold the house to that stranger when he asked for it not too long ago. What was his name? And then Caleb had shown up right on his heels inquiring of the same thing. Had he known Missouri was going to take such a downturn, he would have reconsidered the offers and gotten her as far away from Salty Duck as they could go.

But he couldn't bear the thoughts of that either. Salty Duck raised generations of Pitchkettles, and this house had borne many of them. No, he had long decided to stay put, even when Caleb got downright nasty about it and practically threw a blank check at them before storming out. It wasn't about money, it was about blood ties.

A nursing home. The notion had clambered around in his mind for a while now. But it seemed so cruel. So cruel to his Peaches. How could he do it to her, but how could he not? The desperation in her face and the irrational outbursts were ruining everyone around her and affecting their own livelihood as well. He'd done the best he could and still...

"Leland, we're in danger. I feel it. Something's changed, something's…something's here, or it's coming. But it's all connected to that house over there." She clutched at his arm as if drowning in the quilted coverlets of her bed.

"Honey, you've got to get over this. There is nothing in Salty Duck but the same old things that have been in Salty Duck for sixty years, including you and me and certainly this old house, which has been here longer than the two of us combined. It's safe here, our fortress, remember?"

Missouri shook her head. "No. It's not the same." She abruptly sat up and pushed past her husband on her way to the shrouded window. She pulled the drapes aside.

"Down there. In that house. There is something…unnatural."

Leland stood beside her and peered at the white rental cottage. Nothing stirred but the seashell wind chimes on the tenant's porch.

"Missy, she's a dog trainer, for Pete's sake, and her little girl is an angel. They go to church every Sunday just like you and me. What could possibly be unnatural about that?"

Missouri looked at her husband in horror. "You've talked to them?"

Leland sighed and rubbed his neck. "Yeeeah." It drug out on a long sigh of dread. But he couldn't lie; she would have instantly known. Psychic, as she proclaimed, or not, she was still his wife of thirty-some-odd years and knew him better than he knew himself. Lying was a waste of breath.

"Fraternizing with the enemy, I can't believe it. I can't believe it!" Missouri threw her hands in the air; her bracelets rattled all the way down to her elbows. Leland was used to the sound, the clattering and clanking of good-luck charms and protective amulets she adorned herself with. It was like trying to sleep with Oz's Tin Man bedecked in chains. Yet he managed to tune it out most nights and drift off. This morning the circlets of various metals clanged particularly hollow and loud.

"I don't even know why she's the enemy, Missy! I'm telling you, for your mental health—hell, for *my* mental health—leave these people be and get on with your life."

"Did you just cuss at me, Leland Pitchkettle? Did. You. Just. Cuss. At. Me?"

"Oh good God." Leland collapsed on the bed, his hands dangling between his knees.

A soft rap on the door. Ebby's voice called from outside. "Missouri? Leland? Are you awake?"

"We're awake. What is it?" Leland hollered through the cherry-wood barricade.

"May I come in?"

Leland pulled the bedspread over his bare legs, and good thing—Ebby was already standing in the room before he had a chance to answer her. Her face was pale under her bottle-dyed cap of platinum curls, and a piece of paper trembled in her hand. She looked at Missouri strangely.

"There was a note this time," she croaked.

"A note? What are you talking about?" Missouri went to the woman and snatched the paper. There were two words block written in shaky, bloodred crayon: GET OUT.

Missouri lowered the notebook page, her own face as pallid as the sheet the words were written on. Ebby continued staring at her.

"What?" Missouri snapped at the woman. "You think I did this too?"

Ebby shook her head slowly. "No, ma'am. Not anymore. You better come see."

"See what?" Leland said.

"Please, just come with me."

Leland and Missouri looked at one another.

Missouri wrapped a silk robe around her nightdress and Leland slid on a pair of pants. They followed Ebby down the winding staircase, where Ebby's husband, July, waited.

"I was dropping Ebby off for work when I saw…" July said, his reed-thin neck interrupting the nervous rise and fall of the golf ball mound of his gullet. "I just figured I should wait."

The group joined forces and followed Ebby out the front door. The smell smacked them in the face as soon as they stepped onto the porch. Missouri's scream shrilled through the quiet of Parish Keep, and Leland merely stood with his mouth open and his bare arms pimpling up with morning chill under his nightshirt.

"Damndest thing, ain't it," July said from beside him.

The ocean lay across the front yard, or what it would vomit up after the water rolled in and receded again. From the bottom of the stone porch steps to the iron fence at the street, every inch of the Pitchkettles' front green lawn was covered in dead fish, guts, and blood. Iridescent scales in clotted clumps of slime gelled in the morning sun. Marbled eyes lolled from gouged sockets, and gaping mouths gasped lifelessly from severed tuna heads. Bushes dripped glutinous strings of viscera. The stone pathway to the front gate was slick with a viscid glaze that shone like the wax on the Pitchkettles' hardwood floors. A wavery shimmer seemed to hover atop it all as the stench of rot took on an almost palpable form.

Ebby pulled her apron over the lower half of her face.

"Call the police." Leland found his voice.

"No!" Missouri wailed. "It will only make it worse." She turned to her husband, pure terror in her eyes. "You'll just make it mad."

"Make who mad? Do you know who did this?" Leland's shock was waning. As the sun rose higher, his anger rode up with it.

"Not who. It. It! The devil from my visions. It's a sign." Missouri clutched the neck of her robe as if strangling herself. "Please, Leland, now do you believe me? We're not safe here." Missouri looked as walleyed as the decimated fish heads in their yard. "We've got to get out of here." She ran back in the house, and the group on the porch heard the quick thud of her steps on the stairs.

Ebby looked at Leland, her weary gray eyes asking the familiar question.

Leland nodded. "Put the sedatives in some warm herbal tea with milk this time. When she goes to sleep, unpack her suitcase. That's where she's headed."

"Yes, sir. Leland? Gladys and I can't possibly clean this—"

"I'll have it taken care of. Go on up and tend to Missy."

Leland stared at the gutted aquarium on his front lawn, and for the first time since Missouri started having her violent premonitions, shame engulfed him. He did not believe in the devil or signs or the portent of supernatural evil. But he did believe in inhumanity, and anger was stirring with an emotional elixir of another sort this morning. He feared for his wife's sanity most certainly, but what he feared most at this moment was the danger behind the increasing threats— and the thoughts his Peaches just might be right after all.

24

"I T'S EVERY bit as bad as they'd said. Looks like the whole place was sprayed in pureed fish guts." Caleb walked up to join Ivy and a streetful of scattered neighbors up and down Battery. He shook his head.

"So you heard already," Ivy said, watching the men in white uniforms, armed with shovels, rakes, garbage bags, and plastic gloves, move robotically about the Pitchkettles' yard, plucking goggle-eyed mackerel heads from wisteria vines and stringy innards draped over azaleas. Folks had been in and out of their houses all day observing the commotion at the Pitchkettles' place as if it were, quite literally, in a fishbowl. Ivy was finally overcome with curiosity herself and joined the onlookers. It had been as good a way to pass the time waiting for Caleb as any.

"You could say that," Caleb answered. "The police were at my house bright and early this morning asking questions."

Ivy pulled her gaze off the Pitchkettle carnage to spear Caleb. "What in the world for?"

"For wanting to buy their house a couple months ago instead of renting, like I was forced to end up doing. Looks like acquisition of real estate by an outsider in this town makes you a criminal. The

Pitchkettles got a note tucked in the mail slot telling them to get out, so naturally I devised this diabolical scheme to accomplish it."

"I knew you were a shady character from the first time I met you," Ivy teased. "So how did you do it, pray tell?"

"Wasn't easy. Took me all night and then half the morning to shower. Fortunately, I'd just finished up when Sheriff Buckley banged on my door."

"Ah yes, the evidence of malodor. Wait till the wind changes—that's what we've got to look forward to." Ivy wished she could feel worse for her hateful neighbor who gave her the evil eye every Sunday. She dug down deep for some compassionate emotion, but she could only muster up smug. That wasn't very Christianly either; what would Reverend Holliday and Prill say? Speaking of which...

"Hello, Ivy, Caleb." Mrs. Prill Holliday joined them on the side-walk. "Isn't it awful? Poor thing. Missouri is beside herself. The church ladies have been dropping by all day to console her, but I think we've only agitated her worse."

"Does anybody know anything yet?" Ivy asked.

"Only that the Pitchkettles had other things happen, strange things they never reported because the servants thought Missouri was doing them herself. Obviously, that's not true now. Missouri, in fact, is convinced they're under some kind of curse." The reverend's wife looked at Ivy sideways. "Sweetheart, I have to warn you, she thinks it has something to do with you."

An icy spike ran through Ivy's heart. The last thing she needed was more attention, especially from the police, which just might happen if Missouri was over there blaming her for all this and bad weather in China too. Things had been going so well! Could folks just not leave her alone? And she'd done nothing untoward since moving here, absolutely nothing (*well, except for dumping the Preacher Man's body and eviscerating a dock worker, but they hardly counted, right?*).

"Don't you be bothered over it," Prill continued, laying a moth-erly hand on Ivy's arm. "Missouri Pitchkettle is an odd bird and everyone in the Duck knows it. In fact, the last thing I heard just before coming over here is she's planning a séance. Can you believe it? Matheson will be beside himself, but I'm sure he'll talk some sense into her. Séances." She said it with such disgust Ivy thought the proper Prill might spit or do something really untoward, like cuss. She did neither.

"I like colorful towns," Ivy said.

"Well honey, with the zany things going on around here lately, you couldn't have picked a better place. Now, where is that precious blond button I'm supposed to be looking after this evening?"

Caleb's brows arched. "An evening on the waterfront alone, without our chaperone? I didn't think you were serious."

Prill smirked. "I'd almost believe your disappointment, Caleb, if I hadn't come to know you so well through church. He's a wolf in sheep's clothing, Ivy. Give him a good smack if you need to."

Caleb feigned surprise. "I've been nothing but a gentleman."

Ivy smiled. "Downright boring, Prill. You have nothing to fear."

"Ouch. Why did that sting a little?" Caleb said.

"Better a boring gent than a cad, Caleb," Prill said, only half jokingly. "Remember that. Now you two run along."

"Luna's in the house playing with her turtle, Prill, and the dogs are in my bedroom. Just go on in. We'll be back by ten."

"Take your time. This is my pleasure. Luna's one of the sweetest children in Parish Keep, and she's her Sunday school teacher's favorite." Prill winked. "But that's just between us."

"This is our favorite place to eat—or was, anyway," Ivy said, taking a bite of milky scallop while watching the sky pink up behind the strip of islands across Marshy Bottom. The sun was setting on her and Caleb's first official, up-front, no-tricks date. For entertainment, a royal tern, his shaggy crest of black feathers wavering above grayish wings the color of fog, hovered over the water just in front of them. Within seconds, the bird dove into the sound like a mad dart and reemerged with a squirming bit of silver in its orange bill. The fish vanished quickly and the tern flew off farther down Front Street to hover in predatory silence once more.

"I didn't know we had a favorite place. Looks like this relationship is advancing quicker than I thought," Caleb said, slurping an oyster from the half shell.

"Not *us,* villain. Me and Luna. We ate here our first day in Salty Duck and many times since. Tonight we have our usual waiter, in fact, but that is what has created the stir. This will most likely be my farewell meal at The Bluewater Lady."

"I see." Caleb leaned back in his chair and allowed his flat belly to expand a little. The meal—and especially the company—were too good, and he was indulging himself more than he'd planned. "I thought I detected a connection between the two of you when he lingered over the appetizers and refilled your drink but not mine. Guess I need to be sizing up the competition."

"No need. Luna's gunning for him, so she's taken care of the competition for you."

"I'm a favorite then?" He cocked his head and tried to look more humble than her statement made him feel. It was important that Luna like him.

"One could say you're beating the odds, with Luna anyway."

"In that case," he raised his frosted glass of sweet tea, "I feel honored to be brought to your special place."

Ivy clinked her glass to his and drank deeply as a breeze blew across the outdoor veranda and lifted her hair in a flaxen wave. Caleb stared at her a little too intently and she felt her color rise. Nobody had made her blush since…since Deputy Sanders.

Caleb versus Melvin—an interesting comparison. Both tall, both handsome. Caleb seemed more lighthearted than the serious Doe Springs officer. That was perhaps the confidence of being older. Melvin had been so young when they first met, only twenty-eight. Or perhaps it was the difference in careers. Policeman. Yacht salesman.

But both safe? She'd felt safe with Melvin, and not just because of his occupation. Had he been a gentle potter or poet, she would have felt the same. With Caleb, she guessed it was too soon to tell. Did she want to find out? That might be too soon to tell, too.

"Everything all right over here?" The waiter, less casual for dinner in slacks and a white island shirt open at his thick throat, hovered over them much like the tern before it snagged its meal from Marshy Bottom, and Ivy suddenly felt vulnerable. She shook off the uncomfortable vibe.

"We're good, thanks. Ready for the check I think," Caleb said, barely taking his eyes off Ivy.

"I'll bring it right out. Hey, uh, where's the feisty one with the shellfish hang-up this evening?"

"In bed, I hope," Ivy said. "I'm sorry she's such a pill when she comes here. She's normally a good-natured child."

"Don't worry about it. I admire the kid—she's fearless. But I'd still like to make amends for whatever I did to get on her bad side. I'd hate for you to stop eating here just because the waiter rubbed your little girl the wrong way. My boss has fired people for a whole lot less."

The man set a Styrofoam container on the table in front of Ivy. She opened it to a dark wedge of chocolate cake, rich and dense as fresh brick mortar and smelling of Godiva.

"Wow, this might not make it home, but I'll try my best. Thank you," Ivy said.

The waiter nodded, pleased. "I'll get your check."

They found themselves in a familiar place, only a different time. The moon was up now and had it been full, the scene would have been from the new painting hanging over Ivy's bedroom mantel.

"You painted it from right here, didn't you?" Ivy said, standing at the end of the Marshy Bottom Pier where she'd first met Caleb after coming to Salty Duck.

"Yes, I did. The view of the lighthouse is best from here. Glad you could tell."

"Have you always painted?"

"Just as a hobby. Bruce was one of the first people I met when I came to the Duck, and he convinced me to put some pieces in the craft fair. My professional debut." Caleb leaned on the rail, his back to the intermittent illumination of Pious Cape. Ivy glanced at him, his face above her in brooding silhouette and the lighthouse a halo behind him. He was angelic in the weird aurora of stars and man-made tower, yet mysterious too. An unknown. He seemed to be thinking.

"Ivy?"

"Yes?"

He leaned down and kissed her harder than he'd intended.

"I think I'm supposed to smack you now," Ivy said.

"Does the church lady really have to know?"

"Hmmm. Let's try that again, and I'll let *you* know."

Ivy put her arms around Caleb's neck, and after five years of mourning a lost love, she finally let him go.

25

"Hello, sugar. Surprise!"

Ivy had barely gotten through the front door from her date with Caleb before the mellifluous debutante accent hit her, age only enriching the husky yet musical notes. Ivy stood in her living room, mussed hair at startled attention and a flush to her cheeks that had nothing to do with astonishment, and was no less dumbfounded than if she'd entered upon the Preacher Man, reassembled and lethally mobile once more.

"Miss Ava, is it really you?"

"In the flesh, darlin'." Ava stood there beaming in her lavender Chanel suit worn only for traveling and her hair wound in a lovely knot above a near-creaseless forehead.

Ivy had never seen her ancient step-aunt look better, and it had been a long time indeed, since she left Doe Springs for Canada.

"You're shocked to see me out of my overalls, is that it?" Ava said.

"I'm shocked to see you in my house in Salty Duck. But…but come here." Ivy opened her arms to the only person she still considered family and hugged her tight.

Ava welcomed the embrace, and when Ivy finally released the petite woman's delicate shoulders, she pulled away with a knowing gleam in her eyes. "We'll talk about *him* later," Ava whispered, the man's scent from Ivy's clothes still prickling her nose.

Ivy noticed Prill on the couch then, watching the impromptu family reunion with the same pleasant serenity with which she regarded her husband at the pulpit each Sunday.

"Thank you so much, Prill. I'm sorry I'm late—we lost track of time," Ivy said.

The reverend's wife got up and stretched, shaking out limbs grown stiff from an evening of sitting, drinking hot tea, and talking with the fascinating Widow Pritchard. "Good for you, dear! That must mean you had a wonderful date. From what Ava tells me, you've been alone for too long."

"Oh, well," Ivy said, shooting the widow a look, "that's my aunt. She does love to chat, and I'm usually her pet topic." Ivy wondered just how much info Prill now possessed about her pitiful non-love life. Ava wrinkled her nose teasingly at the disapproving glance from her niece and immediately dismissed it.

"Anyway," Prill continued, "it's nice to see two churchgoing young people find each other. As for Luna, she was no trouble at all, and I've put her to bed already. Oh! Before I forget, you got a call about a dog-training session. Someone wanting an appointment. I left the message on the kitchen counter. And now I'll leave you to your aunt." She turned to Ava. "Widow Pritchard, it was a real pleasure meeting you. I've enjoyed the company, and I hope you'll join Ivy to church on Sunday if you're still in town."

"Why, I'd like that very much." The ladies clasped hands warmly and Prill gave Ivy's arm a gentle squeeze as she went out the door. It closed with a whoosh of inrushing coastal air, the tang of salt and sea redolent on it.

"Well, here we are," Ava said, waiting for Ivy to recover her befuddled senses and act like she was truly happy to see her.

"Ava. Miss Ava. I still can't believe you're here. Sit down. We probably both need to sit down."

They settled on Ivy's couch, knees touching but a distance of years weighing heavily between them. It was painful to feel so distant with one so near to the heart. It was a flaw in her character, Ivy knew, to let loved ones dangle while she flitted about life and expected them to be there when she got back. And looking at her aunt was a deception—the age on the calendar did not match the age in the grand lady's youthful face; it was easy to forget that Ivy's time with her beloved aunt was, indeed, limited. She took it for granted that Ava would always be in her shadow, waiting to leap out of the dark corners and catch her when she fell. But Ivy was on solid ground now, despite the shifting dunes' sands, and because of that she feared she hadn't called on the widow not out of being too busy but just because she simply didn't need her right now.

Ivy hung her head at the realization of her selfish behavior. Ava deserved better.

"I don't know whether to laugh or cry," Ivy said, her eyes tearing up and deciding for her. "I'm so sorry I haven't called or written more. I've missed you."

"Shhh. It's all right, child, it's all right. Come here." Ava pulled Ivy to her shoulder and they sat quietly for a time. Finally, Ivy sat up and wiped her nose with the handkerchief produced from Ava's hand-pearled bag.

"You must think I'm a wreck, blubbering all over you like that," Ivy said, now dabbing at the tears on her cheeks.

"Nonsense. I'm glad you still think enough of me to get all gooey. I imagine you've been on some kind of emotional roller coaster anyway, what with being a single mother and moving about the continent."

"It has been tough at times." Ivy sniffled loudly, signaling the end of the outburst. "But what about you? Have you eaten yet? Are you unpacked? How in the world did you get here?"

"Relax, sugar, I'm fine. I got here by bus not long after you left, according to Prill, and she and I—and Luna—shared banana and peanut butter sandwiches under your oak tree. My luggage is at the bottom of the stairwell; I wasn't sure where you'd want an old bugger like myself to bed down for the night."

"There's a spare room beside Luna's, if you don't mind climbing stairs. It's small, but charming. Luna—what did you think of Luna?"

"She's even more comely than I had pictured. Reminds me of someone else when she was that age, at least by the photographs I've seen."

"Me? Yes. I guess she does look like me."

"Carbon copy, in more ways than one perhaps?"

"I'm not sure if that's good or bad."

"Depends on how you look at it, or who's looking, I'd say." Ava winked. "But enough about that—Luna and I are now old friends. Tell me about this man you're seeing. Caleb, is it? Your hair's a fright—I'm guessing by that he must be one very interesting fella."

Ivy touched her tresses self-consciously. What in the world must Prill have thought? "Ava, there is so much to tell you about Salty Duck, I don't know where to begin," she said.

"Let's start with hot cocoa and see where conversation flows from there. I've got all night."

PART III

*"Neither shalt thou bring an abomination into thine house,
lest thou be a cursed thing like it."*

—*Deuteronomy 7:26*

26

THE CHICKEN pox was over, hallelujah. Officer McKaye was back on duty, and Sheriff Gloria Hubbard was free to do what she needed to.

Right now that meant standing in the middle of the tiny Doe Springs Sheriff's Office and looking around. McKaye was in the cubicle closest to her office, typing a report on his brand-new computer. The unintentional downsizing of the department had upsized their equipment. It was an impulse acquisition to make herself feel better about Sanders's leaving. Now she regretted it. That was taxpayers' money; the old Smith Corona typewriter had worked just fine. Sanders had never complained—Meeks hadn't either, for that matter—but nevertheless, with new blood invited into the department via a want ad, she'd decided it was time for an update in everything else as well.

It was hard to think about—new blood, new faces, new equipment. These brick walls, no more architecturally interesting than a cracker box turned on its side, held the most intriguing personal history. Around her were the remnants and memories of cases solved, mysteries unraveled, teamwork perfectly executed with men she had not just respected as mere deputies but as friends and, to be honest, as family. One, in particular, she had loved.

Tee had been here only briefly, but his presence, his low-key energy, like the hum from a nuclear power plant, lingered larger than life. Like the man himself.

Gloria smiled, remembering the way he would tease her to the point of aggravated distraction just to lighten up her overly serious ways. The way he, with bloodhound Zeke by his side, could loaf around like he didn't have a care in the world, then snap to ten degrees of intensity when a case was at hand, brush popping through the wilderness like a mad Texan, tracking like an Old Wild West Indian, and holding a trail like nobody's business. Nobody she'd ever known or heard of anyway. It had been so nice having him here. She'd had no intention of letting him go back to Montana, no intention of losing him again period. And yet, it happened to spite her, and the tragedy of the not knowing dimmed the corners of this room and sucked the joy from all the successes she had achieved before his arrival and since.

McKaye left his painstaking finger-pecking to look up and catch his chief staring at the wall.

"Sheriff? You okay?"

"What?" Gloria snapped out of it. The picture of Tee and Zeke faded and the wall was just a wall again, cheap brown paneling and nothing more. "Yes, I was just wondering if I'd forgotten any last-minute details before shoving off."

"So you're going now?" McKaye hit the keyboard with finality and frowned when the machine responded with an indignant ping. He shrugged and walked over to her. Tan and stocky, with close-cropped blond hair that he liked to spike with gel right in front, McKaye reminded Gloria of a college quarterback on spring break. But he was a good cop in the making, and sometimes fresh young Silly Putty was easier to mold than hardened old clay that had been around too long. Come to think of it, McKaye was Sanders's age when she'd given him a chance. And look how well that had turned out.

Indeed.

"Yep, I'm hitting the road. You're in charge, Deputy. Think you can handle it?" It was a rhetorical question. Since the Devil of Doe Springs left, life had settled back into its comfortable recliner. Country crime was lazy and ordinary: speeding tickets, farming feuds, an occasional domestic dispute. It was downright boring. Just the way she liked it.

"I'll do my best, Sheriff. Sure wish I could go with you. I bet Miami is great this time of year."

Gloria nodded. "You'd fit right in, McKaye."

"Blue sky and crystal-clear water, just what the doctor ordered." Delores and Shirley had left the front desk to join them. "You're way overdue for this vacation, if you don't mind my saying," Delores continued.

"Bring us back a seashell, and don't worry about Chester—I'll take good care of him," Shirley chimed in.

"Thanks everyone. Two weeks of dawdling around Florida should do me some good. I'll be checking in every day, though, and Police Chief Wilkerson is on standby if you need anything."

"Forget we're here. Just have a good time." The women hugged her, and McKaye, too intimidated to be that familiar, awkwardly shook her hand.

Gloria walked out of the station and climbed into her Cherokee. In the back, underneath a tarp and her luggage, lay her arsenal. Gloria gunned the engine and aimed the Jeep southeast, toward I-40, a small North Carolina coastal village, and the unknown.

"For Tee," she muttered, as the pine-tree-shrouded building and its withering reminiscences disappeared behind her.

27

THE CHURCH bells called them in and Ivy and Luna, in matching cornflower blue, escorted the Widow Pritchard up the steep stone steps of Parish Keep Presbyterian. Prill and Reverend Holliday were already up front, the pastor shuffling papers at the pulpit and Prill finishing a brief warm-up of "The Old Rugged Cross" on the piano.

"Making quite an entrance, ladies." Caleb, in a gunmetal three-piece today, was by their side as they came through the door. He put his arm out for the widow. "Am I to guess this is a special relative come calling?"

The Widow Pritchard took the proffered arm and said, "Am I to guess this is the young man deflowering my niece?"

Caleb's smile crumpled lopsided and froze. A couple seated in the back pew turned to look at them with an admonishing "Shhh!" Ivy covered her mouth with her hand and tried not to laugh out loud.

"Up there looks like some open seats. Come along, then, if you're leading this train. I want to sit down before the sermon is over, let alone begun." Ava allowed Caleb to walk her midway up the aisle. He carefully helped lower her in the pew, then sat behind the trio, the widow's large navy hat blocking his view.

"Did you see how he manhandled me, Ivy? I hope you're taking notes."

"Miss Ava, please be good," Ivy whispered.

Luna stood up on her seat and leaned over the back of it, toward Caleb. "I love my turtle. I've named him Mup, and I'm teaching him and Cali tricks."

"Tricks, huh? How's that working out?"

"Great! Cali can already sit, stay, roll over, and shake hands."

"I see your mama is helping you with some training."

Luna looked put out by the suggestion. "Nope. I did it."

"And Mup?"

"He just sits there with his head all poked in. But I think he'll get it eventually."

"Luna, turn around and sit down. Reverend Holliday is starting." Ivy tugged on the girl's hemline.

"See you later, alligator," Luna whispered.

"After while, crocodile," Caleb answered and winked.

Luna settled in between her mother and great-aunt. Miss Ava smelled so very good to her, like gingersnaps, spice, and fresh cotton. Luna put her little hand over the elderly lady's, who covered it with her other hand in return.

Reverend Holliday, inspired by the large turnouts of the past Sundays, tuned up and let loose with an atypically energetic and powerful sermon about, of all things, loving thy neighbor. As his voice filled the echoing hall of the historical church, Ivy noticed Prill sitting in the front row, nodding her head in agreement with her husband's good words. Ivy couldn't help but think the sermon topic was no coincidence: Prill had put in a good word herself—for Ivy's current predicament with the wretched Mrs. Pitchkettle. But if Missouri was hearing any of it, it was doubtful.

Ava released Luna's hand and nudged Ivy. "Who is that woman who keeps turning around to stare at us?" she whispered.

Ivy sighed. "She lives in the house across the street."

"That's the loonybird you were telling me about?"

"I hate to call her *loonybird*...."

"Why? If the insanity fits, one shouldn't be ashamed to wear it.

It just needs not to spill over onto other people. Crazy I can abide, but rude crazy is another matter altogether."

Missouri seemed to notice they were talking about her. She faced forward again, but if it were possible to have eyes in the back of one's head, Ivy felt them on her now, boring past the cover of the woman's thick braid.

Reverend Holliday, in turn, was looking right at Missouri as his voice boomed, and she sat up straighter, the "how dare he" self-righteous attitude of her countenance snapping her spine straight.

"Widow Pritchard, I was so delighted to see you in the congregation today," Prill gushed as the church members queued past her and the reverend at the door. "Matheson, this is the Widow Pritchard from Charleston, Ivy's aunt."

"I'm very pleased you were able to join us today, Widow Pritchard. And you didn't even fall asleep. That's mighty gratifying for a preacher." Reverend Holliday held Ava's gloved fingers like fragile stems of handblown glass.

"Who could sleep through a good old-fashioned bellowing like that? If I didn't know better, I'd swear you had some fire-and-brimstone Southern Baptist rumbling through your Presbyterian veins, Reverend. Enjoyed the bloody hell out of it, I surely did. Good day, Prill." Ava gave the pastor's hand a hearty lumberjack squeeze, smiled sweetly, and then walked down the stone steps, leaving the Hollidays momentarily stunned.

Ivy caught up to her aunt. "Charleston?"

"Why not? I always wanted to be from Charleston, and I figured you've kept your Doe Springs past under your hat; no sense in me bringing it up. Look—there's that woman over there gawking at us again."

Missouri stood in the street by her black Cadillac, ignoring Leland's efforts to get her folded into it. Indeed, her gaze was zeroed in on the trio like a hungry wide-eyed owl. She made some hand gestures in the air in front of her breast.

"Well, I'll be," Ava said. "I think she just warded off the evil eye, or put a hex on us one. That's it—I think it's time I met your next-door neighbor."

"No, Ava, please. Just ignore her. It's a gorgeous day, and I wanted to take you to lunch on the waterfront. There's a new restaurant we're wanting to try, the Seacharm. I think they might even have blueberry pie on the menu."

"Blueberry pie? Is it homemade?"

"I couldn't imagine it would be any other way."

"Your manipulation of an old woman is not becoming, dear, especially after church. But I'll pretend I'm too feeble to resist your tempting offer. Come along, Luna. I'll meet Mrs. Missouri Pitchkettle another day. You can count on that."

28

Dear Uncle Stefan,

I know it has been a long time—too, too long—since you have heard from me. I've had my reasons. Wanting to put the past and my mother's horrible death behind me. Hurting you for saving me, strengthening me, when you couldn't save her. Running from the pain that you and Germany and my childhood reminded me of.

But there is now, ironically, another childhood to consider. That of my daughter. And with the arrival of a particular black "dog" recently, I realized that you have been a steadfast guardian in my life, watching over my shoulder, despite my hateful attitude, and continuing to protect from afar, first with Aufhocker, who is a beloved godsend, and now with Calopus, the Benandanti. And I realized my folly all this time for trying to shun a part of my family that loves me so deeply.

Mama would have been proud of you—and ashamed of me.

Forgive me, Uncle Stefan. I welcome you into our lives, and I hope that I am still welcome in yours. You have a grand-niece that I would like you to meet.

With all my love,

Your niece,

Ivy

Stefan carefully folded the stationery and placed it back in its envelope. It should convey nothing in his hands—the envelope with his address in feminine cursive that looped and swirled like blue ribbon across the paper. Yet it spoke to him as much as the words written inside. Stefan caressed the wrinkled correspondence, picturing Ivy with her pen and thoughtful expression, scripting the letter that would travel across an ocean and hopefully bridge years of quiet hurt. Perhaps the child Luna had put the envelope in the mailbox, had first affixed the stamp with her tender fingers. Could he smell the girls if he put his nose close; could he feel any love at all, like Ivy had insinuated? The distance was between them all, but through Ivy's efforts and these imaginings, Stefan felt connected.

Which made what he was about to do all the harder.

The phone rang on his mahogany desktop, the private line to which only two others had access—his friend in Salty Duck and the esteemed Widow Pritchard. Three hulking black heads rose from the knotted hardwood floor at the shrilling. Their eyes were incalculable chips of ebony, but to the capable—those like Stefan who could read the wolf, particularly this specially bred kind of wolf—their eyes shone with the venerable wisdom of their ancestors and a rainbow hue of colorful emotions. Right now, however, they were languid, the ringing of a phone a familiar sound.

"Hello, Stefan." It was the American.

Stefan left his grand desk to stare out the window of the red brick complex overlooking one of the canals that furrowed through the *Speicherstadt* from the Elbe River. The Speicherstadt, or warehouse district in Hamburg, was busy today as much from tourists as commerce, but from this height, everything below, all the noise and activity, flowed as silent and serene as the river channel itself. The same could be said for his office, but the arrival of the letter and now, coincidentally, the American's call would no doubt shake up the peace.

"You have good news to report?" Stefan said.

"There's been another incident at the house, and you won't be happy about it," the conversation began.

Stefan heard the disgust in his friend's voice.

"What house? The Victorian?"

"Yes, and I think it's our mysterious friend's doing."

"The one sent by the Order."

"I believe so."

"What happened this time?"

Stefan heard the brief account, of fish tails and scales and mayhem on a poor woman's sanity. It would all end soon enough and her life could go back to normal, if that were possible for one so disturbed as he'd heard this lady was.

"Do you think Pitchkettle will escalate against Ivy until the police get involved?" Stefan asked.

The American swallowed hard and Stefan heard it all the way in Germany. "Too late for that. This latest stunt pulled the police right in. And word in Parish Keep is that Missouri has been none too subtle about pointing the finger at Ivy for everything that's happening to her. The good news is I don't think it matters. The whole town thinks she's a lunatic, including the police, for now. She's got flyers posted down at Leland's store inviting anybody who has the nerve to join her in a séance to—and I quote—'call out the evil spirits.'"

"The police came?" It was all Stefan heard from his friend's ramblings, and the one thing they'd wanted to avoid most of all by obtaining the Victorian. Once Ivy's intentions of moving to Salty Duck had been learned, great care was taken in evaluating the township and its inhabitants. It was a process Stefan had repeated numerous times. His niece's jaunts about the United States and into Canada had been pain free for her for a reason: Her uncle had run ahead and cleared the way, making sure her path lay in a safe zone where she could get herself into the least trouble. Winnipeg had been an excellent choice, but when her sights zeroed back in on North Carolina, he knew only trouble could come of it. Bad enough to be coming home to her state of greatest destruction, and then, of all the houses, she rented the one right across the street from a busybody and self-proclaimed psychic.

Stefan had wanted the Victorian for another reason as well. It was a prime location for observation and ease of carrying out the last step of his plan. Apparently, the Order had shared his idea about the house and were taking ridiculous measures to get it themselves. The unpredictability of whomever they had sent to steal Luna was too unsettling to contemplate—his actions were those of a mad, wily prankster and growing increasingly more bizarre: First, Mrs. Pitchkettle's jewelry and clothes found scattered about the yard in her husband's absence. Then mannequins dismembered and planted in the ruined garden. And now a deluge of fish guts to harass and frighten the elderly couple further. What would happen to Luna if she ended up in such hands? Was he violent as well as unbalanced? He was a Lykanthrop, and Stefan knew the answer to that all too well.

"Relax, Stefan. The police are not interested in Ivy, and she isn't going anywhere right now. I am keeping an eye on the situation."

"I hope you are being discreet. If Ivy gets wind she's being watched, she'll run again. If Missouri Pitchkettle keeps it up, that could still happen. What's worse, we have to be quicker than Simon's man. I think we need to speed up the plan."

"How speeded up are we talking?"

"Take the child at the first opportunity. You will only get one."

29

"Are you ready, Boo?" Ivy asked her daughter as they sat in the Jeep outside Salty Duck Elementary. The building, a typical-looking brick sixties number, was squared up on a couple of acres of half-grass, half-sand lawn. An orange line of "caterpillars," as Luna dubbed the buses, flanked the school in a small parking lot to the left, and a playground with an assortment of equipment—jungle gym, slide, two swing sets, and a blacktop court—peeked from the right. All was functional, but Ivy couldn't help but feel disappointed. She had hoped the school would be as winsome as the rest of the town, but it was new enough to hold no charm, yet old enough to look out-of-date and too institutional to be considered any fun, playground aside. Nevertheless, the parents at church spoke highly of the education quality here, and that was all that mattered to Ivy. That—and something else: "Do we need to go over the rules again, Luna?"

Luna turned an exasperated sigh on her mother. "Be good, don't talk back, listen to what the teacher says, and if something makes me mad, go to time-out."

"That's right, honey. Very important rules, especially that last one. You remember what time-out is, right?"

"Yes, yes, *yes!* Walk away, close my eyes, and count to one hundred. Then count backward from one hundred."

"And what else?"

"Focus only on the numbers, not who made me mad."

"Very good."

"Mommy?"

"What is it, Boo?"

"I forgot how to count to one hundred."

"Nice try, squirt, but I'm being serious right now, okay?" Ivy looked at her sweet cherub, scrubbed and fresh-faced, a pink ribbon in her spiral-curled ponytail, a matching pink jumper bought special down at The Scotch Bonnet (Ivy hated to admit it, but Leland was growing on them—he'd thrown in the hair ribbon for free) all for Luna's big day: her first day at public school.

Pride swelled Ivy's heart; she couldn't help it. Not only was her daughter beautiful, but Luna had easily placed in the advanced kindergarten class because she could already count so well, knew her ABCs, could read short sentences, tie her shoes, and add and subtract simple two-digit equations. But fear tempered the pride. Luna lacked control—could Ivy dare let her out of her sight? She'd considered home schooling so long, they'd already missed the start of kindergarten, but it was Ava who finally convinced her to let the girl go.

"Trust in your own, Ivy. You're suffocating Luna and making her socially inept with your smothering," Ava scolded, and Ivy had listened. Luna was only starting a few weeks late, and with her advanced learning already, it would not be a problem. Luna's new teacher-to-be, Mrs. Flannigan, had assured her of it.

"Can I walk with you to your room?" Ivy asked.

"If it will make you feel any better about me going," Luna answered. Ivy gathered her child's Winnie-the-Pooh lunchbox and they walked hand in hand inside.

• • •

"Welcome, Ms. Cole, welcome. And this must be Luna." Mrs. Flannigan, a pie-shaped woman in a paint-smeared smock, leaned down to examine her new student face to face. Mrs. Flannigan's eyes were the smoky green of moon-dappled sea foam, and Luna saw herself in them, playfully running and snapping at the frothy waves they reminded her of. She liked the older, heavy-set lady immediately.

"Why don't you find an empty cubby over there for your lunch-box, and then join those children at the block station." Mrs. Flannigan pointed from one corner to the next, her last direction landing on a small group of girls earnestly constructing something out of wooden pegs and rectangles. They had given pause to their construction project, however, to whisper in Luna's direction.

"Bye, Mommy!" Luna hugged Ivy's waist, snatched her Winnie-the-Pooh lunchbox, and became a member of the kindergarten class without looking back. Ivy felt a thorn prick her heart.

"Now don't go feeling like that," Mrs. Flannigan said, all straightened up and on adult level again.

"No, I'm fine, I just—"

Mrs. Flannigan held up a dumpling hand to cut her off. "No need to explain, Ms. Cole. Your face says it all. You look like you were just orphaned yourself. But now don't you worry: I see new mothers every single year suffer that same little ache when their babies go wobbling out of the nest. And guess what? They all survive it."

"The children?"

"The parents! You'll be just fine. Look at Luna over there, already making friends."

It was true. Luna was piling blocks and laughing with two freckled twins in pigtails, not a concern at all for her forlorn mother abandoned at the front of the room with a stranger—a kindhearted stranger, at least.

"You're right, Mrs. Flannigan. I didn't expect it to be this hard."

"Call and check on her progress anytime you like, but I can tell, you don't have a thing to worry about. And I have good news. You've got her here in time for what we like to call the Indian

Summer Safari. Several classes team up for one last jaunt to the beach before the weather turns cool. I'll send a note home with Luna about it."

"She'll certainly love that," Ivy said slowly, distractedly. Luna and the other girls continued to balance blocks in an ever-growing pyramid. They were getting along well. Luna would be able to control herself. This field trip, however, could be problematic.

Let her go! her inner voice demanded, only this time it sounded a lot like Miss Ava.

Ivy raced through the streets of Salty Duck, across the Sandpiper Bridge, and into the fishing/industrial port of Lockerman's Ferry. It was only a stone's throw across the water from Salty Duck, but Ivy would probably be late anyway. She checked her watch as the Jeep bounced across the railroad tracks that greeted drivers once exiting the bridge. The narrow Marshy Bottom Sound flowed from the mouth of this greater seaport, its bigger water able to accommodate cargo ships from around the world. Train tracks crisscrossed roadways, and land cranes thrust their necks over concrete-pillared piers to move exotic wares imported from continents Ivy had never seen.

But there was no time to ponder spices from India or any other exotic ware, because true to her nature, she was running five minutes behind, and the quicker she traveled, the quicker her minute hand seemed to spin with the speedometer.

Traffic was more congested on this side of the bridge, and she was glad to find her first turn at last, a left down Ackerman's Avenue. Her next right put her on Fisherman's Quay, but the pretty name did nothing to lift the spirits of the neighborhood. If the Jeep had a top and doors hosting more than flimsy plastic windows, Ivy might have locked up now. She drove through rows of nearly identical saltbox cottages, all worn to the nubs of their nails from a century of overuse and under-repair. Beaten-down trailers broke up the monotony here and there on the cramped streets, which were stippled with flood-washed chuckholes. Addresses on rusted-out aluminum mailboxes were sandblasted to scrawl, and Ivy inched along, her neck and eyes straining, looking for the house number Prill had jotted on the edge of a paper towel. In addition to the address, the caller had left only a last name, Jones, and a time, if she could make it.

Could she make it? Looking about the dispirited community with boats up on blocks and pickup trucks sprouting Confederate flags, she was tempted to think not and turn around. But fishing towns could be like that; in fact, just one street over she could cruise past sorbet-colored houses on stilts that pulled down a cool half mil in mortgage.

No, someone cared enough about their dog to call, and she wasn't about to start her business by blowing off the first client. After facing down the Preacher Man recently, this place was a walk in the park. She'd nearly forgotten all about the appointment anyway while standing in Mrs. Flannigan's class watching her daughter grow up. Okay—granted, kindergarten wasn't exactly off to college, but it was a major milestone nonetheless. She had felt like sitting in the classroom all day, maybe stretched out on one of the nap mats, quietly observing.

Until Mrs. Flannigan took the reins on the situation and threw her out. Politely, of course.

Ivy had walked back to the Jeep, deflated and lonely without the squirt by her side, when she saw the paper-towel note wedged in the cup holder. And then she remembered the earth was still spinning and she had life to attend to.

"There you are," Ivy said, finding the house at last. It was at the very end of Fisherman's Quay, another sad little one-story cottage wedged into a slew of other ones just as sagging and gray. An enclosed screened porch jutted off the back of the house, and Ivy parked in the grassy area beside it. She walked to the front porch, which was scattered with remnants of broken shells. No other vehicle sat in the driveway, and the windows were obscured by shades. The house looked asleep, which did not sit well. Had she gotten the day and time right? Had Prill written down the wrong address? Ivy noticed the nearest residences looked just as vacant. *Note to self: Always bring Auf when making house calls....*

Ivy ran a hand through her windblown hair to straighten it and knocked, certain that no one would answer and she'd just lost her first client. Somewhere in Lockerman's Ferry, a Mr. or Mrs. Jones was patiently waiting for a dog trainer who would never show up and didn't have a return phone number with which to even call and say why.

The door swung inward at Ivy's brief touch. She squinted into the dim room. No furniture. No bulbs in the overhead light. Nothing. Dust swirled in the gloom, a mustiness assaulted her nose, along with another scent more familiar...

A hand snaked out of the shadows, yanking her inside. The door slammed closed.

30

"Hello, there! Anybody home?"

Another house, another knocked door with no answer. The Widow Pritchard wouldn't give the old biddy the satisfaction, though—of turning coattail and running back across the street just because she was so obviously being snubbed. Nope, she'd stand on this porch (not nearly as splendid as the portico on her own Victorian, she sniffed) all day holding this cake if she had to, and set up her feet on the banister for an all-night vigil too. The Widow Pritchard was on a mission and dug in tight. They'd answer the damned door or get used to her living in their entryway one. (But she really hoped for the former. Ivy was gone to kindergarten with the poppet, and the less she knew about Ava's antics in her absence, the better.)

Turns out it didn't take so long after all. A thin but hearty woman in a garish chintz apron answered at the seventh round of insistent raps.

"Yes, may I help you?" the woman asked graciously, as if surprised to find company on the steps despite ten minutes of banging.

"I'm the Widow Pritchard, your next-door neighbor, temporarily leastwise, and I've come to hobnob with the finer class of Salty Duck for a moment. Is Mrs. Pitchkettle home? We've never officially met, save stares in church, and I figured I'd call on her since I hear she's been ailing."

Ebby's eyes darted wearily behind her. A dishrag sprang from her apron pocket then and rapidly wound itself like a nubby ferret through her age-spotted hands. "I don't know. It's probably not a good idea."

"Just take a sec, sugar." Ava pushed past the woman and into the house. It was dark inside, teaked and mahoganied and Persian carpeted to a fault. Cocoa silk papered the walls above walnut wainscoting, and maroon and gold tapestries draped heavily above a stone fireplace better suited to the wilds of Colorado than the gentle clime of the South. Hurricane lanterns cut from Tiffany glass in facets of amber and midnight blue did nothing to lighten the gloom, and Ava squinted to get a better look at the opulent room. *Positively gauche,* Ava thought, *but what should one expect from the nouveau riche?* She put her attention back on the servant, who was now desperately strangling the errant ferret-dishrag tangled about her knobby wrists.

"Madam, please. Mrs. Pitchkettle is indeed not well, and she's sleeping. I will tell her you send your regards," Ebby said, reaching for the cake pan.

"Now where would the poor dear be?" Ava asked, ignoring the servant and sidestepping her in the same breath. The cake pan remained firmly in her grasp. "Up there, perhaps?" Her gaze shifted up a heavy winding stairwell, but stopped at the top step. Mrs. Missouri Pitchkettle stood on the landing staring down at them, the granite set of her eyes grinding away at the sincerity she attempted with a flinty smile.

Ebby let out a deep sigh. The ferret died, hanging limp, and Ebby stuffed it back into her pocket. "Well, there she is then. Good luck to you." She left the room, looking as hunched and defeated as a housemaid could look.

What in the world kind of beast was this Pitchkettle woman to effect such a reaction from her servant? Ava needn't puzzle long, however; the aforesaid was on her way down the staircase in a flurry of scarlet robes, flashing gems at throat and fingers, and jangling bangles upon her wrists and ankles. Ava threw her own flinty smile back on and watched the mistress of the house descend like a reddened peacock in full—if not sonorous—plume.

The women stared at one another in the foyer. Somewhere in the background a cuckoo clock chimed, and Ava suppressed a rueful laugh at the appropriateness of it.

"Missouri Pitchkettle, how nice it is to finally meet you. I hear you have been feeling poorly, so I've brought you a pineapple upside-down cake. I'm the Widow Pritchard from next door, by the way." This is where Ava would normally extend her hand, but she did not want to give Missouri the upper hand by denying to shake it. Instead, she held on to the cake and left the tennis ball in the other's court to see where she might lob it.

Missouri did not smile, and her eyes only briefly darted to the cake pan in Ava's hands.

"A cake? How thoughtful of you," was all she said. A minute ticked by. Two.

Ava waited patiently to be invited in, to take a seat, to enjoy some tea, for heaven's sake. Did the woman have no upbringing whatsoever?

Apparently not. Another minute passed with the two faced off like gunslingers waiting for one's itchy fingers to get the better of her. Or perhaps that was only Ava's imagination, for she was starting to marvel at the other's repose, considering Ava had heard her to be a loose-cannoned lunatic at best. Perhaps there would be no show after all and her adversary was nothing but a sick old woman suffering from delusions. How droll and disappointing. Ava had come armed for battle only to find her opponent frustratingly unengaged. And then...

"You're related to her, I take it?" Missouri said.

Ava's eyes suddenly sparkled. "Related to whom, dear?" Ava knew whom she meant but there was knowledge in description and she wanted to hear Missouri's.

"Her. Across the street." Missouri jerked her head that direction. "I've seen you with her. In the house, around the yard, at church."

"Yes, that's right. I am Ivy's aunt from Charleston. Her step-mother was my sister."

Missouri's eyes narrowed and her head cocked like a curious parrot. "You're not blood kin?"

"Marriage only, but she's like a daughter to me, so that hardly matters. Do you mind if we sit down?"

Missouri shook her head. "No. No, that's wrong."

"My goodness, it's only a request. I'm not far from a century old, dear. I'd think your manners would require one of my vintage to take a seat."

Missouri's gaze, true to her birdish mien, did not blink nor seem to register on a seating arrangement at all. She hung on the widow's former comment. "There is blood there, between you and her. A tie. I *feel* it."

Ava snorted. "I'm sorry. I think I'd know."

"You lie," Missouri stated bluntly. In one hawkish swoop, she grabbed Ava's hand, her heavy jeweled rings gouging the elderly lady's flesh and nearly knocking the cake pan to the floor. Missouri's eyes rolled backward, showing whites tinted the pinkish cast of rose quartz marbles. "You lie...*to her.* About the blood. About..." Missouri struggled, reaching, her sapphires and rubies digging harder into Ava's skin and crawling all the way up her elbow like scrabbling crabs. She trembled, rattling Ava to her bones. "I can almost see it...almost..."

"Stop it!" Ava jerked away, rubbing her tissue-delicate skin. Indentations bit up and down her forearm from the cruel facets of Missouri's rings.

Missouri gasped as the widow broke contact. Her eyes centered and focused. "You and that child. That devil's child," she whispered. "Oh my God..." Missouri's whole body began to quake. "I'm going to tell every soul I know about the evil in that house. I won't rest until all of you are out of this town and back in hell where you belong!"

Missouri yanked a rosary from the bosom of her robe. She brandished it at the Widow Pritchard. " 'Neither shalt thou bring an abomination into thine house, lest thou be a cursed thing like it,' Deuteronomy 7, verse 26."

Ava very gently set the cake pan on a table by the front door. She clasped her bruised hands in front of her and a placid smile spread across her rouged lips. In a soft tone, too hushed for the servant hanging nearby to hear, she said, "My, my, sweet Missy. Such dramatics. You best take care now—you're working yourself up into a might dangerous state. Why, I do declare, some hazard could befall such a weak and ailing thing such as yourself."

"What are you saying? Stay away from me." Missouri backed up a step, the rosary prominent between them.

"Care, Missouri. Take extreme care, would you? Now, enjoy your nice cake I've made before you faint dead away from your fantastical whimsies." Ava took the pan again and pressed it into Missouri's hands. The rosary fell to the floor.

Missouri's rings rattled on the bottom of the aluminum as she shook. "Get out." Her voice wavered, thin and watery, then rose to a shriek. *"Get out!"*

Ebby Brown poked her head into the room at the hysterical sound of Missouri's voice.

Ava's smile unfolded again, all pleasantries and grace. "She seems to be upset, dear," Ava called to the housekeeper. "Perhaps it's time for her medications; her nerves seem to be completely taxed. How inconsiderate of me to tire her so. Don't worry—I'll let myself out." The Widow Pritchard abruptly turned on her heels. As the door closed behind her, she heard the thud of the cake pan against the thick, expensive rug and the clatter of Missouri's feet as they ran back up the stairs.

31

His BACK creaked like the slatted wooden chair he rested on. He'd dug the nearly useless thing from a Dumpster behind the backyard. Never did he think he'd see a time when someone such as himself would be digging through garbage for anything, let alone furniture.

How low he'd sunk. Fitting to his predicament. He was all about self-flagellation these days, why should now be any different? The trash is where he felt he belonged, the gutter a residence of comfort.

So he wrestled the old slatterback from a pile of rusted cans and rotted meat, kicked the worst of the filth off with his boot, and drug it into the house. And now that's all there was—a broken man, a broken chair, and the wait. She was ten minutes late already, and punctuality was a virtue he admired. *Should he punish her for that too?*

Something raw and nasty climbed up his throat and crawled out. The sound was ghastly, like a mummified corpse finding life again, coughing and clawing its way from the grave.

It was—laughter? He expected a puff of dust to follow the unfamiliar sound, a relic pulled from the stored-up attic of his past. No, there hadn't been much laughter in his life of late; no, there hadn't been much of that a'tall.

Tires crunching in the driveway, an engine gunning down. A door thudded. She was here!

He leaped to his feet, the chair smacking the floor in his haste. He moved, lithe as the beast he'd become, to the window and peered between the ramshackle shades. She was standing by the Jeep, looking at the sorry backyard encroached upon by an even sorrier torn-screen porch. She appeared uncertain—stay or go?—but he knew what she'd do. Her jaw locked resolutely, an expression he recognized. She didn't back down from anything, and the only thing he'd ever known her to flee—was him.

"My God, look at you," he whispered. It was the first time he'd seen her in years; there was not even a picture she'd left to remember her by. But time had not diminished her in his mind. She was as effervescent as the first time he saw her. Damn. He had hoped he had glorified her over time, built her up to more than she was. Yet, there she stood, unwaned.

It didn't change things. He shook off the spell. His eyes glittered; there was a cunning there that tempered the mellowness of what once was. Anticipation was a driving force, he'd discovered, and right now, this moment, the anticipation was nearly unbearable: He was on the hunt and the prey was coming right to him, the beautiful ivory wolf masked in the clothes of a doe.

He skirted the windows, slinked through dusky shadows, paralleling her path from the Jeep to the front door. Only a flimsy wall separated them, its congruous particles no more substantial than vellum against his adrenaline-pumped strength.

They made it to the front door together, he on one side, she the other.

She knocked. The door swung inward. Before her eyes could adjust, before her nose could betray his presence, he lunged and viciously hauled his long-lost love inside.

Ivy lay on the uneven boards of the cottage's floor, its wood splintering and moldering from years of ground-in fishermen's tread. The odor was like smelling salts, jarring her back to her senses. Had she passed out? What happened?

Ivy sat up, then shakily got to her feet. The room was just as she remembered it—ugly, dirty, and vacant. So then what—

"Hello, Ivy." The voice came from the corner. She squinted, her eyes adjusting, climbing up the dark figure tattooed by slanted light in the corner. He was big, imposing, his silhouette seeming to loom, even though he was seated. Studying her, waiting for her to steady herself again.

"Hello, Melvin," she said simply. What would have been joy upon seeing him was knocked out of her like wind from a bellows when she was thrown to the floor.

He didn't move. Just continued to stare from his advantage in the gloom. It was a lawman's tactic—sizing up, analyzing, evaluating in silent regard.

It was also the nature of the wolf. His nature now. He reeked of it, like a prurient must.

"You've changed," Ivy continued, then blanched. After five years of no contact and a hundred imaginary, rehearsed conversations between them, that was the best she could come up with? It was a stupid, inane joke.

He got up, his head nearly scraping the low-slung ceiling.

"Changed?" Disgust in his tone, the word growled. "Yes. I have changed…in many ways."

His contempt was unsettling. Ivy looked about, uncertain of what he expected. She longed to put her arms around his neck, but the controlled rage seething off him was telling enough. Time had not forgiven her trespasses in his eyes. He still looked at her as a criminal, no doubt, and concern jabbed at the happiness she should have been feeling to see him again. Was he here to arrest her after all, despite the gift she left him with back in Doe Springs? She had assumed the lupine blood in his veins would help him understand the scaffold of her biological structure; she was a construct of Mother Nature's selection and nothing more. He should comprehend better now than anyone the natural dance between predator and prey, instead of regarding her proclivities as an abhorrent aberration. By now, she had thought he would have embraced his newfound canid knowledge, much older than that of human ideals, and seen the world and its slippery notions of good and evil through whole new eyes. Wolfen eyes.

She thought wrong, apparently, for an awakened man would not have greeted her by throwing her to the floor, then standing his distance with the scorn oozing off him like an unfettered stink.

"What do you want from me, *Deputy* Sanders?" She made his title a slur, and she meant it. She was getting it now, and the hurt was too much. She had tried everything to stamp out the love, but by the look on his stony face—still riddled by shadows that painted him grimmer still—love had left him a long time ago.

"Say something, dammit! Why are you here?" Ivy yelled.

He crossed the room in two great strides. A fist closed on her throat and slammed her against the wall. Chipping, yellowed plaster sprinkled down on Ivy's head, and she gasped as his fingers deliberately dug into the tender flesh of her neck. She clawed at the vise stealing her air, but he gripped her wrists and pinned them to the wall over her head.

"I could kill you with one hand and very little effort, Ivy Cole. I could end your murdering ways right here and now. Don't think I haven't thought of it in a dozen different ways."

"Mel...please..."

"I waited and waited for you to come back," his voice cracked, he caught it, deepened it again with his pent-up rage, "and when you didn't, I reckoned it was time to come find you. And here you are. After five long, messed-up, torn-up years, here you are at last."

His fist squeezed even tighter and Ivy's shock was giving way to her own anger. She struggled against him but he slammed her against the wall again.

"I better hold on, Ivy. That's what I've learned about you. Let go and you run, right? *Right?*"

Ivy didn't answer him, only glared silently with those orange burning eyes she saw no need to hide any longer.

"What you did to those people, Ivy. What you did to me..." His forehead fell against hers, his eyes squeezed shut, his labored breathing fogged moist against her lips. He was struggling with himself, an inner battle she erroneously created by saving his life. *By saving his life!*

Ivy's fury mounted. Her words croaked out, and she spat them at him, around the fingers clamped upon her neck. "What I did to you was save your life, you ungrateful fool. You were dog food to that other werewolf. I could have let you die that night when he was finished. But no, I gave you a gift. *A gift!* Now get off me!"

Ivy's knee smashed into Melvin's groin, a direct, bionic hit. His eyes flared a surprised sun-yellow, his labored breathing hitched and then stopped altogether, and his handsome face, too close to Ivy's own to tell with much certainty, seemed to twist spasmodically as he bent double, releasing her.

He fell against the wall, coughing.

"Well, that figures." He gasped and coughed again, then slid to the dusty floor. Pain quelled the tempest and he looked spent.

Ivy coughed too, the air rushing past the release on her throat. She massaged her neck, praying it would not bruise, then noticed it was too late for her arms. Irregular splotches the color of the shack's gray siding were already rising above her wrists. "Great. Just great." She'd be wearing long Ts through the remainder of the season to avoid explanations to her meddlesome aunt, God love her nosy, overly observant soul.

But back to the moment at hand. Melvin was crouched on the floor, a heap of defeat. Ivy knelt beside him. "I'm sorry, Melvin," she said. For this, certainly, but for everything. She had never meant to hurt him.

Melvin put his head in his hands, his elbows on his knees. "You know what, Ivy? The sad thing about all this is, I believe you." He looked up at her now, the misery in his eyes well beyond the physical. There was wreckage here she had never seen before. Ivy had first met Melvin just coming off being a boy, an up-and-coming officer full of small-town simplicity and big-hearted dreams. This person before her now was a man, a man with a hardened edge. He had grown up in her absence and seemed to surpass her in years. Older, embittered—was the sweetness gone? *Had* she done this to him after all?

"I had so many plans when I came to Doe Springs, Ivy. All I wanted was a good job and a good family. Now, a family is out of the question, and I quit my job. That leaves me here—with you."

Ivy wasn't sure what he was saying. She sat beside him, her back against the wall as well. They stared off into nothing with everything to say, but couldn't. The words were caught somewhere in Melvin's despair and her own sorrow. The fantasies of a life with her sweet deputy dissipated on gossamer wings, and the reality of her and Melvin hit home. They would never be the same.

"Why are you here, Melvin?" she asked him again. It was all she could force out. What she longed for him to say, she knew he wouldn't. *I still love you, Ivy.*

"I need your help."

It was impossible. Sadly so. They had talked and argued into the afternoon with no solution. There was no undoing what had been done.

"There is no cure for lycanthropy, Melvin," Ivy said for what felt like the millionth time. "What you have evolved to does not reverse itself. There are no magic potions to make you merely human again. You are the wolf now, same as I."

They were still on the floor, Ivy facing the deputy with her legs crossed like Luna's when she watched television, Melvin's back still against the wall, his hands on his knees. He was a statue of restraint now, drawn away from her, stiffly so, his gangly legs a barrier between them.

"You made me into something I didn't want to be," he said.

"Is that what you think? That I forced you into this? I didn't make you, Melvin. I fixed you. You could have turned out like the werewolf who attacked you. No conscience. No choice. Just an empty, slavering killing machine with no soul."

"Fixed me? How did you *fix* me?"

"We swapped flesh and blood. That's how it's done to make one like myself, the true wolf as opposed to the werewolf that's driven by man's malevolent side."

"Then why do I still feel the need to kill?"

"It's what wolves do, Melvin. It's what men do. We all eat to live. You have to live, don't you?"

"Not like this. I wish you'd let me die."

Ivy sighed. He was being so terribly morose about it all. "You wouldn't have died. You were too strong. What I did was give you choice, but by keeping yourself chained every full moon, you've not given yourself the chance to exercise it. You do have control, no matter how little you trust yourself. Or me."

"But I...I want to hunt when I'm that way."

"Well, that's the hitch. I said you don't *have* to kill. The 'want' part is another story. I'm afraid it's innate."

A buzzing at Ivy's hip. She'd hooked her cell phone into her jeans before leaving the house. A hated device, she decided she needed one when she became a mother. Emergencies could spring up anywhere with her daughter.

"Excuse me a minute, Melvin." The phone vibrated again like an agitated hornet and she answered it. "Hello? Oh, okay. I didn't realize that. I'll be there to pick her up in a few minutes." Ivy flipped the phone closed. It was Mrs. Flannigan, calling to remind Ivy school let out an hour early today.

"Melvin, there is something I have to tell you."

Melvin turned to her, his face drawn raggedly, his stormy blue eyes showing no reflection of love, understanding, security, safety, nothing. It was as if meeting him again for the first time, when he was a stoic, unemotional lawman doing his job and she was a stranger to him. Luna flitted through her mind and was gone. Ivy could not share her with him. Not like this.

"The Widow Pritchard is in town, staying with me indefinitely. I think it would be best if she didn't see you. I have to go pick her up right now."

Melvin nodded.

Ivy started to stand up, but Melvin caught her bruised wrist. "I've rented this house, so I'll be around for a while. We've still got more talking to do." He started to let her go, then paused for a moment. "And Ivy? Don't run off again. If you do, I'll just come find you, and next time I won't be as nice."

32

IVY JOUNCED back across the Sandpiper Bridge, heading for the outskirts of Salty Duck and the elementary school. The events of the afternoon crashed about in her head with each jolt of the metal against her rubber tires. Her opinion about it all bounced along too, disjointed, confused, disbelieving. How could this be true? How could it have happened? Melvin. Back. In Lockerman's Ferry. Just across the bridge and only a hearty jog from her house. And, let's not forget, a werewolf. Not a happy one, at that.

Ivy glanced at her hands gripping the steering wheel and the bracelets of fingerprints above them. The rearview mirror revealed a sallow mark under her chin that would require makeup to hide. *No, not happy at all.*

She should be filled with outrage herself after their meeting. Truly, how *dare* he? Her bruises throbbed and seemed to darken as she pictured it all, again and again and again. In fact—in fact!—she should be grabbing up Luna and racing home to pack. She should be putting Miss Ava back on a Greyhound and flinging open the Atlas to find the most backwoods hidey-hole on the map to hunker down in till her child was raised. She should be calling her banker right now in the Cayman Islands to wire her a lump of money for traveling that would take her halfway around the world.

She should be doing a lot of things. Instead, the Jeep, very calmly, very pointedly, turned into the elementary school parking lot just as a rolling parade of school buses pulled out. She parked and, with not a hurried step about her, made her way up the sidewalk to the front of the school.

Face it, Ivy—you feel more alive now than you have since Luna was born. Damn the truth of the inner voice. Melvin was back. He was back! And despite the fact she'd have to make him pay for her new bruises later, she didn't want to let him go.

"Mommy, it was the greatest day ever!"

Ivy was wrapped in Luna's arms, Mrs. Flannigan standing quietly behind her. A smiley-face sticker was stuck to the girl's jumper. The classroom was already empty, save for a few straggling parents like Ivy herself, heading down the waxed hallway to the big double front doors.

"We made paper bag puppets and colored sand jars. Look!" Luna held out a mason jar filled with tiers of orange, blue, yellow, pink, and turquoise sand.

"It looks like the sunrise over the sound, Boo."

"It's for you, Mommy." Luna beamed at her mother, and Ivy saw her house as it would be for the next few years: covered in papier-mâché crafts, pottery-sculpted clumps meant to be flower vases, and indiscernible, impressionistic Crayola works of art. A typical family scene. Completely normal. Ivy's heart leapt at the prospect.

"Um, Ms. Cole, while Luna gathers her things from her cubby, I need to speak with you." Mrs. Flannigan's welcoming smile of this morning was no longer in place. She looked strained in a constipated way, as if what she was about to tell Ivy was especially difficult to get out. The cozy knit of normalcy Ivy enjoyed briefly unraveled itself and wound away.

"Go on, honey, get your lunchbox," Ivy said. "Yes, Mrs. Flannigan?"

Luna skipped to the back of the classroom and Ivy followed Mrs. Flannigan to her desk. The teacher pulled a sheet of sketch paper out of the drawer, its blank side to Ivy.

"We also had Paint Station today, Ms. Cole. You see the students' artwork is hanging by the window."

Ivy turned to the large pane of glass that covered one wall from waist level up. A clothesline was strung in front of it. Clothespins held a drooping row of colorfully painted pictures, a divine backlit gallery of kindergarten artistry. Smudgy, pudgy puppies chased undefined children with oval bodies and legs and oversized shoes; stick-figure adults stood over bulbous contraptions on stalks that could only be BBQ grills; sailboats floated on the pointy waves of periwinkle seas.

"They're very nice. Which one is Luna's?" Ivy asked.

Mrs. Flannigan thrust the sketch paper from her desk at the new student's weary-sounding mother.

Ivy's eyes widened. The picture was a glut of red, the paint applied so thickly it coagulated like the blood it represented. In the center of the crimson clot, a figure lay with his eyes wide open, his pupils large and cataractous with death. Dismembered arms and legs were strewn helter-skelter about, and standing over the hacksawed torso was the well-outlined form of a four-legged animal, its body bristly and completely black. Rows of dramatically long white teeth hung from the beast's snout, which was lowered to the ripped body in the wide-open posture of an attack.

Ivy looked at Mrs. Flannigan, whose plumply pleasant face of this morning was now the pasty-floured wash of hardened dough, and just as friendly. What a difference a few hours could make. Ivy had the weird feeling she was about to be sent to the principal's office.

"I...I don't know what to say," Ivy said.

"You need to address it with her, Ms. Cole. Sweet little girls like Luna don't need to have images like these floating around in their heads. Don't you agree?"

"Of course," Ivy said slowly. "But you know how the media is these days, all those violent movies and games. Even the newspaper here lately is showing some grisly material. But I'll definitely be paying more attention to what's on television or lying about the house."

Mrs. Flannigan's lips pursed and her eyes wandered across Ivy's fresh blemishes. "I care a lot about my students, Ms. Cole. If Luna is being exposed to some sort of violence in her household that I should be aware of, it's my duty to contact social services."

"Don't be ridiculous," Ivy snapped, fighting the urge to put her hands behind her back—or around this woman's fleshy neck and award her with her own collar of discolored marks. "There is no violence in the home, not against me or my daughter."

"All right. But I've seen things like this before with other children. Symptoms of a disturbed child can manifest itself in many ways, such as ultraviolent artwork like I have here, or acting out. Which brings me to the next thing. There was an incident today."

Incident. That one word inspired more terrible concern in Ivy than her meeting with Melvin and her recent fight with Marcus Daywright combined. Please, not an *incident*.

Ivy swallowed and tried to look innocently curious.

"Luna bit the Holloway twins," Mrs. Flannigan said bluntly.

"Excuse me?"

"They were getting along wonderfully. You saw that when you dropped Luna off. The girls played together most of the day. Then, this afternoon right after lunch, there was apparently an argument over—well, I still haven't figured that part out—but Luna bit Teena first, and when Neena tried to defend her sister, Luna bit her too."

"Are the twins all right?"

"The school nurse swabbed them with alcohol and put on Band-Aids. As long as your daughter doesn't have rabies, I think that will be the end of it."

Ivy smiled tersely. "I can assure you, she's had all her shots."

"The Holloway parents weren't too upset," Mrs. Flannigan said, disregarding Ivy's sarcasm. "I think they realize children can be unpredictable sometimes, even the very good ones like our Luna here."

The child was back, her angelic face peering up at the adults with bright eyes and happy, flushed cheeks.

"And before I forget, here is the note for the upcoming field trip." Mrs. Flannigan handed Ivy a slip. "Luna says she thinks you won't let her go, but I urge you to reconsider, if that's true. Based on what I've observed, Luna needs a great deal of social interaction with other children in a supervised, yet relaxed, environment. I take it she did not go to preschool, so this could be very beneficial for her. So please, I hope you'll let her come."

Ivy pressed her lips together and looked down at the child by her side. *You sneaky little dickens. You paint a morbid picture of Auf eating the Preacher Man and bite two children to spite me, then you rally the troops to your defense for the field trip.*

"We'll see," Ivy said crisply. "Thank you, Mrs. Flannigan. I will handle everything we talked about. Luna, let's go."

33

CALEB STOOD in his front yard on the corner of St. Mary's and Battery watching Ivy cruise by without a glance in his direction. She was leaned toward the dashboard as she drove, a dour look of determination in her forward demeanor as if she were forging against a particularly strong wind. On the other hand, instead of leaning into the imaginary gust, Luna looked pinned to her seat by it. Normally the child was quivering in her seat belt restraints much like a Jack Russell terrier readying to spring at the first opportunity. He had never seen her so still.

Caleb's wave went unreciprocated, so he followed after the Jeep on foot. He made it to Ivy's house just as they were walking onto the porch.

Luna spotted him first. "Hi, Caleb!" She was all giggles and grins at seeing him, but Ivy's scowl her direction stilled the hug he felt had been coming.

"Hello to you, little sunshine. What's up?" The question was more for Ivy. He'd never seen her this way, and it did not bode well. It had gotten so she seemed to enjoy the attentions between the man and child, or at least tolerated them with a faux irritation that he saw right through. And she knew it. It was a game of safety (for her) but one of acceptance (of him), too. So what had happened?

"My first day of school," Luna said proudly, warming up and beginning to ignore her mother's glower. "I made colored sand and a puppet and painted a picture—but," and here she whispered conspiratorially, "Mommy doesn't like it so don't ask to see it." Then, in a normal voice or perhaps too loudly, "And next week I'm going to the beach with the class!"

"The beach—sounds like that kindergarten is a pretty cool place."

"You bet it is!"

"Luna, go feed Cali. Auf and Mup too. Tell Ava I'll be in in a minute." Ivy opened the front door and shooed the girl inside.

"Bye, Caleb," Luna said quietly, all subdued again, and disappeared into the living room. Ivy watched after her daughter, her arms crossed.

Caleb scratched his head. "I hate to meddle, but you act like you've had a really bad day. Everything okay?"

Ivy didn't feel like talking right now. She'd be facing the Grand Inquisition soon enough, the minute she entered the house, actually. Throwing Caleb into the muddled pot of stew was the last thing she wanted at this moment, and a big hateful brush-off was on the edge of her sharpened tongue.

But that wasn't fair, was it? It wasn't Caleb's fault her life had just turned upside down. That Melvin Sanders had materialized after years of believing she'd never see him again, that Luna had jeopardized her schooling on the very first day, raising suspicions on Ivy's ability to mother.

And yet, yes it was Caleb's fault. Because he'd made her comfortable, made her forget she was anything but normal and could do things like restart her business, have a child in school (okay, that was Ava's fault, let's be fair), enjoy community and craft fairs and having friends...But the most flummoxing part of it all was he had made her feel like she could love again. Love someone else besides the deputy from Doe Springs who obviously hated her for what she was, just like Ava warned he would all those years ago, back when it mattered and she wouldn't listen anyway.

And now, here she was. Falling in love with a yacht salesman from Chicago, to complicate matters exponentially. *Did I just say falling in love?*

Ivy shuddered. The thought only made her grumpier in a sick-in-the-pit-of-her-gut way, and she suddenly wished she were in the backwoods of Appalachia again without a soul around but her four-legged brethren.

She gathered her raw nerves before speaking, her tone as mild and agreeable as she could make it. "Today has been a trial, Caleb, but it's nothing a good hot bath and a mound of chocolate won't cure."

"Sounds intriguing. Can I get in on any of that?"

Ivy blinked.

Caleb tried again. "Okay, I knew the chocolate was pushing it. How 'bout just the bath then?"

"I'm sorry, and don't take this the wrong way, but I really just need to get inside and unwind. I hope you understand." Ivy clutched her arms again, rubbing them. Caleb noticed bruises. His eyes narrowed.

"Ivy, and I hope *you* don't take *this* the wrong way, but I'd stop anybody who was hurting you or Luna. Do you understand?"

Ivy dropped her hands to her sides. The unexpected seriousness of Caleb's implications was too much. It was all too much. "Caleb, there's nothing for you to worry about. I can take care of myself in ways you can't imagine. Please. I'll call you tomorrow." She reached out and caressed his cheek, then went inside. The curtain to the living room window fell in place as an elderly face withdrew.

Caleb brooded in acute silence, staring at an empty china cabinet from the mild comfort of a tatty beige couch. There was only meager adornment in his simple rented home, but he had liked that about it. Empty spaces were uncluttered places, and that helped aid in uncluttering lives. That's what all of this was about to him anyway.

A new start, a new life, a new path entirely. Ivy and Luna were integral to all of that, but today his perfect plan of insinuating himself into their lives, which had thus far been working, hit a snag.

Ivy was seeing someone else, no two ways about it. Women didn't get marks like that by running into walls or wrangling poodles in dog-training class. She'd been in a row with somebody, and that "somebody" could be problematic. It could not have been a stranger who attacked her; she seemed too calm for that. No, this was someone she knew.

Her secretiveness rankled him to a surprising degree. He was hurt she wouldn't confide in him, angry some other man (he assumed it was a man) dared touch her like that, and jealous that whoever it was, Ivy felt the need to protect him. Maybe she was afraid. He doubted it.

Nevertheless, there were other things to consider here, and that brought Caleb out of his brooding stupor. He went to his bedroom and pulled out the bottom dresser drawer. The ancient leather-bound tome of *Lykanthrop* lay atop his T-shirts, and he idly wondered if he shouldn't find a better hiding place.

It had been entirely too easy, acquiring the werewolf historical, passed down from generations from the strongest in the line to the next. He lifted it the day he'd left Ivy's house after hanging her painting. She'd remained in the bedroom, admiring his work, and there the book was on his way out the door, tucked on the bottom shelf of the living room bookcase. Unbelievable. A valuable such as this left so casually about, so casually in fact that she hadn't even noticed it was missing yet. He expected someone would before too long, perhaps the widow, who made him feel like a bug under glass whenever he was in her presence. She didn't like him; he'd heard her whispering to Ivy in church about "the salesman's smarmy, sycophantic ways." That was all right, though. Caleb didn't take offense, as long as it didn't seem to be influencing Ivy any. He got the impression Ava did not like anyone calling on her niece, regarding all men as horny old dogs with no sense and too much heat.

Caleb pushed the book aside and took out a smaller one, a simple, cheap black date book. In the notes section on the calendar he wrote in very neat, deliberate script: "Beach field trip next week."

He closed the book and tucked it in the drawer once more. Then he lay back on the bed and continued to mull in silence.

34

THE CAR sat dark on Battery Street just up from house number 6103 in the historic Parish Keep district of the charming seaside town humorously named Salty Duck. It was black out, even with the pale light of the intermittently spaced street lamps. Backyards were cast in pitch, the cottages and Victorians and plantation-style Colonials blocking all light from the street.

The watcher in the car felt obscure enough. It was an unremarkable vehicle, a rental, and forgettable. The windshield was etched in fragmented shades of purple reflection from the lumbering oaks that lined the street in between the lights, but despite the night, Sheriff Gloria Hubbard could see well enough. All she needed to see really. The house. It was unlit as well, like all the others on Battery Street. But Ivy Cole slept inside, there was no doubt about that. Her comings and goings had been charted for a while.

And that had revealed a horrifying surprise: Ivy Cole was a mother now.

Gloria rubbed her eyes. Her brain was tired, yet it wailed with frustration anyway. Ivy Cole had to go down, but she had a child. An innocent child, who, even from the distance of observation, was obviously loved, and she, in turn, seemed to worship her mother.

Annie had been a sweet child, too, Gloria couldn't forget, before the werewolf devoured her. So then was this blond waif safe, having a mother such as Ivy Cole, an arbitrary creature that could turn like the phases of the heavenly satellite that governed her? Could Gloria protect the child—by orphaning her? She had dove into books for the answer. Wolves made excellent, endearing parents. Would the same apply to homicidal werewolves? Such a bittersweet dilemma. It made Gloria ache in maternal places that she thought were numbed with barrenness by now.

Barren. Could there be any bleaker word? She pictured fallowed fields, their rows puckered like the edges of razor wounds laid open, their soil-mounded lips raw and ragged from the plow. But nothing grows there, and only a hot, dry wind blows over the gray dirt, devoid of life, devoid of any hope of life. Soured. That was her womb as she saw it all right. Sour.

A hurtful word, a hurtful image, but Tee had been so understanding. "It's all right, Glory. You're still you and we've still got *us*." They'd tried for two years before letting police work become the baby they couldn't have.

Tee. Tee. Think of Tee. What would he do now?

"His job," Gloria said to the empty street and the sickle moon overhead. There was time. Still plenty of time. And the answer really was simple. Of course the girl could not stay with her mother, no more than any child should be allowed to live with any murderer. Whatever foster home was provided would be better than the perversity she was surrounded by now. Did Ivy even protect her daughter from the inhuman acts she performed under a full moon? It was too hideous to think about.

What Gloria did think about, and was utterly consumed by, was the when and where of what she was here to perform. A time line had presented itself unexpectedly, however, through the sudden enrollment of Luna Cole in school. A field trip was forthcoming, Gloria had learned through her investigations, and Luna would be out of her mother's skirts for a good long while. The old woman, that pesky Widow Pritchard, was visiting unfortunately, but she would not be in the way. If she happened upon Ivy lying dead in the kitchen by a single, silent gunshot wound to the head, that would be better than Luna coming upon her first.

The gun Gloria finally chose was another story too. Out of the arsenal she brought for protection should something go wrong, none would be the accomplice of the deed. That weapon was a special little number, untraceable and destined for the bottom of a hidden mountain lake as soon as the target was done.

Gloria cranked the car engine, but left the lights untouched. She did a U-turn and drove back up the street toward Sandpiper, through the outskirts of Lockerman's Ferry, and toward the place of her temporary lodging, a nondescript motel twenty minutes away.

Had the sheriff stayed just a few moments longer, she would have been very interested to note a figure creeping stealthily across Battery and slipping into the backyard of the Victorian that sat across the street from 6103 and its slumbering lycanthrope Ivy Cole.

35

SCREAMING. SCREAMING as if the executioner had come. Screaming as if she were seeing the werewolf again, in the kitchen in Germany and her mother lying prone at its bloody feet. Screaming like a lost child in need of its mother...

"Luna!" Ivy was wrenched awake, the scintilla of her dream evaporating like the tail of a comet into a starlit void—but this wasn't a dream. The screams were real, it was morning, and Ivy was running for the bedroom door.

At the top of the stairs already, a black form. Aufhocker. He looked at her and stepped back as she ran past. Ivy crashed into her daughter's bedroom; the bed was empty. *Luna, where are you!* Ivy ran across the room. Luna was curled in a blanket on the other side of the bed, her arms around Cali's thick neck.

"Did you hear it, Mommy?"

The wind rushed from Ivy's relieved lungs; the breath she'd been holding tasted vile. The escaping air was followed by the loud slamming of a door across the street.

"Help me! Oh God, somebody please help me!"

Ivy strode to the window and looked out on a crystal blue dawn.

Salty Duck was just rising, and a lady in an aproned dress stood in the Pitchkettles' front yard. It was much too early to be standing in aprons and screaming in front yards.

"That's Missouri Pitchkettle's housekeeper," Ava said from over Ivy's shoulder. Ivy jumped.

"What in the world is happening? Ava, stay with Luna. Aufhocker, come."

Ava and Luna watched from the upstairs as Ivy, with Aufhocker by her side, ran to the hysterical woman, who grabbed Ivy, clutching at her with one hand while the other stabbed hysterically toward the house. The housekeeper fell to her knees, tears streaming down her face, still clinging to her neighbor and pulling at her pajamas as if she could bury inside the other woman's skin and elude whatever had rattled her so.

"Should we do something, Aunt Ava?" Luna said from tiptoe, her nose pressed against the pane of window glass.

"No. Look—someone else is coming to help."

The neighbor to the right of the Pitchkettles' house came to his porch. Ivy yelled and pointed; the man dashed back inside. He was striding their way a second later, a cell phone glued to his ear. Two cars slowed on the street, and one pulled over. Another woman jumped out, heavier set. Ava recognized her too. It was Missouri's gardener. The housekeeper released Ivy to run into the other woman's arms.

"Does Mommy need us to go over there?"

"Oh no, honey, it will be all right," Ava said, just as an ambulance, tailed by a police car and both with sirens blaring, careened into the Pitchkettles' narrow drive.

Ava pulled the child away from the window. "That was quick. Well, I doubt we can go back to sleep with all that racket across the street. Come on, sugar, I'll go make us a pancake breakfast." They went hand in hand down the stairs, Cali padding after them.

• • •

Ivy walked back home, the surrealness of her dream like a murky, polluted haze she struggled through on her climb back up into wakeful consciousness. For surely, this was a dream, just as she'd imagined when she first heard the screams this morning.

Please, let it be a dream.

It wasn't. It was a nightmare. A very real nightmare that she couldn't even pinch herself to escape. She was wide awake after all, unfortunately, and this would have to be dealt with. But how? As a mother, she was completely at a loss. She could hear Mrs. Flannigan standing over her right now, tut-tutting and shaking a finger. *"It's all your fault, Ivy Cole. I saw this coming a mile away. You're a bad mother...."*

Pebbles and bits of ground-up shell raked at her bare soles, but she did not notice. Auf heeled at her thigh, his head lowered, disturbed by all the people, the sirens earlier, the noise of anguished sobs from the crowd gathering outside the Pitchkettles' yard, now cordoned off with police tape.

Ivy slowly took one step up her porch at a time. Through the front door. The living room. The dining room. She stood under the arch dividing the two rooms and watched her daughter—her precious, beautiful daughter—laughing with her aunt and gobbling down pancakes. The girl turned a sticky smile on her mother.

"Mommy, there you are! We made you some too."

Ivy's eyes moved in slow motion, across the table, the stick of butter cleaved by a spreading knife, the syrup warmed in a gravy boat, to a place setting on the other side. Fluffy, golden brown pancakes with slabs of melted butter sliding off the sides of them waited for her.

"Ivy, your shirt." Ava now, speaking around the juice glass she daintily sipped from.

Ivy idly looked down, her gaze floating through heavy layers of thick water. Down. Down. To a red swipe of blood marring her white pajama top. It was a handprint from the housekeeper. But not her blood, oh no.

Ivy looked at Luna again. In a careful, almost singsong tone, she said, "Luna, go to your room."

"I'm not finished, Mommy."

"Go to your room, honey. Do it now." Steady. Even. Yes, keep control.

Luna slid back from the table and brushed by her mother on her way upstairs. Cali scrambled from underneath the table to follow her.

Ava was staring. Ivy finally turned her head to face her aunt, but the swivel of her neck felt weighted, like the rotation would take a thousand years and her chin was dragging a mountain.

"Ivy, what is it, child? What's happened?"

"Luna. It's Luna."

"Luna is fine, sugar. She ate a whole stack of flapjacks this morning and was about to start on yours. Now tell me what's going on over there before I burst."

Ava patted the seat beside her and Ivy shuffled forward. Aufhocker rested his nose on her lap, and Ivy found comfort in his burly brow. She rubbed him hard, each stroke pulling the skin back to strain the whites of his eyes.

"The housekeeper, her name is Ebby, found them," Ivy said slowly, coming up from the pressured depths now, coming up for air from the weighty zone of disbelief. "Mr. Pitchkettle—Leland—his throat was torn out while he slept. And Missouri...It looked like the killer shook her into pieces. That's what Ebby said. She hit Missouri's arm when she opened the door. She thought it was the doorstop."

"My goodness. That will take the housekeeper a day and a night to clean up, I'm sure. Was there a terrible amount of blood?"

"Ava! Don't make light of this."

"I'm sorry, sugar, but I don't know why you're so upset. Missouri Pitchkettle was a fiend of a woman, always making faces in church. And Leland, well, wrong place, unfortunate time, I suppose. Honestly, dear, what is all the fuss? Somebody's done you a big ole favor, and you act like you just lost your best friend! You've certainly done much worse yourself—*and* on a regular basis, need I remind you."

"But that's my point, Ava. It wasn't me, don't you see? It was Luna!"

"Oh pshaw." Ava flipped her hand dismissively. "You don't know that. She's just a child."

"She is just a child, but what Ebby described...It was a werewolf, Ava."

"So maybe you've got a third one running around town. I'm sure you're not the only lycanthrope who finds the sun and salt air enticing."

Ivy tapped her foot impatiently. "With no full moon? Did you forget about that?"

"You are just determined to be convinced of the worst," Ava said, taking a piece of toast and spackling it with a thick layer of butter, "and I'll bet it's nothing more than Salty Duck has acquired a hatchet-wielding maniac. Does that make you feel any better?"

Ivy frowned at her aunt's lighthearted tone. "Here, let me show you something."

She went to her bedroom and snatched Luna's school painting from the nightstand. She marched back to the dining room, waving it. "It's just like this picture she drew in school. I thought it was Auf and the Preacher Man, but I have no doubt now that this is Missouri Pitchkettle."

"Oh dear." Ava took the drawing and studied the dismembered body, the globs of red paint, the devious wolf form standing in all its lethal glory over the corpse.

"She's hunting without me, Ava. And poor Leland—*he* didn't deserve it. I told Luna he was a good man. I told her! And then there was the man on the beach I told you about." Ivy's shoulders hitched and she put her face in her hands. Tears poured through her fingers and rained over the perfect breakfast her aunt had prepared. She collapsed in Luna's vacant chair. "I can't teach her, Ava. She's just a little girl now. What will she be like when..."

Ava slid closer to hold her niece. "There, there, sugar. Don't fret over it so. Shhhh..."

36

A DOUBLE homicide in Salty Duck, another gruesome murder right on the heels of the mutilation of Marcus Daywright. The town was in shock, according to the newspaper article. Nothing had happened like this since the days of Blackbeard. Police speculation? They weren't saying, but the reporter had an inside source: possible animal attack. A trained predator. Monstrous in size, yes, *monstrous,* to have done such damage. The autopsies should reveal more....

Melvin was back in his chair. He'd moved it to the kitchen this time to enjoy breakfast (coffee from the corner store, black) and the morning news at the counter, its concave surface reminiscent of a swaybacked horse.

Reminiscent. Now there was a word for consideration. In his case, perhaps déjà vu would be more appropriate.

Melvin sipped his coffee and read the article a second time. It was big front-page news in Salty Duck, the headline so large it looked like the announcement of another world war. To a place like Salty Duck *(or Doe Springs),* it might be a fair equivalent.

A cockroach skittered across the counter in front of the deputy, disrupting the flow of words and coffee. It stopped and waggled its antennae his way. Uninterested, the bug continued on its quest to the crack between counter and stove.

"Godspeed to you," Melvin muttered after the roach. He put his empty Styrofoam cup in the rust-ringed sink, along with a half dozen other empty Styrofoam cups. He imagined his six-legged buddy would be back with friends later to scurry through the coffee grounds and leftover backwash.

That didn't bother him much. This house was not about comfort; he'd even turned down the offer of rental furniture to go with it. He had a chair. He had his truck to sleep in. The shower worked. He ate on the road. He was an officer—well, used to be an officer— and comfort wasn't at the top of a policeman's priority list. This was all about function, and the function here was proximity. It was the closest available house to Ivy Cole (that he could afford anyway) without crawling right up her doorstep. Like the roach, in fact.

But after reading this newspaper article, maybe he should be closer. Suddenly a few miles over the bridge felt like a state away. Very troubling, the frequent murders, back-to-back, just when Ivy showed up in town. Bodies beheaded. Torn to pieces. A werewolf's M.O., only...

...only not under a full moon. And not eaten. What was going on? This time could it really be a serial killer, as the newspaper's anonymous tattler speculated, using a trained carnivore? Melvin had thrown that same theory at the sheriff when they'd been investigating the rash of horrible deaths back in Doe Springs all those years ago. But they'd been wrong. Dead wrong. They'd also had a full moon.

No full moon?

Melvin wadded up the newspaper and threw it by the pea green refrigerator to pile atop the other wadded-up newspapers. He bunched his long legs under him and stood up, stretching to his full height. The mirror over the sink did not reveal a pretty picture: Melvin's typically close-cropped military cut was growing shaggy, and the bristly black whiskers stippling his jawline were lengthening every minute it seemed. There was a time when he shaved once, sometimes twice a day, back when an upstanding appearance demanded respect.

Now, what did it matter? He sprouted hair all over his body month-ly—he might as well be the animal all the time. It was less hypocrit-ical.

How did you get here, Melvin? When did you become so bitter? He knew the exact day, the exact hour, would know the exact minute had he not lost consciousness from loss of blood. But Ivy could fill in that blank.

Ivy. Her name padded through his mind, a white wraith on stealthy paws with fervent eyes lambent as the yellow moon that had charmed him.

Ivy. I've seen you every night since you left, running like a quicksilver stream of moonlight through the forest, stalking me in my sleep, chasing me, wanting me, needing me. Why did you leave me?

No full moon. That was what mattered right now. Nothing else.

Melvin needed answers and his mind was made up. It was time to pay Ivy Cole a visit, the Widow Pritchard be damned.

Melvin knocked on the cottage's outer screen door. A plaque hung to the right of it in Old World script engraved with a name and the date 1755. The structure was two hundred fifty years old, and Melvin felt like his weary soul could relate. Nevertheless, the house would probably outlast all of them.

He watched the scene across Battery while waiting for someone to answer. Police cruisers still choked the street, turning it into a one-car, one-way passage. Two officers walked about the porch, and a news anchor was doing a live feed from the fringes of the front lawn. Police tape hung like black and yellow ribbon around the perimeter, giving the residence the air of having been festively toilet-papered at Halloween.

Melvin couldn't believe it, and yet should not be all that sur-prised: The latest murders happened right across the street from Ivy's house. *Reminiscent* ran through his mind again, and he remem-bered Clifford Hughes's torn body in Doe Springs, also drug from the very woods Ivy's cottage nestled in. And yet, who would have ever suspected her?

Yelling across the street. One of the officers had leaped off the porch and was making a beeline for the reporter. Melvin heard the man ordering the camera crew back onto the pavement beyond the fence. The young female journalist was waving her microphone at the officer a little too dramatically, and Melvin wondered if the "melee" would up the ratings for the morning news.

The deaths were only a day old, and this would be big news in Salty Duck for a long time coming, no theatrics necessary. He knew, for Doe Springs had still not fully recovered. People locked themselves in their homes early, despite the sheriff's repeated assurances that the danger had passed. The drone of surreptitious rumors might never cease, rumors of the beast that stalked by the full moon, rumors of the menace that had morphed into legends of the Devil of Doe Springs, as they called it. As they called the werewolf.

The red inner door opened, pulling Melvin from his ruminations and his longing to don a uniform and aid in the investigation across the street.

"Hi!" A nymph with pigtails the color of wheat straw and the greenest eyes Melvin had ever seen stared up at him past a Fudgsicle that had left a mud-colored mustache over her upper lip.

Melvin's brows knit together. He squinted through the screen door, trying to see inside.

Luna looked over her shoulder, then turned back to face the giant stranger filling up the doorway and blocking all the light.

"Who you looking for?" the small stranger blocking the doorway and utterly confusing Melvin said.

Melvin pulled a notepad from his jeans pocket to double-check the address. Maybe Ivy gave him the wrong one on purpose. She certainly didn't want him to actually visit—at least not until the Widow Pritchard was safe and sound back in the Blue Ridge, and he said he would respect that. Until a double murder changed the rules.

The gnome was still there. She held up her Fudgsicle. "Want some?"

Ivy had lied, of course she had, and he had made the elementary mistake of not checking the phone number on her dog-training flyer against the house number before coming. A bogus address, a story about Ava to buy herself time, and she'd fled. She was probably a thousand miles from Salty Duck by now, and he had no one to blame but himself. What did he think she would do once discovered? Stick around just because she was thrilled at seeing him again, just because maybe she still loved him after all?

Don't be such an idiot, Melvin. You should have killed her when you had the chance. But then what? Slink back to Doe Springs a murderer himself and with no cure to his illness? He didn't entirely believe that Ivy couldn't help him figure this thing out, that it was only as cut and dry as "accept it, there's nothing else you can do."

As for killing Ivy, he had to admit it now: He had only been fooling himself.

Melvin sighed. He removed his dark lawman's shades and rubbed his tired eyes. He'd have to start all over now. He'd begin with airports.

"Mommy!" the blond girl hollered back into the house. "There's a giant stuck on our doorstep, and he can't talk!"

"Oh. Oh, no, that's okay. I've got the wrong house. Sorry." Melvin turned and double-timed it down the steps. The black Dodge pickup was pulling away just as Ivy made it to the door.

"He's gone, Mommy. I think I scared him away."

Ivy watched Melvin's truck turn right on Mission Street and disappear. "Yes, Boo, I think you did."

37

"And your name was again?"

"Jack. Jack Cole. I'm here about my niece, Luna. Her mother, Ivy, has asked me to pick her up from school sometimes and I need to make arrangements. Ivy's my sister."

The desk receptionist at Salty Duck Elementary looked up at the strapping man standing in front of her. He had dark brown hair, a neatly trimmed goatee that was both sexy and intimidating at the same time, and the blackest eyes she'd ever seen. She detected a slight accent that he seemed to want to overcome, a hint of Ocracoke Island and its Irish brogue perhaps? She wasn't quite sure, but she herself was from Louisiana, with dialects famous for their Cajun flavor, and unusual accents didn't bother her in the least. She found them deliciously interesting and mysterious, and Iris Rutherford found herself leaning a little too heavily over the desk to better take the stranger in. The left hand was of particular interest, and her whole demeanor puffed up with pleasure when she spied her target, newly freed from his front pants pocket. No gold band in sight.

"Well, Mr. Cole, that shouldn't be a problem. But we'll need to see some identification and get the mother's authorization, of course."

"Of course. If you check your records, you'll see Ivy has already called in. Here's my ID," he flipped the laminated plastic in front of her, "and, oh, I've also got this." Jack handed the attractive forty-something redhead a slip of paper. "I feel kind of silly carrying around a permission slip, but I'm sure you'll want to keep it on file too."

"Yes, we have to document everything now, schools being how they are. A shame, too, isn't it? I bet we'll have a metal detector out here before too much longer, but the smaller schools are taking a lot longer to catch up to the bigger inner city systems."

"A real shame, the need for all that. But you can never be too careful this day and age, although I bet someone as attractive as yourself has to be careful of roguish strangers all the time, eh?" He smiled at the receptionist and watched her face light the color of strawberry wine, a perfect complement to her flame-kissed hair. She barely glanced at the note with Ivy Cole's signature at the bottom.

"No, you certainly can't, Mr. Cole," she said around the dimples in her freckled cheeks.

"Just Jack. And you are Iris Rutherford."

"How did you...? Oh, the name tag. Right." Iris noted Jack's gaze snagged on the small brass plate pinned beside the open button of her blouse a suggestively long time. Quite nervy of him, and yet she didn't mind. That button was undone for a reason. The principal sure was taking his sweet time about paying her any attention; she was starting to think she'd lost her appeal altogether after turning forty. But Mr. Cole, *Jack,* sure seemed to sit up and take notice. She wished her sorry good-for-nothing ex could see her strutting about town with this one on her arm.

"You know, it's been my experience, Iris, that being too careful can also be incredibly boring, don't you think?"

"Interesting theory, coming from an admitted 'roguish stranger.'"

"I don't recall admitting anything, but we can argue about it over drinks one night if you're free."

The school bell rang, signaling lunch, and jarring the moment. Children's voices crowded out the quiet and teachers bustled past the desk on the way to their private lounge. A few gave the stranger and

Iris sidelong glances before moving on. Jack scanned the children's faces outside the office door, hoping he would catch sight of Luna, but the hallway was a waist-deep sea of pigtails and cowlicks, and everyone looked the same in the mob.

"Is everything in order for you?" Jack asked, coming back from his observation outside the doorway to refocus on Iris and the items he'd handed over.

All business again. Iris was aggravated and disappointed at once. Did Jack Cole ask her for a date just now, or did she imagine it all? The timing on her life was forever off. Right when the most promising prospect in forever strolls up to her desk, the lunch bell has to ring and scare him away. Why were men so jittery about asking a woman out these days? It was maddening.

"Wait right here a minute, Jack. I've got to copy your license for our files, and I've also got something you might find handy when you're scheduling your pickups." She'd keep him around a bit longer and let him regroup. Maybe once the hall cleared they could get back to where they'd left off—something about drinks?

She disappeared into another office and was back out in five. "Jack," she beamed at him again, enjoying the familiarity of his first name, "we do have on record that Ms. Cole called this morning to tell us you were coming, and here's a list of upcoming activities and events, plus our regular school hours."

Jack scanned the list, noting book fairs, field trips, parent-teacher days. "This is very helpful, thank you. I notice there's a trip next week to the beach—will Luna be participating in that? I've got a meeting that day that I may have to cancel, if that's the case."

"How inconvenient for you." Iris's brows knitted with concern. "Let me check." She tapped on the computer in front of her. "Her permission slip has been turned in, so, unfortunately for you, Luna is scheduled to go."

"No big deal. I'll work it out on my end. Again, thanks for your help." He started to turn away, then caught himself. Iris held her breath.

"I almost forgot," he said, "could I give you a call sometime, if you're not too busy?"

"Um, I don't know, Jack. What were you saying earlier about roguish strangers?"

Jack's lip curled, an expression that could be interpreted equally as tease or contempt. "I should probably watch how I put things from now on. Got myself into trouble, didn't I?"

"Not as much trouble as you could be in." Iris leaned further across the desk, the remaining clasped buttons of her blouse straining. "The question is, can I trust you?"

"Only about as far as you can throw me." That devilish grin again, those piercing eyes. Iris was lost.

"All right. I like to live dangerously. Here's my number." Iris had it jotted on the sticky note before he'd even asked for it.

He took the number, letting his fingers brush over hers slowly as he palmed it. "Nice meeting you, Iris."

The man walked out the double front doors, feeling Iris's eyes following him every step of the way. As he rounded the corner of the brick building heading for the parking lot and his car, he wadded up the sticky note with the receptionist's phone number and dropped it into the nearest trash bin. The fake ID for "Jack Cole," well, he'd hold on to that for now.

Gage Rowland, waiter for The Bluewater Lady restaurant on Front Street, climbed into his rented sedan and drove away.

Inside the school, Iris Rutherford had watched the handsome stranger walk out of Salty Duck Elementary, the arrogant sway to his shoulders making her heart flutter. When she'd completely lost sight of him, she went to the back office and a file cabinet to deposit the handwritten note into Luna Cole's file. It suddenly hit her, as the white piece of paper fell into the manila folder, that she should have given Jack her cell phone number as well. She was rarely ever home at regular hours. What if he called and she missed him? What if he never called back? Why in the world didn't she get *his* number, to be on the safe side?

These were the unending questions of concern for the newly divorced dating woman. Jack Cole's permission slip from his sister was safe in Luna's file, and Iris closed the drawer. Had she bothered to compare the signatures on the permission slips—the one for the beach field trip and the one for the release of Luna to "Jack Cole"— Iris's concern would have been for an entirely different reason.

38

"What are you doing, Melvin?" The voice came from behind him.

Melvin spun around in the dim room, gun drawn and finger on the trigger. The figure stood in the doorway, the weak bulb from the living room caressing the curve of her form and blinding him to her identity. But he knew that voice well.

"What am I doing? Coming to look for you. Or at least I was, up until a little while ago. I thought you'd be across the country by now. Change of heart?" He tossed the gun into the tangled mess of clothes in front of him. Upon returning to the fisher cabin, Melvin had retreated to this bare bedroom. His clothes spilled out of an open duffel bag on the chair he moved from room to room, and after brooding for an afternoon, he had decided to stuff everything back in. Night had fallen around him unaware, and his grim, defeated mood had left him unfocused and an easy target for ambush. But he never expected to see her here. After hour upon hour of soul-searching, he never expected to see her again period.

Ivy walked into the room, and Melvin smelled the familiar milk and honey of her hair, her skin. Her eyes glittered like ice-sheathed mountain balsam kissed by a thawing winter sun, even in the darkened room, and whether it was the depth of the human spirit or the inner fire of the wolf that lit the hot-cold pupils, he never knew; he only knew it was like the trance between the snake charmer and the cobra when he fell under their gaze.

"I wasn't planning on going anywhere, Melvin. You misunderstand some things."

Melvin closed the duffel bag over the Glock, zipping it inside. "Now that, little lady, is where you are exactly right. My whole life has been one big misunderstanding. I thought I was a good man, a good cop. I failed on both counts. I even failed you, Ivy. I should have taken you in that night, but of course, had I known back then what happens at the full moon, my tactics would have been—how should I put it? Expedited. No, you pulled your shape-shifting stunt and pulled the rug right out from under me. This ole boy sure didn't see that coming. Lollygagging—just another failure that nearly got us all killed and led to this pathetic state I'm in."

Ivy looked at him oddly. "Have you been drinking?"

Melvin snorted. "No, but maybe I'll start. I can add that to my list of sorry endeavors. Pardon me if I'm not acting right to suit you, but just today, after I left that house in Salty Duck—yeah, I tried to see you—I got a few things figured out for the first time in a long time."

"What things, Melvin?"

"Waiting for you to come back, then pursuing you out here just to do nothing—I'm not getting anything accomplished. I'm failing all over again." He shrugged. "I don't know how to stop you, Ivy, and you say you don't know how to help me. My trip here was a big waste of time." He picked up the duffel.

"So you're leaving?" Ivy said. "Just like that?"

"If I didn't know better, I'd swear you sound disappointed. But that's right, Ivy. You're free. I don't know what I was thinking when I came here. I wasn't thinking." He strode past her, into the living room and the glare of the single bulb dangling too low from the ceiling. He crossed the concentric circles of its muted glow, heading for the front door.

"Melvin, wait. Please, wait!"

She ran after him, grabbed his arm. The muscles flexed taut at her touch. Melvin gritted his teeth and brushed her off.

"Melvin," she grabbed him again, her hands strong, demanding. Melvin closed his eyes, opened them, kept walking.

"Melvin, stop. I have to tell you—"

"No!" He whirled around. "There is nothing else you can say to me. I loved you once, and I let you go. If you ever loved me, let me go now. Let me deal with what you have made me alone, away where I can do no harm. That's my only solution, don't you see? There is nothing else you can say to make me stay."

"Melvin," Ivy said, "I have a daughter."

They were in the Dodge pickup, ten miles outside Lockerman's Ferry on a slip of solid ground that stuck into the inlet like a sharp splinter. The eroded bank they parked upon crumbled away to a driftwood beach, which melted into silt beneath the gentle swells that rolled against it. Gulls had serenaded the dropping sun, and now it was quiet save the lapping of water and the night sounds of the maritime forest behind them. If not for the lighthouse far in the distance and the briny scent on the air, they could easily have been parked at a lake in the woods. It was eerily familiar—Ivy could close her eyes and pretend for a moment they were back in Doe Springs, the Blue Ridge wrapping around them and their bellies full from one of Melvin's perfect picnics. She had loved that about him: his joy in simplicity, his consideration for hers—or anyone's—needs. A friend to Doe Springs as well as its protector, Deputy Melvin Sanders had been a hero to her and the town alike. Homesickness mingled with regret, and she pushed the nostalgic thoughts away.

Ivy looked at Melvin now, but he continued to stare straight ahead, out over the water made ebony by nightfall.

"Those eyes," he said finally. "I should have recognized them. The hair too. How could I have missed the resemblance?"

"I meant to tell you that first day, Melvin. But the time didn't ever get right. It was shocking enough, seeing you again after all these years. I wasn't ready to tell you everything."

"You didn't trust me enough, isn't that the truth of it?" His head slowly swiveled her way.

"I had to make sure of your intentions first. It's obvious you've got unfinished business with me—the lawman never got his criminal, right? I couldn't risk your goal being to finally make right on that. I wouldn't let you orphan Luna. You can't blame a mother for that, can you?"

"Is that what wolves do, then? Spirit away the young to protect them?"

"And fight to protect, if necessary. I tried hiding her first."

"Wolves don't hide their young from the pack, Ivy. My new instincts have taught me a lot. The female and the male raise the pups together. I've felt such a longing to find you, but maybe it's been more than my feelings for you that have led me here. Maybe it's been something more primal than that.

"Ivy, Luna is my daughter, isn't she?"

It was Ivy's turn to contemplate the water. The question she feared had found her; she could no longer avoid it. "For the longest time, I thought so, Melvin. She's kind, loving, sweet, but strong, so very strong. All these things I knew to come from you. It was glorious, really, the wolf I knew she would eventually become, one gifted with the lupine wisdom of her mother and the compassion of her father.

"But then, she changed. She...she does unconscionable things, Melvin, just for the joy of it."

"She's only five years old, Ivy. What 'unconscionable' things could she possibly do? Steal someone's juice box? Stomp teddy bears at recess? You're probably overreacting."

"Would you call the Pitchkettle murders overreacting?"

Melvin was quiet for a time. "So we have spawned a killer true to her nature. Should we be all that surprised?"

"You're not getting what I'm telling you, Melvin. It's more than that: I no longer think Luna is your daughter."

His brows dipped to hood his eyes. "How can that be? The time frame is right. Who else could it be if not me?"

Ivy waited for Melvin to think about it, hoped he wouldn't make her say the obvious out loud, for the truth of what she thought was too terrible to utter.

"Wait a minute. *Him?* You think it was *him?* How? When?"

"That last night at the cabin in the woods," Ivy answered, resignation heavy in her tone. "When I thought you had betrayed me by coming to arrest me, and then the sheriff showed up too. What was I supposed to think, Melvin? Aunt Ava warned me against you because of what you are—a policeman—and she told me I should accept one of my own kind. It just seemed to make sense at the time: The black wolf and I ran as mates before the night was over."

"Before you killed him, you mean." Melvin's eyes were hard slits in the dark.

"And saved you, let's not forget. But I'm sorry you had to find out about Luna this way."

Melvin's upper lip curled. "So this is the Black's nature revealing itself in Luna's genes, is that what you're telling me? Luna is the child of another werewolf."

Her voice was a hush, a weary sigh. "Yes, I believe so. She's just like her father, the Devil of Doe Springs."

"Like her father?" Melvin said. "A cold-hearted, cold-blooded, ruthless killer like her father?" He leaned down into Ivy's face, spoke each word with deliberate purpose as if explaining to a slow-witted child. "Ivy, Luna's not like her father. She's just...like...you."

39

R~ED~ IS the color most associated with anger, shades of crimson to denote the rise of blood pressure, the raging flush of the cheeks, the strain of vessels and capillaries as the brain screams stressful signals and the heart pounds to support the outrage.

But in the wolf, anger is a cold beast, and its description might be told as a blankness, the color of steel or blue-white ice that burns just as hot as its scarlet brother. There is no emotion to the stalking wolf, and anger is not in the equation before the strike—a surprise to the prey that comes upon it and falls victim to its intense, furious silence.

This was the fervor that gripped Ivy now as she crossed the Sandpiper Bridge into Salty Duck. Melvin was back at the fisherman's cottage, his lone duffel bag unpacked once more.

He was lucky to still be alive. His implications...a cold-hearted, cold-blooded, ruthless killer? That's how he saw her. That's how he would always see her. She'd about had enough of him and his judgments, and had she been the wolf at the moment or had Auf by her side, his fate might have rivaled that of the Preacher Man's.

And yet...she had done nothing and let her rage simmer in controlled debate as Ivy insisted Luna was not his daughter and Melvin fixated, with frustratingly threadbare conviction, on the notion that she was. But angry as she was, she could not deny that this was the first glimmer of the man Ivy had known before, a spark of hope ignited by thoughts that a family might be possible after all. A dysfunctional family, certainly, but one that could benefit from his upright, guiding hand. Suddenly someone needed Melvin—a little girl in pigtails with a murderer for a mother. Suddenly, he could be the hero again.

Ivy mashed the clutch and jerked the Jeep into second gear. She turned right into the Parish Keep district. It was late; most houses were dark already, including her own. Across the street, police tape billowed around the Pitchkettle residence. The home's seven-foot windows looked out at her accusingly, their arches like resentful, hooded brows. No wonder.

Ivy turned left into her driveway too quickly, nicking the curb as she pulled alongside the house into the yard. She cut the engine and leaned back against the seat, catching her breath, catching control of herself. *Breathe in, out, slowly. Count to one hundred, Ivy, isn't that what you tell Luna to do? Yes, breathe, relax. One, two, three...*She let her eyes close, forced her clenched jaw to loosen...*Four, five, six...*Let the heavy lids fall and her arms rest limp in her lap...*Seven, eight, nine...*

She was not counting for Melvin's sake now. He was not the only reason for the hotness in her chest and the blurring of her eyes as they shaded vibrant green to orange and back again. No, this was not entirely about Melvin and his honorable intentions to be a father (a-whole-nother issue to deal with when she could think straight again). This was about what Melvin had revealed to her later, after another round of yelling had quieted to rational discussion and the pervasive quandary he would not let be: what to do about *his* daughter.

Just as the storm had momentarily seemed to calm, Ivy had posed a question, a simple, ordinary question, and stirred the inner hurricane once more.

"Melvin, there's something I've always wanted to ask you. Something I've needed to know. That night in Doe Springs, when you were waiting for me at

the cabin—you didn't have any evidence. You really couldn't have arrested me with nothing to go on. Just what were you doing there?"

"I wanted to help you. I thought I could persuade you to turn yourself in to a psychiatric hospital." He sneered at Ivy, the stupidity of his former naiveté grossly apparent now.

"I believe that, Melvin. Now I do. But how did you know that's where I would be?"

"Didn't she tell you?"

"Who? Tell me what?"

"The Widow Pritchard. She called me to her house, told me this bizarre story about werewolves and your past. She told me to follow you that night and I would see for myself. The widow was certainly right about that. Prior to that night I thought she was insane—or the best liar I'd ever come across."

Ivy's lids flew up as the conversation played to an end. She'd lost count as Melvin's story had encroached upon the monotone rhythm of the numerals marching through her head. That one nugget of knowledge had been the final undoing of her evening with Melvin, a crazy quilt evening of patchworking as they sorted through a slew of conflicting emotional turmoil that had plagued them both since Ivy left the Blue Ridge.

And now the most unexpected deception of all had been laid bare completely by innocent accident, forcing Ivy's hand. For she could not let this go. She would have to deal with this straight on.

A light had come on in the kitchen. Ivy followed it inside.

Miss Ava turned from the stove, two mugs of cocoa steaming and ready.

"There you are, sugar. I was beginning to worry. Surely you don't normally stay out this late with a wee one at home?"

"Where is Luna?"

"Why, she's upstairs sound asleep, dear, cuddled up between Cali and Auf. Is everything all right?"

Ivy glanced at the cups. It was muggy even this time of year at the coast, but Ava was apparently still on mountain time. "We need to talk."

The widow drew back a little. Her head tipped to the side, and her diamond-rimmed glasses winked in the light of the overhead. She carefully set the mugs on the countertop.

"Perhaps we had better sit down." Ava's tone had hardened to match her niece's.

The dining table was a familiar meeting ground, and they retired there, in the hard-backed chairs, themselves less rigid than the spines reclining against them. Had Ivy been the wolf at the moment, her hackles would bristle to her tailbone. Ava noted the posture, and met her niece dead on.

"It's the deputy, isn't it?" Ava said. "He got to you despite me. It was him made that phone call for a dog appointment, left a phony name. Oh, I should have known better than to fall for that."

"That's why you came here? To keep me and Melvin apart?"

"Somebody has to look out for you. You do a piss-poor job of it on your own. And now there's my grand-niece to consider. That deputy is pure trouble for you. Always has been. I couldn't believe you didn't get rid of him when you had the chance, and I can tell by the way you've got your hackles up you have no intention of getting rid of him again. Yes, I came to Salty Duck to protect you, but I was looking to intercept him here, face to face. I didn't count on him creeping through the back door like that. Sneaky, sneaky."

"That's the pot calling the kettle black, isn't it? How long have you been playing me, Ava? Manipulating what I do? Five years ago you set me up to kill Melvin. You led me to believe he was investigating me to arrest me, when it was you who sent him to the cabin that night in the first place! You knew what I would think, seeing him there. You knew I would have to kill him."

"And look what you did instead—saved his life and killed a perfectly good lycanthrope." Ava shook her head sadly. "Not killing

Melvin was your mistake, Ivy, not mine. He'll be a thorn in your paw until the day he dies, mark my words."

"He was the only man I've ever cared about, Ava. Just what else have you done?"

"Guard your tone, dear. I do what I do for your own good. As for other things I've done to protect you, a little thank you every now and then wouldn't hurt my feelings. I go to great lengths, even recently, to keep you safe from harm."

"Recently? What are you talking about?" Then she knew, and the ugliness of it spiked the anger with a terrible sorrow. But she had to ask, had to hear the words spoken for themselves. "Ava, did you *send* Luna to kill Missouri and Leland?"

"Missouri Pitchkettle was a blight on this community. Don't cry your crocodile tears and lecture me about right and wrong. You know that hateful old bag of bones had to go. Whatever killed the Pitchkettles, consider it a blessing."

Ivy leaned across the table. She clamped a hand over Ava's. Her breath breathed hot in the widow's face. "You answer me, old woman. *Did you use my daughter to kill the Pitchkettles? Yes or no?*"

Ava leaned in to meet her niece nose to nose. "Take your hand off me, you silly pup. You think you've got everything all figured out, but you don't know anything! I'll tell you what you *think* you want to know. But you'll wish I hadn't before it's over, I can promise you that."

40

THREE MINUTES past the witching hour, and the seashell chimes on Ivy's front porch welcomed the crossover into midnight with a clattering against the porch post. Two shells shattered and fell to the beamed floor. Something was brewing up the coastline, something wicked and mean, its whine preceding the force that was to follow. Rain began to splatter against the dining room window, randomly at first, the big drops smearing sideways across the glass as if fired there from a skyward gun. A soughing wind wrapped around the house, under the eaves, through the porch railings, its voice borne by the gale rushing in from the sea. Porch swings rocked by the gusts of tempest ghosts, and the Thinking Tree braced for what was to come.

The Widow Pritchard braced herself as well. This was a tale she did not relish sharing. What Ivy did with her new knowledge could leave them alienated forever, or bond them even closer than before. Could the human in Ivy understand the forces that lay behind the most mortal of intentions? Understand that mistakes could be made at the cost of doing good in the long run? Because that's all Ava ever intended by her actions. Good. In the long run. If some were hurt on that path, well, didn't we all have to make sacrifices somewhere?

Ah well. That was neither here nor there. The time had come to tell Ivy a truth. Ava sighed and accepted it, come what may of them after this conversation. She would love her niece regardless and hope the girl would still feel likewise.

Ava gathered herself and began.

"You were a special child, Ivy, more special than you've ever even realized. The first time Una brought you to see me, right after she and William Cole were married, I felt a connection between us. It made Una green that you would open up to me, a practical stranger, instead of her. Jealously was not pretty on my sister, but she really did want to be a good mother to you. I know you've never been willing to believe that."

"I don't care about any of this, Ava. We can stroll down memory lane later, and then you can defend Una all you want to for stealing my father, destroying my mother, and making me what I am when I was *only ten years old.*"

"Ah yes, the traumas of the very young; such baggage your little shoulders have borne. But Una shouldn't get full credit for your lycanthropy, dear. As I recall, your Uncle Stefan and his pack of wolves had a little something to do with that as well."

"You need to answer my question about Leland and Missouri. I don't care about any of this."

"I'm not being a windbag intentionally, sugar. There is a point to my ramblings." Ava looked out the rain-blurred window. The wind still railed outside, and something thudded against the side of the house, an overturned trashcan perhaps. Cups rattled in the cupboard behind them, and a shutter slammed and flew off.

"There's a bad storm coming, Ivy," the widow said. She looked at her niece. "Are you ready for it?"

And Ava began, as the wind blasted and the rain pounded the house with the staccato beat of jungle drums against the rafters. But Ivy did not hear the maelstrom from outside, for she was held rapt

by the storm from within. The story had started with a visit to Aunt
Ava's one summer when Ivy was eleven. And as the tale unfolded,
Ivy remembered the brief incident herself....

A woman crying, sobbing. Sobbing in the attic. Young Ivy
clutched her Holly Hobbie for reassurance. She knew she was too
old for the doll, but today she needed the extra courage as she
climbed the stairs slowly, one at a time. They creaked with each light
footfall, but the hoarse crying did not pause at her approach.

The narrow attic door loomed above her head, its cream-paint-
ed wood dingy from neglect. This was the highest point in Aunt
Ava's old Victorian house, and children were forbidden to come up
here. Bats and spiders and surely much worse haunted the upper
level, she'd been told. It was not a place where good little girls wandered.

Of course it was those very admonishments that brought her to
the foot of the gloomy stairwell day by day, the first time just to put
a foot on the bottom step. But each visit after, she'd advanced a step
higher, encouraged by the lack of leathery-winged attacks or appearances of evil-intending apparitions.

Today, buoyed by the courage of Holly Hobbie, whom Ivy could
fling at anything that swooped down from above, she had made it to
the middle of the stairs, when the jagged barks and hiccups of the
weeping had reached her. Terrified, she froze, sure that a long-dead
fiend in tattered funeral clothes would throw open the door and
devour her at any moment.

But then a voice broke through the hitching cries; it was her step-
mother, Una, that Ivy recognized. Curiosity released the child from
her frozen stance, and she crept all the way to the top step.

"Are you sure we must do this?" Yes, it was Una's voice, cracked
and shaking as she tried to gather herself.

"It's the only way, he said so."

Ivy leaned down carefully, quietly, and pressed an eye to the keyhole. Inside the pear-shaped slice of view stood Aunt Ava over Una, who was perched on the edge of a steamer's trunk. A handkerchief alternated to wipe her eyes and nose.

"I won't go through with it. I won't let you go through with it." Una looked up at her older sister, pleading with her. "Haven't I done enough to her already?"

Ava knelt in front of Una, Una with her long, licorice hair, pale skin, eyes the strange and haunting color of lilac. She was a vision, even in this pitiful, broken state, and Ivy hated her for it. Her dark beauty could never replace the light of her mother's, no matter how many dolls and dresses and gifts the stepmother bought her. Ivy's true mother was dead and there would never be another, even if Ivy's father were too weak to be loyal to Catherine's memory and put this woman in her place instead.

"Stefan said it won't hurt her, Una. I can't stand being this way. I can't stand being…like you. You owe me this, sister, if you love me at all."

Tears from purple lashes still rained down Una's cheeks. Ava cupped them with her hands. "If you love me at all, you'll let me do this. All I ask is you stay out of the way. That's not so hard, is it now?"

The two women stared at one another, and then a nod, barely perceptible.

"Thank you, Una. Thank you." Ava wrapped her arms around her sister's neck. Una did not hug her back. She stared over Ava's shoulder into the dim, swirling dust, the tears ever streaming down her cheeks.

"I remember," Ivy said. "I was there, hiding behind the door. I heard Una crying and I came up to see why."

Ava nodded. "Then you know I'm telling the truth."

"But what were you talking about? Nothing ever came of it. I was so afraid for a while, too afraid to ask questions, too fearful to even sleep for the next few weeks. And then, I forgot all about it. In fact, I haven't thought about that again until now. What does that have to do with Luna and the Pitchkettles? Can't you just give me the short version?"

"You young people are always in such a hurry. There is so much to learn here, yet your impatience shows complete ignorance. You say nothing came of the conversation. But oh, my sweet child, everything came of it. And you played the center role, you just don't remember. You *couldn't* remember."

Ivy shook her head. "I don't understand, Ava. You're not making sense."

"Just listen…"

"Ivy! Ivy, sugar, come into the house now! You've played in my garden too long. Those fireflies must be exhausted from avoiding you by now." Ava whisked the girl inside, slamming the screen door before any bugs could follow. A few mosquitoes made it through anyway, but that was summer for you.

"I've caught thirteen fireflies," Ivy announced to her aunt. She held up the glass jar so Ava could see.

"That you have. Good job, honey. We'll cut out the lights later and let them entertain us. Better than TV, I'd think."

Ivy beamed and set her catch on the foyer table. Her stomach rumbled, reminding her it was suppertime, but no smells came from the kitchen and the usual suppertime suspects were absent. "Where are Una and Uncle Jeb and Rita?"

"Una has gone into town to buy something special for your father to take back to him in New York, and my lazy husband has decided to turn in early for the night. No since making a big fuss over a meal for two people, so I gave the housekeeper the night off. It's just you and me, kid." Ava tweaked Ivy's nose, knowing full well she was old enough now to really hate that. "I was thinking simple tonight, like watercress sandwiches and caviar?"

Ivy wrinkled her nose, and Ava put her hands on her hips, mockingly aghast. "Not good enough for our little princess? Well, then, how about hot dogs and potato chips, will that do?"

"Yeah!"

"All right then. I might even throw in a cookie or two. Oh, and I've got fresh sun tea, your favorite. Now go clean up while I start getting things ready. I've laid out the prettiest little sundress for you on your bed. It's red as a poppy, I think you'll like it."

Ivy ran down the hall, blond ponytail bouncing, and was back in a minute, the hem of the new dress swishing about her knees. She settled onto a bar stool at the counter and prattled away while Ava prepared a meal fit for an adolescent. Ava smiled and nodded appropriately as Ivy talked, but inside it brought upon her a keen sadness for Una. Here, out from under the skyscrapers and the Cole influence, Ivy seemed as happy-go-lucky as any normal child her age—not all the time, but in lighter moments when she forgot herself, like after spending an evening corralling fluorescent bugs. But to hear Una tell it, Ivy was morose all the time in New York, completely withdrawn, her demeanor curdled and her tone biting if one could engage her in conversation at all. Una worked at being a mother, determined to never give up, but Ava could see for herself that years would not unravel the resentment festering in this child. Ava wondered even then what Ivy would do if she ever discovered what Una had done to Catherine. Seven years later, she was handed her answer.

"There. One hot dog, two chocolate chip cookies, a pile of potato chips, and a frosted mason jar full of iced sweet tea, just how you like it." Ava put the china plate in front of Ivy and folded a linen napkin beside it.

"Aren't you going to eat too, Aunt Ava?"

"Oh no, Ivy, this meal is 'specially for you. Enjoy it. And be sure to drink all your tea, love. I made it fresh this morning. Jeb's already drunk half of it himself."

• • •

Ava watched as the little girl's head rocked lower, then dipped into the middle of her plate. The fingers grasping the mason jar began to uncurl, and Ava caught the glass before it slipped to the floor. She bent down and peered into Ivy's face. Ava's glasses immediately fogged, a good sign. She pulled back one eyelid, then the other, and they closed heavily when released. Satisfied, Ava checked her watch. Una promised she would give her sister two good hours, and the potent little extra in Jeb's suppertime tea would keep him out till dawn.

She scooped Ivy from the bar stool and carried her down the hallway, through a side corridor, and into one of the guest baths at the remotest end of the sprawling house. No one had used it in years and it remained in a state of bored sterility, frequented only by Rita once a month to knock off a layer of dust. Ava had already prepared the room for this night, it was just a matter now of getting the job over and done with. She lowered Ivy gently into the claw-footed porcelain tub, feeling her own back crack in the process. Ivy was a small girl, but Ava was a small, fine-boned lady herself. Had Una not been such a waste of nerves, her help would have been greatly appreciated.

"Rest easy, sugar. This won't take long."

Carefully, Ava rolled the hem of the red dress above Ivy's waist and secured it with two safety pins into the bottom of the bodice. Next Ava removed her niece's sandals and placed them neatly on the floor. The girl's slender tan legs, fashionably scraped and scabbed per her age, stretched out the length of the tub. Ava cradled Ivy's left leg and very gently laid it over the rolled lip of cold porcelain. Her foot dangled limply, the drug-induced slumber making her limber as the raggedy old doll she still sported about.

Ava reached behind her to a silver tray on the countertop. She pulled on surgical gloves with a curt snap, a faint cloud of baby powder puffing from each one. She reached behind her again and removed a scalpel, already sterilized and shiny in the bright bathroom light. Ava's grim reflection glinted in the metal, no less harshly than the determination in the set of her eyes and the thin press of her lips.

Ava held Ivy's left leg at the knee and rolled it slightly outward.

The vicious scar from a werewolf's bite—Una's bite, unbeknownst to Ivy at the time—shined like a jagged white streak of lightning rising out of the summer-bronzed skin of her inner thigh. It would be there the rest of Ivy's life, the only injury to her body that would never completely go away.

And this was where the scalpel laid its sharp edge, in the heart of the scar. Ava drew the blade only a short length of it, barely an inch. It was enough. The blood followed the trail of the scalpel like red lava bubbling to the surface. The line of suspension broke, and red drops spider-webbed down Ivy's thigh to drip onto the spotless white basin.

Ava set the bloody scalpel on the tray and retrieved a second one. She held her left arm over the tub and with a quick slash, slit the underside of her forearm. Ava winced once, then her face steeled again. She was almost through.

Holding her arm close to the girl's face, Ava let the blood stream over Ivy's lips. Ava parted them and waited for the warm liquid to make its way past her teeth, over her gums, down her throat. A minute passed, and she moved her arm over the cut in Ivy's thigh. She pressed her incision tightly over the opened scar, forcing the blood to mingle and stream together: Ivy's blood through Ava's, Ava's blood through Ivy's. It burned as Ava's cut absorbed the vitality of the young wolf. She felt her arm grow hot up to the elbow, then the shoulder. The sanguine fire spread like an enveloping acid in her veins, yet she held her arm firm until the bottom of the tub was a splatter-painted canvas and blood smeared the length of Ivy's thigh from lacy pink panties to the bend of her knee.

Ava started to grimace, but she held firm to the torrid scar, and when enough time had passed, she feverishly pulled her arm away and thrust her face into Ivy's thigh. Her mouth found the open wound and she pulled at it with her teeth, tearing at the edges and sucking blood and bits of flesh deep into her throat. She gagged once, then resumed. Blood flecked her glasses, stained her lips and chin...

"Enough!" From behind her, slurred but firm.

Jeb. Ava turned to the man swaying in the doorway. His eyes strained to focus through the dazzling light and the bleariness of the drug. Blood covered his wife's face, layers of it lapped down her neck and into her neckline; her arm was marred from fingers to elbow. Brilliant red splashed the sides of the tub, the marble tile at their feet. His niece, Ivy, lay still amid it all, like a bled corpse.

Jeb staggered forward, grasping at the wall for balance. "What have you done, Ava?" his voice rasped. "In God's name, what have you done?"

Ava rose from her crouching position and matter-of-factly wiped her hands on her apron. It was a ridiculous gesture, considering the bloody state of the rest of her.

"I did what I had to, Jeb," she said. "I did what I had to do."

41

THE HAIL came after the wind. Ivy and Ava sat in mutual silence and listened to the clicking of the weather against the house, its varying assaults of rain, wind, and ice trying to worry their way in. The lights in the kitchen flickered, dimming the glow it cast into the dining room.

"Why?" It was a whisper, barely audible above the creaking of the cottage against the assailing sky.

Ava adjusted her robe about her nightgown. She was tired tonight and now wished she'd stayed in bed instead of getting up to greet Ivy when she returned home. Already she'd told her niece more than she ever wanted her to know, but the why of it was the crux, and she knew Ivy would ask it. There always had to be a why, didn't there? Or else we'd all just be random molecules turning about the cosmos with no purpose, no motivation, no goal, as meaningful as particles that merely happened to cohere and form a thing or, occasionally, a life. Of course there was a why.

"Una's lineage was imperfect, like all werewolves really," Ava said. "Not her fault. The lycanthrope is what it is, like the one in Doe Springs whom you suspect to be Luna's father. No control, no conscience as a shape-shifted being. Picture a human who has become psychotically savage but also been given the supernatural advantage of teeth and claws to carry out that savagery. They kill whatever they come across with no regard; whatever lies in their path is in danger. Wickedness never became a choice for these characters, just a way of life under the full moon.

"Una gave me that ability, Ivy. Maybe you've suspected it by now. And I wanted it, asked for it, begged her for it, if you must know. But I didn't know for what it was I was asking. What I thought would be a gift was an infection. I *like* control, you know that, sugar, and I despised losing myself in the full moon, losing sense over what I was doing and letting mindless insanity take over. But there was no cure. Or so I thought, until your Uncle Stefan told me about just how special you truly are. There was a cure for my condition, and it was you. He told me how he made you after Una left you that night, told me of what you could do, how I could repeat the process without his wolves and pray it worked.

"And it did work, Ivy. Oh, did it work. You are a talented girl. Your ability to choose goes beyond whether to kill or not to kill and whom. You also have the choice of *when*. Luna's nifty little trick is not innate, sugar. It was passed down by her mama."

Ivy had not moved since Ava began talking, and she was still now, an immovable stone of listening. But did she hear? Was she understanding? Ava wanted to reach across the table and pinch the girl for a reaction of some sort. It was maddening, her sitting there with her dead expression and hostile air.

"Say something, Ivy. I know I've unloaded a lot on you—"

"You expect me to believe all this?" Ivy's mouth moved with no force behind it. Her voice was dull, even, a flat line made even staler by her dispassionate matter-of-factness. "Melvin was right on two counts: You are crazy and you are the best liar I've ever come across."

"I'm not lying, and deep in your soul, you know it."

"That night in the bathtub—you injured me. You cut me. Why don't I remember that?"

"The drugs obviously. I gave you a hearty dose. And by the next morning your leg was completely healed up. Stefan was right when he said you wouldn't be hurt. I never would have done it if I'd believed you would be. Surely you have to believe that, Ivy. I would have fallen on a knife myself before ever hurting you. But you were strong; we all knew you could handle it. Stefan was certain of that much, if not the outcome for me. But after that night, Ivy, the wolf was a new creature, one I welcomed. One I welcomed any time I needed it. And I could stop it anytime I didn't."

"You're wrong about me. If you can do what you say you can, you got it from somewhere else. Maybe from Una after all. She chose my mother and spared me. How did she do that?"

"Oh, sugar, there was no choice there as the lycanthrope. That was all scorned woman in progress. Geography accomplished that feat for my sister, dear. Simple geography. Una put herself at your house and waited to change. As for sparing you, I really can't put an explanation atop that, other than perhaps divine human will overcame the savage for one instance. That's what I like to believe, anyway, although one has to wonder, did Una spare you, really? You were barely alive when Stefan found you. I guess we'll never know what another's human spirit is capable of when challenged by the shape-shifter's influence."

"All right. Fine. But I've never changed except under the full moon either, and I've certainly never stopped it. Explain that."

"You've never had reason to on both counts. I only discovered it myself by accident. Jeb made things very stressful for me after that night with you, and stress seems to bring it about the first time. Surprised the hell out of both of us. Jeb was never keen on my 'moon sickness,' as he called it. You can imagine how he felt staring down the muzzle of a seven-foot wolf in broad daylight. No, sadly, our marriage never was the same after all that, and I have you to thank—and blame, however you want to look at it."

"Stress from an argument with your husband? I've dealt with much worse than that and never had the wolf appear."

"Oh, sweet niece, it was more than just a simple argument. My dearest Jeb decided he might put the old wolf out of her misery before the next full moon came about. I couldn't let that happen. He never tried any of those foolhardy tricks again, but after years of listening to his whining, I decided it was time to let him go. It was for the best, miss him as much as I still do. But that part of the story, you already know."

Uncle Jeb. Poor murdered Uncle Jeb. He'd always disapproved of Ivy, knowing her for what she was, so she couldn't say she was terribly upset when he was gone. But the reasons for his unexpected death—natural causes, it had been determined by medics, due to his age and overexertion in the garden—had been more complicated than Ivy realized. At least Ava had respected her husband enough to give him a peaceful release instead of one by the jaws of the thing he abhorred. Nobody had ever thought to check the quality of the sun tea Uncle Jeb had drunk just before heading out to do yard work that morning, that much Ivy knew, but now she herself had to wonder at the meals she'd shared at Ava's house over the years and the repercussions she was only now becoming aware of.

"Marcus Daywright," Ivy said abruptly, letting Uncle Jeb's memory and his ill-fated love of a poisonous woman and her poisoned tea bury itself once more. "He attacked me. He was going to kill me. Why didn't the change happen then?"

Ava leaned toward Ivy earnestly. "Were you really in danger from the Preacher Man? You knew Aufhocker would save you. But what would have happened if Auf hadn't been there? Then you would have known. With Aufhocker by your side and your meticulous full-moon planning, you have managed to keep your ownself quite in the dark about your abilities.

"But I'm not finished, child. There have been other unexpected positives. You've only to look at Aufhocker, offspring of Stefan's black wolves, to know that part of it. If he had a palm, the life line would run clean down to his elbow. No wolf—no canine of any sort—has the longevity and health of that one. Look at me, Ivy. What do you see?"

Ivy didn't need more light to know her ancient step-aunt didn't look a day over sixty-five and acted fifteen years younger than that. Ivy'd never thought much of it, beyond feeling grateful that Ava descended from hardy genes.

"I'm ninety-two years old, sugar, but the clock slowed down on me that night in my bathroom. I won't live forever, but I'm enjoying the extra time."

Ivy was speechless. She just sat and let the remnants of the passing squall wash over her. The hail had abruptly stopped and the rain with it. The wind, too, seemed to be receding. The calm after the storm was approaching, or was it merely nature's exhaustion after all that mighty bluster was spent?

Her anger was gone. In its place was a lonely, hollowed pit where trust used to be.

"I never detected you. How did I not detect you? I can smell another wolf a mile away," she said.

"Just a little camouflage trick I learned from Stefan. He's smart in our ways, that one. But really now, sugar, were you looking? Would you have seen, even if I'd been less adept at hiding it? Didn't you somehow, deep inside, know about me, but you let denial take over?"

Ivy shook her head. It was not in disagreement, but rather, a motion of sadness and disbelief. Words were increasingly more difficult to come by, but she still had to know this one thing. "Ava, did you kill Leland and Missouri?"

The Widow Pritchard laughed. It sounded like parchment burning in a fireplace, a dry cackling better suited to a crone than Ivy's lovely, cultured aunt. "Of course I did, dear. But don't judge me too harshly. What might Reverend Holliday say about it in his nice little sermon on Sunday? Hmmm. 'And the dogs shall eat Jezebel...and there shall be none to bury her.' That's from the Second Book of Kings, if I remember correctly."

"This is not a joke, Ava."

"Oh, I'm certainly not joking, sugar, but you always did miss the big picture on things. Once again, I just did what I had to do, and Missouri's husband just got in the way. Sadly, husbands tend to do that, even when they mean well. But Missouri sensed you, and Luna too. She picked up on things that could have only caused disaster down the road, and she promised me that was her intention. I say nip trouble in the bud before it blossoms. Besides, you're going to lecture me after the mess of bodies you left piled up in Doe Springs?

Tourism's up forty percent in that town, thanks to you. I think the locals would rather have the Devil come back than deal with one more camera-toting yokel jamming up traffic and flip-flopping along our streets looking for werewolf souvenirs. But I digress. Have I answered your questions well enough?"

"No. There's one more thing. Why didn't you tell me all this before? Why didn't you tell me I could change at will, if that really is the truth?"

"Oh, sugar, I don't know. You seemed to get into enough trouble changing just once a month. Stefan and I couldn't imagine what all you'd get into if you found out you could do this any old time you liked."

"You talked about it? You conspired to keep this from me?"

"Conspired. What a naughty word. What we did was counsel each other on the pros and cons of how to handle your raising. You're young, impetuous, spontaneous, and, let's face it, you've got a chip on your shoulder when it comes to the whole 'fairness' issue. Look at how sloppy you got in Doe Springs, leaving bodies lying around for the police to find, only because you wanted to make a statement on justice. And now, despite nearly getting caught, here you are again, back in North Carolina like everybody would have just forgotten about you by now and you can start your crusading all over again.

"Werewolves should be discreet, Ivy. I've hunted in western North Carolina for years without a soul being the wiser. Even you." Ava tugged her housecoat tighter about her shoulders and looked at Ivy smugly.

A loose cannon, that's how Aunt Ava and Uncle Stefan saw her. Ivy couldn't believe it. She'd spent a lifetime proud of her masterful handling of her lupine abilities and the choices she'd made. Yet here she was, the subject of others' concern about her discretion, or lack of. It sounded just like how Ivy felt about her own daughter, and the way she worried about Luna not having boundaries and good sense.

"I mean really, Ivy," Ava continued, "sometimes it's as if you have no boundaries and good sense."

Ivy jerked, a little startled. No matter how mad she got at the widow, somehow the elderly lady always managed to regain the upper hand and leave Ivy feeling like a reprimanded addle-brained schoolgirl.

She wouldn't let Ava get away with it this time. "I have to be alone, Ava. I have to sort through everything you've said. I don't know whether to feel hurt or just sick to my stomach."

"How about neither? I'd think you'd feel grateful."

Ivy pushed back her chair. She stood over the widow, her silhouette framed by the window behind her. Outside, the night was dimly illuminated by the streetlamp's glow, which had brightened at the conclusion of the storm. Orange eyes flickered out of the darkness, and the widow's sparked in return.

"You're contemplating dangerous thoughts," Ava said mildly. "Careful, dear."

A thin smile spread across Ivy's lips. "Good night, Ava."

She walked to her bedroom and shut the door.

PART IV

"Hello, love. I've come for you."

42

LUNA HUMMED to herself in her bedroom. What a magical day lay ahead—her first field trip with the school and her new friends, off to a beach she'd not been to before. She packed her backpack carefully—there were important things she could not forget. Her towel. Her sunglasses with daisy rims. Her friendship bracelet that Cory Rinehart wove for her out of yarn. She glanced at the terrarium on the dresser across the room. Would Mup like the ocean? She scooped the turtle out of the tank and packed him too.

Cali nudged Luna in the side. "I know, sweet girl. I wish you could go with us." She wrapped her arms around the wolf's neck. "But I can't get you into my backpack. There's only room for Mup, see?"

She held up the powder blue bag with navy trim. Cali was not interested. Her raisin eyes were only for Luna. She wagged her tail and licked the child's face.

"Luna, c'mon! It's seven-thirty already!" Ivy called up the stairs.

Luna threw the pack over her shoulder and scampered down to the dining room where Ivy awaited with sunscreen. She lifted Luna's long T-shirt and slathered the cream around the ties of her bathing suit.

"Mommy, I don't like it." Luna tried to squirm away.

"You'll like sunburn even less, now hold still." Ivy caught Luna's arm and rubbed sunscreen down her other side. Then she popped the lid back on the SPF 45 and opened the backpack to put it inside. She looked up. "Luna, what is this?" She reached in and pulled out the turtle. His legs waved in all directions before realizing his vulnerability and sucking into his shell.

"It's Mup."

"Sweetheart, Mup is a tortoise, a land turtle. You can't take him into the ocean. Besides, pets aren't allowed in school. You don't want to get in trouble with Mrs. Flannigan, do you?"

Luna shook her head, her ponytail bobbing.

"Okay, then. Now go put him back and for Pete's sake, hurry. We're going to be late!"

Luna ran up the stairs, Mup curled in her fist and Cali on her heels. The toaster dinged and Ivy snatched the two oven-tanned pieces of bread. She looked at the kitchen clock: 7:38. No time to eat here, Luna would have to down breakfast on the way. She spread the bread with a thick layer of peanut butter as she went through the day's agenda in her head. *Wrap up toast. Pack in the bag. School's providing lunch. Drop off at eight a.m., pick up at four. Child must provide own towel, check.*

"Luna, it's almost eight. We've got to go!"

"Quit hollering, Mommy! I'm using the bathroom!" the muffled voice from upstairs shouted back.

Someone was banging on the front door.

"You've got to be kidding." Ivy wiped her hands on a dishtowel and strode through the living room.

Melvin Sanders stared through the screen, his hand cupped against it to better see inside.

"Melvin! What are you doing here?"

"I'm sorry it's so early, but can I come in?" He shuffled about on the other side of the door, looking much better than when Ivy saw him last. His face was cleanly shaven and his hair, although still in need of a barber, was slicked back neatly.

Ivy felt something brush her leg. Aufhocker was by her side.

"No you cannot come in. This is a bad time."

"I know. You're worried about the Widow Pritchard. I should have called and warned you I was coming."

"It's not about Ava. Ava is gone."

"Mommy, where are you? I'm ready now. Oh! He's back. See, Mommy, I told you he was a giant." Luna crowded in between Auf and Ivy, with Cali hanging in the background.

Melvin's eyes lit up. He squatted to the child's level to stare at her through the screen.

"Luna. Luna. I can't believe it. You're Luna." He smiled and put his palm against the mesh. Luna raised her hand to touch his, but Ivy grabbed her wrist.

"Honey, go on out through the kitchen and wait for me in the Jeep, okay?"

Luna nodded. She turned slowly, looking over her shoulder at the stranger on the porch.

"Go on, Luna. I mean it."

Luna disappeared through the dining room. Melvin reached for the screen latch, but Ivy grasped it from the other side and held it closed. "No, Melvin. I said not now. This isn't how I wanted you to meet her."

"She's my daughter too. I have to see her."

Ivy rolled her eyes and resisted the urge to yank open the door and smack him. "Look, I don't have time to fight over this again, and you've got some nerve shanghaiing me unprepared anyway. Luna and I are leaving, and I'll deal with you later."

"Everything all right?" Caleb walked up the steps behind Melvin.

And Ivy's nerves went straight to the wood chipper, splintering beyond repair. Melvin and Caleb. Together. On her doorstep at—what?—seven-forty-five a.m., fifteen minutes before her daughter's field trip and a lifetime too late for either one of them. Caleb, she thought she could have loved. Melvin, she once and probably still did. But the only thing that mattered in her life right now was about to miss the most talked about event of her first school year, and Ivy wouldn't let that disappointment happen. After this one magical day on the beach, Luna would come home and they would pack to move again. The broken pieces of Ivy's fractured life stood on her front porch, and she slammed the interior door on both of them.

Ivy grabbed her keys and headed for the kitchen. Luna still stood there, trying to appear inconspicuous as she peeked around the corner.

"All right, kiddo, train's leaving the station. Let's go."

"Finally!" Luna slung the backpack over her shoulder and clapped her hands. They walked onto the side deck and Cali nudged her big head through the door before Ivy could close it. "No, Cali, stay." The wolf worked her broad shoulders through and whined after the little girl climbing into the Jeep. Cali's separation anxiety wasn't usually this bad on a school day.

"No, Cali. Get back."

The wolf fought more frantically to squeeze through the opening Ivy was determined to close. She began to howl after Luna, her front claws digging into the hardwood of the deck and her back legs scrambling against linoleum. Auf appeared just behind her and he too began trying to shove through the door.

"What has gotten into everybody this morning?" There was no time to reprimand disobedient canines. For all Ivy knew, the field trip bus was already pulling out of the elementary school parking lot, and Caleb and Melvin were duking it out on her front porch. She wanted out of here before they took it around back.

"Come on, then. Load up!" Ivy swung the door wide and both wolves galloped for the Jeep. They bounded into the back and Ivy climbed in after them.

"Buckle up, Boo. We got to motor."

Melvin and Caleb had not spoken since Ivy closed the door in their faces. They were at an impasse of sorts, each standing his ground and wondering what the other was about. They both turned as the Jeep backed down the side of the house and onto the street. Auf and Cali shared the cramped back seat, Luna's little blond head barely visible in front of them. She spied the two men on the front porch.

"Caleb! Mommy, it's Caleb!" She waved to him as the vehicle bounced into the road and grinded into gear. Caleb waved back as the Jeep zipped down Battery, Ivy staring stonily ahead and the two bewildered men looking after her.

43

"Mrs. Flannigan! Mrs. Flannigan!" Ivy and Luna ran hand in hand across the school parking lot. The last student had just boarded Bus 58, and Mrs. Flannigan's foot was on the bottom step. Her head turned their direction, and Ivy saw her say something to the driver.

The duo reached her, out of breath.

"I was afraid you weren't coming," Mrs. Flannigan said. Her auburn curls were piled on top of her head this morning in a youthful, casual do, the vibrantly merry hair topping her round face like the spiral top on an ice-cream sundae. Ivy could see the outline of a flowery one-piece bathing suit under the teacher's white blouse and blue skort, which had a hem of smiley-faced apples dancing around her dimpled knees.

"Sorry we're late."

"Late? I'd say you're just in time. Luna, are you ready for the ocean?"

Luna smiled brightly at her teacher and nodded.

"Hop on the bus, then."

Ivy, relieved she'd not failed her child this morning, waved from the Jeep as Bus 58 pulled from the parking lot. Luna appeared at a window and waved back once, then her ponytail was to the glass as another child sat in the seat beside her. Luna was suddenly lost in her friend and the excitement of the day ahead, and Ivy had that pang again, the one of disconnect she felt before, knowing her daughter was stretching the apron strings until they snapped.

"There she goes, guys. Our little girl, off on her first trip without us. How 'bout that?"

Cali answered Ivy with a whine as her muzzle turned to follow the retreating bus.

Ivy reached around to scratch her head. "It's all right, girl. Nothing different today from any other day. Luna will be home this afternoon."

But Cali wasn't listening. She stiffened under Ivy's hand, and her tinny complaint crescendoed into a piercing lament.

"Cali, quiet! For heaven's sake, what is wrong with you today?"

The wolf did not care to discuss it. Her haunches bunched and she leaped from the Jeep. She was running as soon as her paws hit pavement.

"Cali!" Ivy screamed. She cranked the Wrangler and took off after the wolf. Cali stopped at the edge of the school blacktop, the bus already out of sight.

Ivy pulled up beside her. "Cali, come. Calopus, come!"

Cali stood erect, head high, legs square, and back a taut line from neck to tail. Her whole body strained toward the bus's direction even from a standstill, willing it to come back. But the road was deserted and Ivy's voice was but a small sparrow in the back of her mind. She bounded into the road, her long sturdy legs clawing at the pavement and propelling her to forty miles an hour before Ivy could get the Jeep in gear again.

"Cali!" It was no use. The bus was gone around the bend, Luna's wolf disappearing right after it.

44

Bus 58 pulled into the Loggerhead Beach public access behind two other buses from Salty Duck Elementary. Grades K through three spilled out after their teachers and parental chaperones. Ivy had not been invited to chaperone on purpose: Mrs. Flannigan felt strongly that Luna needed time away from her mother, a lady whom she found impossible to label. An educator for fifteen years and a certified school counselor before that, Mrs. Flannigan could sum up a child's home life within fifteen minutes of meeting the parents. But with Luna, it had been different. Ivy had seemed overly protective and clingy that first day of class, but then Luna's behavior seemed to indicate just the opposite: complete lack of attention and supervision at home. It was a conundrum Mrs. Flannigan felt determined to unravel—but not today. Today was about R and R, something she got very little of. With the help of the other teachers and parent volunteers, she planned to enjoy this field trip every bit as much as her giddy young brood of kindergartners.

Mrs. Flannigan was picturing herself laid flat on a cushy mound of hot sand, when Luna filed past her and off the bus. Orvis Rotterman and Eddie Bremmer were close behind, and Orvis was making a point to poke Luna in the back of the neck with each step.

"Orvis!"

The boy looked up at the teacher, a wily expression on his freckled face. He was going to be a menace as a teenager, Mrs. Flannigan was sure of it. *His* home life had been an easy picture to configure: spoiled beyond reproach with not a rule to live by nor a single boundary in place to guide him. His mother had chastised Mrs. Flannigan soundly for trying to govern the ungovernable when he'd been in her class, and Mrs. Flannigan was grateful that the third-grade teacher had not invited Mrs. Rotterman to join them on the outing.

Behind Orvis and his sidekick Eddie came Cory Rinehart huddled up with Neena and Teena Holloway. Cory had left Luna's seat only ten minutes into the bus ride and apparently taken up ranks with the twins shortly after. The teacher noticed Luna's wrist was bare; Cory had reclaimed her friendship bracelet too it seemed.

Mrs. Flannigan shook her head as Luna, a lonely little sprite now, took up her place in line alongside the bus. Her expression was much more somber than twenty minutes ago when they'd left school, and Mrs. Flannigan sighed. This was how it had been during the girl's short tenure in kindergarten. She drew friends easily, she just couldn't keep them, and Mrs. Flannigan couldn't understand why. Had she bitten Cory too, while the teacher's back was to the riders on the bus?

Ah well, just something else to sort out later. Overhead the cerulean sky mirrored the calm azure of the Atlantic, and the sun warmed the day to a toasty eighty-four degrees. The day couldn't have been more perfect for the annual Salty Duck Elementary beach trip and the only real field trip of the whole year. Nothing was going to ruin it.

"Attention, everyone! Attention! Do not lose hands with the person in front of you until we get onto the beach. Stay in line with your group, and we're going to let the third-graders go first. Is everybody ready for some fun in the sun?" Mr. Bennett, vice principal and parent to three third-graders himself, announced to the mixed group of children and adults.

"Yeah!" a chorus of voices rang out, upsetting a flock of gulls on the dunes that blocked the parking lot from the ocean.

Mr. Bennett clapped his hands in approval, and the kids were on the move. It was a wobbly, herky-jerky, backpack-laden, bubbly string of chattering children all grasping hands and dragging each other along to the beach. The classes climbed the steep steps over the dune ridge impediment and broke on the other side into pandemonium. Kids dropped hands and rushed like raiding Indians onto the unprotected shore. It would be an exhausting day for the grown-ups, keeping all the excited fishies within the confines of the school's invisible net.

And, just like schools of fish, errant children began to slowly cluster again in colorful, tropical-clad groups and secretive, giggling pairs. The teachers and parents got settled too, on beach towels and under hut-sized umbrellas. Mrs. Flannigan began to strip down to her own ocean digs, when she noticed Luna, still alone and hanging back by the dunes. Finally, the child approached the ocean and sat by its lapping edge. Some of the parents carried large bags down the beach, from which they distributed pails and shovels. Mr. Bremmer handed Luna one of these, the blinding green of the plastic matching the lime in her suit. He moved on with his Santa sack, and Luna settled down in the sand with what appeared to be the mission of building a sand castle.

Satisfied the child was occupied, Mrs. Flannigan unfolded her own towel and lowered heavily onto the warm, white ground. She would let Luna get her castle underway, then perhaps round up some other children to help her with moat construction. As for now, the sun felt just fine on Mrs. Flannigan's ruddy skin, and she closed her eyes beneath the rim of her favorite floppy hat to doze.

45

Luna dug hard in the sand, her lime green plastic shovel nearly bending double. She'd worked here diligently—alone—for a good thirty minutes, getting everything just right. The towers, the thick walls, the entrance to the castle where the prince could ride his noble steed right inside and get pounced upon by the hiding wolves, who were only trying to defend themselves against the prince's cruel bow.

At least, that was the story Luna was devising in her head, until the tide began rolling rapidly in and lapping at the edges of her toil-heavy fortress. She would lose it to the sea before finishing if...

"Luna Goona, smells like a tuna."

...if Orvis Rotterman did not leave her alone. *Be good. Be good. Mommy says to always be good.*

"Did you hear me, Tuna Luna?"

Orvis Rotterman was eight years old, three years older than Luna, who now sat huddled protectively over her painstaking creation. Three years older, twice as hateful, and about to get it ten times as bad.

Be good! Mommy's voice screamed in the little girl's ear. She'd been hearing that a lot lately, could see her mother standing over her with that doubtful look on her face. *A field trip alone, on Luna's own, with strangers no less? Risky, risky.* "Can you handle it, Boo? Can you make Mommy proud of you by being good?" That's what Mommy'd said, while waving the picture Luna had painted in class and citing the *incident* with the Holloway twins, whom Luna decidedly did not like anymore any-ole-ways. In fact, they could have Cory too, for all she cared. She was doing just fine on her own, determined to make the best of it and not mess up. Not today, on her very first field trip a whole twenty minutes away from home. She was growing up, and she was determined to prove to her mother that she *could* handle it, that she was, indeed, a big girl now, friends or no friends.

All that being said, it was particularly unfair that Orvis Rotterman should be part of the picture.

"She's deaf," Orvis said to Eddie Bremmer, who'd just shown up with chocolate ice cream dripping off his chin and feeding from the bottom of his cone down his elbow.

"Hey!" Orvis bent over, his red-freckled face inches from the sand-dollar-colored ponytail that wouldn't tilt back and show the teary-eyed face of a terrified kid. That's what he expected and always received from the little runts when he could get them out from under their teachers' skirts.

Be good. Luna's shovel gouged even harder into the sand by her knees. *Count to one hundred, and he'll go away.*

"That's the ugliest castle I've ever seen." Orvis was still bent over, trying to get his cheese-wedge slice of nose underneath the girl's bangs to have a better look at her. He figured she was about ready to spout tears like the spray from a whale's blowhole.

*One, two, three, four...*Sand fanned out from under Luna's quickly burrowing shovel.

"Stupid old ugly sand castle." Orvis reached out a dirt-browned toe and nudged a corner of the northern tower. Sand sprinkled down its formidable twelve-inch turret.

*Five, six, seven, eight...*Sand, dig, sand, dig.

"Stupid old ugly house." Orvis's toe pushed in deeper, and the tower shifted again but held; more sand spilled on his foot.

Oh, be good. Be good. Please be good. Nine, ten, eleven, twelve...

"Stupid old ugly Tuna Luna!" Orvis's foot swept the tower clean away, kicking it into the ocean waves.

Luna watched the rest of the castle crumble, all her hard work destroyed. She clutched the plastic shovel until her fingers turned bloodless, while numbers tumbled over each other in a jumbled, out-of-order mishmash in her head. *Fourteen, seventeen, forty-eight, twenty-three...*

Orvis did not notice the inner struggle in front of him and was rather disappointed by the girl's nonreaction. He looked around for another source of torment. Finding no one else of interest nearby, the boy's beady gaze landed on Luna's backpack. "Looky, Eddie, what's this?"

Eddie took a studiously long lick from his ice-cream cone before answering. He and Luna had had run-ins before, the last of which left him plowed into the dirt at the bottom of the monkey bars nursing a sprained arm. Payback versus self-preservation quarreled in his young brain. He opted for the latter. "Leave her alone, Orvis. Let's go play somewheres else."

But Orvis already had the pack in hand and was unzipping all the pockets. He'd get a rise out of the new girl at school or at least get some extra ice-cream money one. Eddie's cone was looking pretty good in this heat, and he didn't want to beat up his best friend right yet to get it. But it was not money he found secured in the side zippered pocket.

"Oh cool!" A reedy grin split Orvis's red cheeks, and Eddie came over to peer inside.

Luna stood up and grabbed at the backpack, but Orvis snatched it away. He pulled out the prize and held it aloft, high over Luna's head. The turtle drew into its shell at the first touch of light on its reptilian skin.

"Don't you hurt him! Don't you hurt Mup!" Luna jumped to reach the tortoise, but Orvis just laughed and pushed her away. She fell, scraping her knees when she hit the ground.

"Mup! What a dumb name for a turtle. You like this ugly old scaly lizard, huh, Tuna Luna?" He loomed over the kindergartner, who was sniffling at last and rubbing her bloody knees.

"You better leave him alone, Orvis." Luna's eyes were downcast, her voice was low. She mumbled to herself. It sounded like counting.

"Or what, Tuna Luna? Here, Eddie, catch!" Orvis tossed the tortoise at the unexpecting boy, who barely caught it. The chocolate cone tilted precariously, but Eddie recovered and held it, ice cream in one hand, turtle in the other.

"I don't want it. Here, Luna, take your nasty old turtle and get out of here." Eddie bent to hand the pet over, but Orvis jumped forward and snatched him back.

"No! Mup is *my* turtle now, and you know what I'm going to do with him, Tuna Luna? Huh, do ya? Do you know?" He wiggled the brown and yellow shell back and forth. "I'm going to see if your only friend in the whole wide world can swim."

Before Luna could find her feet again, Orvis wound up dramatically and whirled Mup into the waves.

Luna gasped as she watched the little tortoise fly end over end in the air and disappear into the roiling water. Standing above her with his hands on his hips, Orvis Rotterman began to laugh.

"You shouldn't have done that," Luna said quietly, the words crippled by a snarl she no longer fought to suppress.

"What's that, Tuna Luna?" Orvis leaned over, his mealy face in hers once more.

Luna slowly looked up at the boy, her bangs parting way to reveal shimmering eyes the color of boiling lava. Still in her grasp, the lime plastic shovel nosedived into the sand a final time and broke in two.

I'm sorry, Mommy.

Luna bolted upright and cocked back a fist in the same motion. Before Orvis could close the surprised gaping "O" of his spiteful mouth, a handful of sand was shoved into it. Then Luna stomped his foot with her hard-soled flip-flop and when the boy bent double, gagging, she grabbed both ears and wrenched his head toward her. Flaming eyes lunged for his face as Luna latched on to the boy's nose and bit down hard.

• • •

Mrs. Flannigan was reading a story, one of diaphanous Milky Way currents, brilliant, quavering stars, and orbiting planets with elflike inhabitants who spoke in the lyrical intonations of...

Shrieking. High-pitched little kid shrieking, to be exact.

Mrs. Flannigan, abruptly time-warped back to planet Earth, stared down Loggerhead Beach toward the noise and directly into the glare of the dazzling sun, blinding her for one disorienting minute. Somebody streaked past her, kicking up sand—it was Eddie Bremmer, terror on his face and chocolate ice cream streaming down his elbow. *A child is drowning. Oh God!* She flung her dog-eared paperback aside and was running toward the noise before it even registered to her protesting body that she had not run anywhere since she was sixteen years old.

Then she saw them, ahead of her, Luna and another child huddled close together as if embracing in a kiss. But as she drew closer, she could see it was only one child screaming and that was Orvis Rotterman, his head held firmly captive by the tender nose clamped in Luna's teeth.

Mrs. Flannigan pounded faster down the beach. Her floppy hat flew off behind her, but she let the sea have it. "Luna! Luna Cole, stop it right now! You let go of Orvis, do you hear me, child? Luna, I said let him go!"

Luna did, and Orvis stood straight up, still screaming and holding the reddened protrusion. He took one look at Mrs. Flannigan, then ran crying down the beach to find his own teacher.

Mrs. Flannigan sucked air and released it like a bellows. Her overweight heart was not meant for such excitement, and she held her side until she could catch enough wind to speak. Luna did not move, just stared up at her teacher with angelic innocence. To Mrs. Flannigan's horror, a perfect ruby pearl of blood balanced on Luna's lower lip. Luna wiped her mouth with the back of her arm, smearing it away.

The teacher struggled between absolute fury and pity. Her class had been topsy-turvy since Luna's arrival, and after this stunt today, she wondered if the girl wouldn't be better served in a special needs class of some kind, or at least put under psychiatric counseling. It was baffling, Luna's behavior with other children. She would share her toys with any student, then attack them viciously when they did not share her point of view. She was a gracious winner and loser in games, but sent Nelson Potts to nurse's aid with a serious kick to the groin when she thought he stole an extra card during a spirited round of Old Maid.

Mrs. Flannigan had tried to explain to Luna that she could not always have her way. Luna had reciprocated with a rather mature argument about right, wrong, and the blurry lines on each of those when it came to *fair*. And her idea of making fair involved a certain amount of bruising and bloodletting. It was reprehensible and heart-breaking at once.

But lessons had to be learned and all children had to be protect-ed—even the rotten ones like Orvis Rotterman. That was the teacher's job, and as bad as she hated to do it, strong action was in order.

"Luna—"

"Are you okay, Mrs. Flannigan?" The little girl was still peering up at her, concern etched on her sweet face. "Do you want me to get some help?" She put her hand on the teacher's arm as if to help steady her.

"No, I'm...I'm all right. Thank you. What happened here?"

"My sand castle. Look what he did to it." Luna motioned to the ground, where there was nothing left but a lumpy heap quickly dis-solving in salted waves.

"You bit Orvis because he knocked down your sand castle?"

"Yes, ma'am. He should not have been so mean to me."

What Luna really wanted to tell Mrs. Flannigan, she knew she couldn't: that Orvis Rotterman was a turtle killer and was about to get a whole lot worse than a bite on the nose if the teacher hadn't come hollering up the beach right when she did.

Luna looked up at her teacher resolutely and held in the sad tears that yearned to fall.

Mrs. Flannigan looked down at the little girl in return while her heartbeat finally slowed and her open-mouthed, goggle-eyed gasping revved down with it. She managed one final, breathless sigh, not out of exasperation but rather, a kind of dolefulness. Luna really did not understand what she had done wrong. It was Orvis's fault, as the girl saw it, and he should have known better.

"Nevertheless, what did I tell you the last time you attacked somebody? Remember? When you pushed Eddie Bremmer off the monkey bars?"

"But he stole Cory's doll and stuck it up there!"

"What did I tell you?" Mrs. Flannigan, re-collected once more, was obviously very angry, her tone firm and pointedly authoritative.

"You said to come to you before I do anything to punish somebody on my own." Luna's voice was getting smaller, lost in the call of the gulls and the ocean wind and the shadow of the woman towering over her with fists on her hips and her hair set wild on her jouncy run down the beach.

"No! What I said was for you to come to me before you *attack* somebody on your own. It's a little different. And did you do that?"

Luna shook her downcast head. Her feet furrowed divots that immediately refilled with liquid sand. She fidgeted until she finally had to say something because Mrs. Flannigan was waiting.

"I'm sorry," she whispered, and Mrs. Flannigan almost believed her. For certain, the teacher felt terrible for what she was being forced to do.

"I'm sorry too, Luna, but that's it for you, young lady. How many times have I told you, no biting the other children! I have warned you and warned your mother repeatedly about hitting, kicking, and *especially* biting, and this is the last straw. You need to learn the consequences of your actions. Come on, we're going to call your mother to come get you right now."

Mrs. Flannigan reached for the slender arm, but another hand reached out and stayed hers instead. Mrs. Flannigan, expecting to see Orvis's teacher or an angry chaperone, maybe even Mr. Bremmer, who was familiar with Luna's antics already, was surprised at seeing a stranger standing beside her.

"That won't be necessary, Mrs. Flannigan. It's quite all right. I'll take her."

Mrs. Flannigan took in the tall, clean-cut handsome man who

had materialized beside them. He wore tailored slacks and a designer shirt, and the timbre of his voice was particularly soothing. After the hectic drama that had just unfolded, Mrs. Flannigan was about fed up enough to turn over the girl with no questions asked. The man looked nice enough.

But Mrs. Flannigan was a good teacher after all, and that miniscule fantasy was as likely to happen as the saga unfolding in the science-fiction novel she was previously reading. This day was just full of unending surprises.

"And who might you be, sir?"

"You mean you don't know? I'm surprised Ivy hasn't told you."

Mrs. Flannigan shook her head. "I'm sorry, but I don't know you."

"My name is Mr. Cain."

"Are you related to Luna?"

"You might say that," the man said. He squatted eye level to the little girl, unmindful that his expensive leather loafers were being soiled by wet sand. "I'm her father."

46

Mr. Cain winked at Luna and stood to face the teacher again.

"Her father? No, Ms. Cole never mentioned you," Mrs. Flannigan said. Pity that. Now this looked like the kind of structured role model a child like Luna required. "I was given the impression Ms. Cole was a single mother."

"She is—now. Divorce is such an unfortunate thing, especially at times like these. I'm afraid there's been a family emergency. Ivy called for me to pick up Luna for her."

"I'm so sorry to hear that. I hope Ms. Cole is all right?"

"She's fine. It's her aunt, Ava. They're at the hospital."

"Well, this is very irregular, Mr. Cain. The only person Ivy has authorized to pick up Luna is her brother, Jack."

"Ah, Jack. Well, it's unfortunate a mother would put her brother down on record and skip the actual father of the child, isn't it? Divorces can be so ugly, but Ivy always did know how to hurt me like no one else could. Backfired on her this time, I suppose. Do you think, just for this one time, we could break the rules? It's not Luna's fault she has parents at war, and her Aunt Ava may not have very long." He leaned forward and whispered over Luna's head. "Stroke. She's ninety-two, God love the dear thing."

Mrs. Flannigan had never been more uncertain. This was a terrible position to be in. Here was this kind man just wanting to help his family, help an ex-wife who obviously let deplorable, abusive men into the home and used her own daughter as a weapon against the father, and yet, school policy was school policy. She couldn't just send Luna off with an unauthorized adult, even if he was the girl's closest kin. And as upstanding as he seemed, Mrs. Flannigan was not a naïve fool. Appearances could be deceiving. What if the man had a restraining order against him? What if Mr. Cain were the cause of the bruises she'd seen on Ms. Cole's arms and not some loutish boyfriend after all? But a hospital emergency, a beloved relative on death's very doorstep...It was all completely frazzling.

While Mrs. Flannigan's inner dialogue quarreled over the vexing dilemma, Luna noted the teacher's pinched expression and knew she had to do something. A reprimand was still forthcoming if "Mr. Cain" did not win this argument. Indian Summer Safari had turned out to be absolutely no fun at all and tragic at best, and she was ready to go anywhere else but here—as long as her mother didn't have to know about it.

"Daddy!" Luna flung her arms around the man's legs and started to cry. "Will Aunt Ava be all right?"

"I hope so, honey. She's at a very good hospital, but we need to get to her as quickly as we can. She's holding on for us to get there." He put a hand on the teacher's shoulder. "Please, Mrs. Flannigan, we need to go right away."

No, no, no. Don't do this to me, Mrs. Flannigan's inner dialogue pleaded. *I was supposed to have a peaceful, relaxing day. Why do things like this always have to happen? Let them go, and I could lose my job. Make Luna stay, and Luna could lose a relative without getting to say good-bye. It's all so unfair. Mr. Bennett!*

"I know this is inconvenient," Mrs. Flannigan blurted, her mind made up, "but you will have to wait until I can get this cleared with the vice principal. Fortunately, he's here with us today. Please understand, it's school policy."

"Of course," Mr. Cain said tersely. He dropped his hand from her shoulder.

"Mrs. Flannigan! Elsa!" Mr. Ed Bremmer was jogging up the beach toward them. "There you are. There's been some kind of row with the Rotterman boy, and Eddie's saying he saw the whole thing. The third-grade teacher is looking for you."

Mrs. Flannigan blanched. "I'm well aware of the row. Luna caused it. Oh, never mind. Is Mr. Bennett up there? I need to speak with him as well."

"They're by the school buses with the first-aid kit. They've called the school nurse as a precaution, and Mrs. Rotterman is on the way. She's hopping mad."

"Oh my." Mrs. Flannigan visibly grimaced. She could swear she just felt all of her insides shrivel up into cords of dried jerky. "There's a problem you should be aware of, Mr. Cain. Your daughter has a penchant for biting children, and today she really attacked the wrong one. Not to say, just between us, he didn't deserve it. I'll take all this up with you and Ms. Cole at a better time, but if you need to get out of here quick, I suggest you wait here while I speak with Vice-Principal Bennett alone. If Mrs. Rotterman is over there, you'll be tangled up in a dramatic, time-consuming mess." She turned to Bremmer. "Can you wait with Mr. Cain while I go talk to Mr. Bennett and make a phone call? I promise I won't be longer than a few minutes."

"Glad to help. That's what I'm here for today," Bremmer said.

Mrs. Flannigan hustled down the beach and vanished between the dunes. Bremmer rocked back on his heels and eyed the man and the child clinging to his leg. He noticed Luna had gone abruptly dry-eyed the second the teacher turned her back and hightailed it away from them.

"So you're daddy of the biter?" he said.

Cain pursed his lips but held a reply.

"You know," Bremmer continued, "she pushed my boy off the monkey bars at school. Liked to busted his arm. Didn't, but liked to."

"Is that right." Cain looked at his watch. Mrs. Flannigan was well out of sight.

"She got a mean streak or what? I mean, that's some temper, pushing kids off jungle gyms and biting noses off and all."

"I didn't bite it off, Daddy," Luna retorted.

"She gets it from her mother," Cain said. "Look, we have a family emergency, and I have to take my daughter to the hospital right now. Will you give Mrs. Flannigan my regrets because I just can't stand around here waiting anymore."

"Oh! Well, sure, sure. If you've got an emergency and all."

"I appreciate it."

Mr. Cain lifted Luna and headed off down the beach in the opposite direction.

Fifteen minutes later, Mrs. Flannigan, accompanied by a husky man with a goatee and wearing cowboy boots, came huffing back. Her face scowled the closer she got to Bremmer, who'd taken up residence on a vacated beach towel and was wearing her floppy hat. He squinted up as the pair approached.

"Ed, what are you doing?"

"What—this?" He gave the hat a good snap with his fingers. "I found it washed up on the beach over there. Looks like it's in good condition."

"Not that! Where is Mr. Cain?"

"Oh, him. He left. Said he had a family emergency."

"You let him go?"

"I could hardly stop him. He was the girl's father, what was I supposed to do? Tackle him?"

The man beside Mrs. Flannigan lifted the brim of Bremmer's hat and peered into his face. "Where did they go?"

"I don't know," Bremmer said. He didn't like the way this fella was handling his new hat, particularly because his head was still in it. But by the look on the big guy's face, he thought better than to bring it up.

"They're going to the hospital," Mrs. Flannigan repeated. She had told him that already, back when he'd shown up in the parking lot right behind the irate Mrs. Rotterman, who was back there flogging poor Mr. Bennett right now with threats of lawsuits and News Channel 12. The only answer Mrs. Flannigan had managed to wrangle from the vice principal before the Rotterman onslaught began was, "Call her mother, I've got my hands full right now!"

"Did he say anything to you different?" the man asked Bremmer.

Bremmer didn't care for the other man's tone either—there was a slight inflection there, some wackadoo accent he couldn't put his finger on—but at least the man had released his hat. There was something about those eyes too, like they were analyzing him from the inside out. And the inappropriate dress for the coast—boots on the beach? No, this old boy weren't from around here, that was for sure. Bremmer hated out-of-towners as much as the next local, and this one didn't even have the decency to act like a regular tourist. And yet, the peculiar package rang a familiar bell....

"Do I know you, buddy? You look awful familiar."

"No," the stranger said through gritted teeth. "Did Cain mention anything other than the hospital?"

Bremmer strained to think. Nope, Cain hadn't told Bremmer anything else; Cain acted like he didn't want to talk to Bremmer much period. But Bremmer was a father too, and he understood. It was a family emergency. But then something came to him. It might not be much help, but...

"Wait, yeah, there is something," he said. "When they were walking away, the little girl was talking about...well, it was hard to make out with the wind and all."

"What? What did she say?"

"I could have sworn she asked her dad something about a boat. Does that make any sense at all?"

The stranger smiled. He straightened up and strode down the beach without another word to either one of them.

"That was rude." Bremmer readjusted Mrs. Flannigan's floppy hat where the stranger had messed with it. "He could have at least said thank you."

Mrs. Flannigan didn't seem to be listening. She was too busy wringing her hands and watching after the retreating man. He made a sharp left into another dune easement and disappeared.

"You look like you just swallowed a goldfish, Elsa. What's wrong with you?"

"I don't know what's wrong, that's the trouble," Mrs. Flannigan said. "I couldn't reach Ms. Cole on the phone, and right after I got back to the bus, that man showed up to get Luna too. He was very angry Mr. Cain was here ahead of him, and he didn't know anything about the aunt."

"Just who was that supposed to be anyway?"

"That was Jack Cole, Luna's uncle."

"Well, I've seen him about, and I'm trying to place him. Wait," Bremmer said, snapping his fingers, "The Bluewater Lady. He's a waiter over there, only I could swear they call him something different. Cage, Page, I dunno. Something odd. Odd name for an odder duck—reckon that's the only reason I remembered."

Mrs. Flannigan looked even more uncertain. "Something is not sitting right with me about any of this. I'm wondering if we should call the police."

"I am the police," Sheriff Gloria Hubbard said from behind them. "What seems to be the problem?"

47

EARLIER THAT morning, while Ivy Cole was rushing to get her child ready for Indian Summer Safari, Sheriff Gloria Hubbard was sitting on the edge of her thirty-dollar-a-night bed awaiting the alarm to go off. Her eyes were open, grim slits in the musty gloom of the cheap hotel room, and they had been that way all night. Sleep refused to come again, but this time her own conscience was keeping it at bay. Gloria was a sheriff of the law, but today the law would be no more. She would have to live with her actions the rest of her life and always wonder if there could have been a better way, a *lawful* way, to have handled this situation.

Gloria's night had been spent in thought on that fact. And thought of all the missing in Doe Springs who had turned up as corpses. About all the blood and rendered limbs and endless terror that was wrought upon her town. About the evil that had taken Tee and Annie by forces that she herself could never explain, let alone get an outsider to believe.

And therein was where law ended and justice would have to be found another way. Plausibility was not on her side; one had to feel the teeth of the wolf at their throat to understand the truth, to accept the irrational, to know that the thing creeping in the dark is not merely a harmless shadow and one's own overactive imagination. No, Gloria had learned the hard way about the credibility of monsters.

So *could* the righteous sheriff live with her actions today, actions that marked her, in her own eyes, as a monster as well?

Gloria caressed the barrel of the .38 in her lap. The alarm buzzed annoyingly. After hours of sitting here patiently waiting, it was finally time to go.

Gloria parked in her usual spot down the street from Ivy Cole's cottage. She knew the morning schedule by heart: Ivy Cole did not let the little one ride the bus—no, she was chauffeured by her mother each morning, then picked up again after school. Mother and daughter generally left the house around seven-thirty, but by the looks of things this morning, they were getting a late start. The Wrangler was still in the driveway and...

What's this?

Gloria scooted forward in her seat, leaning over the steering wheel. She could not believe what she was seeing, and yet, she should not have been all that surprised. Her former deputy, Melvin Sanders, was walking up the steps to the front door. Gloria watched as he had words with Ivy through the screen, and anger seeped into her a.m. malaise. Sanders knew where Ivy was, but for how long? Had they been corresponding since their time in Doe Springs and he left the department to come join her at last? Or had he found her after years of searching and just now confronted her much as she herself planned to do?

It was a question she'd never get to ask the former deputy, for Sheriff Hubbard, to all who would ask, was on vacation in south Florida right now. But here was knowledge that would bother her for years to come. She didn't know whether to feel betrayed or unexpectedly allied. Where did Sanders's heart lie after all these years?

Gloria knew that at one time, it had lain with a white wolf and near-ly cost them all their lives. And seeing him right here on her doorstep did not bode well under any circumstances. Men who loved deeply often did deeply stupid things, even when they thought they might be "over it." Gloria wasn't convinced Sanders ever got over Ivy Cole, even when a darkness grew in him after her departure like a baneful disease.

While Gloria bandied Sanders's motives about, another man she had seen in Ivy's company—Caleb Cain, she'd learned—approached the house as well. Soon afterward, Ivy roared out of her driveway and Cain, who lived in the house just down from where Gloria was parked, left as well. Much to Gloria's aggravation, Sanders did not. He rooted himself on the front porch, apparently waiting for Ivy's return, and did not look to be in any particular hurry about going anywhere soon.

Gloria's gun itched in its holster. Today was the day. The Widow Pritchard had not been seen for some time, most likely returned back home. Gloria would wait in the vacant house. Take out Ivy Cole with one clean shot when she entered the door. Dispose of the gun when she was way out of town, then call the police anonymously so as to protect Luna. Someone had to be there to pick up the child from school and immediately get her into care.

But now Sanders was here, mucking it all up, and Gloria's exas-peration was maddening. He rocked on the front porch swing and his chin dipped to his chest. *My God—he's falling asleep!*

Gloria waited him out for a while, but Ivy Cole was taking an inordinate amount of time getting home as well. With a drop-off by eight a.m., Ivy was usually home by eight-thirty at the latest. That hour had long come and gone. Something was amiss today, and Gloria was starting to wonder if karma were telling her something.

As she mulled this notion, Caleb Cain's white Jaguar backed out of his driveway behind her. He never even glanced her direction.

Gloria's seat was getting numb, Ivy was not home, and Melvin Sanders was going nowhere fast. So where was Cain heading? Perhaps a private rendezvous with Ms. Cole out from under Sanders's jealous eye?

Most likely he was going fishing on that fancy boat of his or just getting a bite to eat. She'd find out. Her day had been altered enough already that a new plan would need devising anyway.

Gloria started the engine and pulled out behind the Jag, keeping a discreet distance. She followed the sports car at a far tail all the way to Loggerhead Beach.

"And that's all I know," Mrs. Flannigan said, her face pulpy red from too much sun and worry. "I'm sure everything is all right, but he took her without authorization. I don't know what's going on with that family, but there's an ache in my bones that something isn't quite right. I'd feel a whole lot better if you could please find Ms. Cole at the hospital and tell her what has happened."

"Don't worry, Mrs. Flannigan, I'm sure when I get there I'll find the whole Cole clan, including Luna, clustered in a waiting room and awaiting news on their aunt." Sheriff Hubbard patted the good teacher's arm.

"Thank you. That makes me feel a whole lot better, Officer Dannon," Mrs. Flannigan said, standing by the buses in the parking lot once more, with Mr. Bennett flanking one side and Ed Bremmer, who had also given a statement, on the other.

"Please, do all you can," Mr. Bennett said. Unlike Mrs. Flannigan, he did not feel much better at all. School policy had been broken and after the beating he just took from Mrs. Rotterman, he couldn't *wait* to meet the irate Ms. Cole tomorrow if an error had been made regarding the pickup of her child—or, if on the flip side, they had not released the girl quickly enough and the elderly aunt passed before Luna could get there. If only Iris, their school secretary, were less attentive to the males that visited and more attentive to her job. For all he knew, Ms. Cole may have authorized a whole gaggle of people to pick up Luna and it never made it to the proper file. Bennett feared a lawsuit could be forthcoming, a double whammy to the school system after Rotterman's threats a while ago.

"I will have this cleared up within the hour, Mr. Bennett. There's no need for you to call anyone else," Gloria said. "Just go on and enjoy the rest of your day." She smiled confidently, reassuringly, and saw her small audience visibly relax.

Officer Dannon, who had quickly flashed her badge and pocketed it again after introducing herself as a policeman on the Salty Duck force, got back in her "unmarked police car" and waved good-bye.

Back on the road, Gloria debated between visiting the hospital per Cain's story or going by Pelican's Wharf per Bremmer's comment about the boat. A phone call to the hospital should quickly dispatch the former option without her driving all over the country first. But what an interesting development: Caleb Cain was Luna's father? Gloria did not get that impression when she saw the two adults together. They acted like strangers getting to know one another, not companions or even, more loosely, acquaintances who shared a five-year-old child. No, theirs was classic dating behavior the sheriff had observed from afar, unless Ivy had a one-night stand so many years ago and this man just reappeared in her life. But Ivy didn't strike Gloria as the one-night stand type. So if all that stood true, then Caleb had lied. But why?

And then there was Jack Cole/Cage, Page, Other (according to Bremmer), another twist in the barbed chain of events. Ivy Cole did not have a brother named Jack. Ivy did not have close family period; Gloria had researched her family tree extensively. So who was this stranger showing up and staking claim to the little girl as well?

Mrs. Flannigan was right. The feeling of wrongness throbbed in Gloria's gut too, and she felt the urgent need to find where Luna had been taken. Suddenly karma's intentions were made clear—there was another child, another Annie, who needed Sheriff Hubbard, and this time she was, ironically or by fate, put in position to help her.

Today was not about Ivy Cole after all. That bit of business, Gloria decided while calling directory assistance for the hospital, would be saved for another day.

48

Luna and her backpack were riding shotgun in a white Jaguar. It was a nice car with its big wooden dashboard full of gadgets she was dying to tinker with. Mup would have liked it, Luna thought wistfully. Cali and Auf would too. They were so cramped, the two wolves *(dogs, Mommy says to always call them dogs)*, stuck in the back of the Jeep all the time. She'd tried hard to get her mother to let Cali ride in her lap, but it was a "road hazard" and "road hazards" were bad. Just like Luna today, against everything her mother had told her the night before. *Be good. Count to one hundred. But above all else, be good!* They'd sat on Luna's bed with the familiar copy of *Where the Wild Things Are* and Luna had promised. Now Mup was gone to turtle heaven and Luna was in trouble at school.

Mommy was going to be soooo mad. Stupid Orvis Rotterman!

"Do we have to tell her what happened, Caleb? Do we have to?"

Mr. Caleb Cain, one hand on the wheel and an elbow stuck casually out his rolled-down window, looked thoughtful. "Who, your mom? Oh, I dunno. How can we not tell her? I mean, you're getting home so early and all. How else could we explain it?"

Luna stared out her own tinted window and watched stilted

houses and cacti'd lawns pass by. "Maybe we can tell her the field trip got over with early."

"Nah. I don't think that would work. She'll see school buses going around this afternoon."

"I know! We could say there was a big explosion and my bus caught on fire and the fire trucks came and you drove by and picked me up."

Caleb tsked. "Hmm. Nope, I don't think she'd go for that either. She'd be looking for it in the news. Then what would we tell her?"

"I'm sick. I can make-believe I'm sick. Watch this." Luna bent over and did a very convincing job of pretending to vomit on Caleb's floorboard. He glanced over a little nervously to make sure the girl wasn't actually emitting anything.

"Impressive. We might could go with that, but your mom's a pretty smart cookie. I bet she could see through a fake sick job. Let's just drive around, and I'll think on it a bit, okay?"

Luna nodded and tried to be quiet so Caleb could think. It lasted all of two minutes.

"Caleb, why did you tell Mrs. Flannigan all that stuff about Aunt Ava and you being my dad? Mommy said Aunt Ava is gone, and I don't have a daddy. That's what Mommy said."

"Sometimes, Luna, we have to tell a story every now and then. Only when absolutely necessary, mind you, but when I just happened to be walking by and saw what was going on, I figured it was one of those times. That was the best I could come up with on the fly to get you out of there quick. Is Mrs. Flannigan usually so mean?"

"No way! I like Mrs. Flannigan. She was just mad because Orvis Rotterman ruined my sand castle and then he threw..." Luna paused. Caleb had given Mup to her as a present. She didn't want to make him mad too. "And then I fixed him, I mean. He won't bother me anymore, so Mrs. Flannigan doesn't have to worry. Have you figured anything out yet?" Being quiet while Caleb was thinking was excruciatingly hard. She wished he would hurry up. The knobs on the shiny dashboard were too intriguing, and her fingers found them despite her best efforts. Caleb carefully pulled her tiny hand away and placed it back in her lap.

"Hey, I think I do have an idea," Caleb said. "You were asking about my boat before. Why don't we go down to the dock and ride around on the *Yellowfin* a few hours? I can drop you off at school later, and your mom never has to know you even left the field trip. What about that?"

"Can we do that! Can we really do that!" The seat belt could barely restrain her. "Can we go to Smitty Pete's Island again too?"

"Actually, you read my mind. I was thinking that's exactly what we'd do."

Luna clapped her hands and beamed at Caleb, the ruined field trip and her sadness slipping behind her. Riding around on the *Yellowfin* was ten times better than sitting in the sand by herself and fighting off castle-destroying, turtle-murdering third graders. And the best part of all, Mommy would never have to know and be disappointed in her. "I love you, Caleb."

"I...I love you, too, Luna," Caleb stammered. The unexpected jerk on his heartstrings caused a foot to reflexively hit the brake. He quickly re-collected his composure and picked up speed again.

"So, Luna, who is this uncle your teacher was talking about—Jack?"

Luna shrugged. "I don't know. I don't have an Uncle Jack."

"I didn't think so."

"I've got an Uncle Stefan, though. He's my great-uncle."

Caleb pursed his lips and turned into the parking lot of the marina. "You don't say. Look, we're at the docks already. How about that?"

49

"CALI! CALI!" Ivy rolled down the street at twenty miles per hour, the Wrangler barely out of first gear and her foot riding the clutch. After following the wolf nearly all the way to Loggerhead Beach after the school bus, Cali had unexpectedly veered down another side street and vanished.

Ivy was as angry as she was scared. She had never had a canine disobey her before; it was unthinkable. But disobey she had, and even worse, the bond developing between Luna and Cali was nearly every bit as strong as what she herself shared with Aufhocker. Could Luna ever forgive her mother for losing such a precious member of the family?

Wolves always listen to me—what has gotten into this one? she thought, as the sign for Battery Street came into view. Was Stefan's line weakening? She didn't believe that. He would let his four-legged prodigies die out completely before mating substandard pairs or inbreeding. It just didn't make sense.

"Cali!" she called for the hundredth time. The coastal sun was a blowtorch on her bare, burned shoulders, and the irony of her speech this morning to Luna about sunscreen only irritated her more. The dust bowl in her throat was not helping either. Cali's name now merely croaked past her scorched gullet between dry, husky coughs. Auf sat in Luna's seat at alert attention, quiet yet vigilant as always. If they were back in the mountains instead of a busy tourist town, she would have cut him loose to go find Calopus and bring her back himself. But there was too much traffic, too many people…he might be run over or picked up by animal control in no time. That fate for Cali only refreshed tears that had dried an hour ago. Ivy was surprised she had enough water left in her body to produce more, and that thirsty, defeated thought was what really had turned her toward home. She prayed the wolf had regained her good senses and would be standing in the front yard when she got there.

Captain Woodside's cottage rose up empty on the left. Cali was nowhere in sight…but Deputy Melvin Sanders was still there, just where she'd left him this morning. He was in the porch swing, hands clasped in his lap and staring at the floorboards.

"Good grief." Ivy parked and strode right past him into the house. She grabbed a water bottle from the refrigerator and downed half of it before coming back out. She locked the house door and climbed into the Wrangler.

"Well?" she called to him.

He looked up. Without a word he pushed off the swing and was in the Jeep beside her, unsettling Aufhocker, whom Ivy was already motioning to move to the back.

"Now just shut up before you even get started, Melvin. I don't want to hear any more out of you right now. I just want to drive around and find my daughter's—"

"Our daughter's."

"No! No more of that. If you want to stay in this car, you will be quiet and help me find Luna's…dog. I can only handle one crisis at a time, and lately they've been landing on my head like a rain of nuclear bombs. Her name is Cali and that's all I want to hear from you. Got it?"

"Cali. Yeah, got it. 'Dog,' huh?" He looked at her sideways and she ignored him, jerking the Jeep into gear and continuing on toward Front Street. She'd follow Marshy Bottom awhile before looping

50

CALEB HELD Luna's hand with his right. In his left he carried a small cooler, one which Luna, with her sharp five-year-old mind, had questioned the minute he brought it out.

"How did you know to pack a lunch for us, Caleb?" she'd asked, putting him on the spot concerning his story about the impromptu, perchance meeting at Loggerhead Beach.

"I didn't know, Luna. I'd planned a picnic for myself on the beach, but there's plenty of food for both of us."

That had satisfied her, and the chatterbox gave him a heavenly three-and-a-half-minute reprieve of silence as they left the car and made their way across the parking lot toward Pelican's Wharf Marina. The main building was a large square, a two-story parallelogram of uninteresting lines but fabulously titanic windows that looked out over this leg of Marshy Bottom and its connection to the Intracoastal Waterway. The top floor was an oyster bar that came alive after six p.m. with everything from jazz to reggae. But at this lazy weekday hour, the restaurant was quiet and the downstairs tackle shop was devoid of customers as well.

Caleb briskly walked toward the boardwalk that led past the

building and down to the pier where the *Yellowfin* was moored. Luna nearly trotted to keep up.

"…and can we swim at Smitty Pete's Island, Caleb? Can we?" The conversation revived itself in mid-course, as if it had never stopped.

"Yes, yes, sure we can." Caleb looked around the grounds and over his shoulder at the retreating parking lot. Then he scanned the boats bobbing in their slips ahead.

"And maybe see the ponies? I love the ponies, Caleb! Can we ride around the Banks to see the ponies like last time, too?"

"Just like last time." He clutched the little hand firmer and lengthened his stride. No one seemed to be here at all, it appeared, nearly all the fishermen on the water or come back in and gone home already. Somebody moved behind the glass of the marina store, then retreated—the clerk returning to the counter, bored.

"Can we fish again, too, Caleb? I liked to fish. Maybe I can catch a fish this big." She held her arms out wide.

"Luna!" Caleb stopped abruptly and spun the girl to face him. "No more questions right now, okay? We'll do everything we did before and it will be a lot of fun, but right now we have to hurry." Caleb glanced over Luna's shoulder. The clerk was at the window again, her arms crossed and watching them. "We have to hurry because we have to be back before your mom comes to pick you up, okay?" He smiled and Luna smiled back uncertainly. Caleb was squeezing her hand too tightly and the one holding the cooler was white knuckled.

"I can be fast, Caleb. I promise. Don't be mad."

"I'm not mad, sweetheart. Just in a rush…Oh no." Caleb saw the marina store clerk looking over her own shoulder but pointing their direction. Another figure materialized in the glass like an oversized apparition beside her.

Luna followed his concerned gaze across the picnic tables and manicured lawn to the store window. Luna's eyes widened. "That waiter! I know him, Caleb. He called me a shrimp and—"

Caleb jerked Luna's last thought away. He grabbed her wrist and was long-striding now, Luna jogging beside him.

"Hey!" someone yelled behind them.

Luna tried to look back. "The...waiter...is coming." Her voice hitched and halted as she struggled to keep up.

Caleb did not look back. Instead he grabbed up Luna and ran. Luna wrapped her arms around his neck, but staring behind him now she saw something amazing. She started to squirm, her voice screaming in his ear:

"Cali! Cali is here! Caleb, stop, it's Cali! Come, girl, come on!"

The wolf did not need encouragement. She charged across the parking lot toward them just as Luna's personal nemesis, the waiter, emerged onto the marina lawn and charged at them as well.

"Luna, we can't wait for her. I'm sorry." Caleb was sprinting hard, but Luna was struggling, desperately screaming for her dog. "Cali! Calopus, come!" And then: "The waiter is chasing us, Caleb! What's happening?"

"He's a bad man, Luna. He wants to hurt you. We have to get to the boat."

"Then we have to wait for Cali!" Luna no longer sounded scared or confused. She was starting to get mad, and tiny fists grabbed the hair above the back of Caleb's neck. Already she had lost one pet that day; she would not lose Cali too.

Caleb felt a tuft of his hair rip loose and another ear-piercing shriek skewered his eardrum: *I want my dog!*

"Haskell! Haskell, push off!" Caleb yelled at the deckhand, who stood by the *Yellowfin* with his hand cupping visorlike over his brow. He was motionless, like the familiar old pelican and marina namesake balanced on the piling above him, watching the race across the marina lawn. But at Caleb's booming voice, he jump-started to life and began untying ropes and slinging them on the boat's deck. The motor was already warmed and ready, its quiet idling a purr against the murky water.

The boat rocked and pulled taut against the one rope remaining in Haskell's hands. Caleb pounded down the weathered wooden pier toward him, a child bobbing in his arms.

"Push off, I said! Let it go!"

Bewildered, Haskell followed orders anyway. He threw the last dock line into the boat and watched it drift backward. It was eight feet away when Caleb ran past Haskell and went airborne. Child, cooler, and man landed squarely on the boat's bow. Caleb was at the helm and backing out of the slip fast before Haskell's mouth had a chance to close. Clear of the pier, Caleb throttled up hard, ignoring the no-wake zone and sending a wave of spray over the deckhand.

Another man, the big fella who had been chasing Caleb, pulled up beside Haskell, heaving heavily. Just down from them, a large black dog stood rigidly, its body seeming to strain toward the fleeing boat.

"Dammit t'hell," the man said. "Where's he going? Do you know where he's going?" His stabbed his fist the *Yellowfin*'s direction.

"No, don't have no ideay. Mr. Cain just called the marina and said to get his boat ready. That's all I know." Haskell felt smothered under the other man's shadow.

"Bloody hell!" Gage kicked a piling, unseating the pelican. It flapped off in the direction of the Regulator, which sat a hundred yards out idling. Gage glared at the boat and the man at the helm.

Caleb smiled and saluted toward shore, then turned the boat sharply, kicking up another fan of white spray.

Behind it, at the pier, Calopus leaped into the water and began to swim.

51

"SHE WENT this way, I saw her!" Ivy whipped the Jeep left, cutting off oncoming traffic and careening into the parking lot of Pelican's Wharf Marina. The last time she'd been here was a storybook day spent aboard a beautiful boat manned by its strong and handsome captain. Now she was back, accompanied by her bitter long-lost love from Doe Springs and chasing down a wolf that was dangerously close to being shipped back to Germany on the next available flight out of the States. How things could change in such a short length of time.

Ivy had never been so angry with a canine in her life. The wolf had run from her twice now, once this morning, when she'd taken off after Luna's bus, then again when Ivy had spotted her on the waterfront, nose to air and ground intermittently and moving determinedly this way. It wouldn't be long before Ivy would have to pick up Luna from school, but thankfully, the chase may have just come to an end. If she and Melvin could corner Calopus down on the pier, she'd drag the wolf all the way back to the Jeep by the scruff of the neck and try not to kill her on the ride home. For Luna's sake.

Ivy stopped at the top of the boardwalk leading from the manicured marina storefront and restaurant down to the boats. "Do you see her? Tell me she's not gotten away from us again."

Melvin scanned the near-deserted grounds, save for a store clerk watching from the tackle-shop window and two men down by the boats on the pier. Aufhocker leaped from the Jeep to come stand beside Ivy. His head was up, ears perked in the direction of the waterway beyond where the boats were docked. Melvin followed the wolf's gaze.

"Ivy, look." He pointed at the water where a black speck bobbed. "Is that her?"

Ivy shielded her eyes and squinted. "It can't be, but I think it is. How did she get out there? Calopus!" Ivy's tennis shoes thudded quickly on the boardwalk leading down to the boat slips, but from behind her: "Sanders, Ivy Cole, wait!"

Melvin wheeled around at the familiar commanding voice. Sheriff Gloria Hubbard was running toward them, her khaki blazer flapping behind her and revealing a .45 on her holstered hip.

Melvin's blood turned to rivulets of ice. It couldn't be true, and yet there it was: Sheriff Hubbard had followed him to Salty Duck, and he'd led her right to Ivy.

Ivy turned at the voice as well, then looked at Melvin with the same shock he saw in her face that night in Doe Springs when the sheriff had miraculously appeared out of nowhere and Ivy was sure Melvin had betrayed her. It was that moment in the woods relived here on the coast, and Ivy's hurt expression begged only one question: How could you do this to me again?

However it looked right now, one thing was certain: Ivy was in danger, and Melvin was in the middle of a situation that was about to escalate from bad to worse. Would Hubbard try to arrest Ivy? Detain her indefinitely for questioning? Shoot them both on the spot, him for conspiring with the enemy and Ivy for heinous reasons too numerous to name? All this ran through Melvin's head while the sheriff pounded toward them. He debated whether to face her now, or just grab Ivy's hand and run. Hubbard would never shoot a fleeing suspect in the back, no matter how angry or to rights she was. And Ivy wasn't even *that* officially, in the eyes of the law. Her record was as clean as Melvin's starched uniform hanging in the closet at home.

But Melvin wasn't a coward, and running from someone he respected as much as Gloria Hubbard wasn't in him either. Melvin would have to deal with this head-on, right now, good or bad. He hoped Hubbard at least respected him enough to let him explain that he had not betrayed his department, merely came here seeking answers himself. To what, she didn't need to know.

He couldn't run, but as for Ivy...

"Ivy, I swear I didn't tell her where you were. But it doesn't matter now—you've got to get out of here. I'll talk to the sheriff and see what she wants."

"I don't know whether to believe you or not, Melvin. Just when I think I can trust you again..." Ivy shook her head violently. "No! I'm not running anymore, and I'm not going anywhere without my little girl's companion. You handle Hubbard, and remind her she has no evidence—or jurisdiction—to arrest me for anything. If she tries to, I'll sue her department for everything it's worth, and I've got the money to round up enough barracuda lawyers to do it. Excuse me, but I'll be down at the pier trying to get Calopus back to shore." Ivy started to walk away when Gloria called her again.

"Ivy, wait! You need to hear this. It's about Luna!"

That stopped her cold. She stood by Melvin as Sheriff Hubbard finally made it to them.

Gloria paused a moment, catching her breath, when she saw Sanders and Ivy were not going to force her to pursue them. It might well have come to that; she couldn't imagine what they must be thinking at seeing her here, in Salty Duck, at the Pelican's Wharf Marina. She was completely out of context, a main character in the wrong setting, and that could be unnerving to say the least. And yet, it was completely beside the point because there was no time to explain or go to war over the past. They'd save that for another day, although Gloria's cover was blown all to hell, unfortunately. Again, couldn't be helped. What she'd just witnessed was of utmost importance, and every second spent jawing was counting against them if what Gloria thought she saw was correct.

"You're wondering why I'm here," Gloria said with her second wind. "I'm only going to say this once: It doesn't matter right now." She looked directly at Ivy. "You and I have unfinished business, Ivy Cole, but I have to ask you a very important question: Do you know where your daughter is?"

Ivy looked at Melvin, confusion marring her pretty face. "What is all this about? Melvin, do you have something to do with this?"

"He doesn't know anything, Ivy. Just answer me, where is Luna?"

"She's on a field trip at the beach with her kindergarten class."

"She's not with the school," Gloria said.

"Of course she is. They're all at Loggerhead Beach right now. I saw the bus leave this morning, and she was safe and sound on it."

Ivy didn't know, and Gloria believed her. "Look, there is no time to explain things, so you're going to get the short version, and you're just going to have to trust that I'm telling the truth.

"I've been watching you, Ivy, for a while now. Today I was at Loggerhead Beach, where I followed Caleb Cain. Mrs. Flannigan said Cain, posing as Luna's father, picked her up to go to the hospital, and your 'brother,' Jack Cole, came in right behind him to get her as well. I got here just in time to see Cain and Luna leave on his boat, and that man, the bigger one," Gloria pointed at the pier, "was after them. I don't know what the hell is going on, and if you don't know anything different, we'd better get down there and start asking some questions. I think your little girl may be in trouble."

52

"WHAT YOU suspect is true. That man—Caleb Cain, you say his name is—has kidnapped Luna. I was trying to save her." Gage looked at Sheriff Hubbard, Deputy Sanders, and Ivy Cole in turn. He put his big palms over his face and wiped downward as if trying to wipe away his frustration and utter despair. "This could not have gone any worse. Ivy, I am so very sorry."

Ivy knelt on the pier, trying to get a handle on everything the man was telling her.

"I don't understand any of this. You're a waiter at The Bluewater Lady. Caleb is a yacht salesman on sabbatical from Chicago. What would either of you want with my daughter?" Ivy's voice cracked; she was trying hard not to lose it. But…Caleb had kidnapped Luna? Caleb was a diabolical fiend? Caleb, the man whom she thought was falling in love with her family, the man whom she thought she just might be falling in love with herself? She felt as if her whole life had gone haywire, a typically ordinary occurrence considering her topsy-turvy past.

But this time she couldn't very simply drop everything and hit the road, saving herself and moving on toward new adventures. This time, she had a child, a child who was suddenly the center of the maelstrom. And Ivy was responsible. She had let Caleb in.

"I'll try to explain this as simply as I can," Gage said, "but we should talk in private. What I have to say may not sound reasonable to mundane types, and I do not want my sanity questioned." He glanced at the deputy and the sheriff.

"I may be *mundane,* sir," Gloria said, "but I'm not uninitiated. I know about werewolves, and if it's in regards to that, you can talk freely. When it comes to the child, I'm here to help," Gloria said.

He looked to Ivy for affirmation and she nodded.

"Fine. My name is Gage Rowland, and I work for Ivy's uncle, Stefan Heinrich. We've known Luna was in danger for some time, from the Order. You're familiar with them?"

"Yeah, I'm familiar with them; I have their bible, *Lykanthrop.* But it's a relic," Ivy said. "That organization is defunct now, isn't it? Disbanded after Uncle Stefan left?"

"Hardly. These wolves are very active and particularly interested in Luna's abilities. They want to study her. They want to…dissect the cause of her talent. Stefan sent me here to protect Luna, but I misstepped, and now their man has her." Gage pointed out to sea. "He's in a boat with Luna heading that way. We're too late."

"Like hell we are." Melvin had heard enough. A few hours ago he was standing on Ivy's porch beside the very psychopath who had stolen his daughter. Now, the policeman in him jarred to life, and the father in him steeled to do whatever was necessary to get Luna back. "You!" Melvin jabbed a finger the dockhand's direction.

Haskell stood a few feet away, just outside the group but close enough to hear everything. Bunch o' nuts, that's all he could figure, but all this werewolf talk sure would make fine fodder for conversation around the fishing hole. Now the tall gent was yelling at him, what he appreciated none too much a'tall, but he also figured it best not to argue with loony types out on a pier with no witnesses. "Yea, whatcha needing?"

"A boat," Melvin said, "right now. You got keys for any of these?"

"Nah. I just help clean the fish, tie off when the charters come in, gas up when they're heading out, that type of thing."

Gloria pulled out her badge and showed a glimpse of the Glock tucked underneath her blazer. "Surely you can help us somehow."

Haskell scratched his balding head. He grimaced, but looked down the length of the pier. "Yah. I got a boat. You can have it, if you want. Not as fast as Mr. Cain's Regulator by any stretch, but it's a dogged little vessel. It'll get you where you need to go."

"Show us," Gage growled, and they followed Haskell as he passed one beautiful craft after another. He stopped.

"It can't be. We won't even make it out of the wake zone with this thing," Ivy said. The group stood in front of an old wooden fishing boat, its battered pilothouse windows cracked and the boards of its hull splintered and fighting rot. It was the same crappy, barely upright little wreck that Ivy had mistaken as Caleb's their first time to Pelican's Wharf.

Haskell looked offended by Ivy's nautical assessment. "She's battled nor'easters in Maine while pulling up lobster and tropical storms off the Carolinas while collecting crab pots. She's survived where better boats didn't, and she'll get you out to sea and bring you back, no worries."

"It's better than nothing." Gage climbed aboard and started untying dock lines. "Ivy, do you have any idea where Cain might be taking Luna?" he said.

Ivy thought a minute, scoured her brain for anything that could be significant. "I only know of one place, and it is in the direction you say he went. It's an island on the other side of the Banks, set off to itself a ways. It's called Smitty Pete's Island. But why would he take her to a deserted island? Is he going to kill my daughter?"

Ivy's voice was level. Gage looked into her eyes, expecting to see the edge of motherly hysteria. Instead, the pupils were a dead zone.

"He might go there to hide for a while," he said, "or it could be a rendezvous point. Whatever, it's as good a place to start as any. We've got nothing else."

Gage was untying the last dock line when Melvin caught it. "What do you think you're doing, Rowland?"

"This will be dangerous. I need to go alone. Now let go of the line."

"We all go," Ivy said. "Where's the sheriff?"

"Here." Gloria had slipped away and was now striding toward them down the pier, her arms full. "I thought we could use some reinforcements."

She handed Melvin the pump-action rifle. She held the shotgun out to Ivy. "You know how to handle one of these?"

"I've never had a need for guns." Ivy's eyes locked on the sheriff's. They glared at one another.

"I know how to use it," Gage said. Gloria tossed him the Remington.

"Here, take this," Gloria said. She handed Ivy the .38 revolver and tried not to smirk at the irony of it. "I think this was made for you. Just point and shoot."

"Thanks," Ivy said. She did not like the look on the sheriff's face when she handed her the gun. "I promise I won't shoot you with it."

"Marksmanship is the last thing I worry about when it comes to you, Ivy Cole."

The remainder of the party, including Aufhocker, climbed aboard Haskell's boat. Gage was already in the pilothouse, the engines running smoothly. A few minutes later, Melvin was scooping Cali out of Marshy Bottom Sound and the boat traveled unwaveringly the same direction she'd been swimming, toward Smitty Pete's Island.

53

Luna sat shivering on the boat's cushioned bow, a towel wrapped around her shoulders. Tears streamed down her face—she was not afraid, these were tears and tremors of anger.

"You left her," she said above the wind whistling around the center console, where Caleb stood at the wheel. His eyes scanned the horizon in front of him, but more often than not, he turned to survey behind the boat, too. He had every paranoid right to be looking over his shoulder. The other man was coming. Caleb knew this with absolute certainty. Somehow, some way, "the waiter" was back there, hunting them like a—

"...wolf! Did you know that? She's not a dog at all, she's special. And you just left her! She might have *drowned*."

Luna's voice wailed on the last word. She still saw it clearly—Cali diving off the pier to follow her, paddling as hard as she could, her black fur a slick upon the water. They were safe on the boat, the bad man couldn't get her, and yet Caleb left Calopus out there in the water anyway. And he refused to listen even now. What was wrong with him?

Luna got up, walked behind the man, and kicked him in the back of the knee. The boat revved down so hard, she faltered forward, catching herself on the edge of his seat.

Caleb turned to her as the boat idled in the water. "Do we have a situation here, Luna?"

She looked up at him, her eyes blazing a disturbing amber hue that was brightening by the second. Her hands were on her hips and she looked about ready to draw back and kick him again. Caleb took her by the shoulders.

"Luna, you have to listen to me, honey. I'm sorry about Cali. But she's a big girl, she can take care of herself. Wolves are incredible swimmers and when she gets tired, she'll go back to shore."

"Then we should go back too. I don't want to go to Smitty Pete's Island anymore. I want to go home. I want Cali and Auf. I want Mommy." The eyes flared alarmingly.

Caleb's brow broke into a sweat. He knelt down, spoke in his most reassuring tone. "We can't go back right now, sweetheart. You're not safe in Salty Duck while that man is still there. We'll go to the island, wait awhile, and then I'll take you home. Okay? I bet Cali will be right there waiting for you."

Luna's lip snarled upward. "No, she won't. She's coming for me, and you left her. You left her, Caleb, and I don't think I like you anymore."

"Luna, calm down."

"I want Cali."

"Luna—"

"I want Cali."

"Luna, what are you doing?"

"*I want Calopus!*" The scream echoed across the open water, scattering the gulls that had followed their wake. *Be good, Luna, just this one time. No, Mommy, I won't....*

The towel dropped to the deck, and Luna fell to all fours after it. Her fingernails dug like claws into the boat's pristine flooring, her spine hunched upward against her T-shirt. Spiny vertebrae stood out against the white cotton, and Caleb watched as more vertebrae seemed to rise up from somewhere deep within the girl and attach themselves to the knotty spinal chain. The shirt ripped as her back lengthened, and coarse white hairs emerged around the strings of her bathing suit underneath it. Her ponytail hung around her face, but a fierce glow emanated from her downturned head. It was her eyes, brighter now than the sun, glittering above elongating cheeks. Pearlescent fangs, sharp and daggerlike, bejeweled the lengthening jaws within seconds. Soon the transformation would be complete.

Caleb scooted backward, away from her and the jowls that were starting to snap even as they formed. There was only one thing he could do, save for jumping overboard and swimming for it. In one comical moment, he pictured himself passing Calopus in the ocean, her still paddling steadfastly toward the *Yellowfin* and him stroking as fast as he could away from it. But the comedy was short-lived. Caleb grabbed for the cooler beneath his seat. Inside lay only one thing on the ice—a syringe. He tapped the sides of it and squirted a bead of clear substance onto the pointed tip.

"Hold on, Luna! Just hold on, this won't hurt much!"

Luna was no longer small. Her roached back was thick with muscle and nearly as high as Caleb's head where he knelt. New, taut skin twitched and quivered underneath hair as white as egrets' wings. Two gimlet eyes stared at him above a muzzle that could snap his thighbone in two. She lunged, and Caleb held the syringe in front of him like a pitiful spear. He raised both feet to catch her staggering weight, then jabbed the needle deep into her throat.

The wolf, not quite wholly formed yet, emitted a high-pitched bawl, part animal, part child in pain. Caleb depressed the plunger and let his feet topple the young werewolf to her side. The effect was instantaneous. The animal seemed to suck in on itself, claws and fangs retreating, bones and sinews contracting, until nothing but a wisp of a little girl lay still.

Caleb leaned up on one elbow. Luna's face was slack, lips parted and eyes closed. He put his ear to her mouth and found steady breath, then let loose a shuddering breath of his own. He stood up, his sea legs shaking and useless. He grabbed the back of his chair for support and stood there a minute, five minutes, pulling himself together. *That was close. Good God Almighty, that was close.*

Caleb picked up the satellite phone from his console and called.

"I got her. It wasn't easy, though, and I'm sure I'm being pursued. And I hate to tell you this, but I had to use the serum. I tried to be careful not to hurt her, but she would have killed me, I'm certain of it."

He paused to listen on the other end.

"I'm all right, and she's sleeping. But you never told me it would be like that. I'm telling you, I was meat. If I didn't have the syringe…"

German ranted in his ear.

"She would have killed me, I don't care what you think. You weren't here. Listen, I'm almost at the island. I'll look for you within an hour."

Caleb hung up and looked at the sleeping child on the deck. She was in an uncomfortable heap, her clothes in tatters. Caleb wrapped her in one of his own T-shirts, then worried about her exposure to the harsh sun. Days like this he wished he still owned a yacht, but the fisherman in him had finally won out, and he'd traded in that lifestyle for one of rods and reels and outriggers. Never would he have dreamed he'd someday need a comfortable cabin in which to lay a drugged, five-year-old werewolf. As it was, he carried her to the head, where on the floor by the toilet he prepared a soft pallet of towels. Caleb laid Luna gently on the makeshift bed and went back up to the helm to check his location on the Global Positioning System. Smitty Pete's Island blinked on the radar beside it. He was almost there.

54

"So you're a skipper, too," Gloria said, standing behind Gage at the helm and watching the bow bounce over the rolling waves in front of them. They were the only two in the pilothouse, Melvin choosing to stay on deck with Ivy and her conspicuous black "dogs." They were all thankful at least one in the group could pilot a boat; otherwise, the unwilling Mr. Haskell would have been their only hope, and Gloria was against bringing civilians into dangerous situations.

"Yeah. Learned the water when I was growing up in Texas, the Gulf side." Gage didn't turn around. His attention was on the GPS, which was picking up some static. Haskell's boat was a piece of crap, and the instruments weren't much better. For all Gage knew, that old man navigated by constellations. He tapped the GPS screen with an impatient finger and the picture cleared for a minute, only to go fuzzy again.

"Texas? Huh. I wouldn't have pegged you as a Texan. I was thinking Ireland, especially with the tattoo. Celtic, isn't it?"

Gage fiddled with the controls, his broad back blocking her view of the helm. He grunted, and that was the only answer she got.

"Hey, could you get Sanders in here?" he finally said. "I need to see if he knows anything about wiring. We're about to lose our navigation system."

"Sure." Gloria fetched the deputy, and the two men standing shoulder to shoulder quickly filled the small space and crowded her out. She needed some fresh air anyway.

The werewolf and the sheriff stood stern of Haskell's hardscrabble boat, while Melvin assisted Gage inside. It had left Ivy and Gloria uncomfortably alone, and now Ivy cast sidelong glances at the woman beside her. The sheriff still wore her cocoa-colored hair tied back in a slick, no-nonsense ponytail; her eyes were still that same impenetrable shade of police officer steel. But a few more lines engraved the corners of her mouth, making the hard set to her lips appear parenthetical, and the crease between her eyebrows was deeper than Ivy remembered. It gave her an appearance of unrelenting consternation, and Ivy wondered if she herself were responsible for permanently etching those worries into Gloria's handsome face.

When Ivy had moved to Doe Springs to live in contented Blue Ridge Mountain bliss, she had unknowingly created a hell for Sheriff Hubbard and her deputies. Gloria's loathing was absolutely understandable, and Ivy regretted that. Except for the sheriff's attempts to arrest her, Ivy admired the other woman and was saddened they could never be friends.

"Is there something you want to say?" Gloria said, still staring out to sea. Conversation with Ivy Cole was the last thing she wanted right now, but the woman had been studying her since she replaced Sanders by her side. Gloria had rather stay focused on the mission rather than cross words with an "inhuman." A plan was trying to formulate itself, but how could she devise a strategy when she didn't know what they were up against? Would Cain be alone on the island? Or would they encounter an entire werewolf cult out for blood? The moon was not of issue, but murderers were murderers. What would keep them from killing her small group and tossing them all into the ocean on their way back to whatever hole they crawled from?

Furthermore, would Cain and Luna even be at Smitty Pete's when they got there? Their current destination rested on pure assumption alone, a werewolf's hunch borne from air rather than concrete. It was all a shot in the dark, but they had nowhere else to go. Tooling around the ocean hoping to run across a big yellow fishing boat would certainly get them nowhere fast, and time was paramount in a kidnapping case.

Then there was Gage Rowland—a stranger supposedly on their side, and yet he had shown up at Loggerhead Beach to steal Luna himself, without Ivy's knowledge either but supposedly to "help." Plus there was the obvious lie, over seemingly nothing. Gloria might be a hick from a hick town, but she was no fool. Rowland was from Ireland, not Texas, and she knew this with certainty no matter how hard he tried to bury one accent and fake another. No crime being from Ireland, so why hide it? Was it possible that Cain and Rowland could be in cahoots somehow? Nothing was making a lot of sense.

And still, as all these jumbled thoughts clashed and dickered in Gloria's head, Ivy continued her blatant visual analysis as if dissecting a frog under glass. That was usually Gloria's job, and it annoyed her further that someone else—especially this someone else—use her own tactics against her.

"You didn't answer my question, Ivy. Is there something you want to say to me?"

"I was just wondering..."

"Why I'm helping you," Gloria said.

"Yes," Ivy answered simply. "And no. I think I understand why."

Gloria turned to face her. Strands of hair had loosed from the austere pull of the ponytail and blew in nearly romantic wisps around her face. "Do you? I want it to be perfectly clear. I'm *not* helping you. I'm helping Annie."

"What did you say?"

"Luna. I said I'm helping Luna. She's the one I'm protecting, and don't think for one minute you're excluded from whom I see as one of her enemies. But I can't do my job if I don't know everything.

What was Rowland talking about back there? Why do these Lykanthrops want Luna so badly?"

"They think she can do something special."

"Special. Like change into a wolf, you mean."

"That's right."

"And can she do that?"

"She's just a little girl, Gloria." Ivy arched an eyebrow, and truth lay in her expression. Gloria suddenly knew. Luna was anything but just a little girl; she was a wolf who could do something so amazing it had caused all this, and honestly, when Gloria dug down deep to examine the situation, she was not that surprised. A wolf would spawn a wolf, wouldn't it? That was Mother Nature 101. But the new knowledge changed nothing; Luna suddenly needed Gloria more than ever.

"Look, Sheriff," Ivy continued, "I know about Annie. The child who vanished in Uwharrie, the one who you and your husband—"

"Don't say his name. Don't you dare say his name."

"—tried to save and couldn't. But Luna is not Annie, and I had nothing to do with what happened to her or your ex. I'm grateful you're here to help Luna in any capacity, but if your goal is to separate me from my child, I won't let that happen. I won't let you do what these others are setting out to do. Do you understand?"

Ivy's bright emerald gaze locked on the sheriff's gunmetal glare. The boat rocked and swayed, but the two women seemed immobile, lost in their own intimate battle.

"Ivy!" Melvin stuck his head out the pilothouse door. "Gage needs you to help spot the island. The radar's not working, and the GPS died. All's left is the compass and our eyes."

Ivy nodded and followed Melvin inside, the heat of the sheriff's glower a hot poker in her back as she went by.

"We're in the vicinity," Gage said. "Does anybody see anything out there?"

Ivy and Melvin squinted through the pilothouse windows, but nothing created a bump in the thin, straight line of horizon ahead. Off the bow there seemed to be only increasingly large waves and a few metallic quivers that were, surprisingly, flying fish. Ivy didn't know fish could really fly, but there they were, launching themselves airborne to splash down yards away.

"I don't see land," Ivy said. "Are you sure we're going the right way still?"

Gage checked the charts spread out by the helm. "Yeah. According to the GPS of fifteen minutes ago we are around here somewhere. And the compass is telling me we're still dead on course." Gage stabbed the map with a meaty finger to show their location.

Ivy leaned over the strange configuration of lines and points to see for herself, but it may as well have been an astronomy chart he was asking her to decipher.

"Whoa!" Gage yelled, as the boat cast sideways in the water. Ivy felt Melvin's arm go around her waist to steady her from falling. The boat listed hard and recovered.

"What was that?" Ivy yelled over a sudden rushing wind.

"I think I just found our bread crumb trail. Look there," Gage hollered.

A chopper appeared in front of the bow, its blades churning the waves and spraying the pilothouse with saltwater. It skimmed the ocean directly in front of them, then abruptly pulled skyward again.

"Dropped down to have a look-see, did we?" Gage said through gritted teeth.

"Who the hell was that?" Gloria said, charging in.

"Our competition, I'll wager. We're going after them!"

Gage throttled the engines to their maximum speed, thrusting the groaning vessel after the helicopter and, Ivy prayed, her daughter.

55

"Caleb? Caleb?"

"It's all right, sweetheart. You're okay now."

Caleb sat on the beach in the warm sand, Luna cradled in his arms. He was hoping she'd be out longer, but the drug would prohibit any transformations for a while yet. He was safe from her for now, but what of his pursuer? And where was the helicopter? His eyes scoured the sky as well as the sea. If another boat approached, he would have to seek shelter in the island forest behind him, a thought he did not relish. He remembered the wolves from the last visit, a pack he did not want to meet up with again under the cover of their own territory. They'd most likely run from him, but could one ever be certain? After his close encounter on the *Yellowfin,* he was not looking forward to meeting anymore wolves today, even the shy red ones of Smitty Pete's Island.

Luna rubbed her groggy eyes and burrowed in closer to Caleb's chest. She gave a mewling cry, then was asleep once more. Caleb's attention came inland then and his heart turned over at the baby nestled against him. He suddenly pictured Ivy's face. She must be shattered with worry by now, and he felt shattered by guilt. Nothing was as he thought it would be. The reward he'd been offered to help carry out this plan was not worth the cost. He'd nearly lost his life on his own boat to a preadolescent werewolf. He'd fallen in love with the mother of the child he was sent to abduct. And then there was the child herself, Luna. What would become of her after this was all over? Caleb had been promised she would bond with a new family, that she'd forget Ivy, that her life would be protected and better in Europe, that she would be safe.

But Luna didn't need any of that. Luna needed her mother. That bond was unbreakable no matter what Luna's age—he'd learned enough of the wolves by now to see that. And he suddenly felt he had made a big mistake.

"I'm sorry, Luna," Caleb whispered and kissed her smooth forehead. She tasted of salt and kelp and the sea. A sea wolf.

The sound of helicopter blades. Caleb looked up and shielded his eyes. It was a big black hawk of a machine, sleek and cool and lethal looking, just like the man who owned it. That was not a comparison Caleb would have made, until now, until today. The chopper rocked the Regulator anchored offshore, then hovered over the beach a hundred feet away. Caleb hid Luna's face in his shirt to shield her skin from the abrasive flying sand. The chopper set down easily and the blades slowed.

A tall, thin man in a black overcoat and black hat stepped onto the beach. His gray beard was trimmed to perfection, and a smile filled his distinguished face at the sight of Caleb and the girl. He approached them.

"Caleb. It's good to see you, my American friend," he said.

"It's good to see you as well, Stefan. Let me introduce Luna, your niece's daughter."

56

"THERE THEY are! I see the helicopter!" Ivy pointed straight ahead. Despite the loss of their technical equipment, the good old-fashioned compass—and a Eurocopter EC 120—had led them straight to Smitty Pete's Island.

Gage coasted the fisher boat in to shore as close as he dared. "We swim from here," he said, turning from the helm at last to reach for the shotgun Sheriff Hubbard had so thoughtfully provided. The corner where he'd wedged it was empty. He glanced up to see Gloria standing by the pilothouse door. The others were already on deck and climbing over the side; Gage heard a loud splash as the biggest wolf hit the water and started to paddle.

"Looking for this?" Gloria said, holding the Remington.

"Yeah" was all he said.

"Here you go then." The sheriff tossed him the gun, and he caught it in one fist.

"Thanks," he said gruffly, squinting, sizing up her tone. She was hard to read, and that bothered him. The whole predicament bothered him. He was supposed to be here alone, taking care of the "situation" and skirting back to Ireland to personally hand Luna over to

Simon, a Lykanthrop lieutenant disciple, at his father's hundred-acre farm—a sprawling establishment, by Irish standards, although not even viable when measured by the wasteful, land-grabbing American ranchers' yardstick. Kilderry Downs had become the western seat for the Order in Europe, an honor bestowed on the Rowland family after generations of loyal service. Fitting that there was a time in Ireland's history that the country was known as "the Wolfland," and Gage liked to think his family—a family of gentle sheep and dairy farmers by day—had a little something to do with that auspicious moniker.

But instead of things going perfectly to plan, he had lost the girl and acquired an armed entourage, all of whom would need to be dealt with before he could leave the States. Reinforcements were already waiting in the wings—a brief call after leaving Loggerhead Beach had alerted them that he may need help, and then his one private moment in the pilothouse had secured for his fellow Lykanthrop brothers their final destination and the heads up that some "waste removal assistance" would be in order. Fortunately, Haskell's radio was more functional than his GPS, and even though it was a call Gage had dreaded making, his confidence in the mission had returned, knowing it hadn't gotten completely screwed up beyond repair. The prize was still there for the taking, and getting rid of the excess baggage would now not be so problematic after all.

"I'm right behind you, Sheriff Hubbard," Gage said, hefting the gun in his hand, feeling its weight and imagining the damage such a weapon could inflict. Effective, but not nearly as fun as what he could do to the sheriff if night were upon them and the moon were ripe.

Gloria nodded, as if agreeing with his deliciously wicked thoughts, and then she turned to follow the others into the ocean.

It was only waist deep, the water where they anchored, and Ivy pushed through the surf, thick and tepid as pudding, as fast as she could. Melvin was ahead of her with the sheriff breathing down her neck from behind. From shore, Caleb and a tall stranger shielded by his hat watched their approach. And then yelling—it sounded like German: "Start her up! Start the engines back up!"

The chopper blades began their slow circuit, and Auf and Cali were spurred by it. They charged out of the crashing waves, their black manes lathered by foam, as if thrust from the sea by Neptune himself.

"Luna! Luna!" Ivy screamed. She could see her child at last, curled in Caleb's arms as he sprinted for the helicopter.

"Caleb! Stop!" Finally free from the ocean's drag, Ivy raced down the beach after Melvin and her wolves. Gloria was in step right beside her, their footfalls landing in an awkward, squishy cadence on the water-scoured beach.

The chopper blades whirred faster. Caleb offered Luna into the belly of the machine just as Aufhocker dove onto his leg with full force. Calopus latched onto his arm and Caleb toppled, rolling Luna into the sand. A bearded face appeared and the wind from the chopper blades snared his hat. It blew toward Ivy. Her eyes met those of the tall man in black. It was Stefan Heinrich. Her Uncle Stefan with Caleb, stealing her daughter.

"No!" Ivy ran harder. Beside her, Gloria pulled her gun without missing a step. And down the beach, Stefan was stepping into the fray of wolves attacking Caleb. Ivy saw Aufhocker and Calopus draw back, uncertain, confused, but instinctually knowing to obey Stefan's words that harkened to their days before Ivy and Luna, back to puppyhood and the respect of the elder pack leader.

Melvin reached the chopper first. Ivy and Gloria were only seconds behind him. They—Melvin, Ivy, Gloria, and the wolves—faced Ivy's uncle and cohort. Caleb lay bleeding on the ground. He staggered to his feet and glared at Stefan. "You said the Benandanti wouldn't hurt me." Blood coursed down his elbow, and his pants were stained dark above the knee.

"My mistake," Stefan said evenly, his English perfect but guttural in its German inflection. "Her bond is with Luna now. I did not realize how strong it would be this quickly. She only wants to be with the child."

Caleb did not appear mollified, but he held his tongue upon realizing the wolves were not their only concern here. A .45 and a rifle were aimed at his and Stefan's chests. Ivy had fallen into the sand beside Luna, clutching her silently and stroking her head.

"Shut the chopper down," Melvin ordered. "You're not going anywhere right now."

Stefan grimaced and glanced nervously out to sea. "You're making a mistake, Deputy Sanders."

Melvin blinked, surprised the man knew his name. "I said tell that pilot to gear down."

The deputy's eyes glinted with an inner yellow flame for only a second, but it was Stefan's turn to be surprised. He turned to the cockpit and in German: "Shut it off!" The pilot immediately responded, and the blades slowed once more. Stefan faced Melvin again, but his attention quickly moved to his niece. Ivy still knelt with Luna, rocking her quietly, feeling her heartbeat, gently trying to rouse her from her somnolent precipice, a blissful but precarious place between wakefulness and unconsciousness. The drug was still heavily in effect, but time was wasting, and Stefan wondered which would be worse for him momentarily: the Lykanthrop's arrival, for surely the other man was still out there pursuing them, or perhaps the swelling anger of armed police officers (wolfen officers?) who thought he was a felon, or maybe the awakening of a young she-wolf who suddenly decided Uncle Stefan wasn't a very nice man at all and she needed to do something about it. Just for Mommy. Yes, that would be ironic, wouldn't it.

At Stefan's age, the idea of death did not frighten nor complicate his moods; it only left him with entertaining contemplations about the significance of how it should occur. Really, he didn't care what happened to him today at all. But he cared about what happened to Luna—and Ivy—a lot.

"You're not safe," Stefan tried again. "I saw another man on the boat from the helicopter—"

Caleb cut him off. "Another man? Was it the man from the pier? The one who was chasing me?" He looked at the officers.

Ivy rose to her feet beside the helicopter, lifting Luna to balance on her hip. The little girl's arms wrapped around her mother's neck and her head rested on Ivy's shoulder groggily. "Yes, and it seems he's deserted us." She looked around. Haskell's boat appeared empty in the distance, and the beach they'd run across held nothing but their footprints rapidly vanishing into the rising tide. "His name is Gage Rowland, and he told us Caleb works for the Order. He said he worked for Stefan. Hello, Uncle Stefan, by the way. You'll pay for this, but you already know that, don't you?"

Stefan smiled, a thin upward crescent that bore no cheer, only a steely calm tinged with weariness. "Hello, my dear. It will be a privilege when the time comes."

He bowed slightly, keeping his distance at her cold implications but wishing he could hug her just one time instead. The last time he saw his niece in person, she was painfully young and still bearing the scars of tragic and recent loss. *But look at her now,* he thought, *all grown up and just as lovely as her mother.* It was like looking at a reflection from the other side, a spiritual remnant of his dead sister come to life. Somehow, it just made him sadder.

"You're Stefan Heinrich?" Melvin said.

"Yes, my boy, and you're Melvin Sanders and this must be Sheriff Gloria Hubbard. Not quite the company I expected Ivy to still be keeping these days."

Gloria snorted. "So this is *the* Stefan Heinrich. Somehow I thought you'd be smarter than this. The *law* will take care of you two," Gloria said, glancing pointedly at Ivy, "but first, you've got some explaining to do."

"I'm sorry, Ivy," Caleb burst out.

Melvin walked up and knocked him down with one punch. "Try that for sorry, you piece of—"

"Sanders! Let him talk," Gloria said.

Caleb lay moaning on the ground, his ripped arm bowed across his chest and his uninjured hand cradling a broken nose. The black wolves paced by Ivy's side, the bloody scent from downed prey heady in their sensitive nostrils.

"Please," Stefan said, "no more violence. That's not what we wanted. It's what we wanted to avoid." And Stefan told them, about

Simon, about the Order, about their intentions to experiment on Luna to find the genetic key to her abilities. "She'll be a lab rat. Without my Fenris and his lineage—the wolves that helped make you, Ivy—Luna became their only chance."

"Why didn't you just tell me all this instead of trying to take her from me? I can hide. I can protect her," Ivy said.

"Not like I can, and wolves don't desert their young. I knew you would never give her up. But I can hide one more effectively than two, and there are foster families already in place to take her month to month, year to year, until she's grown, just like how my family raised the wolves they protected generation after generation. Luna will thrive the same way they did. The Order would never be able to keep on her trail."

"She's not one of your endangered species. She's a person, a little girl, my daughter, and this is all insane. How do I know you're telling the truth?"

"Because he is," Caleb's voice was muffled and nasally. He sat up and leaned his head back, stemming the flow of blood from his nose.

"Prove it then," Ivy said.

"All right," Stefan said. "I know the Rowland family; they're well initiated in the Order. This Gage person, if he is who he says, will have a tattoo."

"On his bicep," Gloria said. "I saw it."

"And does it look like this?"

Stefan removed his overcoat and rolled up the sleeve of his gray silk shirt. A symbol resembling a Celtic knot adorned his upper arm. Looking at it closer, however, the lines of the ink in the center of the tattoo converged not to make the intricate patterns of the knot, but to make an abstract head, a wolf's head, with an exaggerated peaked muzzle and keen, almond eyes. The canid was so expertly drawn as to be nearly camouflaged within the design.

"It's the mark of the Lykanthrop, the same brand stamped onto the cover of the book you possess," Stefan said.

Ivy thought back to her and Luna's first meal at The Bluewater Lady, the bottom edge of the tattoo peaking from beneath the waiter's shirtsleeve. She pictured *Lykanthrop* at home, how the bottom of the symbol would look if she covered most of it with her hand.

"That's it," Gloria said, interrupting Ivy's thoughts.

"And he's armed," Melvin said.

"This is most unfortunate." Stefan looked up the beach; nothing was there but large stands of tortured driftwood, smooth and bleached like whale bones. "I wonder, just where did our Irish lad run off to?"

"Here I am, Heinrich," a voice said from the other side of the helicopter, "with a little surprise for all of you."

57

THE PILOT made not a sound as he slid from the cockpit and onto the sand at Ivy's feet. A ragged necklace of red wrapped around his throat, the gash spurting blood from the severed jugular.

Gage Rowland jumped out of the cockpit behind him. He'd climbed into the helicopter from the pilot's side and managed to ambush them all while they'd stood around trying to figure out what to do next.

The frustrated rage in Melvin elevated another notch, and his eyes sparked alarmingly. He didn't want the sheriff to see, to know what he had become, but the beast in him was fighting hard with the rational side of the lawman, and every part of his being was ready to tear this Black Irish stranger apart with his bare hands, werewolf be damned. He didn't *need* to change to accomplish murder; his paternal instincts were taking over and self-defense by ultimate death suddenly seemed so...reasonable.

"Hidey-ho, Sheriff," Gage said in his best fake Texas drawl. "Thanks for the Remington." The weapon was pointed at the group. "Now toss your guns over here please."

Gloria aimed her automatic at Gage's head. "You first."

"Sheriff, what are you doing?" Caleb looked back and forth between the two, his injuries forgotten.

Gloria's eyes never left Gage's.

His lips spread into a cruel, thin smile under the mustache of his goatee. "Pretty confident, aren't we? What makes you think I won't blow a hole through one of you right now?" He grabbed Ivy by the arm and yanked her to his side. In the same motion, he threw the shotgun at Gloria and pulled a nine-millimeter from his waistband. He pointed it at Ivy's head. "Now, really, Sheriff, do *y'all* think this good ole boy from *Tex-ass* would be so stupid as to barge into a gun-fight without making sure the gun my compadre gave me wasn't loaded first?" He stressed the words contemptuously, well aware they already knew who he was not—a Texan, a Southerner, hell, not even an American. He ground the pistol into Ivy's temple with relish. The disguises were off; it was better this way.

"He won't shoot her," Stefan said quietly. "Not with Luna in her arms. It would be suicide—Simon would never forgive it if Luna got hurt, and that's a death no cur wants to face, not even this one."

Melvin glanced at Stefan, his questioning expression clear: *Are you sure?* Stefan nodded.

The deputy charged, his rage unleashed in one furious, lightning moment. And yet, the whole thing unreeled in his head like slow-motion film, where he saw it all in painstaking, deliberate detail. Leaping toward Gage, his hands outstretched for the gun and the other man's throat. The gun pivoting off Ivy, Gage actually pushing Ivy and Luna out of the way as the barrel swung, and swung, and swung toward Melvin, who was now within point-blank range. And then a shot, just one.

Falling, Melvin falling, and the ground grabbing him and sucking out his breath with one brutal, beating whoosh. And then fire in his shoulder and a boot stamped on his own throat. He grabbed Gage's leg and wrenched it, wrenched him to the ground till they were rolling together, and Gloria shouting in the background as she circled with her firearm trying to get a split-second make on the target, and then more shots coming from...*the beach?*

And then everything stopped.

• • •

"It's about time you got here." Gage shoved Melvin off him and climbed to his feet. He kicked Melvin in the ribs and again in the shoulder, right below the gunshot wound. Six men in black pants, T-shirts, and boots surrounded the group, their own guns leveled at them. They grabbed Gloria's pistol and slung Melvin's rifle into the surf.

"The ocean's up. There's a small-craft advisory out," one of the men said. "It wasn't easy getting here in ten-foot seas."

Gloria was closest to him—the one who had jammed a gun into her back and then ripped it away as she'd been trying to get a hit on Gage. She studied him now with her hands in the air. His professional slicked-back hair coupled with an articulate British accent put him oddly out of place on a beach in North Carolina. A law office in London might have been more fitting, and yet, there was a conscientious nothingness about him, a void that pulled him away from justice's reasoning. In his eyes, Gloria saw a wasteland swept by wind and ice, and it brought back harrowing memories of familiarity: Here were the Lykanthrop, the werewolves in human disguise, and Gloria feared her sadly outnumbered group was about to die.

"Rowland, let me help Sanders," she blurted. It was a diversionary tactic, if not one of futile kindness. *Keep them talking, keep the situation stalling, keep the moment from filling again with gunfire.* "You've got our guns, there's nothing we can do. I just want to stop the blood."

But Gage ignored her. His dark, brooding eyes narrowed and then widened as he scanned the faces of the surrendered: Sheriff Hubbard. Stefan Heinrich. Caleb Cain. And the deputy on the ground.

There was no Ivy Cole, no Luna. Even the black wolves were gone.

"Bloody hell! They've gotten away!" Gage turned in circles, seeing no sign of the woman or child anywhere. Tracks ran into the forest and his nose prickled as he drew a breath of them in. "They've gone that way. You!" he jabbed a finger at the Brit and a short, stocky man with red hair standing beside him. "You two cover them, and the rest come with me. We've got to find Luna. As for anybody else, shoot whoever moves."

58

SAND PULLED at Ivy's feet made heavier by the weight in her arms. Luna was still in and out of consciousness, her dazed cries of rousing interrupted by a shallow drift back into sleep. The wolves flanked Ivy on either side, their pace slowed to match their mistress's. Together they plowed up dunes, through sharp sea grass, and slid down the embankments when Ivy lost her feet. Her shoes were full of sand and the grit abraded her soles and ankles. But on she ran, deeper into the interior of the small island and the forest that had managed to survive there. Low, spiny trees with weird twisted branches ripped at her cheeks and hair, and she pulled Luna's face into her chest to protect it. Somewhere behind her was the yelling of strange voices, her pursuers. And gunshots.

"Auf, Cali, halt." She stopped, looked back. Whatever was happening, it was still on the beach. Ivy was torn. She needed to get Luna to safety. She needed to go back and help. The .38 the sheriff had given her was still wedged in her waistband. She lowered Luna gently to the ground and pulled out the gun. She popped the cylinder. The chamber was empty.

Sheriff Hubbard had given her an unloaded gun.

Ivy growled in frustration and slung the revolver through the trees, her feral eyes orange as twilight. She looked around, getting her bearings, looking for a hiding place, a safe den in which to stash her child till she could figure out what to do.

They were in a marsh thicket. It was a dark, interior place with mud swamp and thick, green, slime-covered plants. The breeze off the beach had ended when she entered the forest, like a closed-in tropical blister, trapping heat and keeping all else out. It bubbled with decay and bacteria and the breaking down of flora to fuel the rich mire.

It was an eerie, unwelcoming, forbidding, dank bog, and Ivy was so grateful to have found it. And there was a path. The sand had petered out to solid ground inside the forest, and here a thin ribbon of earth wound through the swampy ooze.

But there were no hiding places that the Lykanthrop wouldn't see, other than sliding into the muck itself. It was not out of the question. Ivy grabbed a broken stick and poked it into the black mud. It was only a foot deep, shallower in other places. Ivy stabbed a deeper area only to find it suctioned like quicksand. She wrestled with the stick, then gave up and let the swamp have it.

Aufhocker's head suddenly rose into the fetid air, his stygian eyes unusually bright. There was movement ahead of them on the path. Not one approaching, but many.

The Lykanthrop soldiers! How did they circle in front of us?

Ivy's mind raced while her heart seemed to stop. The tops of the trees leaned closer over her head, their branches knitting tighter, squeezing more fresh oxygen out of the air and compacting what was left like fumes from an exhaust. She felt lightheaded, gassed, trapped, the wolf in the snare with the gunman approaching. They were known to chew off their own paws, desperate wolves in that situation, and Ivy now understood their panic. But it was not for herself that she feared.

They can't take my daughter. They can't take my daughter. Ivy's knees buckled, and she sank to the ground beside Luna. The outward light of her irises seemed to burn inward too, scorching her eyelids and eliciting a fiery ache in her head like from a solar burst.

They can't take her. The air compacted even tighter, denser, as if she were trying to breathe the mud itself from inside a box. A super-heated, swampy box. Or a coffin.

Can't take my daughter. Ivy's hair fell wildly around her face in moist, clingy tendrils. Sweat rolled between her shoulder blades in rivulets, then what felt like rivers. Her hair swung over Luna, brushing her cheeks. The girl's slumber was so peaceful; her sun-tinged cheeks were pink and her eyelids fluttered with a dream.

Ivy's heart wrenched, looking at her child. She'd never wanted children, never even imagined that a family—a normal life—could be part of her future. But Luna had come into her life anyway, had stolen every moment of her time, burdened every single bit of freedom she'd ever had, intruded on every private introspective aspect of her being, been the source of numerous sleepless nights—a child was the last thing she'd ever needed, let alone wanted, and to lose her now after only five short years together...

Ivy had lost much in her life to horrible circumstances: parents, family, friends, her one true love. She'd weathered it all and come out stronger on the other side. But she could not survive this. Not this loss.

A pain ripped through the center of Ivy's axis, from the core of her spine and radiating outward. And then Ava's words whispered hot in her ear. *Luna's nifty little trick is not innate, sugar. It was passed down by her mama.*

The pain wracked her again. It was familiar, and not. It shuddered her bones and spread outward through her blood to boil against her skin like molten lava.

Ivy staggered to her feet and stood over Luna. A wolf flanked each side of her, and she threw back her head...

My child...

...her arms spread wide to receive heaven...

...*my only child...*

...and an inhuman howl burst through the tropical tangle overhead.

"You won't take my daughter. I won't let you."

Ivy's eyes flared bloodred, and her declaration to no one slurred and growled over emerging fangs. She fell to her knees again between the black wolves, and the transformation began.

Ahead on the path, the hunters emerged.

59

THERE WERE ten of them in all. They stood in a graduated cluster on the path, lupine "soldiers" in scattered formation against a giant white wolf, two black ones that rivaled their Arctic brothers in size, and a sleeping girl. A wolf girl.

They were red wolves, the same pack that had greeted Ivy and Luna on their first visit to the island. Four more had joined the ranks since that serendipitous encounter.

Wa'yaaa...

The alpha's ginger-tipped ears perked toward the white wolf as the word floated through his brain. It was a human term uttered in a canine voice, and he knew it. It was of him, of them, the core of their soul, of what they were, or once were: regal upon the whole southeastern lands. Roamers of fens and bayous, farms and fields, marshes and beaches. Predators of deer and the smaller animals of the East, and masters at maintaining the balance of the ecosystems they inhabited.

They were respected by the Native American, and persecuted by those who had run the Indian farther west and the red wolf into the lowest, netherest regions of Louisiana and Texas—until the land petered out, and there was no where else left to go. No place for them on this earth, no use for them.

And then they came here, were placed here, but no matter. They were free to live as wolves lived. But today something new had set down among them, the likes of which they had never seen. A great white beast of *Canis* blood and common ancestry, and her curious wolfen offspring, whom they remembered from before.

The alpha's ocher eyes locked on the white wolf's. A moment or a century passed between them, as the sounds of the forest and even the present faded into a subdued lull in their ears, like the hollow muffling tune of the conch in its imitation of the tide. They were in another time, another place, as an era of instinctual connections passed between them. It was mutually understood, this one thing: the wolves' way to defend territory, to mark what belonged to a pack and drive away, or even kill, their rivals. But...they were as familiar as different, these trespasser wolves and their island cousins, and the red wolf felt only a kindred yearning toward the august animals before him.

The white wolf broke the spell, turning to gallop toward the beach, the largest black wolf right behind her. The red alpha paused only a moment, then broke into a steady lope after them, his pack following. They forked around the other black wolf and the girl, their coats blurring like sands washing through a rushing current as they picked up speed. There was another scent on the wind, new visitors on the beach, and the wolves comprehended in their canine brains that the pearl-crested waves of their pristine shoreline would froth hot and red before the hour fell.

The hunt was on.

60

THE BRIT and the redhead had moved off a short distance from their hostages, giving themselves a broader view of the perimeter. They scanned the shoreline repeatedly, perhaps hoping Ivy would get turned around and flounder back onto the same beach she'd attempted to escape, or maybe she'd make some gallant gesture and come back to save her "friends" and they could waylay her. Or, maybe, they were just hoping for the return of the group so they could get the hell out of here and back to Europe. Whatever their thinking or strategy, Gloria took advantage of the breathing room. She knelt by Melvin, who was sitting up now and holding his shoulder. Blood squeezed through his fingers, but it was a trickle compared to what Gloria expected.

"Let me see it, Sanders," she said, pulling his palm away and examining the wound. It was low, near the armpit. The bullet pierced the skin like a skewer but thankfully seemed to miss anything of substance. "His shot hit the fleshy part of your shoulder. Looks like the bullet has gone through."

"Lucky me." Melvin moved to stand and Caleb helped him. He winced as Caleb hoisted him up by his good arm, the kicks to his ribs by the steel-toed cowboy boots hurting worse than the hole in his shoulder. The men exchanged glances, two bloodied enemies who now, unexpectedly, had become unwilling allies.

"I'd say very lucky you." Gloria squinted at Sanders. He was different, and she couldn't put her finger on it. The gunshot wound was superficial, and yet she'd sworn Rowland had gotten off a point-blank shot on the center of his shoulder. It should have splintered Sanders's scapula. Not life-threatening, but much worse than the flesh wound he was sporting now.

"I'm fine, Sheriff." Melvin abruptly turned to Stefan. "They won't hurt her, will they?"

"Hurt? By hurt if you mean kill, then no, Luna will be safe. But Ivy..." Stefan could not say the final words, even as his gaze did not lower and he met Sanders's hate-filled glare, even as the shame he felt engulfed him because he was responsible for all this, albeit indirectly. Ivy had not desired contact with her family. If he'd left her alone all these years like she wanted, perhaps the Lykanthrop never would have found her. "I only meant to help," he said, his voice steady, despite the grief-stricken shattering of his heart. "I love Ivy and Luna, you must believe that."

"I don't know what to believe, but you can believe this—whatever happens to them today, I'm holding you responsible, and you won't like the consequences of that."

Gloria stepped between them. "Enough, both of you. You can settle differences later. Right now we've got to deal with the moment at hand, and I say we can stand around waiting for these yahoos to shoot us, or we can take control of the situation and get Luna back ourselves."

"What do you want us to do?" Caleb said. He dreaded the answer, but she was right. They were all good as dead as soon as the Lykanthrop found what they came for. He hoped Ivy had run far and hid deep in the brief time she'd had to escape. His own injuries, ironically mostly from Sanders, seemed very inconsequential to finding himself shot and thrown overboard in the middle of the ocean.

"They only left us with two guards, who seem more interested in watching the beach than us," Gloria said.

"You got a plan in mind, Sheriff?" Melvin said.

"Good ole bootlegger ambush tactics," Gloria answered.

"What is that supposed to mean?" Caleb said.

"We rush 'em," Melvin said. "There are two of them and four of us."

"I don't think that's going to be necessary." Stefan pointed down the beach. "My niece has come back. And she's brought friends."

The two guards at the front of the helicopter were not prepared for what was coming toward them at long-limbed run: the white werewolf, larger than any of them at their own transformations and certainly larger than a five-year-old werewolf should ever be, followed by the black wolf and a pack of other canids that appeared, remarkably, to be *Canis rufus*. They ran with the silent lope of skilled hunters, and the gunmen realized they had a choice: defend themselves against the very child they'd been sent to capture, or become prey, an ironic predicament for men such as these who heralded themselves indomitably ferocious at the onset of the full moon.

The redheaded guard did not have to think long. "Fire! Fire!"

The white wolf was on him before the round could discharge, and the red wolves immediately circled the men, cutting off any escape. Two red wolves dove from out of the woods and latched on to the Brit, hamstringing him quickly while his gun fired wildly into the air. Another red wolf leaped onto his face, grabbing at his nose and throat, while Aufhocker launched at him from behind. Teeth buried into the muscles of his back and all went numb as his spinal cord unzipped through the flesh of his body. He was down in seconds, alongside his Scottish chum, and they both became lost in a flurry of fur and teeth and claws.

When it was over, the red wolves regrouped and surrounded the chopper. Aufhocker left his prey to stand beside the white wolf, which had moved off the dead Lykanthrop to face the four humans.

Gloria crouched to reach for one of the fallen's guns, but Melvin grabbed her arm and pulled her back.

"What are you doing, Sanders? We're next, don't you see that?" Gloria hissed.

"Wait. Just…wait."

The wolves drew closer in on the huddled group.

"Uh, Stefan?" Caleb looked around anxiously. He knew about the Lykanthrops' transformation abilities, had been Stefan's friend for years and studied his lupine line, had even agreed to help Stefan on this dangerous, ill-gotten scheme at the promise of his own loyal familiar like Aufhocker as a reward and, quite possibly, becoming a lycanthrope himself one day.

But seeing it in full bloodied form before him—awe inspiring and horrible at once—shed new light on his old ideas. He saw the werewolf for what it really was: a killer, a carnivore, an eater of human flesh. Instead of courageously basking in the she-pup's glory, like he expected once he met her face to face, Caleb felt only terror. Had she fully transformed hours earlier on the boat, he would be long dead by now with no remorse on her part. He peered hard into that wolfish face. She was too big, too raw, her presence too magnificently malign. Where had the child gone?

"It's not the child," Stefan said, reading Caleb's thoughts. "This is Ivy."

"No," Gloria said. "It's impossible. The moon?"

Stefan didn't answer. He was both saddened and relieved that Ivy had found her inner strength at last. Another mistake on his part to keep it from her, but she had discovered it on her own, just as he and Ava suspected she would one day when backed into a corner.

The white wolf stood only a few feet away, her coat shining with ocean spray and blood. She lowered her head to study the group through eyes that blazed like coral from the sea floor. She advanced a step forward toward the group, the rest of the pack holding the periphery.

Melvin felt Gloria stiffen and he released her arm. "Please, Sheriff, trust me."

He took a step forward to greet the wolf. The last time he knew her this way, it was indeed by a full moon's light, glowing like a hallowed nimbus above the evil dark of the Appalachian woods. He had feared it would be the last time he would ever see Ivy—but now he faced the wolf again, and again, his life was in her hands.

"Ivy, it's me." Melvin held out his blood-stained palm. The animal was more than waist high; if she stood upright, as she easily could, she would tower over him.

The white wolf stepped closer till she could touch him. Her nose stretched to sniff his fingertips, breathe in the blood which was the deputy's own. Fire-touched eyes found their way to the wound in his shoulder, its flesh already reknitting around the ragged bullet hole. The wolf's pink tongue flicked out and grazed the injury, tasting the rapid healing in Melvin's repairing skin.

Melvin fell on his knees, face to fang-filled muzzle. His eyes glimmered orange behind the blue and the white wolf acknowledged it. She pushed her nose against his chin, into his neck, the hair across his forehead.

"She'll rip his throat out. Let the sheriff get her gun," Caleb whispered to Stefan.

"Be still, Caleb."

Melvin reached out and stroked the white wolf's ivory-mantled head. "So beautiful…" She was not how he remembered, when it seemed a monster from his nightmares was upon him. Her face, now that the fear and misunderstanding were shed from him, was bewitchingly noble, enchantingly benevolent. She held him raptly with the gaze of the wise, not the fierce intenseness of an insentient slayer. There was purpose to her, and those like her, who were only those of true *Canis* blood.

"I never saw before…" Melvin's words sighed on the ocean breeze, and suddenly they were alone with the surf and the wind and the gulls calling overhead.

An unexpected longing pulled in Melvin's heart, a longing to drop to the sand and gallop through the peaks and valleys of the waves. To be free of human form and constraint, to love as the wolf loved and know nature and instinct as the mother of justice. His body felt suddenly confining, his skin too restrictive, his entire life too hemmed and suppressed. But the freedom of the wolf, the way of his beloved Ivy...

Come with me...

"Yes, Ivy. Always."

Voices from up the beach. Yelling. Running. The Lykanthrop poured out of the woods.

The white wolf glanced back at them; then, like a dervish conjured from the dunes themselves, she and Aufhocker melted back into them, and the red wolves charged up the beach to greet the island's invaders.

61

GAGE AND the four men behind him moved with as much precision as they could muster, but it wasn't easy. They were knee-deep in slime-covered muck, fording through some God-awful southern America jungle and not even sure if they were heading in the right direction. Gage's mood darkened with each footfall, and his frustration mounted to match it. Were they the wolf at this moment, Ivy's trail would have blazed like a path of iridescent paint laid out in front of them. As it were, however, the human in them dulled those senses to a near-useless degree in this chameleon terrain.

Shouts in the distance. A scream. Most unnerving—a man's scream.

Gage held up his hand, halting the group. "Listen!"

They waited, guns poised, mud oozing around their legs and into their boots.

All was quiet again. No gunshots. Robert and Sean were ordered to shoot first and ask questions later. Had Stefan and his ragtag band of patriots managed a coup in Gage's absence? Without his men getting off one single shot? The whole thing did not sit right with him. "Let's get back to the beach."

The group retraced their steps, slogging as quickly as the slop would allow, till the ground firmed and the trees thinned out to dunes, grasses, and white sand once more. The Lykanthrop soldiers emerged at different points down the tree line, and all picked up a run toward the helicopter and the source of the noise. As they drew closer, a horrifying scene came into view: their two brothers down and spilling hot blood onto the hotter sand. The woman and men, their captives, were firing on them from the cover of the chopper, and a pack of dogs was charging full-tilt up the beach.

No, not dogs. Wolves! Gage could not believe what he was seeing. The tide on the island had turned dramatically in his brief absence, and the Lykanthrop were now the prey.

A bullet whizzed by Gage's head, and he dropped to the ground like the others around him. But that was no cover. The red wolves hurtled into the men, and chaotic gunfire from the surprised Lykanthrops shot into the air, over their heads, into the trees, the dunes, the ocean. Wolves yelped but continued to attack, such unnatural behavior for the timid coastal animal, and Gage could only guess at what supernatural motivator lay behind it. *Luna.* Stefan's man, the fool, had apparently not given the girl enough serum to quell her transformation any longer. Gage was even more impressed that one so young could organize an army against him, but where was the young werewolf now? Guarding her mother, most likely. Ivy had proven most troublesome, and dispatching her had just made top of his list. Luna would hopefully gentle up at losing good ole Mom; the extra tranquilizers should finish the job.

A man fell in front of Gage, a red wolf on top of him and worrying at the soft of his stomach. He clutched at the reddish gray ruff of the animal's neck, but small as it might be, the seventy pounds were pure muscle intent on its quarry. Another wolf joined its pack-mate, and its jaws clamped on the man's face and ripped up, taking jowls and an eye with the force. A third wolf grabbed for the flesh of his thigh, ripping open an artery and spraying itself with blood.

Disgusted, Gage fired a round into the animal's side, then crawled away from the carnage. Were it a full moon, everything on this island would lay dead before them. As werewolves they were unstoppable, the one who lost his face in front of Gage, case in point. His name was Thomas, a ruthless hunter under nightfall. Gage had seen Thomas kill an entire family in one night, gorging until not a trace remained. But by day, by the majority of the calendar month, Thomas, Sean, and the rest of Gage's soldiers were just men, men who suffered the weaknesses that humanity bore upon them.

Damn it all! Simon would not care about any of that, about *excuses*. And Gage had made unforgivable mistakes. It was supposed to be a simple child abduction. A lethal child, granted, but a little girl who could be controlled with drugs just the same. No, the problem was he'd underestimated Stefan, and that's really where things had gone wrong. Simon, sitting back there on his cushy throne in Nuremberg, would not understand this at all. His punishments could be particularly long, particularly creative, and particularly cruel.

Gage had to find Luna.

At the tree line again, Gage climbed to his feet. Wolves and men lay dead across the beach, but it was the wolves who were clearly the victors. Six of them moved among the bodies, as many of which were mowed down by bullets as teeth. Stefan and his newly armed companions would be leaving the cover of the helicopter soon. Gage had to hurry.

62

GAGE PLOWED through the mud once more, the suctioning of his steps quieted as much as he could manage. Crabs and some kind of weird island lizard scurried away from his path and he cursed America under his breath. He swore, after this was over, he would never set foot on this damnable land again. On that note he paused, gathering his bearings and scouting the surroundings for any inklings of a wolf trail. Overhead the close tree line created a hooded canopy that was shielding the last of the late afternoon sun, and he was losing visibility fast. He didn't have a flashlight—why would he? He was supposed to be well on his way back to Europe by now. Funny how life continued to throw these charming little twists into his otherwise perfect plans. Pursuing a werewolf under cover of darkness was not an encouraging thought by any means, and suddenly his weapon felt paltry. He should have grabbed one of the fallen Lykanthrop's rifles before diving back into the jungle. It was that kind of impulsive bullheadedness that had gotten him thrown out of the Irish navy a long time ago anyway.

Couldn't be helped now. Gage put a new clip in his nine-millimeter and checked the real weapon that would bring the wolf to her knees: a syringe tucked in his belt. It was loaded with no ordinary tranquilizer but rather, a nifty contribution from Stefan Heinrich himself. After losing Catherine unexpectedly to a rampaging Lykanthrop more than twenty years prior, Stefan had presented the Order with his own "werewolf antidote," a serum that suppressed shape-shift abilities with a harmless sedating effect. He'd followed his remarkable presentation with an appeal to the Lykanthrops' human side: Stop the bloodshed. That, of course, was laughable, but the Lykanthrops had welcomed the drug just the same. Its uses were not for what Stefan had originally intended, and how ironic that now Stefan's creation should be used against one of his beloved own. Gage felt some satisfaction from that, and of the knowledge that once he'd secured the wolf, he was going to track down Stefan's entourage and kill them one by one. Stefan he'd save for last, and strangle the old man with his bare hands.

"Lu-na," Gage called in a singsong voice. He was anxious and surprisingly not afraid. He'd so enjoyed her visits with Ivy to the restaurant, where he could observe them for at least an hour and catch moments to even banter with the little spitfire. Yes, a spitfire by all means. She'd disliked Gage from day one, when he'd inadvertently insulted her, and he wondered if the chocolate cake he'd sent as a gift had won him any favor.

Not that she ever had to like him or anybody else in the Order, for that matter. Liking life was not the point of what this mission was about. The point was function in life, and Luna could enhance that function greatly. No, like did not have to be part of the equation, it would merely have made things easier. Kudos to Stefan and his man for taking that obvious approach. Hate would most likely rule Luna's future once they wrestled her out of the clutches of her mother, whose death Gage was relishing the thoughts of more and more with each step deeper into the interior quagmire. He would blow her brains out right in front of the little she-wolf, shattering the pup's deadly focus and confidence, and then dispose of the black wolves just as easily. He should have done it this way from the beginning— the delay had cost the Order dearly. Gage pictured the dead men on the beach, and his resolve cemented itself with a seething venom.

Simon had shrugged off Gage's earlier suggestions; maybe from here on out, the lieutenant would listen to him.

"Luna, come get me! I'm here!" Gage threw his head straight back and howled. Nothing answered, even the birds were still. Gage trudged on until, thankfully, his boots found firm ground again. The thinnest thread of a path unwound before him, its moist soil torn by the four-toed indentions of wolf prints heading toward the beach. Gage ignored the tracks and continued on the trail the same direction he'd been heading—deeper into the swamp. His nose had suddenly caught wind of something, something that prickled his sinuses and tickled his nostrils, nearly making him sneeze. It was musky, a headier perfume than a red wolf would carry. Gage's black eyes flashed—he was on the scent, literally.

If you won't come to me, I'll come to you, little pup. Gage started to jog. He held his gun in his right hand and pulled the syringe from his belt with the left. He would have to get uncomfortably close to make this work, but if he could get the serum in the wolf's system before she managed to fatally injure him, whatever damage she did inflict, he could recover from quickly.

And there she was. A white mass of fur hunkered on the forest floor. She was crouched, lying belly to ground, her back to him and attention elsewhere. The two black wolves were to either side of her, their backs to him as well. But their heads swiveled his direction as soon as he rounded the bend in the path.

"Hello, love. I've come for you."

Gage aimed, his trigger finger ready to fell whatever charged him first. And then...he stopped.

The white wolf slowly rose to face him. And rose. And rose. Gage's eyes widened as the wolf climbed to her full seven-foot height. At her clawed feet lay a form, a child's form. It was Luna.

"My God. What are you?" The gun in his hand took on a trembling life of its own, but it was excitement more than fear that motivated it. And then he knew. It was impossible, and yet, the truth faced him now with the disquieting gaze of the predator fixing on its target. "You're...you're Ivy." Gage shook his head, incredulous. "All these years we followed Luna, waiting to see what she would blossom into, and here you were, you beautiful majestic beast, available to us the whole time."

The wolves stood in front of the child, shielding her. The smaller black wolf shifted her weight side to side anxiously, her patience undeveloped by youth. Here was the man, the one, the enemy whose designs were to take Luna away. She smelled the evil intentions leaking from his pores as easily as she could have tracked an ailing moose from a mile away. The larger black wolf turned his head, but before he could act to quell the overeagerness of the younger, it was too late. She bounded at Gage, her jaws open as she leaped for his throat. A loud crack, and then the wolf fell to the ground, still.

Gage looked at the animal, then the gun, as if it had acted of its own accord. His gaze traveled through the murky dim of the low light to see the white wolf's hindquarters bunching, her eyes blazing so brightly as to illuminate the path between them. She roared into the charge, and Gage fired again, but the shots were like pebbles to the werewolf's hide. He turned and fled, praying that if she leaped he could jab the syringe into her thick arctic fur before she tore him apart.

Gage had only rounded the bend again when he ran headlong into Melvin Sanders's oversized fist.

63

"How do you like it?" Melvin kicked Gage in the ribs three times in rapid succession. The man lay curled on his side, moaning through his busted mouth. A shaky hand managed to snake out and pilfer through the dirt regardless, searching.

"Looking for this?" Melvin waved Gage's gun and drew back to kick him again.

"No," Gage gasped before the toe of Melvin's boot connected and doubled him up again. Through the pain in his rib cage, Gage's eyes frantically searched the dirt for the syringe. It was gone, lost when the idiot deputy knocked him down, no doubt.

"Pull it together, Sanders. Do you hear me?" Gloria gripped his arm—his bad arm from his injured shoulder, which Sanders seemed to have gained full use of once more. The solid punch to Gage's face when he'd suddenly come upon them had hammered the Irishman straight to the ground.

Sanders's head whipped to face the sheriff, and she released him, startled. For a second she thought she saw...

"Oh no, Sanders."

The deputy licked his lips, his eyes darted away from her.

A dreadful suspicion churned in Gloria's stomach, but there was no time to address it now. First they had to find Luna. She trained her gun on Gage, while Caleb hauled him to his feet.

Stefan leaned into his face. "Where are they?"

Gage spit out a tooth and grinned, the bloody gap in its absence hideously comical. "Where are they? You'll get the answer to that soon enough. She's right be—"

"Behind you!" Gloria shouted. Everyone turned.

The white wolf stood on the path before them, two powerful haunches holding claw-tipped forelegs upright. She stared at the group, her muzzle slightly open to reveal rows of daggerlike teeth, her orange eyes flickering like ember fire in the lowering light.

"Give him to her," Stefan said. "Give him to her! It's what she wants."

Gloria's head snapped toward him. "No, Stefan. I can't do that. I'm a police officer, and he's still a human being."

"You couldn't be more wrong about that, Sheriff." Gage, while Gloria's head was turned, reached out and grabbed her gun hand by the wrist. He forced the weapon upward while lunging the same direction. Melvin hurtled forward but Gage was ahead of him. His thick arm was around Gloria's neck, the gun at her head. He braced her in front of him, a human shield.

"Those bullets won't do you any good," Stefan said. "You're a dead man."

Gage smiled crookedly. "They may not do much to the likes of her," Gage motioned the gun in the white wolf's direction, "but one shot will tear this one to pieces. Now, Stefan, call off your dog."

"I can't."

"Call her off!"

"She won't listen to me."

The white wolf lowered to all fours abruptly and advanced. Gage shoved the gun barrel against Gloria's temple. "Call her off!"

"Sheriff..." Melvin looked helplessly at Gloria. Her face was cold, resolute. *Don't you give in to him, Deputy. He'll kill all of us.* That's what her eyes said. He didn't care.

Melvin jumped between Gloria and the werewolf. "Ivy, stop."

She moved closer, her head lowering, her body flattening into a stalker's stance.

"You know me, Ivy. Please. Don't let him kill Gloria." Melvin was unsure if his words were heeded, did not know if Ivy could even understand them as the wolf. But he thought she did. He believed she did. He believed in her. She would listen, she would never hurt him or anyone he loved. Yes, he *believed.*

The white wolf sprang full into Melvin's chest, knocking him onto his back. His breath expelled in a whoosh as the terrible weight of the animal momentarily crushed his lungs. *Ivy, no!* He swung at her sides, grappling, trying to take hold of the shaggy coat to at least slow her attack by dragging him with her.

At the same time, Gage Rowland shrieked, his bloodcurdling agony echoing out of the forest all the way to the ocean.

Stefan and Caleb jumped back as blood spurted in a torrent from the nub of wrist where Gage's gun hand used to be. A red geyser spouted across Gloria's face and hair.

Another white wolf was by Gage's side. It slung its head angrily and the gun with hand still attached flew into the sludgy waters of the bog.

The white wolf atop Melvin sprang off his chest and barreled into Gage, knocking Gloria to the side. Fangs buried into the side of his neck, and then more movement out of the woods as Aufhocker ripped into the man's thighs.

Gage went down in a heap, the three wolves gnashing and rending meat. Fleshy chunks stripped from Gage's sides, his chest, his abdomen. Bloody spray formed a growing puddle around the pack as their screaming prey grew sickeningly silent, and all the sound was the breeze and the gulls and the distant waves lapping at the shore somewhere beyond them.

64

THEY DIDN'T say a word on the way back to the dock. Ivy sat huddled at the stern of Haskell's boat, wrapped in the clothes she'd pulled from a dead Lykanthrop after transforming to human once more. Luna was snuggled up tight against her mother, staring quietly at nothing. Occasionally a tear slid down and dripped off the tip of her chin. The depth of sadness was nothing her mother could fix this time, for beside them on the deck rode only one black wolf, not two.

Inside the pilothouse, Caleb sat at the wheel. Gloria stood to one side of him, watching the mild waves through the glass. The ocean had quieted again since the afternoon; whatever storm was looming when the Lykanthrops rode in seemed to have passed, its bluster all bluff. Nevertheless, it would be dark soon, and Caleb hoped they'd make it back before total night was upon them.

Melvin hovered just outside the pilothouse door, not sure where he belonged. He was not comfortable in close proximity with Caleb, yet he didn't fit in Ivy and Luna's intimate circle either.

And just behind the fishing boat tagged the *Yellowfin*, piloted by Stefan alone. His helicopter remained on Smitty Pete's Island for now, but by morning, it—along with the pilot's body—would be taken care of. As for the rest of the dead on the beach, the red wolves had taken care of that. Someone would come upon the Lykanthrops' abandoned boat eventually, but what they would make of it would be hard to tell. It would be yet another mystery surrounding the haunted island.

The lights of Salty Duck grew larger at last, from tiny pinpricks in the distance to storefront silhouettes that seemed to move on their own as early evening shoppers and diners walked the waterfront cobblestone streets. A gap of darkness in the festively lit shoreline marred the gay scene, The Scotch Bonnet's empty interior a solemn reminder of the Pitchkettles' tragedy.

The two boats drifted silently by, and then finally the marina was in view. Again, not a word as Caleb expertly guided the old boat into an available slip, and the *Yellowfin* pulled into place beside it. Melvin jumped on the pier and tied off Haskell's boat first, then ran over to assist Stefan. Caleb helped Ivy and Luna onto the pier but stepped back when Gloria's expression clearly indicated she didn't want the likes of him to touch her. Aufhocker jumped off last and stood beside Ivy on the minutely swaying wooden planks.

The pier was deserted, thankfully, and the group stood together in an uncomfortable assembly. Minutes passed.

Luna shifted in Ivy's arms, her sniffles buried in the hair lying over her mother's shoulder. "Mommy, I want to go home."

Ivy squeezed her tight. "Yes, sweetheart. Me too." She looked at the faces around her. Then she turned and walked away.

"Ivy Cole."

Ivy kept walking.

"Ivy Cole, stop right there."

Ivy heard the click of a Lykanthrop's gun in Sheriff Hubbard's hand, knew it was pointed at her back right now. Ivy turned around.

"What is it, Gloria?"

Gloria's rueful smile was weary. "You know."

Ivy shook her head. "After all we've been through?"

"It's a shame, isn't it? I feel like if you weren't what you are, we could have been friends."

"Funny. I had that same thought, too. Even after I saved your life. It's not too late, perhaps?"

"You know the answer to that. But thank you, Ivy, for saving me. I owe you that."

"You're welcome, Gloria."

The sheriff nodded. They paused, looking at each other intently.

"Give her to me, Ivy. You know I can't let you take her."

Ivy laughed, a small sound that was more doleful than sardonic. "And you know I can't let you have her. You gave me an unloaded gun back there, by the way."

"What?"

"The revolver. I would have found that useful had you trusted me enough, but in a way, *I* should thank *you,* Gloria. Being without it forced me to learn something new about myself. Something I can do at any time. Something Luna can do at any time."

"Are you threatening me?"

"I'm simply warning you, for your own good, like friends do."

"This is for the child's own good, Ivy. What happened today is proof she's living a nightmare."

"And just how do you plan to help her? You saw what Luna is. What makes you think life with you would be so much better? She's a *wolf,* Gloria, a creature of the forest, of the wild, of Mother Nature. There's nothing you can give her."

"I can get her help. There's got to be a way."

"I'm telling you no, Sheriff."

"And I'm telling you, you won't leave this pier with her."

"Ladies, please," Stefan said. "We've been through so much today. Can't we just part ways peacefully?"

"It's all right, Stefan," Ivy said. "Sheriff Hubbard *has* been through a lot, and not just today. You see, I ruined her town, in her eyes. She lost her best deputy because of me. And she lost her husband, Tee Hubbard. Somehow I'm sure that's my fault too."

Stefan glanced between the two, ready to speak again, when Melvin barged in. "It's not her fault I left the department, Sheriff Hubbard," he said.

Gloria snorted. "You don't have to say another word, Sanders. I already know why you're here. You're one of them."

"Sheriff…"

"It's all right, Deputy," Stefan said, his voice fatherly, the German clip to his English words commanding and comforting at once. "Let me talk to her."

Stefan moved to Gloria's side, mindful of the firearm pointed at his niece. "It's going to be all right now." He put a reassuring hand on Gloria's shoulder. She started slightly, and then looked at the elderly gentleman with questioning surprise.

"What…" she breathed. Her arm fell slowly down, down, down, as if incrementally sinking through measured depths of water, the pressure and weight on her wrist increasing with each second of descent. An enveloping somnolence pressed against every nerve and every recess of her wakeful mind. It promised sweet rest, and try as she knew she should, she simply could not resist it.

Stefan slipped the gun from Gloria's slackening grip and tossed it to Caleb. With his other hand he withdrew the syringe from her neck; then he put a strong arm around her waist and helped lower her carefully to the pier. As he lay her gently down, he whispered in her ear, "I leave you with this, my good sheriff: Your ex-husband Tee—he is alive."

Gloria's excruciatingly heavy eyelids fluttered with stunned acknowledgment of his words. Stefan smiled kindly as the burden on Gloria's consciousness became too much, and she slipped away into an abysmal hinterland that beckoned her to join it.

"What did you do to her!" Melvin grabbed Stefan's shirt collar and jerked him up. He shook the old man and shouted again, *"What did you just do?"*

"Let him go, Sanders!" Caleb tackled Melvin and knocked him to the pier, toppling both of them. Melvin landed on his back with both fists swinging. Another hard right slammed solid into Caleb's jaw, throwing him backward. Melvin dove onto the prone man and caught a brutal jackhammer to the chin, rattling his teeth and upping his fury another notch.

"Stop it, both of you!" Stefan stepped into the fray, trying to break the men apart. Their rolling bodies and flailing fists nearly pitched him over the side of the pier into the water. He crawled on his hands and knees away from them, toward Ivy, who stood help-lessly watching the two men. They'd gone completely feral and there was nothing she nor Stefan could do but let the anger wear itself out.

Luna wiggled in Ivy's grasp, struggling to get down, her teary eyes wide at the sight before them. Ivy set the child on her feet and she broke away from her mother, running at Caleb and Melvin.

"Daddy, no!"

The brawling men froze, fists in midswing, bloody noses and chins and mouths suddenly, inanely, preposterous under the circum-stances. The tension deflated in both of them as both of them sat up to stare at the little girl. Caleb looked from Luna to Melvin and back again, and even Stefan was hushed.

"What did you say?" Melvin said.

"Please don't fight, Daddy. Caleb didn't mean it."

Ivy stood by Luna's side. "Why are you saying this, Luna?"

"Because Caleb is our friend."

"No, Boo, the other thing. You don't know Melvin."

Luna looked up at her mother. "Yes, I do, Mommy. I know him deep," she pointed to her chest with a tiny finger, "in here. He is my daddy, I feel it."

Melvin's eyes reddened. He tried to hold on, but his vision blurred anyway and one lone streak of water wound down his cheek. He held out his arms. "Come here, Luna."

Luna looked at her mother again, and Ivy nodded. She ran to Melvin and he hugged her close.

Stefan and Caleb climbed to their feet, and Caleb held out his hand to Melvin. He looked up at his former adversary, his face ruddy from the fight and emotion and pure unending fatigue, and then took the hand offered him. Caleb pulled him up and they squared off, but this time there was no fight, only a little girl, between them. Caleb nodded at Melvin and stepped back, and Melvin felt Luna's fingers curl around his own.

"Deputy Sanders," Stefan said, "your sheriff will be all right." He held out the syringe. "This is a highly potent sedative, an elixir made especially for lycanthropes. Rowland dropped it when you attacked him, but I know the serum. I developed it. Gloria will be asleep for some time, but she'll awake feeling just fine. Maybe hung over with a twinge of a bellyache, but overall healthy nonetheless. I promise."

Melvin wiped his eyes with the back of his dirty sleeve. "Thank you."

"How much time have we got?" Caleb asked.

"Twenty-four hours at the most. We have to make good use of it."

"What about the sheriff? We can't just leave her here," Melvin said.

"I'll see to it she is put in a safe place until she wakes up," Stefan said. "For now, you must go get ready to leave. Ivy, I'll be in touch with you by morning."

Ivy nodded. She was tired, and there was no use disputing it: She needed Stefan's help.

Someday, she thought through the utter exhaustion that encumbered every limb and clouded every rational fragment of her thinking, *someday the running will be over.*

Today was not that day.

65

EARLY MORNING lingered behind the cover of darkness yet, the last beam of the lighthouse soon to fade as dawn embraced it. Off behind Pious Cape the horizon was brightening, another beautiful day in Salty Duck held in its glowing promise.

Ivy and Luna would not be here to enjoy it, however, and Ivy reflected on that cheerless notion just as her own reflection wavered in the water beneath her feet. This morning she stood at the end of Marshy Bottom Pier for the last time.

"Saying good-bye?" Caleb walked up beside Ivy. She'd smelled him before he'd announced himself, clean and crisp as he was, like the ocean he would miss even more than she. But a whiff of something else followed him now, as well—the scent of blood and injury. Ivy looked up at him, his handsome face marred by a black eye, a white bandage taped across the bridge of his nose, a swollen lip. For an absurd moment she almost laughed. After all the danger they had encountered on Smitty Pete's Island, it was Caleb who had come out the worse for the wear, and all mostly due to an irate deputy with a mountainous temper who would have probably made a fine fishing buddy under different circumstances.

"Yes," she said, the momentary lightness leaving her. "Just seeing it once more before we go. How did you find me?"

"I had a feeling you might be here. That, and Sanders told me where you were."

"Ah," Ivy said, nodding thoughtfully.

Caleb leaned on the rail beside her, enjoying the briny air and homesick for it already. He and Ivy had both come to Salty Duck to change their lives, and each was leaving with that very result. Ironic they were not the changes either of them had intended. "I met you right here, Ivy. Seems like an eternity ago, doesn't it?" When she didn't reply: "So it's good-bye to me as well then?"

There was hope in his voice, even while knowing it was hopeless.

Ivy turned to him, a gentle sweetness about her face that belied everything he'd seen that she could be. Her eyes told him the answer well enough when she didn't speak. Words seemed useless after everything between them.

"You could come with me, Ivy. Stefan and I will be flying to Europe in a few hours. He has a place already prepared—"

"Stefan already has a place prepared for me here, Caleb, in the States. This is my home. And I intend for it to be Luna's home."

Caleb sighed. Stefan had been very busy over the course of the night. His heart twinged a little that his friend with his worldwide connections had been so effective at relocation. If he and Ivy had been given more time, he might be able to set things right between them.

The Pious Cape Lighthouse shut off with his thoughts, and behind it rose the rim of the sun. The fiery crescent reminded Caleb of wolf's eyes in the forest, burning with the passion of life and freedom, the hunt as well as play. He had seen beauty as he had never seen it before—fierce and wanton and undeniably wild. He was sure he never wanted to see it that way again, and yet...

"I love you, Ivy. And I'm sorry. We meant well."

Ivy put a tender hand against his cheek. It alighted there for just a fluttering moment before she pulled it away. "I believe that now. All of it. Take care of yourself, Caleb."

Ivy walked away from him, the blond woman he longed for, the ivory wolf who would haunt his every nightmare.

"Ivy!" he called to her from the end of the pier.

She paused to look back.

"He's waiting for you, Ivy," Caleb said, a sad acceptance grinding against the grief of his loss. "Don't let him go."

Ivy walked back up Battery Street, relishing the feel of a final dawn in Salty Duck. A young paper carrier pedaled by and flung the day's news with one expert flip and a "Good morning, ma'am" before rounding the corner onto Mission Street. At the edge of the nearest yard, a fluff of white charged from behind a hedge to bark at the bicycle. His owner soon came to the porch in a housecoat and called the staunch little bichon sentinel inside. In the distance came the grating rumble of steel as the Sandpiper Bridge lifted to allow passage of its first tall vessel of the day. And through it all whirled a morning breeze that lifted Ivy's hair softly and fought against the humidity of a summer floundering unwillingly into fall.

Ivy embraced the sounds and moments and stored them away as she came to Captain Woodside's cottage at last. All their bags were packed, all possessions sorted to their meagerest for traveling. They would be leaving behind all but the barest of essentials, including the book *Lykanthrop,* which Caleb confessed to possessing. Ivy gave it to Stefan with good blessing—the book had caused her nothing but trouble and heartache in the past anyway. She was relieved to be rid of it, to let someone else be its keeper. Whatever important secrets it might hold for the Lykanthrop themselves, she didn't care.

The front porch steps were suddenly very inviting, and Ivy sat on the top one. Auf got up from a listless snooze in the yard and flopped down again beside her. Melvin sat on her porch swing, raptly engaged in a string game of cat's cradle with…his daughter.

"Hi, Mommy. Look what I learned to do." Luna looped the string through her fingers with some difficulty but then pulled the ends quickly to produce a perfect design. "Ta-da!" She held her entangled hands out for her mother to see.

Ivy inspected it. "That's about the finest cat's cradle I've ever seen."

Luna beamed and dropped the string to start working on it again.

"Boo, can you go inside and make sure we got everything? I need to talk to Melvin for a minute."

"Sure, Mommy." She used Melvin's knee as a springboard and catapulted off the swing. Aufhocker trotted after her, the screen door nearly catching his tail.

Melvin rocked slightly and patted the vacant seat beside him. "Join me?"

Ivy cocked her head. A simple question, with an underlying implication. There did not seem to be a good answer. Perhaps looking for the good or right answer was her perpetual mistake. Maybe she should be looking no further than what made her happy. No further than what would make her daughter happy. And that would be good enough.

She stayed seated on the security of the porch step anyway.

"You know what I am, Melvin."

"I accept that."

"You know what Luna is."

"Yep."

"You'll try to change me. Us."

"I might." Melvin gave her a cockeyed grin, half serious, half kidding, he'd let her decide. But in truth, Stefan had given him a supply of the serum, enough to last through many moons until he could at least get a handle on the illness and discover how to control it. With Ivy's blood in his veins, Stefan felt fairly certain Melvin possessed the same ability to change—or not change—as Ivy did. The hope in him had buoyed his spirits, and it inspired him this morning to be playful.

"Then why?"

"Always making it harder than it is, Ivy, since the day I met you. Luna is my child. She needs me, she needs a role model. And no matter what you say, you know it's true. I think if you'd lower your hackles for a minute, you might see you need me, too."

"I've never needed anybody. I don't even know what that's like.

But Luna..." Luna did need more, she deserved more. A stable home life, two parents to depend on. Living on the run with her mother—what kind of maladjusted young woman would she grow up to be? Already she had been through too much; all Ivy wanted was to protect her. It's all everyone had wanted apparently, in their own misguided way.

"Stefan has a new home for us that is far away from here," she said casually. Overcasually. And more pointedly: "For Luna and myself."

"I know. He told me."

Ivy's eyebrows shot up. "What did he tell you?"

"That the new place is small, but plenty big enough for a three-member family."

A black stretch limousine pulled up in front of the cottage and interrupted the conversation. A driver got out, his uniform and hat very formal against the coastal vacation backdrop.

"Are you Miss Cole?" he called from the street. Ivy looked at Melvin, and he shrugged.

"That's me."

He nodded curtly and walked to the back of the car. He opened the door and leaned in to take something in his arms. When he turned back around, Ivy gasped and even Melvin jumped to his feet.

"This is for you, Miss Cole," the driver said. He bent over and set the wriggling bundle on the ground.

"Rex!" Ivy leaped off the porch and the little gray terrier scampered to her. Ivy fell to her knees in the grass, and Rex leaped into her arms from three feet way. He smothered her laughing face in kisses and his tail beat in a frenzied fuzzy blur.

"Ahem. Miss?" the driver stood over the reunited, an envelope of expensive canary linen in his hand. "This is also for you. Good day." He tipped his hat and climbed back into the limo.

Melvin came down the steps beside Ivy. "What does it say?"

Ivy tore open the card while Rex dashed around her, jumping up again and again to deposit more kisses.

"I don't believe it," she said, shaking her head. "It says 'Thought you could use the sight of an old friend. Please forgive me. Love, Aunt Ava.'"

Ivy lowered the card, and Rex immediately grabbed hold of it, shaking it back and forth like a captured mole.

"That old woman always did know how to play me," Ivy said, but she felt herself giving in to it, giving in to the sheer joy of having Simple Rex back in her life, the sheer gratefulness for yesterday's outcome, the sheer appreciation for the loved ones surrounding her…The hard feelings toward Ava crumbled with each lap Rex ran around her, and the burden of anger and a desire for revenge slipped away.

Ivy's cell phone rang, startling Rex, who made a dive for it before Ivy snatched it back. She recognized the number Stefan had given her and answered. "This is Ivy….Yes, we're ready….Okay, we'll leave for the airport as soon as we get our bags thrown in the car….Yes, Uncle Stefan, I know. I love you too."

She flipped the phone closed. "Well, Deputy, I guess this is it."

"Looks like it." He leaned down and scratched Rex's head.

Ivy waited, but the only affection forthcoming seemed to be aimed toward her furry friend. Exasperated, Ivy threw up her hands. "Well, good-bye."

She moved to stomp around him back to the house when he caught her arm. She started to protest but he kissed her anyway, while Rex yipped and yapped around their knees.

"You've got the rest of our lives to tell me how wrong we are for each other, Ivy Cole, but right now we've got a plane to catch."

Ivy opened her mouth, but excuses and arguing were pointless. No reason she could think of to keep him from coming was very convincing anyway, not even to her.

"You're biting off more than you can chew, Deputy Sanders," she finally said.

"I've taken on werewolves and lived to tell about it. You let me be the judge of that."

Eyes flickered, and a wildfire danced behind green irises. "We'll see, Deputy Sanders. We'll see."

Ivy smiled.

About the Author

Photo by Karl Farago

Winner of the New York Book Festival Award and top finalist for the Compton Crook, IPPY, and Benjamin Franklin Awards, Gina Farago is the author of *Ivy Cole and the Moon,* the first book in the Ivy Cole series. Her studies have included research on werewolf legends and lore, and personal interaction with a gray wolf pack, observing firsthand the animals' social behavior and hunting techniques.

Farago's other works include coauthoring *Making Do: How to Cook Like a Mountain MeMa* with Lois Sutphin. Farago lives in North Carolina with her husband, Karl, and their numerous four-legged friends.

For more information on how you can help the red wolves of North Carolina or wolves everywhere, please contact—or donate to—the Red Wolf Coalition, www.redwolves.com, or the Defenders of Wildlife Wolf Fund, www.defenders.org.

www.GinaFarago.com